THE MOTHER ELEMENT

MONICA ENDERLE PIERCE

GOLDEN
FLOWER

STORIES THAT STAY WITH YOU

Copyright © 2019 Monica Enderle Pierce
Cover Illustration Copyright © 2018 Qistina Khalidah
Developmental Editor Maia Driver
Copy Editor Mel Sanders
Cover Design by Scott Pierce
Ebook ISBN-13: 978-0-9859761-8-7
Print ISBN-13: 978-0-9859761-9-4

"In the Gloaming" poem © 1874 Meta Orred; music © 1877 Annie Fortescue Harrison (public domain)
"Swing Low, Sweet Chariot" © prior to 1870s unknown origin (public domain)

For all the women with steel spines

THE MOTHER ELEMENT

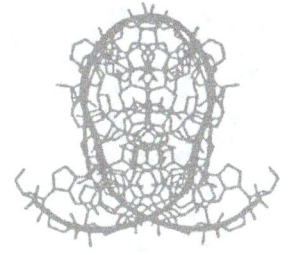

PART ONE
CARBON

ONE

I STARTED HEARING voices six months ago, the day after I bashed in Cyrus's skull with a wrench. I thought my flashbacks and grief had died with him.

I was wrong.

"We are one."

Yeah, yeah, you said that already, I thought as I turned a small wooden puzzle piece between my fingers, the newest of four pieces Ehtishem had carved for me, presenting each with no explanation.

At first, the voices were an indistinct hum I assumed was *Dathusha's* engines. They came and went, sometimes loud, sometimes soft. But a few weeks ago they grew more distinct and I realized they were speaking to me. Which meant I'd stopped having flashbacks only to start hearing voices?

Not. Fair.

"You're distracted, Rachel Pryne." Ehtishem ran his fingers through my short brunette hair, tilted my head back, and kissed me. He had broad gentle hands and like all Ohnenrai his skin was dark brown and his nails were black and iridescent. But his were the hands of a soldier, a killer, my lover. He released me and buttoned his shirt.

"Only by your touch," I said.

"*We are one*," the nattering voices repeated. They were the real distraction.

Ehtishem replied, "Flattering but a lie."

"Alright, I'm distracted by the mystery of this puzzle." I held up the piece. "When are you going to solve it?"

"*We are one.*"

I told no one about the voices, not even him. Hearing imaginary voices wasn't a good sign and I'd happily put off diagnosing myself as looney for as long as possible. Besides, they weren't hurting anything. They only said, "We are one." Maybe I had multiple personalities trying to integrate. Maybe ignoring them would make that happen faster.

"It's your puzzle to solve, Pairika," he replied as he closed the last button on his shirt.

"Trying to make me crazy?" I mused in Ohnenrai. Always Ohnenrai. I dreamed in Ohnenrai instead of English now. And I heard voices. Maybe I already was crazy.

"I thought you enjoyed challenges." Tall and broad enough to more than fill a doorway, Ehtishem had almond-shaped hazel eyes and black bones beneath his dark skin. He made me feel tiny and that was saying something considering I was six feet and solid, especially now that I wasn't starving.

I smirked. "Because I'm with you?"

We were in his bedroom aboard the civilian ship *Dathusha* having showered and changed after hand-to-hand combat. He called it training, but it was more like kissing the floor for me and swatting a gnat for him.

He looked up from tucking his gray uniform shirt into his matching trousers and gave me a brief dazzling grin. "Exactly."

I treasured the rare gift of his smiles. Toothy, charming,

almost boyish, his smiles weren't the kind you'd expect from a man who'd conquered worlds, crushed enemies, and snapped his own uncle's neck with his bare hands.

"Monster." I clutched the puzzle piece, another precious gift from my Ohnenrai lover.

This life was closer to "normal" and "family" and "love" than I thought I'd ever find again. Which, of course, made me afraid to lose it. Stars winked beyond the room's wide viewport, alien stars seen from an alien ship. How strange my life was six months after the rainy evening on Earth when a wounded Ehtishem showed up in my muddy yard, wanting to give and receive aid.

He shrugged into his coat, the sun of his smile extinguishing. Seven green and gold bars marked both sleeves over his biceps, his left collar, and circled his cuffs. His high rank and high deeds were stitched all over the chest of his charcoal gray uniform, row upon row of colorful insignias on one side, a circle of seven blue and seven gold stars surrounding a white dog — Draxtu Mainyu — opposite. The same symbol decorated his guards' uniforms. It meant determination no matter how shitty the situation got.

I also wore a uniform, the gray-and-red of Ohnenrai medical staff. Its wide stripes designated me as a low-rank ops worker. "Funny this life," I mused. "How did a nobody from nowhere get to be your lover, Zosh Mahle?"

His brow furrowed for a second then smoothed out. Controlled, always emotionally controlled. Vairim, his people called that self-command, and Ehtishem had mastered it. He brushed his fingers along my jaw. "I asked you never to call me by my title."

"Technically untrue. You told me never to call you 'Thrai'." That was his former title, third in command of the Ohnenrai. He'd killed his uncle and taken the top spot. Not that he'd wanted to do either, not that Isphahan made it a choice.

He laughed, humor he quickly stifled. "Eresh."

"Yes, I know it's true," I said following him into the third floor hallway and down the wood and glass stairway.

"I'm off to OSCG for a few hours then to *Pohru-Mahrko* to oversee the jump to Fisk-Vayat and the water runs once we arrive." We reached the first floor. "I'll be gone for forty-five hours. Pearl and Audie are military, so they'll join their trainers aboard *PM*. You'll remain on *Dathusha*."

He crossed the room to the Terran grandfather clock that was absurd and appropriate in equal measure in his quarters. He retrieved the winding crank from the cabinet's lower drawer, wound the clock, and watched the pendulum swing. "Huorem and Mahzel will take you to and from the CMSD while I'm gone."

It was his mother Ahremena's idea that I work in *Dathusha's* Civilian Medical Supply Depot. Ehtishem didn't love it, but he knew I'd go stir-crazy if left in his quarters with nothing to do. Besides, as his mother — the head of Ohnenrai Genetics — pointed out, this exposed me to more Ohnenrai, so I seemed less like a frou-frou lap dog and more like a contributing member of the ship. I preferred a med tech position and a lot more freedom, but those weren't options. Not everyone appreciated a Terran sharing a bed with the Supreme Command General of the Combined Ohnenrai Military and Civilian Defensive Forces.

"Anywhere else?" I asked.

"The firing range for practice."

Huorem and Mahzel were training me to handle a mass ammunition pistol.

I sucked a deep breath then released it as a slow sigh.

He joined me in the kitchen and kissed my forehead. "These restrictions won't last forever."

"I know."

"When we reach Fisk-Vayat, I'll give you a tour of *Pohru-Mahrko*. Your last experience aboard my ship was unpleasant. In many ways, she's more home to me than this place." His gesture indicated his expansive three-story quarters, starting with the elegant wood furnishings and art glass on the open first level and ending with the window ceiling that revealed all the stars and planets *Dathusha* passed as she and her military escort hurtled through space.

I looked up. "That would be nice."

"Ushta." He retrieved two cups from a tall cabinet and poured suxra into one. He took a sip and frowned into the cup.

"What?"

He dumped the red tea back into the pot. "It's cold." Folding his arms, he leaned against the wide counter. "I had a report from Pearl's tahkaesha about her and Audie."

"Good, I hope?" My eight-year-old daughter and our dog were training to be a cathru-at-namandar — a military dog-and-handler team.

"They're making excellent progress." He watched my face as he added, "So much so that they're scheduled for their first in-field exercise. They'll go dirtside with a team when we start our water run on Fisk."

"That's awesome."

"You think so?" He sounded a little surprised.

"Why wouldn't I? They've worked hard for this." I laughed and kissed him. "Thank you," I said in English.

"You're welcome. I'm happy to keep them together. That dog will protect her with his last ounce of strength."

"Yes, he will. I also like that she's getting self-defense and weapons training."

"It's one of many things that's overdue."

I arched a brow at him. "Oh yeah? What else?"

His gaze caught and held mine. Intense. Wanting. Maybe a little worried?

"Whaaat?" I asked, suddenly nervous.

"I want to register our bond."

"Okay. What does that mean?"

"It's rarely practiced because it's irrevocable. And Ahremena won't approve."

"But what does that *mean*, Ehtishem?"

"Hathevar — absolute fidelity."

My jaw dropped. The most eligible and attractive Ohnenrai bachelor was taking himself off the market in a big and major way. For me. "Are you asking me to marry you?"

"That's the closest Terran word for it. But it's more complex. Severance is not an option. Infidelity is criminal and carries harsh penalties. And, because you're property, it requires the dissolution of my ownership. And you must renounce your Terran allegiance."

I sucked in another breath and released it with a whoosh. "Well, that's not the most romantic proposal I could imagine."

His lips twitched, almost a smile.

"I mean where's the diamond ring and the kneeling and the horse-drawn carriage and all that bullshit?"

His brows furrowed. "Did I do something wrong?"

"Nava." I pressed my hands against his chest, the fabric of his uniform stiff under my fingers, the thread of the insignias smooth. "Those things always seemed a bit silly to me."

He placed a finger beneath my chin, tilted my face back, studied me. "You're sure you don't want all that *bullshit*?"

"Well, maybe I want the ring so I have something to pawn when you get your big carcass killed in some stupid battle."

"I'll see what I can do." His finger slid along my jaw. "I'm not exaggerating about the fidelity and the renunciation."

"I know. And I've dealt with infidelity accusations before. That got thrown at me a lot in Suffer." I looked away from his intense gaze. "But allegiance is trickier." His finger stopped. "I'm still trying to figure out who I am here. I don't know if I can or want to give up being Rachel Elizabeth Pryne from Earth. It feels like a betrayal of myself, my planet." I met his gaze again. "My parents."

He pressed his finger to my lips. "Think about it and discuss it with Pearl. This isn't a decision to be made lightly or quickly. It cannot be undone." His gaze intensified and his voice deepened as he added, "I want you to know beyond all doubt that I consider you more than a weapon to be used and forgotten. I won't leave you behind, Pairika."

I nodded and he feathered his fingers past my ear and into my hair. He pulled me to him, brushing his lips against mine as he whispered, "Mem kam-va, Rahzhel, upairi anghu."

He loved me more than life. I slid my arms around his neck and kissed him.

Ehtishem grasped my waist and lifted me to sit atop the counter. The world slid away, lost to the feel of his hands and his lips, his tongue and his body, lost to the sound of our breath and words whispered in Ohnenrai and English.

"When you're done eating each other's faces, I need you to braid my hair, Momma."

We froze. I peered over his shoulder. Pearl stood at the bottom of the stairs dressed in her pale-gray uniform with a brush in her hand. Her brunette hair was a wild mass of curls cascading over her shoulders and down her back.

"How long have you been standing there?" I asked.

"Long enough to be grossed out."

I laughed. Ehtishem shook his head and said, "I see you're getting stealthier, Ushika."

Her grin revealed gaps where she'd lost two teeth. "Isn't that why you call me that? 'Cause ushikas are sneaky?"

Aevadasa Gahlen entered Ehtishem's quarters through its frosted glass doors. Aevadasa Tinish was on his heels.

"Troublesome little critters, too," Gahlen said. He'd suffered a mouth wound some years ago and couldn't properly enunciate long O's and U's. They came out short and sometimes I had to listen a little closer to understand him.

Ehtishem stepped back. I immediately missed his warmth and strength.

"Troublesome how?" I slipped off the counter and gestured for Pearl to bring me the hairbrush. We shared the same heart-shaped face, pale skin, and wild hair. Only our eyes were different. Unlike my bottle green hue, hers were the blue-green of sea ice. She'd inherited them from her father Cyrus, the man I hated.

The man I'd killed.

"They nest in narrow spaces, like walls, coming and going without your knowledge until the day they gnaw a random cable or water pipe," Gahlen replied.

"But they're effective ahzish control," Tinish pointed out. He was the eldest of Ehtishem's guards. Silver dusted his eyebrows and peach-fuzz hair.

Ahzish were Ohnenrai snakes and Ehtishem muttered, "If only they were effective against the Azatem."

Pearl said, "Momma will be."

His gaze found me and he murmured, "Zant." He straightened his coat and strode toward the door, pausing to chuck her beneath the chin. "Stay sharp today. Someday maybe you'll get your chance to fight them too, little ushika."

She grinned at him. "I will, Payu."

"Ash-ush." He left with Tinish and Gahlen on his heels.

I sat at the dining table. "C'mon. Lemme at that rat's nest." Pearl wrinkled her nose then turned her back to me. We began the morning taming of her hair.

"Are you gonna marry Ehtishem?"

"Something like that. The Ohnenrai call it hathevar." Her hair crackled around my fingers as I worked out the snarls in small sections.

"You should. I told you he's — Ouch! — good for you."

"Sorry," I murmured. "I remember you saying that a while back." Pearl trusted Ehtishem almost from the first day we met. "But it's more complicated than Terran marriage," I added.

She held up a yellow hair tie. "Why? You love each other. That's what matters."

"Well, yes, but there are Ohnenrai laws and citizenship implications. And there's Ahremena's genetics work and the Azatem are still out there hunting us."

She shrugged. "I don't see why any of that matters."

Of course she didn't. I finished braiding her hair and secured it with the tie. "Maybe it shouldn't, Pearly Girly." I kissed her cheek.

She turned and hugged me. "I want Ehtishem to be my dad."

"You mean officially?" She already called him Payu — Father.

She nodded.

"I think he'd like that. And so would I."

She stepped back. "It's settled then," she said and scurried up the stairs.

"I guess so." I touched my lips and laughed; they still tingled from Ehtishem's kisses.

TWO

WITH A BASIC BLACK DESK, a wooden swivel chair, and a pair of metal chairs for visitors, Ehtishem's office in the Offices of the Supreme Command General were spartan. He hadn't hung pictures or brought in any personal items, except his woodcarving knives. No point getting comfortable; he didn't intend to hold the position for long. The only positive about the office was its expansive window to his back. It afforded a view of Barathrishma's lush, green grounds.

Ehtishem scanned the list of complaints on his paper-thin reader. Governing Council members were publicly and privately demanding he immediately deploy Rachel against the Azatem. Ohnenrai Genetics had chimed in to push for it too. Never mind that it was a military matter and his military hadn't yet settled on a plan for deployment and retrieval. The council was overstepping its mandate. Rachel's handling was his responsibility, not theirs, and he was damned tired of explaining that.

His gaze traveled past the reader to a wooden orb perched on a small holder on his desk. He picked it up, balanced it on his palm, and studied the topography he'd carved into it as a boy and refined as a man. Ohnenrah, the Ohnenrai home world, decimated by the Azatem before he was born. Like all his people, Ehtishem was born aboard *Dathusha*, pieced together by Ohnenrai Genetics in a lab and incubated in a surrogate's womb.

He'd carved the orb when he was in training under Sree. She thought woodcarving would calm his mind and control his fists. She was right. She was always right.

Almost always.

His compad sounded. He tapped the blinking screen and Sarem Ahremena Mahlei's face appeared on the device with Ohnenrai Genetics' logo in the background. "Zant, Mother?"

"Two things." She was elegant and intense, with ebony skin and impeccable control over her beautiful face's expressions. "One: Your DNA deposit is overdue. Do I really need to remind you that there are buyers waiting on your sperm, Ehtishem?"

"And they'll keep waiting. I have better things to do than come in a cup for you."

He didn't know why she still insisted on selling off his genes. OG had succeeded in conferring Azatem immunity only to him. That functionality hadn't passed to anyone with his DNA. His genome wasn't better than any other Ohnenran's, but it was sliced and diced, auctioned, and distributed by lottery. Ahremena had convinced an entire generation that Ehtishem Mahle's DNA equalled a superior future and they all wanted a piece of him, no matter how small.

She gazed evenly at him for a moment then said, "Two: Meet me in my lab before you—"

"Contact OSCG about my schedule. I'm unavailable for the next forty-five hours."

"This is significant, Ehtishem. Some unexpected test results."

"Will they alter within two days?"

Her mouth pinched, a millisecond change that conveyed a lifetime of information to Ehtishem, who knew his mother all too well. "Nava."

"Request a meeting through my office or find me on *Pohru-Mahrko* and get in line, I—"

"See me before you leave."

"—have other priorities today," he finished to a blank screen as she ended the connection. The damn woman was trying his very thin patience. There were two hundred thousand soldiers ahead of his mother. He pushed back from the desk. Ahremena believed her work was the most important factor in Ohnenrai survival. She so easily dismissed the day-to-day operations of their ships. Without potable water, her efforts were pointless. Although *Dathusha* and *Pohru-Mahrko* recycled and generated the bulk of their water, the ships still took on fresh supplies when the opportunity arose. Fisk was a graveyard, but she did have plentiful water.

He swiveled his chair and considered Barathrishma's expansive gardens, the sparkling blue lake at its center, the vibrant pink, red, white, gold mahle flowers. If he opened the window, he'd smell the blooms' heady aroma, fresh grass, and the lake's water. He'd hear laughter, conversation, maybe a dog barking. The park's green lushness stood in stark contrast to Ohnenrah, the barren dirt clod their ships were orbiting.

He pivoted back, propped his elbows on the desk, and sandwiched the orb between his hands, rolling it gently, feeling its ridges and curves. He caged it with his fingers and rested his chin upon his hands. "We need a new home." The obvious choice was Terra, but how would her people react to permanent occupation?

And the planet had been noticed by the Azatem. Possibly stripped of life by them already, just as they'd done to Ohnenrah.

He sat back and tossed the wooden orb from hand to hand. "You're getting ahead of yourself, Ratheshtolo." It was something Sree often said. Patience was another of Ehtishem's ceaseless battles.

He exhaled a long breath and winced as nerves around his ribcage twinged. He cursed, "Aiya." That wound still reminded him of how close he'd come to death. "Vairim, Zosh. Vairim," he muttered then pulled up *Pohru-Mahrko*'s medical supplies report and scanned its summary. The Military Medical Supply Depot needed bandages, analgesics, antiseptics, hypomatic cartridges, wound staples. Nothing extraordinary and all available in *Dathusha*'s CMSD storage. He added his approval code to Timsai's and sent the request on its way.

Two more tasks to do before he left for *PM*.

He summoned an assistant into his office.

Nahnesh strode in, tall and sure. The irony of her comfort wasn't lost on him. She'd been ordered to assassinate Ehtishem not so long ago. She'd refused and as a reward he'd offered to make her an aevadasa — a first-level commander — and elevate her to Sub-Elite status, but she'd turned down the promotion. She'd slipped out of the military ranks and had become accustomed to the anonymity of civilian life in the Middle Caste. Qualified to serve an Elite in an assistant role, she'd asked for a position in the Offices of the Supreme Command General. Ehtishem gladly approved her request. She was efficient, flexible, and comfortable with him, a quality few assistants demonstrated.

Nahnesh showed that ease with her greeting. "You look grumpy, fra."

He glowered at her.

"Nava, that word's not strong enough. Barethri Rachel would call it...pissed. You look pissed off."

He *was* pissed off, and tired of fighting morons. "I'm sending a confidential document to your reader. I want it filed with OMCR immediately."

She nodded. "I'll do it now, fra."

His chron chimed. Ninety minutes until he wanted to be aboard *Pohru-Mahrko* to oversee jump prep. He tossed the orb into a desk drawer, transferred a highly-confidential file to Nahnesh's com, then swiped his reader off. "Make sure that private data gets registered with top-level indemnity." It was the first step in freeing Rachel and making her his wife. "I'll finish reviewing the day's complaints aboard *Pohru-Mahrko*. I'm too accessible here."

"Know when you're defeated?"

"Know how to change the field of engagement before you're defeated."

"Will you hear some advice, fra?"

He sat back, met her gaze, nodded.

"Vent some steam before we all pay the price." Wise enough to run after dropping a bomb, she saluted and left the office.

Ehtishem exhaled a slow breath. "That bad, huh?" His vertebrae crackled as he rotated his head. Stress was part of the job. He shrugged and contacted Gahlen. Three hours until the day shift ended. He wanted to review the drop strategy for the water runs before anyone set foot on Fisk.

"Fra?" the soldier answered.

"Please notify Panca Command that I want a readiness report by eighteen-hundred hours."

"Zant, fra."

A notification popped up and chimed on his compad. Nahnesh had scheduled him for a meeting with Ahremena, just as his mother had demanded. He shook his head and denied the item. "Unexpected test results." More problems and delays? "What else did you get wrong about the Azatem Code, Mother?" One more reason why he was postponing deploying Rachel.

The Azatem Code conferred immunity against the alien Azatem's genetic weaponry and, in the laboratory, made Rachel a weapon against them in turn. Whether or not the Azatem Code would cripple their powerful enemy in practice remained to be seen. She was the only carrier of a full code and Ehtishem wouldn't risk her until he was certain she could fulfill her function *and* be retrieved. The latter half of the equation was controversial. Most Ohnenrai considered her expendable.

He did not.

He opened his desk drawer, retrieved a small parcel, and pocketed it. He stood and straightened his uniform, tugging the sleeves down and smoothing a crease from the front. His troubles and challengers would wait. Certainly they wouldn't go away or give up. He picked up his reader, pausing to consider a quick message to Rachel, then slipped it into his pocket. She didn't expect to hear from him until after they reached Fisk. He'd promised her a tour of *PM* and that was one promise he could easily fulfill.

Ehtishem stepped off the lift into the gray austerity of *Dathusha's* prison block. He checked in with the Bilge officers and was escorted to a cell at the end of a long, empty ward. They let him into the rectangular pen, a space large enough to accommodate a bunk, a toilet, and a wall-mounted table and chair.

Vent some steam.

Nahnesh had meant a trip to the Nest for sex, but Ehtishem hadn't wanted anyone except Rachel since the day they'd met. However, he wouldn't bed her angry. That would be a dangerous mistake. Nava. Relief would come in the form of pummeling his sparring partners later. Now, however, he could find some peace in speaking with an old advisor. He hoped.

"Should we stay, fra?" one of the officers asked.

"Leave. I'll summon you when I'm finished."

They saluted him and marched back toward their station.

The woman occupying the cell had close-cropped silver hair, a face creased from age and experience, and a dark unflinching gaze. She was small for an Ohnenran, though taller and broader than Rachel.

"About time you came to see me." Sree paused in doing pushups. "I'm pleased you're still alive, Ratheshtolo." The nickname was hers alone to use; it meant Little Warrior. She resumed exercising. Though she was almost three decades past Ehtishem's forty-two years, Sree was solid muscle.

He dug his fingers into his side where his uncle had knifed him between the ribs. The muscles still ached. "I don't like seeing you here. You were the one person I thought I could trust. This cell reminds me of how wrong I was."

She paused at the bottom of her next pushup, pulled her feet up beneath her, and stood. "I did what I believed was best for the Ohnenrai. I didn't mean to kill that boy or destroy your trust."

"Meant to or not, Adam's dead. Your disobedience nearly killed all the Terrans. You endangered Rachel. Pearl. Even the Ohnenrai."

She brushed her hands on her yellow-and-white-striped pants. "I thought I was making the best decision for our people."

"You didn't trust me."

"I put my faith in genetics. I don't know if that was a mistake or not." Sree's low voice matched his. "When Rachel was brought aboard *Dathusha*, Ahremena emphasized this was a military operation and told me to guarantee access to her remained unfettered by Isphahan, the Purists, or anyone else. I was to exterminate any threat to our success."

"How was a fourteen-year-old Terran boy a threat?"

"He put himself between Rachel and me."

Ehtishem didn't bother to hide a scowl from her. "And if it had been me stepping between you? Would I be dead, too?"

Sree folded her legs beneath her as she sat on her thin bunk mattress. "Of course not. You'd only be incapacitated. As I was trying to do with Adam."

"Slim comfort for me, none for him."

"Why are you here?"

He folded a hinged seat down from the wall and sat. He stretched out his long legs and crossed his ankles and his arms. "I'm calling in favors and you owe me."

Her brows arched. "Do I?"

"You're still alive despite a conviction for treason. Who do you think intervened in your sentencing?"

Her chin lifted and she side-eyed him. "I'm listening."

"I'll commute your sentence if you pledge to give up your freedom and your life to protect Pearl, and if you agree to train her to fight as you trained me."

Her head tilted. "You've grown fond of the girl."

"I have an obligation." Pearl was more than a responsibility, but Ehtishem still didn't understand his relationship with Rachel's daughter. He just knew he wanted her happy and safe.

"What does her mother think of this?"

"Rachel doesn't know and she's no longer your concern.

Your sole purpose will be Pearl's well-being and training. Do you agree or not?"

Sree stood. "Agreed. Ferahi-va. I won't fail you, Ratheshtolo."

"You'd better not. Your life is guaranteed by that child's. If she dies, so will you."

THREE

"THIS IS SO AWESOME!" Pearl sat opposite me in the eating area motoring through the grayish-green gruel that had replaced two out of three daily meals aboard both ships. "I can't wait to get into the field with Audie. We had the top scores again last week. Did I tell you, Momma?"

"Yes, at least five times. Being in the field won't be all sunshine and roses, you know." I poked at the sludge in my bowl. Knowing what was in the mixture didn't make it more appealing — powdered grubs, powdered vegetables, vitamins and minerals. It also came in an equally disgusting and almost un-chewable hockey puck shape. No matter the form, it tasted like salty banana, grass, and dirt. Ohnenrai restricted rations were altogether disappointing.

"I know. But I don't mind hard work." Finished eating, she washed her bowl then headed upstairs to fetch Audie from his kennel.

I put my bowl of nastiness in the kitchen cooler. Food couldn't be wasted. When I got hungry enough, it would taste better. Starvation made anything edible. I knew that from experience.

Aevadasa Huorem and Aevadasa Mahzel came through the apartment's front doors. As members of Ehtishem's inner circle they wore the same charcoal-gray uniform he did, decorated with the same dog head symbol and almost as many commendations.

"Will Pearl and Audie go to *Pohru-Mahrko* before or after the jump?" I asked Huorem as he sauntered into the kitchen whistling between his teeth.

"Probably after, but the trainees won't go dirtside until Recon signals all-clear."

I filled a cup with suxra. The stuff tasted shittier than muddy water, which was another memory I'd rather not relive. I took a gulp. The bitter red tea had grown significantly more flavorful with the introduction of bug paste to my diet. "How do all of you grow so big eating squashed insects?"

Mahzel said, "They're highly nutritious."

"And wholly disgusting," I replied.

Mahzel was the straight man to Huorem's smart-ass, the one always on watch with eyes the same unusual hazel shade as Ehtishem's. He didn't make me laugh the way Hu did, but I trusted him implicitly. His quiet presence often felt like a substitute for my lover's. Mahzel made me feel protected. Huorem made me forget my worries.

Hu sat on the wide countertop. "I understand why you don't like eating insects. Terra's aren't as tasty as the ones we raise shipboard."

"Nava. I don't like them because they taste like starvation." I sipped the suxra. "Ohnenrai bug paste reminds me of some of our leanest times in Suffer."

Pearl reappeared at the top of the stairs, ready for her day and still bouncing. Audie charged past her and into the kitchen.

He skidded to a stop beside me, all wiggles and wagging, and nuzzled my hand. I fondled his floppy, brindle ears as he gazed at me with adoration in his brown eyes. Mahzel crossed the room to scratch Audie under the harness. The dog arched his neck, so my bodyguard could reach just the right spot.

Huorem grinned at Pearl. "Excited to go dirtside, Ushika?"

"Very." She attached a long lead to Audie's harness. The dog wagged from nose to tail and nuzzled Mahzel's hand when he stopped scratching.

When Pearl said, "Audie, va'jam," the dog's attention went immediately to her, the scratches forgotten. He knew when she meant business.

Mahzel approved. "Ushta, Pearl. You make a good team."

Her answering smile reminded me of sunshine, the real kind, not *Dathusha*'s artificial daylight.

"Ready to leave, Barethri?" Huorem asked. I nodded and we all headed for the security pass-way and the locked Master Lift beyond it. Just another day in space aboard *Dathusha*.

The world outside the window blurred as the bullet-shaped car our small party rode in shot down its track toward Ahn Maidhya Terasca — the Central Cross.

"We are one."

Okay, got it. I heard you the first time, I thought. *You can shut up now.*

Pearl nudged me. "Earth to Momma."

"Hmm?"

She studied my face. "I said, I wish I had a mahle bloom on my face instead of this nasty snake."

"I wish you didn't have that ahzish or any other mark." I stroked her fair cheek and looked past the gaping jaws of the

Uahdim family's mark — a white, fanged serpent winding from the middle of her forehead down her left cheek to her jaw. Isphahan made her his property. His death made her Ahremena's. Ahremena traded unfettered access to me for Pearl's freedom.

She reached up to trace the white blossom — more a brand than a tattoo — that marked my face. Her fingers followed the vines and leaves that twined past my eye and around my temple to end in an unfurling bud on my forehead. "At least your mark is pretty."

Snaring her fingers, I kissed them then pressed her small hand between my palms. "That's beside the point. A mark isn't a good thing." I glanced at the broad backs of the two soldiers who accompanied us.

"I know, I know. I'm no one's possession. Neither are you." She'd heard this from me plenty of times.

"Legally?"

She shrugged. "I don't care about legally, Momma. Ehtishem doesn't think of you as property."

The car shifted tracks and slowed, leaving my stomach a few feet behind as it pulled into the crowded main hub for all the automated cars zipping people and products from one end of *Dathusha* to the other. The Ohnenrai ship was nearly the size of New York City and home to eight million Ohnenrai citizens and a scant handful of Terrans — two dying races. The lights above the car door changed from green to purple and the neighboring cars stopped and shifted from track to track, up and down, making way for our transport. The purple traffic lights coloring Ahn Maidhya Terasca brought all eyes to our car as it stopped at the loading platform. Purple meant important. It meant Elite. It meant everyone noticed me, whether I liked it or not.

"Barethri." Huorem gestured for us to precede him as

Mahzel opened the door, his shock rifle at ready-rest and his head turning from left to right as he scanned the crowd.

"Anghu framarez pantham, vana." Mahzel's voice boomed above the crowd. He'd ordered them to clear a path as Pearl and I stepped from the car.

The crowd strained against curiosity and a wave of murmurs washed over our little group. We proceeded through the opening in the flickering amber energy wall protecting Ohnenrai citizens from the thundering cars on the tracks below the platform. Pearl and I were oddities — Terrans who'd gained the affection of their zosh.

She hopped lines in the flooring, her brunette braid swinging to and fro as our group proceeded toward another lift. Audie trotted beside her. His perked ears and keen eyes meant he was protecting his pack, not playing.

Many brown Ohnenrai gazes followed our progress toward Barathrishma, the park that dominated the center of *Dathusha*. I wondered how many opinions were unfavorable in that sea of beautiful faces. We were aliens. And we were property. Their last leader conquered and nearly destroyed our home world, yet Pearl and I received a military escort and had the ear of the zosh. We lived in luxury.

At the park entrance Pearl hugged me. "See you at Fisk, Momma." She and Audie jogged down the path toward a group of students and their animals — mostly Terran dogs but a few of the larger, wolfish Ohnenrai pa'cashmem. I stood at the top of a rolling, tree-lined hill and watched her return the salutes of her trainers and fellow trainees.

"She's earned their respect," Mahzel said beside me.

I nodded. "'She may be small but she is fierce.'"

"It doesn't hurt that the zosh hasn't hidden his affection for her."

I looked sidelong at him. "Favoritism? You sure that's not a hindrance?"

"Not for her, Barethri. She's military." He nodded toward the group of handlers. "She's one of them."

Huorem grinned. "One of us."

"We are one."

"I don't need you here right now," Judilei said as I entered the CMSD. The lead tech of the Civilian Medical Supply Depot jerked her thumb at three junior techs packing supplies and toting bins.

I stopped at the door. "I'm on the schedule." I waggled my compad as if it would refute the supply tech's point.

"I don't need you here," she repeated. "I have my morning staff."

I shoved the com into my gray jumpsuit's thigh pocket. "Then send me on deliveries." We had this conversation all too often.

At first, I'd walked on eggshells around Judilei, intimidated by her surliness, her hulking fists, and her dour looks. Then I'd decided the bug up her butt had a bug up its butt and there was no reason not to do my job and do it well. But her displeasure at having a Terran in her department still grew. Last-minute scheduling changes and kicking me out to run minor errands were her newest tactics to keep me away.

I could say something to Ehtishem about it. But I wouldn't. I was pretty damn sure Judilei wanted me to cry and run back to my protector. She knew Ehtishem wanted me seen working side-by-side with the Ohnenrai and pulling my own weight. But my efforts and weight didn't mean squat to her. So I stayed in her hair and didn't back down. Her bitchiness made me more determined to sit under her nose.

"You're on the afternoon shift. Go home, Terran. "

Go home. That stung. I folded my arms. "Which home do you mean, Ohnenran? The one with a bed where I screw your zosh? Or the one your former zosh screwed all to hell?"

Behind me, Huorem sniggered. In front of me, all work stopped.

Her gaze was flinty. "What did you say?"

"Send me on deliveries."

Judilei considered me with a set jaw and narrowed dark-brown eyes. Slowly the head tech turned. She considered the wall chron then grabbed a black canvas satchel off the floor and tossed it onto the long counter between us. "Replacement cartridges. Take them to Dvaidasa Dahmircan, then finish your hours on *Pohru-Mahrko.*" She picked up her com and turned away, muttering, "I don't need an Elite plaything underfoot."

I bit back a reply that might require my guards to save my ass, instead opting for, "Will do, boss." I hefted the satchel onto my shoulder, pivoted, and left the CMSD, but not without noticing the speculative gazes of the junior techs.

Back at Ahn Maidhya Terasca, Huorem, Mahzel, and I passed through the doorway set into the coppery energy barrier. Cars flashed past the platform or gently stopped to release and accept passengers.

Huorem huffed a loud sigh. "I hate lines. You know that, Barethri?"

"Yep."

The pressure in my ears expanded and contracted as cars thundered past. The Central Cross was a hive of activity. Ohnenrai soldiers dressed in dark-gray uniforms marched past with smart purpose. Civilians wearing jewel-toned tunics and gowns strolled and chatted. Lower Level workers in dingy coveralls lumbered by us, the weight of their thoughts seeming to slow them. All moved through *Dathusha's* primary transportation hub to and from every part of the massive civilian ship. Bridges arched between the platforms and the cars passed beneath as they entered and exited the interchange. Those releasing passengers rose out of the lanes as oncoming traffic thundered through. The deck rumbled beneath our feet, a ceaseless manmade earthquake. Tunnels and lanes shot off in every direction. The Cross's levels spanned thirty stories of the cavernous ship, but access was restricted at the highest levels.

Huorem muttered, "There's nothing wrong with taking the Elite Line."

Mahzel replied, "You know Barethri Rachel's to be seen."

"And that I hate the Elite Level citizens," I added. "They pretend I don't exist."

"Or run away like you're a diseased little freak," Hu said and laughed when Mahzel elbowed him.

I snorted. *Typhoid Rachel.*

We shuffled forward with the crowd. Mahzel scanned the area, his shock rifle at ready-rest and his eyes keen. Huorem, despite his jokes and complaints, also kept a sharp eye on the people around us.

Mahzel said, "Judilei should've sent the cartridges with another tech and let you serve your scheduled time here."

"I know. But she didn't, and I'm not going back to Ehtishem's quarters to sit with my thumb up my butt all damn day."

"The zosh will be displeased," he added. Ehtishem had cleared me to work in the civilian MSD but not *Pohru-Mahrko's* military MSD.

"Pissed off, you mean." I tugged the bag up on my shoulder. Judilei made it look light, but it definitely wasn't. I faced Mahzel and added, "The zosh doesn't need to hear about this."

He stopped scanning the crowd to meet my gaze. "But we all know he will. Somehow."

Huorem said, "And we'll be deader than dead."

I rolled my eyes. "Yet you're not stopping me from going."

Hu snorted. "What? Miss a chance to break the rules and blame it on Judilei?"

I laughed and he nodded, a wicked grin on his face. The man's humor was indomitable and infectious. He was the most animated Ohnenrai soldier I'd ever met.

Mahzel murmured, "I would not mind seeing her torn down by the zosh."

"I don't know how she stays upright with that big ol' chip on her shoulder," I said.

The crowd's rumble ebbed and flowed with the movement of the vehicles. With a deafening *hiss* and *clunk* two massive grappling arms dropped one of the cars into place on the track while four passed in the lower lanes. The line of passengers moved forward. I looked up as I stepped into the car. Rows of suspended transports gently swayed above the platform on massive hooks. It was too easy to imagine being crushed by one of those things if the clamps failed.

I found a seat. Huorem and Mahzel stood back-to-back before it, preventing anyone from sitting beside me.

"Is that really necessary?" I asked.

"Zant." Mahzel didn't turn. Huorem just started whistling.

It was a familiar argument I never won. Ehtishem had charged them with my protection and they would not fail their zosh. Mostly, I was grateful. "Sometimes the hovering gets annoying, you know."

They ignored me as more passengers shoved in and the car filled to standing room only.

"Rachel?"

I looked around at hearing my name. Lot Jones, my dead best friend's widower, eased though the standing crowd. He was one of the few Terrans still aboard *Dathusha* and had a history — good and bad — with Ehtishem.

"Hi, Lot." I moved over and patted the seat beside me. "Sit." He glanced at my guards. I elbowed Huorem in the hip. "Move, aevadasa. Let him sit down."

He and Mahzel eyed Lot before slowly stepping aside.

"Uh, ferahi-va," he said and sat. Neither responded.

No longer slave labor, Lot wore a mechanic's green coveralls with Draxtu-Mainyu embroidered on the chest and back. Ehtishem rewarded loyalty. Lot and his crew had earned it by helping free thousands of Terrans enslaved by Isphahan. Their selfless actions resulted in them being trapped aboard *Dathusha*, but the few times we'd talked Lot hadn't expressed any regrets.

"Where are you heading?" I asked.

"*Pohru-Mahrko.* The zosh's personal transport is scheduled for service. Since he's taking it to the cruiser-carrier, we're going too."

"It can't wait?"

"Anyone else's could, but we don't put off inspecting and servicing the zosh's ship."

I nodded. Ehtishem was as important to my few fellow Terrans aboard the Ohnenrai ships as he was to his own people. Maybe more because it was his word that kept us safe. No one believed Isphahan's xenophobia had died with him.

"How's Pearl?" he asked.

"Really good. She and Audie will go dirtside with one of the teams when we reach Fisk."

"Proving themselves, huh?"

"Growing up faster than I'd like, but doing it with grace."

He nodded and looked down at his hands. His sons had died in Suffer with his wife, murdered by Cyrus. That monster had destroyed so many lives.

I squeezed his hand and let go. "I'm sorry."

He met my gaze, his mouth a thin line, his eyes filled with well-worn grief. "I know." He stood. "My stop's coming up." He slipped around Huorem and Mahzel and headed for the closest door, disappearing into the crowd as the transport slowed for the next platform.

I spent the rest of the ride to the Southeast Shipping Bay staring out the window at the passing blur, remembering Lot's wife Judith and his boys, their sunshine-yellow kitchen, her sweet smile. She was kind to Pearl and me even though the rest of the community rejected us. I helped deliver her baby boy just before I fled Suffer. I closed my eyes. That baby, Judith, her two older sons, and all the people of that community but Lot, Pearl, and I were murdered by Cyrus.

Cyrus. My tormentor. Pearl's biological father. The last time I saw him, his blood was oozing from his broken face and gaping mouth. His brain showed through the massive gash I'd made in his skull with a wrench. I opened my eyes. I still felt his spittle sliding down my cheek.

The car pulled into our stop at the shipping bay and my escorts guided me through the noise and order of hundreds of troop transports ferrying soldiers to their duty stations aboard *Pohru-Mahrko*.

"Elite force, SSW," Huorem muttered and nodded toward a figure speaking with two soldiers in flight suits.

Ahremena. Her gaze followed me as Hu, Mahzel, and I boarded one of the gray, beetle-like transports. I expected her to stride across the flight deck, stop our ship, and question me at length. Instead, she turned back to the men and continued her conversation.

"Think the sarem will report us?" Huorem muttered as we found open seats.

"She didn't stop us." Mahzel shrugged. "And we're following Judilei's orders."

"Exactly," I agreed. "If our chops get busted, so will that battle-ax's."

Huorem snorted. "Battle-ax. I like that."

Mahzel stowed my bag in the overhead compartment as I secured my five-point flight harness with a few hard tugs. He settled to my left. Huorem sat on my right. This trip would take us from civilian ship luxury to the austere functionality of the super-heavy cruiser-carrier *Pohru-Mahrko, Dathusha's* escort and protector.

As the transport filled, the soldier who took the seat opposite mine, considered me then looked at Huorem. "Still babysitting?" he asked. The sneer in his voice didn't show in his disciplined expression.

The small ship lifted off the flight deck, its motion making straps and netting sway all around us. Metal clattered and squeaked. The floor juddered.

"Zant, Rivan," Huorem answered. "Mahzel needs all the coddling he can get." He jerked his thumb at me. "That's why Barethri Rachel's along." He leaned forward and the humor left his voice as he added, "She's got more in-field kills than you."

Rivan's gaze flicked from me to Mahzel who held up five fingers. Rivan's eyebrows lifted then he blinked and settled back. "Good thing you've got her to protect you."

Mahzel nodded slowly as Huorem slouched in his seat and closed his eyes. I did the same. No point in staring at the Ohnenrai soldiers around me.

Let them wonder, I thought.

Besides, military drops were rough. Better to focus on deep breathing than to challenge doubters then barf on my own boots. Reinforcing that fact, the transport jolted as it settled into the waiting arms of a small guide ship. Metal scraped metal and some of the soldiers pounded their fists against the inner hull and shouted insults at the pilots.

Static came over the intercom followed by a nerve-grating squeal that garnered more protests. "Quit whining, you babies," the pilot said.

Artificial gravity pulled me against the seat as the airlock doors thudded overhead. An alarm sounded, red and yellow lights strobed, the ship plunged from *Dathusha's* belly into the dark nothingness of space. With a flip made nauseating by the sudden loss of gravity, the transport rolled down and away from the civilian mother ship then shot toward *Pohru-Mahrko*.

More static came over the intercom, then the pilot's feminine voice filled the cabin again: "Grab your boobs and your balls, girls and boys. We're running fast and landing hard."

Beside me, Huorem was already snoring.

The Ohnenrai built *Dathusha's* wide halls, arched walkways, and open boulevards with civilian life and luxuries in mind. *Pohru-Mahrko*, on the other hand, was every inch a warship and the comfort of the crew came second. With the exception of her cavernous launch bays, the cruiser-carrier was cramped. Her bulkheads and overheads sprouted cables, conduits, and gauges. Access panels hid all manner of equipment. Food and supplies took any spare space.

I ducked through another low-clearance doorway and maneuvered around soldiers on the way to the MMSD, the bag slung across my chest to keep it from snagging equipment.

Huorem peered down at me, his long stride easily keeping him at my side. "You seem comfortable here."

We stopped at the east lift on Deck H. The depot was twelve decks above. "I like small spaces." We stepped in and Mahzel directed the computer to our destination as I added, "My dad took me on a tour of an American fast-attack sub when I was a kid. *PM* reminds me of that."

"What's a sub?" Huorem asked.

"Submarine," Mahzel replied. "A deep-water vessel that relies on speed and stealth to surprise and destroy enemy ships. They remain submerged much of the time they're on duty."

I peered at the aevadasa. "I didn't know you were into Terran military vessels, Mahzel."

"Ocean-going vessels are the closest equivalent your military had to our ships. I find the parallels interesting."

"Huh." I put down the heavy bag and leaned against the cold lift wall as it took us upward. It felt good to stop and breathe and not have so many gazes assessing me.

We reached our deck and traversed two more narrow passages to reach the medical storeroom. *Pohru-Mahrko* kept only enough supplies on hand to cover a ninety-day deployment. Hypomatics were the preferred method for injecting medicines, but their pressure cartridges required regular scrubbing, filling, and pressurizing. Hence my visit. The MMSD had gotten two faulty cartridges from *Dathusha's* CMSD and all other cartridges from their batches were rejected as potentially unreliable. I pitied whoever had made that mistake. They'd be scrubbing the heads for a few weeks; standard military punishment across the galaxy, it seemed.

"Weren't your parents in the United States military, Barethri?" Mahzel asked as we entered the depot's receiving room.

"Just my father."

Like in the MMSD, a shiny metal counter ran from one end of the room to the other. I pulled the cases from my bag and stacked them on it. Standing behind the counter, Dvaidasa Dahmircan ignored me. He was in charge of all the medical supplies and supply personnel aboard *Pohru-Mahrko*. While I counted the filled med packs hanging on the vertical supply conveyor — a wall of hooks that moved downward through an opening, carrying the filled packs to a dispersal room below — he refilled a bin with rolls of gauze, counting as he stocked, and updated the ship's inventory on his reader. Finished with his task, he straightened and eyed Huorem and Mahzel then turned his black gaze on me. "You brought replacement hypo cartridges?"

"Zant, fra." The fra, *sir*, was unnecessary from me, but a little deference from a civilian never hurt.

Dahmircan slid a blade into the top case's seal and flicked the point through the membrane to pop it open. "Aeva, dva, thrish—" He began counting and checking every cartridge to verify that all thousand were properly sealed and dated.

Huorem leaned against the counter, his back to it and his elbows propped on its cool surface. "I thought your father was an interpreter, Barethri."

"And a pilot. My mother was a civilian physician." Dahmircan shot me a look that commanded silence. I passed it on to Hu as I rolled up my sleeves, and got to work filling med packs for the away teams.

I'd been on depot duty for almost six months and had finally convinced Huorem and Mahzel that they didn't need to hover over me the entire time I was working. My insistence that they skedaddle was helped by Judilei's surly attitude. Dahmircan's was no warmer. Once the supply master approved the replacement cartridges, the two soldiers headed for the closest firing range. With ten hours before the jump ships opened a wormhole, I could put in seven hours on *Pohru-Mahrko* and still make it back to *Dathusha* before the departure. Ehtishem would be none the wiser.

"Civvies aren't permitted aboard *PM* during military maneuvers," Dahmircan remarked.

"Tell that to Judilei. This was her idea." I slipped hot/cold packs into the bag I was prepping. "Let's hope the zosh doesn't find out."

Dahmircan picked up the new cartridges. "It'll be her ass in a sling, not mine. I'll send back a load of spents with you." He disappeared into the supply warehouse, leaving me alone.

Or so I thought.

"We are one."

The voices were so loud, I looked around, almost expecting someone to be screwing with me. No luck. Just my multiple personalities.

"Shut up," I muttered.

"We are one."

I didn't feel like having this one-sided conversation for the next seven hours, so I started singing to drown them out.

"In the gloaming, oh, my darling, when the lights are dim and low." I pulled a brown-and-green camo bag that was bigger than Pearl from a wheeled bin and flopped it up on the counter. "And the quiet shadows falling, softly come and softly go." Opening and unfolding it revealed compartments and holders for every type of medical equipment a med tech could want while dirtside. "When the trees are sobbing faintly with a gentle unknown woe."

In went a backboard and an inflatable cervical brace. "Will you think of me and love me, as you did once long ago?" A vitals scanner found its pocket and thermal blankets snugged in nearby. "In the gloaming, oh, my darling, think not bitterly of me." Gauze and bandages, suture staples, a stapler, a hypomatic and its cartridges found their way into pockets and behind straps. "Tho' I passed away in silence, left you lonely, set you free."

Cauteries, clamps, and retractors were added. "For my heart was crush'd with longing, what had been could never be." Analgesics, antiseptics, cortisone, and clotting agents followed. "It was best to leave you thus, dear, best for you and best for me." Antibacterial cleansers, saline, anti-convulsants, blood replacer, and emergency oxygen were stowed and secured, too. "In the gloaming, oh, my darling, when the lights are dim and low." A pre-packed host of other medications to keep soldiers alive completed the kit. "Will you think of me and love me, as you did once long ago?" I rolled, folded, and closed the compartments then the bag, and the song ended with a grunt as I pulled the weighty kit off the counter and swung it onto the conveyor's hooks.

One down, ninety-nine to go. I grabbed another camo bag and started the song and the packing again. Though I wasn't treating patients, I was saving lives. Indirectly, yes, but that was something to be proud of, nonetheless.

FOUR

"ZOSH ON DECK!"

Thrai Timsai met Ehtishem as he exited the lift onto *Pohru-Mahrko*'s command deck. "Pre-jump preparations are running smoothly and we're on target to hit our mark at oh-sixteen-hundred, fra. The last transports are in line to complete personnel transfer within the hour."

"Excellent."

"This trip is well-timed, too."

Ehtishem studied his thrai's stony expression. "Trouble?"

"More fighting's been reported."

"What's causing the increase?"

"Considering that most of the instigators were stationed on Terra, I'd say they're frustrated with being ship-bound."

Ehtishem nodded as he settled into the commander's chair. He understood. After twelve years under Terra's open sky, *Dathusha* and *Pohru-Mahrko* felt small and cold. "We're not meant to be trapped in a tin can beneath artificial lights for so long. Those who've never set foot on a planet don't know any better, but the soldiers returning from long ground ops are missing real sunlight and fresh air." He surveyed the quiet industriousness of the command deck crew. "Let's consider an extended stay on Fisk."

"Agreed."

Ehtishem had a canvas roll and a leather-covered wooden stropping block in hand. As he untied the roll's straps the deck lights turned amber and a klaxon sounded. He looked at Timsai and arched a brow. "Did someone forget to set their chron?"

The thrai's fleet scowl said he'd chew someone's head off. It was replaced with concern when one of the jump techs said, "Wormhole formation, fra."

Timsai responded, "We haven't deployed."

The tech replied. "It's not ours, Thrai." Professionalism and training couldn't quite hide the note of fear in his voice.

Ehtishem thought, *The Azatem tracked Rachel.* He said, "How long until emergence?"

"Estimating seventeen minutes."

"Call the count, please," Timsai said. "Deploy the paradox lock and jump ships. Let's get that array out in record time, pa'nerem. Our lives depend upon it. I want all transports berthed double-time. No time to secure them. Just get them inside."

"Zant, fra. Initiating hangar lockdown. All bay doors sealing in five minutes."

Ehtishem said, "Com, relay orders to *Dathusha*. Initiate emergency engagement protocols. We'll jump to the Fisk Juncture. Nav, input the coordinates."

Timsai said, "Open a ship-wide channel."

"Channel open. Go ahead, fra."

"This is your thrai speaking. We have enemy wormhole formation. Lock and slings have been deployed. All personnel report to action stations. All transports dock and lock immediately. This is not a drill. I repeat, this is not a drill. All personnel report to action stations."

"Deploying lock and slings."

"Calculating coordinates for the Fisk Juncture."

"Transports are heading home. Emergency docking procedures in effect, fra."

"Ushta," Ehtishem said.

Timsai turned to his weapons techs. "Ready full loads. Give me status on the shields and countermeasures."

"Sixteen minutes until emergence."

"Shields at sixty-eight percent and climbing steadily."

"Countermeasures coming online now, fra."

A communications tech said, "*Dathusha* is hailing us, fra."

"On screen," Timsai replied.

Fravaz Ahnoru, *Dathusha's* captain, appeared on the command deck's wall-length bank of screens.

"Problem, fravaz?" Ehtishem asked.

"Zant." Ahnoru's relaxed expression reflected none of it. "There's a transport heading your way with orders to dock aboard *Pohru-Mahrko*, rather than returning to the closer berth in our belly."

"Who's the idiot behind that order?"

"Sarem Mahlei. Apparently, she's aboard and refusing to obey protocol."

"I see." Ehtishem didn't let his anger at his mother's insubordination and recklessness creep into his voice.

Timsai ordered his crew to locate the transport in question and hold the nearest docking bay open.

Ehtishem finally unrolled the canvas kit — his woodcarving tools — and slipped a straight gouge from its compartment. "Think I should take the opportunity to shoot her, Ahnoru?"

"I can see how that would be a great temptation, fra,"

Dathusha's captain replied. He'd long been one of Ehtishem's closest allies and they shared a dislike for Ahremena.

Timsai said, "The transport's four minutes from Launch Bay C East."

"Inform them LBC East will close in three minutes." Ehtishem placed the wood block on his thigh, leather face up, and slid the gouge across its surface with a sure, even stroke. "And tell my mother to move her ass. We're not at liberty to wait for her today."

"Zant, fra," a communications tech replied.

"Anyone who doesn't want to meet the Azatem should be berthing by now," Ehtishem said. "Sarem Mahlei knows that."

The command crew murmured and heads nodded all around. This eventuality had been drilled into all of them from the time they were old enough to walk. Ahremena was breaking protocol, and Ehtishem wouldn't delay their escape for her.

Ahnoru nodded. "We're in agreement. *Dathusha* out." The screen went dark.

Timsai turned to his crew. "Stay focused, pa'nerem."

Hush returned to the deck, the only sounds made by the ship's computers, chairs creaking, commands and responses, the steady scrape of Ehtishem's tools being honed. The rhythmic task focused him and helped him block his crew's turbulent emotions so he could maintain vairim.

On the largest overhead display, two small, orange, bullet-shaped ships and a cluster of smaller silver ships emerged from *Pohru-Mahrko's* forward and aft Lock Bays. The jump techs, well-practiced after six months of wormhole travel, maneuvered the orange lock ships into place on *Dathusha's* nose and *Pohru-Mahrko's* tail, and ringed the convoy with the silver sling ships.

Timsai said, "Paradox lock status?"

"Lock is engaged and holding steady on *Dathusha*'s nose and our tail, Thrai."

"Slings?"

"Powering up."

Ehtishem checked the array and said, "Record time, pa'nerem. Ferahi-va. Wormhole status?"

"Fourteen minutes until emergence, fra."

"Give me a visual on the emergence field, *Dathusha*, and the lock," Timsai said.

A jump tech replied, "The computer's having trouble predicting the field, fra."

Ehtishem stopped honing and looked up. "Why?"

"Unclear. We're getting indications of the field across multiple vectors."

"Show me," he commanded and leaned forward.

The calculations appeared on another screen, an ever-changing array of numbers and directions.

Ehtishem scanned them. "Utha."

Timsai saw the pattern he did and started barking orders even as *Pohru-Mahrko*'s proximity alert started blaring. "We're in the emergence field. Take evasives. Now."

"Warn *Dathusha*," Ehtishem snapped.

"Already have, fra."

A jump tech said, "*Dathusha*'s pulling the lock and sling ships with her. The rear lock is still on our tail, but the net's stretched to max. It'll fail if she pulls away. What are your orders, fra?"

"*Dathusha* is on screen," another tech said.

The wide overhead display showed opaque clouds of roiling gases obscuring great swaths of space. *Dathusha* — the massive Ohnenrai civilian ship — fired thrusters to reorient her position in the paradox lock formation. A single orange vessel at her nose formed the point of the paradox lock. The silver sling ships ringed her like a belt. In concert with *Pohru-Mahrko* and a second lock ship bringing up the rear of the tethered formation, the array manipulated space to open and close wormholes. But now *Dathusha* was breaking formation. The space around her and *PM* shimmered and undulated like an unstable iridescent bubble.

Formation alarms started blaring, a discordant cacophony with the proximity alarm. The view warped further. The Azatem ship's wormhole exit was forming between the two Ohnenrai ships.

"Get us out of this field," Timsai ordered.

Ehtishem knew it was suicide for *PM*, but he made the only decision that might save the majority of his people. "Release the rear lock. Order *Dathusha* to jump without us. We'll meet them at Fisk."

Fear rippled through the ranks as soldiers shifted in their seats, looked at each other, or stared at the overhead screen.

Ehtishem gripped his carving tools and reached deep for vairim to block the crew's emotions. He needed calm, control. He needed focus. There was no time for fear or doubt if he was going to keep his soldiers alive. He said, "Nav, we need an escape route. Find one fast."

"Zant, fra."

"Rear lock disengaged."

"Taking evasives." The cruiser-carrier shuddered beneath them as she fired her engines and accelerated away from the forming wormhole. *Dathusha*'s engine's flared. The civilian vessel began moving in the opposite direction, but she was still pulling the rear lock ship into place.

"*Dathusha*'s realigning the lock, fra. She's preparing to jump."

"There's no time, Ahnoru," Timsai muttered. "Com, tell her to run now, jump later."

"We have wormhole formation."

Space warped and the red Azatem leviathan, *Maso-Vohu*, emerged from a wormhole to dwarf *Pohru-Mahrko*. Caught out of alignment, the Ohnenrai rear lock ship exploded as *Maso's* leading edge rammed it. The jump net failed in a cascade of golden energy. Free from tension, the remaining net ships spun wildly, firing their thrusters to control their trajectories and escape the Azatem ship's path.

Timsai ordered, "Go to tactical."

"Going to tactical."

The central screens changed to a representation of the situation with markers for *Dathusha*, the Azatem warship, and an ever-changing overlay of measurements and calculations. Other screens maintained the exterior view of *Dathusha*, some focused on the Azatem leviathan, others the exterior of *Pohru-Mahrko*.

Ehtishem was calm. Combat always blocked his worries. There was only the enemy and the will to survive, to win. He slid the gouge blade across the wood block as he studied the scene. "Thrai, let's draw her attention and her fire away from those civilians. Give them a chance to escape."

"Helm, cross *Maso's* nose. Short burn," Timsai said. "Fire pulse missiles at will. Target arrays, radar, weapons systems, anything sticking out of that beast that might be useful. I want her deaf and blind when we run."

A grim chorus of "Zant, fra," filled the command deck. Doubtless many of them didn't think they'd survive long enough to run anywhere.

"Stay focused," Timsai said.

"Missiles away," a senior weapons tech announced.

"*Dathusha's* recovered the remaining lock and sling ships, Thrai."

"Targeting reports one hundred percent strike rate. The Azatem aren't deploying countermeasures."

"*Maso's* firing on us."

"Release countermeasures."

"Brace for impact."

Klaxons sounded. Lights strobed.

"Countermeasures ninety-two percent effective."

"We've taken damage."

The impact wasn't felt. Wherever the missiles had struck *Pohru-Mahrko*, they were too far from the command deck to be noticed. But Ehtishem imagined that he felt every death they brought to his crew.

Timsai called, "Damage report."

"Fire doors triggered in Engineering and Navigation."

"Hull integrity?"

"Sensors show breaches in C-Six and D-Six; A-, B-, and C-Eleven; and D through G Compartments Thirty-two through Thirty-seven, fra. Enemy missiles are detonating before impact. They're using pulse laser warheads."

"The target isn't decelerating, fra."

"Evasive maneuvers, Helm," Timsai said. "Let's not get rammed. Are teams in place to patch those breaches?"

"Evasives programmed."

"Breach teams moving in, fra."

"I want a casualty report," Ehtishem said.

"Engineering reports the fire is under control. Generators are fully functional, fra."

"Ash-ush," Ehtishem replied. "Navigation status?"

"Enemy is firing again."

"Navigation reporting," a tech replied. "Systems are offline, but coming back on. Crash teams are on the scene."

"Countermeasures intercepting enemy salvo."

An announcement came over the ship-wide com: "All available med techs report to medical bays E, J, O, T, BB. Med techs to Medical Bays Eresh, Jivyam, Oyum, Tarad, Baresh-Baresh."

"*Dathusha*'s accelerating away."

"Ash-ush," Ehtishem replied, a part of his brain recognizing the good in that.

"Countermeasures ninety-one percent effective. Brace for impact."

This time *Pohru-Mahrko*'s shudders were felt on the command deck and the lights dimmed. Two screens flickered and went black. Techs droned the damage reports as they poured across their screens.

A wall of yellow lights appeared on screen and streaked toward the enemy ship as *Pohru-Mahrko* attacked again, but the Azatem monstrosity didn't slow or alter its path. It fired on *Dathusha*'s engines and explosions rocked the rear of the civilian ship. Fires plumed along her flanks. Debris spread in her wake.

Having crippled one target, *Maso* rolled like a Terran whale, reorienting her main weapons bank on *Pohru-Mahrko*.

"Enemy ship is firing on us again, fra."

"Release countermeasures," Timsai said.

"Countermeasures away."

But even as the Azatem ship attacked *Pohru-Mahrko*, it continued toward their crippled mother ship.

"*Maso*'s moving to intercept *Dathusha*, fra." As the tech said it, a massive bay opened near the front of the Azatem ship's belly, a red maw opening to engulf its prey.

Pohru-Mahrko shuddered and the lights dimmed again. Four more of the overhead screens went dark.

"Damage report," Ehtishem said.

"Full salvos," Timsai commanded. "Helm, bring her around. Put everything we've got right down her throat."

The ship shuddered again, harder this time. The control

team worked frantically, but *Pohru-Mahrko* continued to hold her course.

"Helm?" Timsai crossed the deck to their station.

Pohru-Mahrko's pilot and crew looked up, helplessness written across their stricken faces.

"She's not responding, fra," a tech said. "We've lost the forward northeast thrusters."

"Then use the southeast thrusters and spin her like a top," Ehtishem growled.

But even as he said it, *Maso* ingested *Dathusha*, a blue whale swallowing a tuna. *Pohru-Mahrko*'s crew watched, silent, stunned.

Ehtishem's gut twisted into an unfamiliar knot. He'd failed. He'd lost his lover. He'd lost his family. He'd lost his people. He'd failed to protect everyone and everything he'd ever cared about.

"Zhek," someone mumbled. "Zhek-zhek-zhek."

Timsai broke the silence. "Focus shields to our rear. Helm, give me a sustained burn, full throttle. Let's escape while we can."

Still the silence stretched out, even as *Pohru-Mahrko*'s crew performed their duties and the last Ohnenrai ship accelerated away from their worst enemy.

Ehtishem looked down at the gouge and block in his hands. He loosened his fingers. They ached from his death grip. He inhaled slow, deep, deliberate. "Did Sarem Mahlei's transport safely dock?" His voice was even and sure. That gave him grim satisfaction, the only satisfaction he expected to have for a very long time. He began the methodical, muted scrape-scrape-scrape of metal over leather.

A tech's voice cracked as she replied, "Zant, fra."

Timsai said, "Nav, give us an escape route."

One of three navigations techs said, "Iodiq is six hundred

twelve hours from our present position if we cut through the Kevrian Formation. No course correction needed. We can do a hard burn and outrun *Maso*."

"Nav," Ehtishem addressed the other navigations techs, "what's your opinion of the Kevrian and Iodiq?"

Timsai ordered, "Fire another salvo, please. Let's keep hurting *Maso*."

A tech called up images of a glowing, dense cloud of brown dust and rainbow-hued gases. "Kevrian's doable, but a rough route, fra. The damage *Pohru-Mahrko* sustained in this fight will make her hull vulnerable. A forming star system isn't paradise."

The third tech said, "Iodiq is a third-rate junkyard, at best. She has pump stations to serve the shipyard and passing fleets, but they're old."

"How old?" Ehtishem asked.

"Abandoned for more than a century, fra. We'll be lucky to find anything more than rust."

"Any other viable options?"

"Nava," all three techs said.

Ehtishem nodded. "Set our course for Iodiq."

"Zant, fra," they replied.

Ehtishem met Timsai's grim gaze. The thrai nodded. Ehtishem scanned the command crew. "You all performed admirably. Now we're wounded and bleeding. Our charge has been captured. We can't help *Dathusha* if we're dead. We run now, lick our wounds, and come back to fight another day. This. Is. Not. Over."

"Agreed." Timsai turned to the ship's pilot. "Helm, sustained burn, take us up to full speed. Let's put a wide gap between us and *Maso*. Someone get me the status on the debris shield."

"Engineering is working on it, fra."

"Tell them to work harder or the Kevrian's debris will finish what *Maso* started."

The senior helm tech said, "Beginning sustained burn now."

"Weapons, until the shield is functional, you're to obliterate any debris large enough to scratch our hull," Timsai ordered.

Ehtishem schooled his expression to stone even as his thoughts turned to Rachel and Pearl. "Thrai?" He refocused on Timsai. "Are all the water teams fully assembled aboard *Pohru-Mahrko?*"

Timsai shook his head. "We still had med teams and the animal handlers to bring aboard." The thrai stepped closer and lowered his voice to add, "Pearl and Audie are still on *Dathusha*. Is Rachel there?"

Ehtishem nodded. "She's what they came for."

Timsai's mouth pressed into a thin line. "The Code."

A tech announced, "We're pulling away from *Maso*. She's not pursuing us, fra."

Ehtishem nodded slowly. "The Code."

FIVE

"WE'RE in the CMSD aboard *Pohru-Mahrko*, Barethri, and we're safe," Dahmircan said, his voice low and calm, like he was soothing a wild animal. Which he was, in a way. When the first explosion had cracked like thunder and heaved the floor, he'd lifted me off my feet and dived across the counter.

We sat with our backs to it as the packed kits slammed against the wall, supplies scattered, and I jolted, trembled, whimpered with every boom and shudder beneath us. The walls groaned and so did I. A klaxon sounded incessantly, amber lights flashed. Everything was getting hazy, including my connection to my own body. I didn't know what was here-and-now, what was long ago and far away. Fear was bridging my past and my present and dangling me over a void.

Somehow Dahmircan knew.

"Tell me your name," he said and nudged my arm when I didn't respond.

I looked at him, blinked, tried to focus on his face, his words. "I... What?"

"What's your name, Barethri? Where are you from?"

My name. "I'm Rachel Pryne."

"We are one," the voices screamed in my mind.

"And? Where are you from?"

The floor heaved. I closed my eyes. "Oh shit, oh shit, oh shit."

"Rachel Pryne, where are you from?" His voice was equal parts soothing and commanding. His hand came down on mine and his grip was tight. "Look at me and answer the question."

I did. His eyes were so dark they were almost black. "Suffer. I'm from Suffer. That's on Earth — on Terra."

"Where are you now?"

"We are one."

I stared at him. His questions meant something. "Am I having a flashback?"

He nodded. "Zant." He pressed my hand to the floor beneath his and repeated, "Where are you now, Barethri Rachel?"

I hadn't had a flashback in six months, but the sudden thunderous sounds had triggered me.

The metal floor was cold. His skin was warm. I focused on my palm, looked at our hands, then his face. His nose was crooked, broken sometime in the past. *"Pohru-Mahrko.* I'm in the CMSD and you're Dvaidasa Dahmircan." I sucked a deep breath, exhaled slowly, and nodded. He'd centered me. "How did you know what to do?"

He didn't smile, but there was a softness around his mouth I hadn't seen before, empathy in his eyes. "Not all of us are cut out for combat, Barethri."

The main door squealed as it opened. Huorem squeezed through.

"Rough ride, eh, Barethri?" he said. His light tone and words didn't hide the concern in his eyes. He crouched before me and took my hands. "You okay?"

I nodded. He pulled me up. "Zant. Thanks to Dahmircan. He kept me safe."

"Ferahi-va," Hu said.

The dvaidasa nodded and circled back around the counter. "There'll be plenty of work waiting when you come back, Barethri." He disappeared into the storage room.

"Where's Mahzel?" I asked. "And where's Pearl? What's happening?"

"The Azatem found us."

"What? How?"

He led me into the hallway. "Mahzel reported to his action station in Engineering. I'm here to take you to mine. You heard the call for medical personnel?" When I nodded he continued. "Ash-ush. You're a trained medic, so you're coming with me. We're heading to the closest trauma bay. They need all the help they can get. We've got a lot of wounded soldiers and techs."

"But Pearl—" Panic was crawling into my brain and through my belly.

He must've heard it in my voice. His grip tightened and he leaned close. "Her trainers will protect her. Trust them to do their job, and you come do yours. People are dying all over this ship." He held my gaze, his dark-brown eyes intense, unblinking, devoid of his usual bravado. "We need your help, Barethri." He glanced at soldiers hurrying past and added, "Show them what you're made of. Show them why the zosh chose you."

Medical crisis. I knew how to fix broken people, how to stitch wounds, relieve suffering, save lives. The Ohnenrai needed me. Huorem was asking for my aid. I nodded. "Okay, but promise me you'll find out where she is."

"I will." We continued down the hall, picking up the pace to a jog. "I'll get her status as soon as possible. I promise."

We crowded into the closest functioning lift with three weapons techs.

"We are one." The voices were so loud in my skull it felt like my brain was vibrating.

I know, I know. We're all in this together, I thought. *You can shut up now!* It wasn't making me feel calmer, but as far as coping mechanisms were concerned, I'd take it over another flashback.

The elevator's computer, polite as always, requested our destination: "Gatu, vana?"

Huorem slapped his hand on the lift pad. "Deck O, no stops."

The door closed and the lift dropped, juddering and squealing all the way. The ship had taken a beating. So had her crew. The soldiers around me stood stone-faced and silent, like the statues I remembered from the old churches in Germany when my father was stationed there.

Hu touched my arm. "We'll escape, Barethri. We may be smaller than the Azatem monster, but we're faster."

"But what about *Dathusha?" What about Pearl?* I wanted to scream. I didn't know if she and Audie had gotten to *Pohru-Mahrko* or were trapped on the civilian ship without me. I didn't even know what had happened to *Dathusha.*

Huorem said, "Patience. I'll keep my promise, you know that."

I nodded. I did trust him. Huorem had never let me down.

The lift doors opened and a trail of blood pointed the way to the controlled chaos that had overtaken the Deck O Trauma Bay. Bodies — damaged, dying, dead — were lined up to enter. The cacophony of war's aftermath assaulted me: groans, moans, screams, clipped conversation and the rattle of examination tables, the hiss of loading hypomatics, the clatter of surgical tools against metal containers, and the gurgle of suction tubes and beeping machinery.

We stepped into the madness.

Surrounded by carnage, Ahremena moved around the injured soldiers, gathering supplies into a tote and ignoring their suffering. She glanced up and spied me. Hefting her load, she advanced. "Aevadasa Huorem, I'm sure they can use the barethri's skills here."

"Zant, Sarem. That's why she's come."

She studied me for a long moment then nodded and strode through the crowd toward the lift, unmoved by the destruction and chaos around her.

"There goes one cold bitch," I muttered.

Huorem frowned for a split second before turning and leading me into the bay. "I'll introduce you to the Senior Med Tech."

He found the red-clad tech with her hands buried in an unconscious soldier's shredded abdomen. "Barethri Rachel's a skilled med tech. How can she help?" Hu said.

The SMT didn't look up. "Can you close wounds, Barethri?"

"Zant."

"See Dasa Aihaman in Triage. She's the acting TIO."

Hu and I wound back through the ward, dodging med techs and the wounded, to reach the bay's staging area. Trauma Intake Officer Aihaman gave me supplies and I set to work side-by-side with Ohnenrai med techs on the reassembly line. When I ran out of staples, someone handed me more. When those ran out, I took over suturing from another tech, who moved on to dressing wounds. There wasn't time to worry about Pearl. The trainers were with her. Audie was with her, and Ehtishem was right, that dog would die to protect her.

God, if you exist, please don't let it come to that.

An announcement came over the intercom: "*Pohru-Mahrko* is now beyond torpedo range." A cheer went up.

I closed my eyes and whispered, "Thank you."

Huorem appeared beside me, pulling on surgical gloves. "I'll take burns."

I cleaned debris from the gaping wound on a soldier's palm. "I didn't know you're a trained med tech," I said to Hu.

"We're all cross-trained. Multiple disciplines." He peeled back the bloody dressing from the left side of a soldier's charred scalp. The man's clawed grip on the table edge said everything his controlled expression didn't. "The zosh will be tweaked to see you working in Trauma."

"The zosh will be tweaked to see me aboard *Pohru-Mahrko* period. But he can suck it if he thinks I'm gonna do nothing while people die."

Huorem snorted and flashed a fleet grin. "I'll convey that message."

"You do that." I irrigated the soldier's wound.

She grunted and asked, "Why are you here, Barethri?"

I looked at her over the magnifying surgical loupes perched on my nose. "Because I have needed skills. Which the zosh damn-well knows."

She nodded. "Clearly. But you don't have to get your hands bloody."

A hypomatic hissed and Huorem's patient relaxed his grip on the table.

"We're all in this together." I rummaged in the bin behind her until I found more surgical thread. And keeping busy kept my fear at bay — fear for all of us and, most of all, for Pearl. Focusing on the wounds before me meant I didn't notice the ship's rumbles and shudders, I didn't plummet into a flashback.

"We are one." The voices resumed their useless litany, echoing what I'd said to the soldier.

The metal floor was made of jagged grating and I tried to dodge the water as a tech flushed the ward's subfloor. Blood, fluids, and wastewater dripped through the grating and he hosed it toward central drains. The surgical tables consisted of rubbery padding over metal. After the patients moved on, the hinged table faces were tilted, washed down, swiped with an antimicrobial device, and righted, ready for the next procedure.

A group of med techs moved from injured soldier to injured soldier administering two intravenous shots. I nodded toward them. "Hu, what are they giving the wounded?"

He glanced up, saw whom I meant, and said, "Engineered stem cells and growth factors to speed healing."

"Wow," I mouthed. That kind of off-the-shelf stem cell therapy had been in clinical trials back on Terra when the Ohnenrai had showed up. As I considered the kinds of wounds the med techs treated around me, I realized Earth had never stood a chance against their forces and technology. Wounds like these would've meant certain death back home.

At the far end of the ward, a large lift transported patients up to Recovery or down to the morgue. Despite Ohnenrai medical advancements, too many bagged bodies were descending. My hosts could do incredible things to save lives, but their Azatem enemy could do even worse to destroy them.

Finally, the flow of fresh wounds ebbed. Twenty-one hours after *Maso*'s attack, aches and pains I hadn't noticed while I was working suddenly made themselves known. I leaned on a freshly washed table, not caring that my forearms were getting cold and wet. My shoulders and back throbbed, my feet had gone from hurting to numb to hurting again.

The SMT moved through the room, checking on her staff and assessing supplies. She paused by me. "You're relieved of duty, Barethri. Ferahi-va." She saluted me and other med techs acknowledged me as I staggered behind Huorem from the med bay.

"You worked like one of us," he said.

"What do you mean?"

"Like a machine."

I shrugged. "Just doing my part."

Intra-ship transports ferried soldiers, technicians, and supplies from one end of *Pohru-Mahrko* to the other. There were far fewer of them than on *Dathusha* and even fewer now that they'd powered down much of *PM*, so we waited for forty minutes in near darkness until one arrived that we could squeeze onto.

"I'm not sure where to bunk you." Huorem led the way to an open space beside a gray pole. The upper grips were too high for me to reach.

Mahzel had rejoined us and stood guard as usual. "The zosh's quarters will be sufficient," he said.

Hu squinted as he considered the idea. "It's against regulations."

Mahzel replied, "Since when do you care about regs?"

"With tensions high? I care. And so will the zosh. You know how he is about regulations and impressions. No one can afford attachments and he won't want to appear like he's making an exception."

"Keeping Barethri Rachel safe means making exceptions to the rules." Mahzel gestured at two soldiers in seats beside me. "Up," he ordered.

I caught his arm. "Don't. Please."

The soldiers' gazes skidded past me to look at him. Their faces, hands, and uniforms were stained and torn. They stood. One mumbled, "Will you take our seats, Barethri?"

I stared at the woman for a moment then shook my head. "Nava. You're tired. You've been working hard."

Her male companion stepped aside. "We insist." Their words were as cold as the void of space.

Mahzel nudged me. I dropped onto the hard, gray bench, unhappy that they'd been pushed aside but grateful to be off my aching feet. Huorem sat beside me and shifted his shock rifle off his shoulder.

The transport's air was warm and heavy, thick with the acrid stink of electrical fires, ozone, and sweat. I watched the glowing strip lights on the walls beyond the windows, rocked by the car's sway as it covered miles in minutes. Everything else blurred past, but those luminous lines only skipped when the car passed other tunnels. It didn't offer the smooth ride of *Dathusha*'s cars.

Mahzel shouldered his weapon and addressed the soldiers he'd just unseated. "What deck were you working, Vehl?"

"Deck W, Compartments One thirty-five and One thirty-six, fra."

"How bad is it?"

"The outer berth took a direct hit. We got life support and electrical rerouted, but five teams are still working to close the breach."

"The inner seal failed?" Hu asked.

"Partially, but the bulkheads did their job."

The soldier who'd spoken to me cleared her throat and added, "There's no gravity in there and everyone was obliterated by the laser heads and shrapnel. It's grisly."

"Aiya."

Vehl added, "Coulda been worse. Most of the soldiers were at their duty stations so the berths and rec room were pretty empty."

I swallowed and looked down at my hands. There was dried blood under my fingernails. The same blood stained the soldier's uniforms. "Goddamn Azatem bastards," I whispered.

Huorem, Mahzel, and the two soldiers nodded.

Three others joined the conversation. They were hydro techs. Parts of Deck C and D were flooded. They'd sealed the breaches and rerouted drinking and wastewater.

"Engineering will be working round the clock to set up extra filtration measures. We lost one of the primary purifiers and about a third of the ship's potable water."

One of the hydro techs turned to Mahzel. "Aevadasa?"

"Zant, narem?"

"Were you on the command deck?"

Mahzel shook his head but said, "I've spoken with Aevadasa Gahlen, who was. Why?"

"Are the rumors about Fravaz Ahnoru true, fra?"

"That depends on the rumors."

A female soldier said, "He was slow to obey orders."

"Nava-nava," Mahzel said. "A transport violated protocol and delayed *Dathusha*. *PM* released the rear lock and drew enemy fire to protect the civilians, but there was nothing she could do to stop *Maso* from firing on *Dathusha*."

I stiffened. Huorem caught my arm and pinched muscle to bone to distract me.

Mahzel leveled a hard, steady gaze at the soldiers and added loudly enough for the whole car to hear, "*Pohru-Mahrko* bled so that innocent citizens would not. Fravaz Ahnoru is not to blame from *Dathusha*'s capture."

The soldiers around him nodded, and someone said, "I knew Ahnoru wasn't an ahzish."

I stared at the blurry tunnel outside the window. I swallowed and tried to focus on the pain Hu was sending up my arm. But all I could think was, *Pearl. Oh, god, oh, god, oh god.*

Ehtishem's quarters were located at Deck JJ, Compartment Fifty-two, ten levels below the command deck. They were austere. And small. One room held a tiny galley with a table that folded flat to the wall and two folding chairs that hung beside it. A fat, hard-cover book took up a third of the counter, *The Complete Works of William Shakespeare*. It was so like him to have a piece of my world in his inner sanctum. An adjoining space had a bunk above a dark-gray couch. There was a tall, personal locker recessed into the opposite wall and a tiny bathing room with a shower and toilet. The sink sat above the toilet so its wastewater flowed down to serve double-duty as toilet tank water.

The same amber emergency lighting I'd seen on the walls and floors throughout the ship pushed back the darkness here, but failed to brighten my bleak imaginings. I still didn't know where Pearl was, if she was safe, if she was scared. And worse things I didn't dare think. I wrung my hands and pushed those possibilities back with the frantic fear of a mother who knows they're way too close to probable.

Mahzel said, "The zosh will be on the command deck for the next ten hours. We'll find suitable quarters for you tomorrow. Meanwhile, you can get a shower, a meal, and some rest."

Huorem answered a knock at the door. There was barely enough room to admit another soldier, but two crowded in. Dasa Leilei and Dasa Nadera were Hu and Mahzel's relief. After introductions, the women took up stations outside the door, keeping me safe.

"Ferahi-va for taking such good care of me," I said to Huorem and Mahzel.

Hu offered a brief, weary smile. I matched it with a shaky one of my own. "We serve you and the zosh, Barethri. We serve the Ohnenrai." He touched my arm, gently this time. "We'll find Pearl. I won't forget."

They directed me to the cabin's clothes locker and showed me how the tiny shower worked. "Be efficient. The water's rationed, so you'll only have five minutes before it shuts off." After they left, I showered, changed into a clean, gray pajama shirt — ridiculously oversized because it was Ehtishem's. I didn't bother with the pants.

Compared to the luxury of his wood-and-glass quarters on *Dathusha*, this was a shoebox. Ironic that it was smaller than the little shit-hole cabin on Terra that Pearl and I had lived in, the cabin where we'd met him.

I climbed onto his bunk and stared into the dark. My chest tightened. My scalp tingled. Fear. Anxiety. Helplessness, which was worst of all.

"Stop it, Rachel." I pressed my palms against my eyelids. "There's nothing you can do about anything that's happening right now. Trust the trainers to protect Pearl. You don't know that she's still on *Dathusha*. She's probably being bunked on one of the lower decks. Assume she's fine. Trust Ehtishem to keep *Pohru-Mahrko* away from the Azatem."

The rah-rah speech didn't make me feel any better. I rolled over, buried my face in the pillow, and groaned. "Calm down and go to sleep. Worrying about things you can't change will only exhaust you."

"We are one."

The voices weren't shouting anymore. In fact, they were quiet and weirdly soothing. My fear and paranoia eased. The muscles across my shoulders and back relaxed. I exhaled, closed my eyes, felt calm, sleepy.

Maybe hearing voices isn't such a bad thing after all.

SIX

"DAMAGE REPORT, ZOSH."

Ehtishem looked up from the holographic galactic map he was studying as Timsai entered the captain's office adjacent to the command deck. It had been twenty-five hours since *Maso*'s attack and *Dathusha*'s capture. He squeezed his tired eyes shut, shrugged the fatigue out of his shoulders, and gestured to the seat opposite him. He didn't want to hear this.

His fingers followed the curves and angles of a carved sleeping dog, a piece of work to distract himself from the emotions careening inside his mind. The sharp knife of his soldiers' agony and the cold fear that accompanied it magnified his own worry. His stomach soured with the nauseating thickness of their anxiety and rage. Their agony made it almost impossible to maintain vairim, and worry for Rachel and Pearl crowded in. This had been his lifelong battle, this emotional storm. No one knew how great a struggle it was for him, not even Rachel.

Pairika. The Azatem had tracked them by following her: he was certain. It was as Ahremena had planned but sooner than she'd predicted. *Dathusha* and all that ship's inhabitants — with the exception of Rachel and, possibly, Pearl — would soon be dead. He turned his attention to Timsai to redirect it from the situation he couldn't fix, the worry he couldn't relieve.

The thrai sat at the small conference table and read from his compad. "*Pohru-Mahrko* sustained damage to Navigation, Engineering, the Deck AA Medical Bay, water purification, water and dry food stores, and the forward Northeast Launch Bay. Hull breaches are reported in the following compartments: C Seventy-two and D Seventy-two and Seventy-three, Decks K, L, and M Eleven and Twelve, Decks W through AA Compartments Thirty-two through Thirty-seven. We've lost a quarter of our dry food storage, one third of our potable water. Purification System Three is a complete loss; two warheads decimated the East Central Bilge." He glanced up. "Don't go down there without a mask, the sewage stench will melt your sinuses. Water filtration is functioning at half-capacity and wastewater is building up in the remaining Bilge overflow tanks."

"Why?"

"Engineering rerouted much of the lower deck cooling systems to control reactor temperatures while one of the primary heat sinks is replaced."

"Which has raised the ambient Bilge temperature."

Timsai nodded. "The area is a hot, stinking sewer. I pity the soldiers working down there."

"Swing the shifts more frequently and relocate any bilge rats to temporary cells."

"Already on it." Timsai looked at his notes. "That's not the worst news. Total casualties: Five thousand seventy-four dead, thirteen thousand two hundred thirty-five missing and presumed dead, and twenty-two thousand seven hundred eighty-six injured."

"Aiya. Casualties and losses number nearly forty-two thousand?"

Timsai nodded. "We've moved into the Kevrian Formation. All systems except basic life support and internal med bays have been idled and speed is holding steady. No sign of *Maso-Vohu*, but there's no telling how long that'll last.

"All breaches except those at D Seventy-two and Seventy-three have been temporarily sealed. The fusion drive remained stable throughout the exchange. Countermeasures were ninety-four-point-three-five percent accurate. I have commendation requests coming from all department leaders. Also a complete list of casualties is being compiled."

Timsai looked away from the screen and his face softened. A rare micro-expression of regret twisted his mouth, then he reasserted vairim and continued. "I know risking *Pohru-Mahrko* was a difficult decision, Ehtishem, but you have the crew's support."

"Ferahi-va." He wondered if that support would hold once the ranks realized the Azatem had found them by following Rachel to *Dathusha*. He scowled. The Code wasn't supposed to be active yet. It didn't make sense that they could find her. Unless Ahremena had lied or failed to understand her own experiments.

They faced a juggernaut. The Azatem had captured eight million civilians and maimed or murdered tens of thousands of soldiers. And the surviving two hundred thousand of them were left without a food source. "Food compromised."

Timsai nodded. "And water."

Dathusha, as the civilian ship, was set up to create, process, and distribute all basic living necessities. *Pohru-Mahrko* had enough supplies to keep her populace alive for ninety days. Except that one of the hardest hit decks was a major storage section. They'd be fine if they reached Iodiq, and if they found working pumps, viable water wells, and unbreached food stores on the planet. Those were some big ifs.

"Iodiq." Ehtishem steepled his fingers. "Assuming we continue to evade the Azatem battlecruiser long enough to reach that planet, the native species are highly food-motivated."

"And big."

Ehtishem nodded. "Window, fifty percent."

The opaque floor-to-ceiling window became transparent. Gas and dust greeted him, dark and swirling against the brilliant form of a new star. The Kevrian was a solar system being born, filled with opaque blue, brown, and red dust clouds, planetesimals, careening asteroids, and wicked gravity. Only desperate travelers would venture into the dangers of a protoplanetary disk. Travelers who'd been crippled by an Azatem battlecruiser, for example.

"Someday, you bastards," he said.

Timsai nodded. "That's a promise." His com buzzed and he read the message.

Ehtishem stared out the window. He'd stayed busy, focused on keeping *Pohru-Mahrko* moving, visited wounded soldiers in the med bays, reviewed the plotted course to Iodiq. But with any lull, his thoughts went to Rachel and Pearl and his lost civilian ship, and his blood began to boil.

He slammed his fists on the desk, creating a hairline crack in its polished surface, then he met Timsai's gaze. "I want crews working non-stop. Let's repair *Pohru-Mahrko* and find *Maso* before all our people are dead. If my mother's plan worked, and it seems like they've taken the bait, they'll focus on Rachel. That'll give us an opportunity to strike."

"So they did follow her." Timsai's face was an exercise in neutrality. "The Azatem Code was activated early?"

"Not with my knowledge."

"Aiya," he exhaled. "That's treason."

"Possibly. I'll be questioning Ahremena at length and with little pleasure. She failed to notify me of the danger. The blood of *Dathusha*'s citizens is on her hands." Ehtishem sat back. He bumped his fingers along the carved spine of the wooden dog. "How quickly can we make repairs?"

"I've drawn up a shift schedule." Timsai proffered his screen. "We'll activate anyone who's not currently assigned. No one's on break, no excuses. Only the injured and the dead are exempt."

Ehtishem studied the plan. "I can always count on you."

"Zant, fra. And I on you. We'll get through this, haxan."

Ehtishem nodded.

Timsai straightened and folded his arms across his chest. "Ahremena's set up shop in Recovery Bay Nerem Forty-nine. I've had complaints about her displacing the wounded."

"I'm sure you have."

"Sorry to add to your growing list of problems."

Ehtishem dismissed the apology. "She's one problem I'm well-practiced in handling. The question is, why did she disobey protocol to board *Pohru-Mahrko*? She never comes here."

"Eresh. Something about the Code? Maybe she was trying to warn you."

"Maybe. But she didn't have to come here to do that. A message would've sufficed until we had time to meet." Ehtishem put down the dog. It reminded him of a boy he once knew on Terra. "Logan," he murmured.

"Who?"

"Logan." He tapped the carving. "He was a Terran boy I met. I gave him a carving like this. That kid went through hell and back, and kept going."

"Terran children are surprisingly tough and resourceful."

Ehtishem met his oldest friend's gaze and found compassion there. "That gives me hope."

Two long, semi-oval tables faced each other in *Pohru-Mahrko*'s Central EXO briefing room. Behind and above each table was another longer semi-oval table. The configuration created a curved fan shape with an open area for a speaker to roam from one end of the tables to the other. Ehtishem sat at one end of the fan. A large display was opposite him, and his divisional leaders and the Draxtu-Mainyu Brotherhood were arrayed around the tables. The screen showed multiple charts and lists: a summary of *Pohru-Mahrko*'s damage and casualties, the shipboard resources that were available for repairs, combat, and survival, and a deployment plan for Iodiq. Holographic maps of the Kevrian, Iodiq, and surrounding solar systems appeared in the middle of the room.

"If we scrap more of the supply transports, we'll have the necessary raw building materials, fra, but that doesn't solve our water problem," said *Pohru-Mahrko*'s Chief Engineering and Systems Officer.

"It also slows restocking when we reach Iodiq's supply depots." Ehtishem studied the map of the Kevrian. It showed their current position and the location of the nearest inhabitable planets and moons. "Iodiq's still our best bet?"

A navigations officer nodded and popped his knuckles. "Fisk-Vayat would've been the better choice, but it's too far without wormhole capabilities." The man was lanky and drooped over the table, like a Terran willow tree with a voice as raspy as dry leaves.

Pop went his large right index knuckle. "There are a few other possibilities, fra." *Crack.* "Stenos-171 and one or two moons orbiting Haegun, but we don't have confirmed liquid water on those." *Crack.* "Iodiq has surface and subterranean water pumps, and unmanned purification facilities." *Pop.* "Plus our supply depots at her southern pole and dry stores located in both hemispheres. Lots of food in those according to our records."

Ehtishem unrolled the leather pouch that held his carving knives. He itched to stab a V-gouge right through the officer's hand, spear it to the table and put an end to the knuckle cracking. "Aevadasa, is Chief Navigations Officer Hamayei injured or occupied?"

"She's dead, fra."

"You were her second?" The man nodded and Ehtishem added, "I regret the loss of such a competent officer. Ash-ush. You're the new CNO." He caught and held the man's gaze. "Stop cracking your knuckles before I cut your hands off."

A few soldiers chuckled at that.

The new CNO flattened his palms upon the table. "My apologies and my thanks, fra."

"Zosh?" Gohra had spoken. "Iodiq offers a native population that will either eat us or tear us apart, then eat us."

Berk looked up from the animal he was creating from folded paper. "Just another day in the Ohnenrai military."

"Or Berk's personal life," Anchal muttered.

That got laughs, and Berk flashed a grin at the senior weapons tech. "You're just upset that I haven't screwed you since the last hamistayeca tournament."

Jeers and calls followed. The emotions of the crew careened around the room. Small tells gave them away — the nav officer's knuckles, Berk fiddling with paper, the CMO's bouncing leg, even Ehtishem's own woodcarving. The barbs and taunts. The whole crew was on edge. Instead of stabbing his officer, Ehtishem pulled a diagram and an irregular cut of wood from his coat pocket and studied them. His voice rose above the taunts and laughter. "Any pertinent objections to Iodiq for water and orbital repairs?"

A chorus of "Nava" circled the table.

Timsai said. "Helm, steady on to Iodiq."

Ehtishem asked, "Any sign of *Maso*?"

"Nothing, fra," the thrai replied.

Ehtishem nodded and pushed back from the table. "You know what needs doing, pa'nerem. Let's get it done."

The officers stood, saluted, departed singly and in groups. Timsai caught Ehtishem's sleeve and held him back as the others left. "You need sleep."

"You first." Next on his agenda was hunting down his mother and removing her liver with tweezers.

"I already did while you were keeping your mind off Rachel and Pearl and *Dathusha* by keeping it focused on a million details that are already being handled by *Pohru-Mahrko*'s very competent crew."

A flash of anger surged through Ehtishem. He sucked a breath to chew his thrai a new asshole but caught sight of his own reflection in the polished table top. He exhaled, nodded. "You're right. And smarter than me, as usual. I'm going to my quarters for a few hours of rest." He straightened, squeezed Timsai's shoulder, grateful for his old friend's level head and even temper.

Ahremena could wait. He'd be an idiot to confront her with exhaustion dulling his brain and making vairim a greater struggle. It had been thirty-one hours since *Maso*'s attack. He'd put off sleep to avoid dreaming. Vairim didn't work in his dreams, and his concerns about Rachel, Pearl, his crew, and his citizens would come screaming out of his brain. Besides, Ahremena would just push him over the edge and into doing something rash, like killing her.

He wound through *Pohru-Mahrko*'s cramped, gray corridors, returning salutes and stopping to speak with bandaged soldiers, until he finally reached the officers' bunks and turned the corner down to his small quarters. Ahead, Nadera and Leilei snapped to attention and saluted.

Ehtishem returned their salutes automatically, reached up to press his palm to his door's access panel, then stopped.

Nadera and Leilei.

He considered them through narrowed eyes. "Why are you here?"

"Doing our job, fra," Leilei answered.

"Your job isn't to guard my empty quarters, dasa."

Nadera replied, "It's occupied, fra."

He looked from soldier to soldier. Their faces remained stony, too stony. He palmed open the door. The room's lights came on.

Rachel bolted upright in his upper bunk and smacked her forehead on the overhead. "Ow! Shit!" She fell back against the pillow, hissing and pressing her hands against her head. "Ow-ow-ow! Dammit!"

"What are you doing aboard *Pohru-Mahrko*?" His voice was harsh and low, filled with repressed worry and even more repressed relief. The door squealed shut behind him.

"Jesus H. Christ, Ehtishem!" Still holding her forehead, Rachel squinted at him. "Kill the damn lights!"

"Lights twenty percent." The room's computer reduced the glare. He grabbed her arm and waist and pulled her off the bed. She gasped though he caught her and set her on her feet within the confines of his arms, but he didn't embrace her. Instead, Ehtishem gripped her upper arms and repeated, "What are you doing here?" He stared into her bottle green eyes and knew his feelings for her hadn't changed. He loved her no matter what hell her DNA brought down upon them and, more than ever, he wanted — *needed* — to keep her safe.

Her glare held fury, hurt, confusion. She snarled, "I'm trying to sleep after twenty-some hours on my feet fixing mutilated soldiers and worrying to death about Pearl and you and every-goddamned-thing!"

He was an idiot. And he was being cruel. Ehtishem slid his hands up to cup her face. He kissed her hard, still unable to find his center and control the sickening mixture of anger and relief flooding him. She made a noise — something between a whimper and a moan. He broke the kiss, pulled her against him, and pressed his face to her short, wavy hair. "Rahzhel," he murmured, "why didn't you send me a message?"

She sucked a deep breath and pulled back. He let her, though reluctantly, and kept his hands on her. Rachel, in turn, held onto the front of his uniform and said, "Because we were both busy."

He shook his head. "I had time to read a message."

"Well, I didn't have time to write it. I was knee-deep in blood."

"I would not have authorized that." He studied her expression, her tone. She was on the edge of breaking.

"Which is another reason I didn't contact you." She pushed him back. "The trauma bay couldn't afford to lose a pair of capable hands."

"You're not a combat doctor—"

"Bullshit I'm not." Her jaw set and her hands balled into trembling fists. "I've been dealing with combat trauma since I was a kid, thanks to the Ohnenrai."

He grimaced.

She closed her eyes, opened them and met his gaze, contrite. "I'm sorry. That wasn't fair."

"None of this has been fair," he said. She had a sizable, red lump forming on her forehead. "Let's get something cold for that knot on your skull. If we don't stop the swelling, Huorem will start calling you Knot-head."

"Not if he knows what's good for him." She touched the spot and winced.

"Since when does Hu know that?" He led her to the small galley — a privilege found only in the cruiser-carrier's top commanders' quarters — and pulled a cold pack from the refrigerator. He wrapped it with a thin towel. She held it to her forehead as he directed her back to the couch.

She sat and exhaled a shaky sigh. "I still don't know where Pearl is." She clutched his arm. "Huorem promised to find out if she's safe, but he hasn't sent word. Do you know anything?"

He sat beside her, took her hand. "Zant." He sandwiched her palm between his hands. It was small and made her seem delicate, but that was an illusion. Considering her fragile was a mistake. More than once she'd proven herself the strongest woman he'd ever met. "Pearl is aboard *Dathusha*." He didn't soften the blow. She wouldn't appreciate equivocation.

Her chin slowly lifted as she held his gaze. She inhaled and hissed, "Shit!" then stood.

She was fighting despair with anger. He knew it and approved. Better rage than the kind of fear and hopelessness that made her catatonic. He'd seen that in Logan's stepmother. It had killed the woman.

Rachel turned. "How the hell did this happen?" she snarled. "How did they find us? I want answers, Ehtishem. I want to know who I have to kill for this."

He stood too. "You don't want those answers."

"The hell I don't. Tell me, right now, or I'll start tearing through this ship asking every damn person I see until I get satisfaction."

"Rachel."

"Don't 'Rachel' me. Tell me who's to blame. I deserve to know. I have the right to know who got my daughter killed!" She was shaking, fists clenched, eyes flashing.

"We don't know their fate." He wasn't ready to consign Pearl and the others to death.

She got in his face, an admirable feat considering the difference in their heights. "Answers, Zosh."

He gripped her upper arms, but his voice was low and gentle when he replied. "You. They followed you."

She pulled against his hold. "Is that supposed to be a joke?"

He frowned. "Why would I joke about that?"

"You tell me, 'cause I sure the hell don't know why you think I'd bring the Azatem to us!"

He centered himself to take her emotions, drew a steadying breath. "You're a beacon they homed in on. It's part of the Azatem Code's design."

Rachel staggered. His grip held her up. "But...but they never found me before." Her anger had become anguish. "Did they?"

He released her arms, turned, stepped away. Shame churned his gut. How could he tell her this?

"Ehtishem?" she whispered.

"This is my fault."

"What?" She grabbed his arm and moved to see his face. "What do you mean? You just said it was mine. I don't understand."

"I should've anticipated this," he replied in English. There it was, the guilt and shame he'd fought since the first day he saw her scared and alone in Suffer, standing in a frigid creek and scrubbing violation from her skin. "I knew the Azatem Code was meant to draw them. I should've taken precautions, put procedures in place to detect them sooner."

"Fucking hell," she exhaled, staring at him, her expression

caught between grief, shock, and rage. She'd trusted him with Pearl's life, and he'd gotten the girl captured, maybe killed. She'd grown so still he was sure she'd stopped breathing. "You knew they could find us because of *me*?"

"Yes. If you need someone to blame, I'm that person."

Suddenly rage won the battle of emotions and her voice held a mixture of fury and hysteria as she snapped, "Why didn't anyone tell me?" He recognized that mother bear side of her, knew she was seeing red and wanting blood.

"Rachel, calm down."

She jerked back. "Don't patronize me! Why didn't you tell me this could happen?"

"I thought it had to be triggered."

"Triggered how?"

"By Ohnenrai Genetics."

Her expression hardened, her eyes narrowed. "Did Ahremena do this?"

"I don't know."

"But she's the only one who could. Right?"

His silence was all the answer she needed and Rachel turned for the door, murder in her eyes. "That bitch!" she snarled.

Ehtishem grabbed her. "I will handle my mother. This isn't your place."

"Not my place?" She pinned him with a glare that could melt ice. "Like hell it's not."

He pulled her back, his hand manacling her arm. He was being rough, had to be to get through to her. She wasn't thinking clearly. She didn't understand the ramifications of violence against a sarem. She just wanted revenge. "If you go after my mother, lay a finger on her, who do you think will have to lock you up? Hold you accountable? I can't play favorites. I don't have that luxury. So I need you to be calm, Rachel, level-headed. I need everyone to maintain vairim until we get this ship repaired and figure out how to find *Maso*. If you go after Ahremena, it'll be one more problem and I have more than enough of those." He drew her closer, lowered his voice. "Can you control your temper?" He'd had to ask her that once before, when his uncle had threatened Pearl. Rachel had managed then. She could do it now. He was sure.

She shook with rage, looking away from him. When she met his gaze, her anger wavered, collapsed, and despair rushed in. She collapsed into his arms and sobbed. Ehtishem held her, stroked her hair, kissed the top of her head. "I know you're frightened. But Pearl isn't alone. She has protectors."

"Audie?" She shook her head, hiccuped a sobbing laugh. "He's only so much help, you know."

"I asked Sree to shadow her."

Rachel's head jerked up and she tried to push away. "Sree? Adam's murderer? You asked *her* to protect my daughter? Are you nuts?"

"You mean crazy? Nava. Not that I know of." He kissed her damp cheeks, drew her back against his chest. "She'll keep Pearl safe, Rachel. She's as deadly as Ohnenrai soldiers get. If anyone can protect her, it's Sree." He led her back to the couch.

She sat, covered her face with her hands, and moaned, "This is a nightmare."

He pulled her hands away and wiped tears from her cheeks with his sleeve. "We'll repair *Pohru-Mahrko*. We'll find *Maso*. We'll free *Dathusha* and we'll save Pearl."

She whispered, "Not if she's—"

He pressed his fingers against her lips to stop her words. "Don't think that. Don't."

"But—"

"Pearl has the Azatem Code. She has Sree, Audie, Ahnoru, the pa'tahkaesha, her fellow trainees. She's a fighter, as tough as her mother. She'll survive and be waiting for us. Trust me, Pairika."

She chewed the inside of her cheek and searched his face as if looking for some trace of doubt, some sign of uncertainty. Finding none, she nodded. "Okay."

"We won't stop until we've recovered them."

"You promise?"

"I promise, Rachel. I promise."

She bit her lip. "Ferahi-va."

"You don't have to thank me. I care about them, too." He scooped her up and lifted her back into the bunk. He showered and changed into pajamas. She was asleep when he climbed into bed and spooned around her. She didn't even move.

"Syscom, set an alarm for oh-five-hundred. Verify."

"Verified. Alarm set for oh-five-hundred," *Pohru-Mahrko's* systems computer responded.

Ehtishem closed his eyes and fell asleep, lulled by the sweet scent of Rachel around him.

SEVEN

POHRU-MAHRKO'S INTERIOR WAS DARK. She'd been running for forty-five hours. Her air pumps circulated fresh air throughout the cramped ship. Her temperature control system kept space's sub-zero chill at bay. She still hurtled through the galaxy, of course, and Ehtishem had assured me she could maneuver again, but all non-essential power was off while repairs were made to the engines and reactors.

After his brief stay with me in his quarters, Ehtishem hadn't returned to sleep with me, hadn't told me what had happened with Ahremena, hadn't updated me on the repairs. I tried not to let it bother me. He was more than preoccupied. My anxieties were low priorities. But I sucked at sitting still when there were things to worry about. Hunkering down in the dark offered too much opportunity to imagine the horrors Pearl was facing and devise ways to murder Ahremena. With nothing to do, I only grew angrier and more anxious by the hour. I started imagining I felt Pearl's fear, and that didn't help my sanity. I was her mother. My job was to protect her, comfort her. Instead, I'd failed her and continued to fail her with each passing minute.

I sighed. At least the voices had shut up. Maybe I wasn't so crazy after all. Or maybe I was completely bonkers now and that's why Ehtishem was staying away — so he didn't inadvertently trigger me.

Tired of fighting my own demons, I changed into my uniform. As I tightened the straps on my boots, a request for entry came from Huorem at the door.

"Enter." I squinted in the glare of his helmet light until he dimmed it.

"Good morning, Barethri," he said. "We're relocating you to Thrai Timsai's quarters. Do you have any belongings to take?"

"You are?" I stood and gathered a few new carved puzzle pieces Ehtishem had left on the galley counter for me. I shoved them into my pocket with the others.

More separation from him. No surprise. *Pohru-Mahrko* was a military ship; sexual activity was discouraged on board. That's what *Dathusha*'s Nest was for. Ehtishem would go out of his way to avoid the appearance of privilege, though he'd already violated his own standards.

And as much as it killed me not to confront his mother, I understood the horrible position I'd put him in if I bashed the woman's brains out. His focus had to be on his ship and crew, not my mania or things he couldn't fix right now. My vengeance would wait. I wanted him getting *Pohru-Mahrko* repaired so we could find *Maso* and Pearl. Survival and patience, those things I understood.

"Where's the thrai bunking?" I asked Huorem as we left.

"In Northwest Torpedo Bay Four with its crew."

"Sleeping with the torpedoes like the old American submariners did."

"Did they? I didn't know that."

I nodded. "Will you thank the thrai for me?"

"I will."

Bouncing dim lights cast strange jolting shadows as a phalanx of soldiers jogged toward us. Huorem gestured for me to step into the recess created by a closed door while he took the opposite one. The living areas were tight and hallways were wasted space when so many soldiers needed to be packed in.

The men and women ran past, flipping quick salutes to the aevadasa. Their steel-toed boots thudded a rhythm on the metal flooring and their leather weapons harnesses creaked along with the beat, metal clasps and buckles jangling a counter tune.

I stared at the floor. The sound of those soldiers reminded me of the day Pearl and I were captured and taken from Terra. We were separated then, too, and I'd thought my daughter was dead. I swallowed.

Pearl will be fine. I had to believe that. The alternative was unthinkable, crippling.

The soldiers passed through a bulkhead and Huorem stepped out of the recess. "Just around the corner, Barethri."

Shouts and commotion spilled out of a room ahead of us as a soldier stumbled into the corridor and bounced off the wall. Throwing curses and fists, another soldier followed and swung at him. She missed and her opponent used her momentum to knock her feet out from under her. But she was up fast and they circled, fists up, faces grim. The man's nose leaked blue blood in a steady stream. The woman spat a tooth at him. A small crowd followed them into the corridor.

Huorem stepped me into another door recess. "Stay put." He pushed through the crowd and intercepted the woman as she made her next move. Her arm swung back to pummel her foe and her fist clocked Hu's jaw. His head snapped to the side. But he didn't go down, didn't stagger.

She gaped. "Fra! My apologies, I—"

Huorem's hand cut her off as he slapped her hard enough to knock her into the wall. Her opponent crowed until he received the back-hand of the slap. He, too, kissed the wall.

Hu straightened and wiped his hand on the sleeve of one of the watching soldiers. "I don't want to know who started that. I don't care. Neither will the zosh." He gestured at the group of bystanders. "We are not enemies and we can't afford to be at odds. The Azatem will slaughter us if we can't work together." He grabbed the two soldiers by their collars and shoved them toward two arriving security officers. "They can resolve their disagreement while scrubbing all the heads on this deck."

"All?" the male soldier said.

"All. And I'll inspect your work personally, so they better shine." He started shoving the onlookers down the corridor. "The rest of you get back to work or you'll get assignments too."

Some of them noticed me and nodded as they passed. Huorem gestured for me to join him and we resumed our trek.

"Tensions are high, Barethri. This is what happens when Ohnenrai field soldiers are afraid. Not that they'd ever admit to their fear."

I studied his profile as we walked. He was a bit broader than Ehtishem, his skin a bit darker, his eyes deep mahogany brown. He had a quick grin and laugh lines around his eyes to prove his humor even when it wasn't on display. Of all the Ohnenrai I'd met, Hu was the most animated, the most relaxed, the most open with his emotions.

"Are you afraid?" I asked.

He looked down at me, his expression calm, his eyes thoughtful. He held my gaze and nodded. "Zant."

We continued, our silence broken by his quiet whistling, until we passed through a coded door with the approval of its security computer.

"Is Ehtishem?" I asked, returning to the conversation.

"Is the zosh what?"

"Afraid?"

He stopped whistling. "I'm not sure. He's worried, I know that. Focused on solving our problem, keeping *PM* going. But I don't think he's afraid." He squinted, considering, then added, "I've never seen him afraid. Don't think he feels fear."

I knew that wasn't true. Ehtishem had confessed to feeling fear one night as we'd talked in the dark of my rickety hunter's cabin outside Suffer.

"We feel, fear most of all," he'd said. It was the reason he practiced vairim so rigorously, to block that fear. But I didn't tell that to Huorem. I didn't think he wanted to know his zosh shared the same weakness as the soldiers who were fighting. It would break the spell Ehtishem seemed to have over his troops. Crack the visage to expose the ugly truth and the whole tenuous hold the Ohnenrai had on their existence might fall apart too.

Changing the subject, I asked, "How long did it take you to find your way around this maze?"

He gave me one of his quick, bright grins. "I can't say. I was fresh from the Nest when I got stationed aboard *Pohru-Mahrko*. I did latrine duty for almost a year before I was identified for combat specialist training."

"You scrubbed heads for a *year*? Who'd you piss off?"

He grinned again. "Thrai Ehtishem Mahle."

"This I've gotta hear."

He shrugged. "I got in a brawl with another trainee, but I wasn't smart enough to leave it behind on the hamistayeca grounds. I brought it onto the training floor. The thrai saw my intentions. He yanked me off my opponent and sent me to scrub toilets until I figured out how to lose."

"And that took you a year?"

He rapped his knuckles against his temple. "I'm a slow

learner." We reached the end of another corridor and turned left. "I still haven't figured out how he knew I was itching to bust Mahzel's nose."

I stopped. "You were fighting with Mahzel?"

"Zant." Huorem cocked his head toward me and added, "Don't let his quiet demeanor fool you. He's an ahzish, fights dirtier than any soldier I've faced. And there's no better fighter to have at your back." We stopped before a door. "Keep that in mind." He entered a code into the security pad then pressed his palm to the ID reader and presented his face. The door lock clicked. Huorem slid it open. "The Draxtu-Mainyu Brotherhood is here to support you and the zosh, frei."

He stepped back and the door closed between us with a *screak*.

"Someone should oil that thing," Ehtishem said from the dark and his hand on my waist made me jump.

"Jeez Louise," I said. "Don't surprise me like that."

His grip tightened and he pulled me into his arms. "I'm sorry. That was poor judgment."

I exhaled a long, slow breath that was tainted with an old terror. "I forgive you. You're tired and it was an easy mistake to make. No harm done."

He kissed the top of my head and asked, "Who's Louise?"

I snorted. It was still funny when he interpreted Terran slang literally. "No one important or helpful."

Ehtishem's arms tightened and he kissed me again. "I came to take you to lunch."

"What's being served?" I knew perfectly well what was on the menu.

"Filet mignon with a generous helping of protein paste and very strong tea."

"Can I have the filet mignon without the paste?"

"Of course, but then you'll only be eating air since I lied about the filet mignon."

"In that case I'll just have the tea."

"You're not hungry?"

"Not for bugs." I stood on my toes and pressed my lips to his throat, pressed my body against his. "Can't that enticing lunch wait?" I suddenly felt a different kind of hunger.

"I have meetings."

I worked the fasteners loose on his jacket. "They'll wait for their zosh."

"I shouldn't even be here." His voice was husky.

I yanked his shirt from his trousers and shoved my hands beneath it. "But you are." His abs contracted beneath my touch as my fingers headed south.

"Rachel," he groaned, tilted my head back, and crushed his mouth against mine. His lips released my need and longing. Fear was behind the urge to be closer to him, but I wasn't going to fight it. Fear may have been my lifelong companion, but Ehtishem was a much better lover.

We inhaled each other's breath as our lips parted and our tongues touched.

His arms tightened around me. He stepped back, sat on a couch, and pulled me onto his lap. "Rahzhel. My love." He trailed his lips down my chin, my neck, my chest. He pressed his face to my skin and inhaled, ran his hands over my breasts, stroked my skin, my stomach, my thighs.

I moaned, longing spiraling out like a net to ensnare us both. I pulled back from his lips, feathered my fingers across his brow, down his cheekbones. I stared into his large hazel eyes, looked at his beautiful full lips, and lost myself in his kiss, his passion, him.

As Ehtishem stripped me, I pulled his grey shirt over his

head, tugged off his belt, and pushed at his trousers. I dragged my fingernails up his spine, delighted by the moan I elicited.

He pulled my mouth back to his. With one arm around my waist, Ehtishem lifted me, shifted me to straddle him. Then he was inside me, and I gasped and moaned as he lifted me, slowly, easily, kissed me, stroked me, licked me. He moved me closer and closer to my only escape. God, it felt so good to have him inside me. For just a little while I could forget fear and rage, I could just feel good, safe, loved.

He groaned and whispered in English, "Rachel, my Rachel, I love you." Our breath, bodies, longing in synchrony. "I love you."

I was lost in the taste of our skin, our lips, our tongues, our fingers. We went deeper and deeper, faster and harder. And then there was nothing but us, our bodies, our release.

I clung to him, drowned in ecstasy, held him as he groaned and pushed up into me again and again. I collapsed against him, my face on his shoulder, my lips against his neck, and shuddered as spasms rolled through me.

Ehtishem wrapped his coat around me. He pressed his face to my hair and inhaled. "You smell sweet, like strawberries and lilac, like summer in the wildflower fields of the Upper Ribbon Trail."

I smiled and murmured, "Thank you."

"For what?"

"Treating me like a person, not a tool, or an alien, or a broken weirdo. For letting me freak out one minute and jump you the next."

Ehtishem smiled. "I love you, Weirdo."

"I love you, too, Stranger."

"We are one."

The low murmur floated though my mind, followed by an

overwhelming sense that Pearl was scared and cold and needed me. Covering my face with my hands, I whispered, "Oh, god."

"What's wrong?" He tugged my hands down. "You seem... unhinged? Is that the Terran word for unstable?"

I nodded, got off him and fled to the bathing room. "More unhinged than usual?" I asked when he appeared in the doorway. "Is that really a surprise considering the circumstances?"

"Nava." He crowded into the tiny space, trapping me. "But there's something you're not saying."

"How do you know that?" I was too surprised to pretend he was wrong.

"Proximity to the Azatem rattles everyone, but some of us more." He reached past me to turn on the shower.

The voices.

I studied his handsome face, wondering how it would change if I told him.

"Pairika?" He touched my cheek. "Stop."

Only then did I realize I was chewing the inside of it raw. *Damn.*

Ehtishem leaned down to look into my eyes. "What is it?" he said, coaxing, gentle. "You can tell me."

"Do you hear voices?" I whispered. "Do you hear them in your head, louder when the Azatem are closer?"

He shook his head, but his expression didn't change and I loved him even more for that. "What do they say?"

"'We are one.'"

He straightened. "Lunch will wait. We're going to see Ahremena."

EIGHT

HE'D PROMISED to deal with his mother, but there hadn't been time. Or maybe, if Ehtishem was being honest with himself, he'd avoided it because he hadn't wanted to add one more battle to his roster. He *had* ordered her moved to *Pohru-Mahrko's* small military lab and he'd bunked her with the grunts. Both decisions she'd taken as the insults they were.

Ehtishem led Rachel through Recovery Bay Nerem Forty-nine to reach the lab. He nodded and spoke with more injured soldiers as he went. It took a great deal of vairim to project an image of control. Rachel gripped his hand hard enough to hurt and her distress did nothing to quiet his misgivings. *PM's* situation was bad. He'd led campaigns and seen plenty of battle wounds, but nothing this devastating on his own turf. And he didn't believe her assurances that she was emotionally prepared to face this horror. It had to be dredging up memories that were best left buried. He glanced at her more than once. She was chewing her cheek again, but the resolve in her eyes said she was winning the war with her volatile emotions, for now.

The lab's doors rumbled open and Ehtishem strode into the

room, Rachel beside him. Two techs assisted his mother. He pointed at them. "Both of you are dismissed."

Ahremena straightened from looking into an electron microscope. "Stay put and finish your work."

"Out. Now." The assistants glanced at him, then her, saluted, and made themselves scarce. "What are you doing aboard my ship, Sarem?" His tone was as hard as granite and a whole lot colder.

Ahremena returned to her microscope. "You told me to find you here."

"I told you to get in line."

"I did. Looks like you've dealt efficiently with all two hundred fifty thousand demands queued up ahead of me."

She was heartless. Ehtishem folded his arms. "Rachel is hearing voices. Presumably the Azatem. It's obvious they tracked her."

"Hearing? How interesting." Ahremena turned and dissected Rachel with her gaze. "What do they say?"

Ignoring that, he asked, "When did you trigger her immune response?"

"I didn't." Ahremena's expression betrayed none of her thoughts. "Just Pearl's. The child's immune system destroyed the Azatem as effectively as yours always has."

Rachel sucked a sharp breath. "Are you serious?"

Ehtishem slammed his fists on the table beside his mother, making vials and beakers jump.

She eyed him. "Struggling with vairim lately, Zosh?"

"A bit," he said through clenched teeth.

She shrugged. "I had to know if code functionality was inherited by the girl. She's perfectly healthy. No harm done."

"You bitch!" Rachel lunged at her.

Ehtishem caught her forearm and stopped her from strangling his mother, though the temptation to allow it was great.

"No harm done?" he said. "Tell that to the forty-two thousand dead and wounded soldiers on this ship. Tell that to everyone aboard *Dathusha*."

"No. Harm. Done. Pearl is the one I infected, but she's no more attractive to the Azatem than you are."

He straightened. "Which means they're tracking Rachel, and *that* means you activated her code against my orders."

"Wrong." Ahremena cocked her head to consider him then Rachel. "You did that." She folded her arms across her chest. "Though, I don't believe it's fully functional yet or they wouldn't have been distracted by *Dathusha*. We still need to boost the signal before we drop the weapon in their path."

"Don't play games with me." He released Rachel and stepped forward, menacing. "You did this, Sarem Mahlei."

"Sperm and spit." Ahremena arched an elegant brow at him. "You started the process when you exposed Rachel to your DNA. I warned you to limit your contact with her. I told you it would be a struggle. Why do you think I insisted you master vairim?"

Rachel gaped.

Ehtishem stepped back.

"Did I surprise you? How unusual." Ahremena flashed a rare smile. "You weren't supposed to engage with her sexually. I'd expected you to be protective, but you took it to the next level. Had I thought of it, I would've specifically warned against intimacy with her."

"Utha." He grabbed a chair and yanked it forward. Its feet stuttered across the floor as he pushed it towards Rachel. "Why didn't you tell me she'd been triggered?"

"Because my initial tests indicated she hadn't. That appears to have changed with ongoing, low-level exposure." Ahremena pulled up some results and turned the screen toward him. "These readings are based on the first blood draw I had from the day she was brought aboard *Dathusha*. They show non-reactive T-cells." She indicated another set of information. "These are the most recent, from just before this last encounter with *Maso*. You can see the difference. However, while her immune system is now reactive, the Azatem Code remains latent. I'm guessing your initial encounters didn't introduce enough DNA to trigger her, but repeated exposure has nudged her immune system. It won't take much more to activate the code." She closed the file and eyed him. "You might consider curbing your natural inclinations where she's concerned, Zosh, until you're ready to deploy the weapon."

"Obviously." He folded his arms.

"Why didn't you warn us?" Rachel asked.

Ahremena looked down her nose at her. "Because you showed no outward signs of code activation. I couldn't be sure the appearance of the Azatem in Terran orbit wasn't just coincidental."

Ehtishem nodded at the screen. "Your 'unusual test results'?"

She returned to her work. "Zant."

He growled in the back of his throat. "I've had enough of your secrecy and paranoia, Sarem. If you'd brought your suspicions to me sooner, perhaps we could've avoided that second Azatem attack."

"You're the one who can't keep his pants on."

Ehtishem cursed beneath his breath. As much as he hated that she was right, his damned weakness may have doomed them all.

Ahremena's tone was somehow equal parts smug and conciliatory. "Ehtishem, don't condemn yourself. Not even I foresaw how strong that attraction would become. I don't think anyone has the willpower to withstand the strength of a drive that exists on a cellular level."

He shook his head. He could chew on his own bitter mistakes later. "You knew her immune system had become reactive but failed to inform me of the increased risk to the Ohnenrai. Why?"

"I had only a theory to go on, some empirical observations of blood and DNA." Where his tone was accusatory, Ahremena's had gained a brittle edge. "I didn't know with certainty that the Azatem could track her. And converse with her." She looked at Rachel again then turned back to him. "Would you have acted on supposition alone?"

"This whole experiment is based on supposition, mother."

"It was. Now it's based on fact. The Azatem tracked Rachel. They crossed how many light years to come to her exact location?" Her eyes glittered with excitement when she met his gaze. She grabbed his arm. "The Azatem Code *works*, Ehtishem. You should be pleased."

He shook her off. "We don't know that it works, only that it paints a target on her." He glanced at Rachel. Agitation was morphing into something worse in her expression. "Deploying a weapon we're not fully ready to utilize is going to get all of us killed."

"Ready? The only person unwilling to fully activate and wield that weapon is you," Ahremena said. "This is another reason why I warned you against attachment."

Rachel leaned forward. "What happens if I'm deployed?"

"You'll kill them." Ahremena sat and began entering information into her compad. "But if Ehtishem doesn't utilize you, they'll track you to *Pohru-Mahrko* and kill everyone aboard to get to you. I'm sure they've already finished tearing through *Dathusha* and realized you're not among its populace. After *PM*, they'll likely return to Terra. So much life to harvest and consume there."

Rachel gasped.

Ehtishem steadied her with a hand on her shoulder. "Do you ever stop being manipulative, Ahremena?"

"Don't be insulting," she replied.

"Why not? You've insulted me by withholding vital information." He jabbed his finger toward the full med bay. "Their blood coats your hands."

She straightened and her veneer cracked with the slightest rise in her voice. "I kept my secrets because I had to."

"You kept them because you wanted control."

"Isphahan and his Purists threatened to destroy everything Ohnenrai Genetics had accomplished. Even if every one of us dies, Ehtishem, the Azatem still must be stopped and she is the mechanism of their end." She jabbed her finger at Rachel.

"I'm very well aware of Rachel's purpose and I had matters in hand aboard *Dathusha*, yet you failed to provide me with complete information. How can I protect our civilians and ready my troops for battle if you keep secrets from me? We are supposed to be allies."

"We are. But you're incapable of making rational decisions where she's concerned." Ahremena glanced at Rachel. "That was evident the moment you rescued her from the Stoaca Varefshar." She deliberately straightened the vials and jars that his earlier outburst had jostled. "You're driven to protect her, even when that means going against logic, duty, and the survival of everyone else. That's the Azatem DNA in your genome influencing you — an unforeseen flaw in our plan that's now laughably obvious." The tiniest smirk lifted her lips as she added, "You can't deny it."

Ehtishem couldn't, though he wanted to slap the smirk off her face. Before he met Rachel, he'd crushed anyone or anything that stood in his way. Now he'd walk away from his own people to be with her. He'd nearly done just that on Terra until Isphahan's ambition had intervened.

Rachel's voice was surprisingly calm as she asked, "How much time do we have until they find us again, and how do you boost the signal?"

Ahremena regarded her with a steady gaze. "There's no way of knowing how much time we have." She nodded toward the electron microscope. "I'll show you how the Azatem Code functions."

Ehtishem moved behind Rachel to give her a clear view.

"Contamination occurs through DNA exchange, through physical contact." Ahremena donned protective gloves, removed a small container of clean glass slides from a shelf, and placed them on the table. She opened a portable cold-case and removed two vials. She held up one that contained bright yellow liquid. "These are Azatem bacteria, stained for differentiation." Then she indicated the other vial filled with red blood and said, "Rachel's cells." She gestured toward a com screen. "Watch."

She used a syringe to place two drops of the Azatem on opposite sides of a glass plate then slid it into the microscope's sample chamber. "The Azatem are a highly-organized colony of sentient bacteria infecting and hybridizing any living thing they encounter. They strive to evolve and are compelled to remain together."

Rachel asked, "Why?"

"They're a single entity made of billions of microorganisms." The geneticist nodded toward the magnified cells on the screen. "Like Terran ants, they work for the good of the whole colony and don't see themselves as individuals."

On the slide, the yellow drops shivered and slowly oozed together to create a single drop. Ehtishem glanced at his mother, but she nodded her chin toward the screen as Rachel leaned forward, her brow furrowing.

Ahremena opened the chamber to access the slide. "Introduce new DNA to be assessed and possessed, and their frenzy increases." She lanced her finger and squeezed a row of cyan-hued blood drops onto the plate.

The Azatem moved to absorb the cells with a swiftness that Ehtishem always found unsettling. The drop began to turn green.

"*Jee*-zus." Rachel sat back.

"Family is drawn together, Rachel," Ahremena said. "And you're particularly attractive to them, by design." She placed one drop of Rachel's red blood onto the plate, far away from the rest. The Azatem slowed their assault on Ahremena's blood. They stopped. They reversed course to quickly join Rachel's blood, turning the drop a muddy hue.

"What does that prove about me?" Rachel asked.

Ehtishem replied, "You're an antimorph."

She shook her head. "I don't know what that is."

Ahremena answered, "We've fooled them into recognizing you as one of their own, but your DNA is disruptive." She nodded toward the screen. "Watch." Once again, she added her own blood to the plate, but this time the Azatem didn't so much as twitch. Even when she ringed the sickly-brown drop with her own bright-blue blood, the Azatem didn't respond.

"You're accepted as normal, but your DNA is capable of paralyzing their entire colony." She held up the vial of Rachel's blood. "These are your stem cells. The Azatem seek a host, alter its genome to create a suitable environment, then move on in search of the next host. An ever-evolving species. But your DNA was designed to interrupt that drive. The Azatem stop seeking new DNA to focus solely on clonal reproduction, ultimately leading to mutational meltdown."

"Meaning?"

"They mutate until they destroy themselves." Ahremena

smiled. "It's an elegant solution to a difficult problem. Use their own nature against them."

Ehtishem caught Rachel's hand in his. "Are you certain this will work on a large scale? And at what cost?"

His mother nodded. "Her presence destabilized Cyrus's psychological balance. She caused you to alter your path to her own gain. She prompts the Azatem to behave against their nature, against their own survival."

Her expression was smug when she looked at Rachel. "You're a carefully created biological weapon." She perched on the edge of the table and filled a new syringe from the vial containing the yellow Azatem bacteria. She placed it inside a metal cylinder, screwed on its cap, and held it out to Rachel. "For you."

Ehtishem took it. "What will this do to her?"

"It's the booster she needs to push the Azatem Code out of latency." Ahremena grabbed Rachel's wrist and said, "You are powerfully disruptive to the Azatem societal order and breeding processes."

Rachel jerked free.

"Our weapon is ready." Ahremena's controlled expression never wavered as she looked down on Rachel. "My only doubt is whether or not you will aid us. Where nurture influences nature I have little sway." She turned her cool gaze to Ehtishem and said, "That's your part to play, my son."

He folded his arms, mirroring Rachel's stiff posture. "I won't utilize this weapon until I know my troops can act on the damage it causes, completely destroy the Azatem, *and* that we can recover her afterward."

"That was never part of the plan." Ahremena sat, picked up her compad and swiped the edges.

"I'm altering the plan. And I'll keep altering it until I think it's optimized. She's our only fully functioning weapon. We have to assume there are more Azatem than those aboard *Maso*. We can't sacrifice her only to be surprised by another battlecruiser. I won't repeat the mistakes of my ancestors."

"Fine." She glanced up at them from beneath her brows. "But don't forget why she exists."

Ehtishem towered over his mother. "Rachel's not your tool."

"You are both components of a complex weapon my predecessors and I designed to destroy our enemy." She met his guarded gaze. "Don't forget that."

He led Rachel to the door.

"Rachel?" Ahremena called, "What do the Azatem say?"

"Fuck you," she replied.

NINE

EHTISHEM SWALLOWED a spoonful of bug paste and studied me.

We sat in an officer's booth surrounded by sound-proof glass. Around it, Ohnenrai soldiers ate, talked, and shot us furtive glances. I tried to ignore them. Ehtishem didn't seem bothered by eating in a fish bowl. Then again, he'd spent most of his life being watched.

"You're not eating," he said.

"I'm still not hungry enough for bugs." I pushed aside my bowl and shoved my hands into my pockets. One held a jumble of puzzle pieces; the other held the cool, smooth syringe case. I fingered that, pulled it out, and placed it on the table between us.

Azatem.

He eyed it. "You do realize we're the only people on this ship with Azatem immunity, correct?"

I nodded. "That's why I'm not leaving it sitting around." I folded my ams on the table, rested my chin on them, and looked past the tube to my lover's face. "Tell me everything I don't already know."

He gulped scalding suxra like it was iced tea and asked, "About the Azatem?"

"And the Ohnenrai. And the Terrans. And Ohnenrai Genetics. And me." I sat up. "Everything."

He scanned the mess hall then met my gaze. "Centuries ago, Ohnenrai Genetics altered a simple, benevolent bacterium to aid in genetic engineering. They also developed it into not-so-benevolent bio-weaponry as part of a military program. The result, an aggressive Azatem strain, escaped containment, became a pandemic, and irreparably damaged the Ohnenrai genome. It turned my people into its hosts and became the unstoppable threat we see today." He paused to drink more suxra.

"I thought they came on a ship and destroyed Ohnenrah."

"They returned home to Ohnenrah aboard a ship of their own making just as we were on the brink of recovery. That's when they destroyed the planet."

Jesus, I thought. The Ohnenrai had created the means of their own extinction. "And the Azatem Code?"

"Was developed by Ohnenrai Genetics in response to the Azatem pandemic. Seven hundred Terran years ago, OG visited Earth and introduced it into the human genome expecting it to spread, planning to harvest the improved DNA and reverse-engineer it back into our genome. Instead, it fragmented as Terra's own Black Death pandemic triggered a massive die-out. Meanwhile, the Azatem destroyed Ohnenrah. OG's only recourse was to return to Terra and rebuild the Azatem Code one gene at a time, culminating in your birth."

"A new weapon they hope to control better this time," I said.

His metal cup clattered on the aluminum table as he set it down. "Zant."

"You have Azatem immunity." I slowly rotated the dull metal tube. Light winked off it. "Were you exposed to this too?"

He nodded. "I was seven the first time Ahremena administered a booster."

"Just a boy."

"Death would've been more pleasant."

I let go of the vial and sat back. It rolled a few inches toward me before stopping.

He added, "I don't think it'll be so agonizing for you."

"Why?"

"Pearl tolerated it well. She inherited immunity from you."

"Damn it," I said beneath my breath. "She never said anything about it."

"She probably doesn't know."

"Eresh." I nodded. "What effects does it cause?"

"Temporarily — fever, muscle pain, delirium. Permanently — elevated Azatem immunity and rapid healing." He ran his hand over his short-shorn black hair.

I studied him with dawning realization. "You heal like that."

"You noticed on Terra." He leaned his forearms on the table.

"I *knew* sepsis should've killed you." He'd recovered remarkably fast from a blood infection and a broken ankle.

"I'm glad it didn't."

"Me too." I inhaled slowly through my mouth to quell a wave of nausea then bit down on the raw spot on the inside of my cheek, welcoming the familiar pain it brought. "I'd rather not think about Suffer."

"I'm sorry I reminded you. I regret you were thrown into

that crucible." Ehtishem squeezed my hand but didn't hold on. There were too many soldiers watching us.

"You and me both. Why did Ahremena send me there?"

"To hide you from Isphahan and, I think, to see the effects of exposure to you."

"Because Cyrus had Azatem DNA too." I nodded. "She wanted to see if I'd alter his behavior."

"And hoped I'd have enough vairim to stop you from changing mine." A slight smile curved Ehtishem's lips but disappeared as he lifted his cup to drink more suxra. "A failure I consider an unexpected benefit," he murmured into his drink.

I turned the metal tube in tight circles on the table. "If being around me pushed you to act against your training, and that's while most of my *abilities* are latent, wouldn't it be a bad idea for us to proceed with this right now? With all that's going on?"

He arched his brows. "Do you think I'll become a lunatic like Cyrus?" I shrugged, and Ehtishem gave a brief laugh before schooling his features and demeanor. "It hasn't happened yet. We don't have much choice, Pairika. The Azatem are tracking us. Despite the enormity of space, they've found us twice since you came aboard. It's not coincidental."

"Could they be following stored Azatem DNA?"

He shook his head. "I considered that, but we've had it aboard both ships for decades." He caught the tube as it rolled his way. "The last time they caught up with *Dathusha* and *Pohru-Mahrko*, the ships had returned to Ohnenrah and lingered in orbit for nearly fifty years. I can attribute that to coincidence and logic on their part." He passed the tube back. "Not these times. They're following you. And ending latency will be a signal boost to them."

I picked up the Azatem DNA. "Which means this

weapon," I tapped my chest with the tube, "needs to be prepared when they find us again."

"Zant." He drained his cup and added, "It also means that these weapons," he indicated himself, the ship, and the crew, "need to be at maximum readiness, too. You're designed to cripple. My troops are trained to kill." He reached for me and his fingers slid down my wrist and across my knuckles, over my fingers, and took the tube. He set it on the table and added, "It's still your decision."

I nodded and shoved my hands under my armpits. "I guess I'm afraid."

"Of?"

"Oh, you know, being eaten alive." I watched three soldiers cross the mess hall with their dogs at their sides. "Losing you too." I shivered and surveyed the crowded hall. So many soldiers who were afraid, angry, suffering but still doing their jobs because of the unwavering commitment of the man sitting across from me. "Do you feel emotions more acutely than the average Ohnenran?"

He shrugged. "Probably."

"Another effect of the Azatem in your DNA?"

He finished his tea. "Devotion on a genetic level. Isn't that what Ahremena said?"

"What about love?"

He studied me. "The Ohnenrai don't think about love."

"You do. And you're not one hundred percent Ohnenrai."

He flashed a smile, there and gone in a blink. "Eresh."

"That must've been unbearable when you were a boy."

"What?"

"Growing up in a society where everyone's expected to control their feelings."

"I had Sree to teach me vairim." He surveyed the mess hall too. "She comforted me when the struggle was at its worst."

"You trust her, even after she betrayed you? Even after Adam's death?"

He met my gaze. "Sree is more a mother to me than Ahremena ever was. Her betrayal hurts like a festering wound, but I understand her reasoning. And I don't believe she meant to kill Adam. She made a terrible mistake."

"You're making excuses for her?"

"Nava. There's no excusing what she did, only understanding it."

"You're more forgiving than I am."

"I doubt that."

We were silent for a few minutes.

"I hope I can't sense all their emotions." I jerked my chin toward the crowd. "I can barely handle my own." I shook my head. "I don't know how you do it."

"Practice. And, when vairim doesn't work, I pummel someone." Ehtishem stood and gathered our dishes.

I rose, but two soldiers shoved their chairs back and into my path as I stepped from the booth. Both glanced up as they stood. One immediately moved aside and said, "I apologize, frei."

But the other soldier looked right through me and left his chair in my path as he turned, picked up his tray, and sauntered toward the exit.

"Nerem." Ehtishem's voice boomed over the crowd and smothered the chatter like a wet blanket on a fire.

The soldier stopped in his tracks but didn't turn around. "Zant, fra?"

"You disrespected our guest. Was that unintentional?"

The man turned. He still didn't look at me, but he met Ehtishem's gaze and replied, "Nava, fra."

"You disapprove of a civilian being aboard?"

"Nava, fra."

"You disapprove of a Terran being aboard?"

The soldier's gaze skipped to me for a second then returned to his commander. "Zant, fra."

I marveled at the man's cool demeanor under the pressure of Ehtishem's questioning. It took balls to admit he didn't like me being there. It also scared the shit outta me 'cause I knew he couldn't be the only one.

"Barethri Rachel is here by invitation of your zosh and with the approval of your thrai. When you disrespect her, you disrespect the Office of the Supreme Command General, you disrespect the Ohnenrai Military Command, and you disrespect me." As he spoke, Ehtishem closed the gap between himself and his soldier.

"I mean no disrespect to you or to Command, fra."

"Actions hold more weight than words, soldier. I won't have my guest, my office, my command, or my decisions disrespected by you or anyone else." He removed his coat and rolled up his sleeves. "Four strikes, nerem." The soldier put down his tray and clasped his hands behind his back. Ehtishem punched him in the face. The man stumbled back and fell hard. A group of senior soldiers pulled him up. Once again his hands went behind his back and once again his zosh doled out punishment.

I winced with each blow — four altogether — but I stayed quiet and watched the man take a beating. *Pohru-Mahrko* was a military vessel. The Ohnenrai believed in unbending military discipline. Questioning command and disrespecting an officer could be punishable by death. Ehtishem, fortunately, wasn't that fanatical. He didn't need to be. The fourth blow knocked out the soldier. The zosh wiped blood from his knuckles as the unconscious man was tended by two med techs.

"Does anyone else require aid to solidify his or her faith in my command?" he asked. His voice carried to the back of the cavernous mess hall. His soldiers presented stoic faces and direct gazes. "Ushta." He clasped his hands behind his back. "Remember, pa'nerem, if one of us falls, we all fall. So you must help your fellow soldiers stand. It's been brought to my attention that many of you have engaged in pointless brawls and barbs. Such disagreements will stop. Now. Any soldiers found fighting or behaving disrespectfully will face my fists and the floor."

He turned away. Clatter and chatter returned. The techs pulled the fallen soldier to his feet. Ehtishem checked the man's eyes, shook his head at what he saw, and sent him to the closest med bay.

"Don't make enemies on my behalf," I said as he led me toward the exit.

"You're mistaken, Pairika. That was discipline, not a battle, and it was the most fun I've had in weeks."

"Right. When vairim doesn't work you pummel someone?"

"Zant." He considered his bruised knuckles, stopped in the doorway, and pulled his com from his pocket.

"This is your zosh speaking." His voice came through the ship-wide com. "Many of you are concerned about our circumstances. Perhaps you are fearful and question my decisions. Tensions are high. Many of you need relief. So ready your marks. We'll hold a hamistayeca forty-eight hours from now."

That brought cheers, clapping, stomping from the soldiers around us. Whatever a hamistayeca was, *Pohru-Mahrko's* soldiers wholeheartedly endorsed it.

When it quieted, Ehtishem continued. "We are a ship afloat in a sea of stars, but we are neither rudderless nor homeless. We will see *Dathusha* again. We will rid ourselves of our dauntless enemy. I know this because I was once lost in the wilderness, surrounded by those who would destroy me, but I returned home and I defeated my enemies. We will not rest until *Dathusha* travels under our watchful eye and protective arm again. We are Ohnenrai. We fight as one. We bow to none."

———

When we reached Timsai's quarters, Ehtishem dropped onto the couch with a groan, rubbing his side and grimacing.

"Still sore?" I left the syringe and puzzle pieces on the galley counter.

"Zant. *Zhek.* I'm glad I snapped my bastard uncle's neck."

I laughed. He rarely cussed in front of me and hearing it in English was even funnier than Ohnenrai.

"Forgive me for my language."

"You don't need to apologize to *me* for cussing." I tugged his sleeve. "Lift your arm, I want to see your ribs. Has anyone examined the wound recently?"

"Nava." He raised his arm, resting his wrist atop his head. "I'm just sore. But I know better than to fight you."

"Uh-huh, you haven't seen a med tech because you're too special to develop complications." I pulled up his shirt and added, "But wait, that's right. No. You're. Not."

The incision was pink and well on its way to healing. "There's no sign of infection."

"Disappointed?"

"Maybe a little." I rested my hand against his abdomen. His secondary heart thumped a slow rhythm. Laying my head against his chest I smiled to hear the percussion section that was the Ohnenrai cardiovascular system — a primary heart located between his lungs, just like mine, and a larger, slower secondary heart located near his gallbladder. "What's a hamistayeca?"

Ehtishem stroked my hair. He wrapped his other arm around my shoulders. "A game."

I waited. When he remained silent, I nudged him. "What kind of game?"

"The kind where soldiers bloody each other. A lot. And there's a ball."

"Of course."

He pressed his lips to my ear. "You should watch. It's a rare chance to see Ohnenrai soldiers having fun."

"You guys know how to have fun? No way." The syringe caught my eye from its place on the galley counter. I pushed away from him and let my head fall back against the cushions. I laced my fingers with his. "How're your knuckles?"

"Fine. His face was soft."

I shook my head and checked his hand for swelling or fractures but his solid fist was only a little bruised.

Ohnenrai fingernails, like their bones, were black, and Ehtishem's were iridescent when the light hit them just right. He had long, strong fingers and kept his nails even and trimmed. Mine were jagged from biting and from filling med packs.

"What's wrong?" he murmured.

"Can't hide anything from you." I bit the inside of my cheek and stared at the damned metal tube. "Shit, Ehtishem." I sat up and slapped his knee. It stung but made a satisfying *thwack*. He looked at me from the corner of his eye as I clenched my teeth. "Just *shit*!"

"Rachel."

I stood. "Don't. Just don't. I'm cornered again! I finally got away from Cyrus, but I'm no better off. You finally got rid of Isphahan, but you're no better off." I faced him. "You know what? This sucks donkey dicks!"

He stared at me for a second, then laughed as he stood and hugged me. "That's another reason why I love you, Rachel Pryne. You say exactly what you mean and you never hide your feelings." He leaned back, cradled my face in his palms, and added, "Don't ever change."

I pushed away. "You can't ask that of me. Because if I don't change, we'll all die."

There it was, the reality of my choice. "I thought I was finally free of being controlled, but I never really had a chance. I was manufactured, nothing but a tool." I met his gaze and added quietly, "We both are. And the choice really isn't ours."

He bowed his head with a slow nod. "I wish there was another way."

"But there isn't. Either I do this or the Terrans and the Ohnenrai will disappear." I took the tube from the counter. "You heard Ahremena. If I use this, I can disrupt the Azatem and you can attack. Then you can find *Dathusha* and Pearl."

He closed his hand over mine and the syringe. "Don't let my mother use your fears to control you." He took the tube from me and returned it to the counter. "You're not doing this tonight, Rachel, because we're not ready to attack." He cradled my face and tilted my head back to look into my eyes. "But when we are, we'll strike hard. Then we'll recover *Dathusha* and Pearl together." He lowered his head and kissed me.

I raised my hand, my pinky cocked. "Pinky promise?" I said against his lips.

He drew back, confused. "Pinky what?"

I took his hand and hooked our little fingers together. "Pinky promise. Something my mom and dad used to do with me."

Ehtishem's expression turned solemn. "Pinky promise."

I couldn't sleep.

"We are one."

The voices were back, soft, almost inaudible, and knowing they weren't imaginary wasn't making me feel any better about them.

The metal tube glinted in the cabin's low light.

All the bodies descending to the morgue kept passing through my mind on their way. The sounds of suffering from the Trauma Bay echoed too. The stoicism of the soldier hosing blood and guts and lives down the drains made me cringe. The footage I'd seen back aboard *Dathusha* of the Azatem pa'vikeret digesting soldiers threatened to invade my brain next, and with it, shimmering around my consciousness, was the strange out-of-body feeling of a flashback.

Goddamn it.

I thought I'd gotten through *Maso's* attack and the after-math unscathed. But Ahremena had rattled me. I'd always kept my shit together for Pearl. She made me a rock. Without her, my resolve was crumbling. No matter how strong she seemed, she was still my weakness. Now my baby was beyond my help again, and those monsters would kill her if Ehtishem and I didn't stop them.

"We are one."

Screw you, I thought and slipped from the bunk. *I'm not like you. I'm not.*

His voice thick with sleep, Ehtishem mumbled, "Pairika?"

"Just using the head. Go back to sleep." He rolled toward the wall and his breathing deepened.

I needed to get grounded in the here and now or a flashback would take hold. The reflection of light off the metal tube caught my attention again. I stared at it for many long minutes. Finally, I grabbed it, retrieved Ehtishem's belt from his clothes locker, and went to the bathroom. Squinting from the light's glare, I sat on the toilet and unscrewed the tube's cap. I tipped out the transparent syringe. Bright yellow Azatem stem cells crowded against the side of the syringe in my palm. That color was a warning. It said, "Danger. Turn back. Proceed with caution."

"There's no choice," I whispered. "If I don't do this, we're all dead." I angled the syringe, but the Azatem cells began a frenzied dance and moved against gravity to remain close to me. "Pearl. Ehtishem. Do this for them." I remembered him hugging Pearl before we were separated from him on the side of a mountain in the American Pacific Northwest. I smiled and the cells slowed to a waltz. "Weird. So you really do respond to me."

Ahremena had called them sentient bacteria.

Watching the Azatem, I pictured Cyrus's twisted, obsessive expression, felt the panic when he'd surprised me in my muddy, overgrown yard. The Azatem cells went mad. Like a storm raging inside a little bottle, they careened from one end to the other. My own panic threatened to surge and suck me into that flashback. I fought it with thoughts of Ehtishem, the feel of his lips and his skin, the taste of his tongue. And the storm eased. Once again the cells waltzed around the syringe and a sense of tranquility relaxed me. They were weirdly soothing, just like the voices had been after *Maso*'s attack.

"I'll be damned." I considered the tiny world in the palm of my hand and made a decision. I fashioned a tourniquet with the belt and brought up a vein on my left arm. A recessed wall box yielded antibiotic wipes. I cleaned my skin then uncapped the needle. With the bevel up, I pressed the point to my vein.

I hesitated, staring at those yellow cells. "Promise me we'll be friends, okay?" The Azatem gathered close to the needle, as if they knew the party was about to start. "Jesus-fucking-Christ." I watched the moving bacteria, afraid if I didn't do it now, I wouldn't have the nerve later.

There was a sharp sting as the needle broke my skin. I

pulled the plunger back just a little. Blood appeared in the syringe; I'd hit the vein. The Azatem cells continued their frenzied celebration.

"*I'm sure they've already finished tearing through Dathusha.*" Ahremena's words invoked my fears.

"*Double-edged sword. Strike when you need to.*" My father's words had buoyed me during the darkest days.

"*We're not ready to attack. But when we are, we'll strike hard.*" Ehtishem's words gave me hope, and made me pause.

He trusted me to trust him, trusted me wait, trusted that I wouldn't chicken out and let them all die. I swallowed a lump and whispered, "I'm coming, Baby Girl," even as I removed the needle, pressed my thumb to the puncture to stop any bleeding, and placed the still-full syringe in the sink. "Soon. Very soon. I promise."

I couldn't do something stupid and endanger everything Ehtishem had worked so hard, sacrificed so much, to accomplish. "Get your shit together, Rachel. If he says Pearl is protected, then she is. Don't be a dumbass. Don't be jerked around by Ahremena. And don't let your emotions control you."

I rested my face on the cold metal edge of the sink and watched the Azatem as their frenzy died down. They gathered close to me like they were watching me and wondering why the hell I'd stopped. "Sorry, guys. Party's been postponed." I capped the syringe and returned it to its protective tube.

I left the tube on the galley counter and slipped into bed.

Ehtishem rolled over and pulled me against him. "Did you ever have a dream, an ambition? Before all this happened?" He spoke English and the timbre of his voice told me he was more awake than I'd thought. Did he know what I'd almost done?

"No. Your people arrived just after my birth. The only

dream I ever got a chance to have is the dream of being free, of Pearl living without fear and with freedom. What about you?"

"No." He rolled to his back, tucked his hands behind his head, and looked at the overhead, his profile lit by the dim glow of the wall chron in the galley. "The only dream I've had was to see the day when my people don't live in fear of disappearing from existence. I've always lived in the shadow of our impending extinction."

"Our dreams aren't so different."

"Except, I destroyed yours."

"Huh. How magnanimous of you to admit that."

He looked at me.

"You don't know what that means, do you?"

"No."

I laughed quietly. "It means you're an asshole." I rolled onto my side to face him. "Does that explain it?"

"Yes. That word I'm quite familiar with."

TEN

"THE INTERIOR HULL breach is closed. Electrical's back to eighty percent capacity but water purification is still unavailable. However, this is what I brought you down here to see, Zosh. You should have the scan on your visor now. The deformations are evident where the joints were stressed." Aevadasa Sezenei, *Pohru-Mahrko*'s Chief Structural Engineer, drew Ehtishem's attention to his helmet's visor as four of her assistant engineers slowly slid an electron scanner over Sector Eighty's magstenite main beam.

Ehtishem nodded and studied the visuals as they appeared on the inside surface of his visor. "Aiya. That's unmistakable." He, Timsai, and the engineers all wore bio-suits, atmospheric suits, and helmets.

Beside him, Timsai peered into the hole that had been carved out of the subfloor by an Azatem laser warhead. "How far does this damage extend?"

"Through Y, Z, and Double-A decks, W and X are solid. I've got a crew checking Double-B through Double-D."

Timsai nodded. "At what point does this go from a repair job to a rebuild?"

Ehtishem waited for his visor screen to go dark and minimize before he blew out a long breath and scowled as his CO_2 monitor squealed a warning in his ear; he was tired of telling Ops the thing was too sensitive.

He'd received departmental briefings in the small command deck meeting room all morning then had met with Timsai and Sezenei to discuss battle damage and repairs.

This area of the ship had housed a major trauma bay and taken injured patients directly into the ship through launch bay doors that now were a tangled mess of slag. A temporary transcrete airlock was being erected to stop the ship's atmosphere from leaking into space. The Kevrian's dust and protoplanets could be seen beyond the jagged opening.

Pohru-Mahrko hurtled through space, fifty hours out from Iodiq. Stars became streaks, gas and debris clouds were smears. Only skittering flashes of light, as the ship's repaired deflection field obliterated debris, indicated they were passing through a star system in its infancy.

He gestured into the ship's gaping wound. "What's the final word here?"

Sezenei replied, "With those main beams cracked, our biggest concern is instability between the decks."

Ehtishem's atmo-suit creaked as he leaned forward. "One wrong move and they'll pull apart?"

"Zant, fra. And we'll have decks falling beneath each other's weight. This is one of four primary beams showing stress fractures."

Ehtishem nodded. "If one goes, we could lose all of them and *PM* will implode."

"Exactly. Unless we can fix this, she'll come apart in the next battle."

Ehtishem clenched his fist. "Keep me informed. If a retrofit can't be accomplished in transit, we'll scrap and rebuild this whole section when we reach Iodiq."

The engineers murmured agreement then returned to their scanners.

Timsai proffered his reader.

Ehtishem took it. "What's this?"

"Funerary procedurals."

Ehtishem scanned the information, input his approval code, and passed the compad back. Most of the dead had been prepped for release. Iodiq's sun would be the final resting place of the ship's lost soldiers. "Two days from Iodiq and still no sign of *Maso*."

"Luck finally swung our way."

"When we're done here, I want you to get some sleep, Thrai. You've been carrying more than your fair share of work. Don't think I haven't noticed."

Timsai nodded. "Of course you did. Nothing escapes you." They turned from the gaping hole in the floor of the traumatized trauma bay. "I'll do that. And you should do the same. We need a rested zosh when we reach Iodiq, Ehtishem."

"Agreed. I'm ready for a long rest. I haven't been sleeping well or much."

Timsai nodded. "You're not alone. There was another fight in the mess hall during the midday meal today."

Ehtishem grimaced, willing to show displeasure and other emotions to his oldest friend. "What's there to fight over? We're all eating bug paste."

Timsai pocketed the reader. "Paranoia's setting in and knowing *Maso*'s still out there doesn't help. They're looking for something to blame for our string of bad luck."

Ehtishem crossed his arms. "Superstitions cause more problems than the actual problems blamed on them. The Azatem are responsible for our current situation."

"Tomorrow's hamistayeca can't come soon enough."

"It'll do a lot to alleviate tension."

To describe hamistayeca as a rough sport was an understatement, which was why the Ohnenrai soldiers enjoyed it. Forty soldiers, one ball, two opposing goals, and no rules. Blood, sweat, and broken bones — the Ohnenrai idea of a good time.

Timsai said, "That'll blunt their edge before we reach Iodiq."

"Walk with me."

The thrai strode with Ehtishem as they headed for the only working lift that serviced the damaged levels.

Timsai said, "A rebuild could take a year." The doors of the lift closed and they removed their helmets as it pressurized.

"Possibly more if the depots on Iodiq have been compromised. The records are unreliable. Some show a shipyard there, others don't. And the dates don't help. We could find fortune on our side or nothing."

"Let's hope for good fortune. We need more."

"Zant. It's been long in coming and short in supply."

They were quiet for a few moments, two friends who knew each other well enough to be comfortable with silence.

Ehtishem's com buzzed, breaking the peace. He glanced at the incoming message and muttered a curse.

There's more you need to know. I'm in the lab. Make this a priority.

"Bad news?"

"Ahremena."

Timsai was all too familiar with Ehtishem's troubled family relationships. He indicated the zosh's com and said, "I sent you the most up-to-date information on Iodiq's facilities, as well as the landing team's recs on recon, the troop dispersals we discussed with a few modifications based on CO input, and ship personnel rotations."

Ehtishem kneaded the back of his neck. He responded to his mother: *Tell me before the team briefing this afternoon.* Then he called up Timsai's data. "All right. Take me through this."

When all his closest officers and advisors were seated in *PM's* Central EXO Briefing Room, Ehtishem stood the wooden piece he was carving on edge and surveyed his inner circle. They were the women and men whom he'd come to trust and rely upon. They called themselves the Draxtu-Mainyu Brotherhood because they all considered him their brother. And truly, they were a family. More than ever he needed them to believe in him and trust his leadership because he wasn't sure that what he was asking them to do wasn't tantamount to suicide.

Ehtishem indicated his mother. "Sarem Mahlei is here to answer the questions that will result from what I'm about to tell you. There's a great deal to explain and, as always, where genetics and biology are concerned, it's complex and ever-changing information." He picked up the wood, ran his fingers around the rough edges. "The sarem has brought to my attention research she has not been at liberty to share for fear of reprisals from Zosh Uahdim. That research involves an unusual connection between the Terrans and the Ohnenrai created by the introduction of Azatem bacteria. And it presents another significant step toward freeing ourselves from our enemy." He pointed at the ceiling and said, "Windows full dark. Lights off.

"You've heard of the Azatem Code, but you don't know the

extent of its influence on our present and future actions. You have only a fraction of the truth.

"The Azatem are colonial bacteria. Their influence upon each other drives them to be together. And that drive is compelling them to follow Barethri Rachel, the person genetically designed to attract and influence them to act against their own well-being."

Boots scuffed. Chairs creaked. His soldiers were uneasy.

He looked to his mother. "Sarem Mahlei, please explain."

She stood and gestured at the overhead display. "In the final days leading up to Ohnenrah's destruction, as you all know, a team of soldiers took an assignment to infiltrate and destroy the Azatem harvester in orbit. Their success was widely reported. What wasn't made known was that samples and data were obtained for Ohnenrai Genetics. That information revealed a connection between the Ohnenrai and the Terrans and helped shape the Azatem Code to emphasize parthenogenesis."

"Partho-what?" Anchal asked.

"Asexual reproduction," Ahremena answered.

Huorem leaned across the table and said, "Making babies without having the fun."

Ahremena eyed him. "The Azatem continuously mutate using DNA obtained from captive species, but they never jeopardize their colonial connections in doing so. My predecessors and I saw opportunity there. We designed Rachel Pryne's Azatem Code to be highly attractive to the Azatem. So much so that they'll forego obtaining outside DNA in lieu of utilizing her genome for their genetic growth. Essentially, they'll copy and recopy her genome to their own detriment, eventually resulting in mutational meltdown and colony collapse."

"I don't understand what most of that means, frei," Gahlen

said. "I do hear you saying Barethri Rachel will kill them, but what will stop them from killing her?"

Heads nodded around the table, and Ehtishem withheld a smile. His soldiers were loyal to Rachel. That's what he'd hoped to see.

"Genetics," she replied. "It's the same thing that compels you to ask that question, Aevadasa."

"What do you mean?" Mahzel asked.

"All of you have Zosh Ehtishem Mahle's DNA in your genome, therefore all of you have Azatem bacterial DNA. And all of you are now compelled by that DNA to protect Rachel Pryne. I want to know how far her influence extends."

As Ahremena further explained her findings and suppositions, the soldiers shifted and fidgeted. They murmured and glanced at Ehtishem. Of course they knew they had his DNA, but that it included Azatem genes and drove them to protect Rachel was stunning news.

Uncertainty hung in the air, so thick he couldn't block it. Ehtishem studied the sketch of the puzzle box he was carving for Rachel, the meditative task helping him maintain vairim. He scanned the diagram and turned the wood; this was the final piece. The grooves and patterns within the block showed him what to cut and shape. The wood always told him which direction to move the knife, where it would give, where it would fight, and where it was vulnerable and required careful handling.

Timsai spoke. "You believe our shared Azatem DNA connects the Ohnenrai and the Terrans on an instinctual level. And we can use that to our advantage. Do I have that right, Sarem?"

"That's correct, Thrai. We also want to understand how the Azatem communicate with each other and with Rachel." Ahremena sat like a stone goddess, sure in her manipulation of the mortal lives around her. But was that security unfounded? Was she guessing and hoping, hiding flaws in her assumptions? Ehtishem's fingers tightened on the wood. There was a knot there, hidden below the surface. He picked up an ink stylus and marked the puzzle pattern with sure strokes. *You're keeping a secret*, he thought.

Mahzel said, "Wait. They're communicating with her?"

"Zant," Ahremena replied.

More shifting and throat clearing met her statement. The Brotherhood hadn't expected that.

Timsai said, "I'll ask the question no one else wishes to. If they're communicating with Barethri Rachel, is she responding and revealing our location deliberately?"

"Nava," Ehtishem replied. One last curve marked, and he set down the wood. "Rachel believed the voices were a manifestation of her anxiety. She was as surprised as you are to learn the voices she's hearing are the Azatem."

Ahremena added, "I believe it's a previously-unknown aspect of the Azatem Code at work. Our enemy followed her because she was designed to attract them. She's fulfilling her purpose."

Timsai asked, "How do we proceed?"

What Ahremena had explained about Azatem communication and emotional influence bounced around Ehtishem's brain. How could he use Rachel's impact on his emotions to his advantage? And, maybe even more importantly, could other soldiers be positively affected by her? Could she aid them in the coming battles with the Azatem?

As if reading his mind, Ahremena said, "I require a small volunteer group to work with Barethri Rachel in testing non-verbal communication and emotional reactions. Your interactions will be carefully observed. This will be a test of your vairim unlike any you've experienced."

Ehtishem murmured, "Doubtless," to a few knowing laughs.

Mahzel asked, "What about Barethri Rachel? How will this affect her?"

"Has she even agreed to be involved?" Huorem added.

"Not like she ever had a choice," Tinish muttered.

Heads nodded around the table at that. Including Ehtishem's. "Good questions," he said. "Rachel wears her emotions on her sleeve, as most of you already know." That understatement drew more laughs. "She has many reasons not to help us." And that uncomfortable truth brought more chair creaking and throat clearing.

Under Isphahan's leadership, the Ohnenrai had murdered the majority of the Terran populace, including Rachel's parents. She had every reason to let all of them die, even if it meant suicide in the process. The only thing stopping her from doing that was Pearl. And Ehtishem, he hoped.

He continued. "I don't know what, if any, advantage this gives us, pa'nerem."

He looked from face to face. Mahzel and Huorem, whom he trusted with Rachel's life, Gahlen and Tinish who protected him, Gohra, Stig, and Anchal, the fiercest fighters on his force, and Timsai his staunchest ally since boyhood.

"What I do know is that with *Dathusha* gone, we are hanging by a thread. Any possible strand that appears to aid our survival is one I'll grasp with all my might. I'll do anything I can to buoy my soldiers — my *family* — as we face the coming battles. There's no longer an Elite Caste, no Middle or Lower Caste. There are only survivors. And something I learned during my years on Terra is that family is a bond the Ohnenrai have been missing." He gazed around the room. "No longer. Everyone on this ship is my family. And we are going to use the strength of that bond to survive, just like the Terrans did."

Heads nodded around the table. The Draxtu-Mainyu *Family* was with him.

When all the officers' questions were answered and six volunteers had been selected, he dismissed the soldiers. "Sarem Mahlei will contact our volunteers to begin testing. You need to be closely monitored, so we'll adjust assignments to cover everyone's duties."

Ahremena lingered, scanning her files and watching the soldiers.

"What more do you have to discuss?" Ehtishem had finished the rough cuts of the puzzle piece and was refining the design.

"A detail I didn't clarify. I think only you should see it right now. I'm trying to be considerate of Rachel's *sensitivities*, so I thought this information should come from you."

He put the wood down, slid his narrow spoon gouge into its leather pocket, and folded his hands. "All right."

She nodded toward the overhead display where a visual file depicting Rachel appeared. Only it wasn't Rachel, it was her twin. The woman had a bruised cheek, a cut above her left eyebrow, and wore her dark hair elaborately coiled atop her head. She also wore a white, sleeveless gown, and there was something in her eyes that said she could see right into anyone's soul.

Ehtishem stared, not bothering to hide his confusion or the dawning realization that the woman Ahremena was showing him wasn't Rachel. She wasn't Terran. He sucked in a sharp breath and pushed back from the table, rejecting a sickening awareness. The image changed and now he saw two sets of DNA sequences. They matched but for their identification codes: *Terran/PNA625969/Rachel Elizabeth Pryne* and *Azatem Humanoid/AZ000001/Yazadami.*

"You understand what you're seeing, Ehtishem?"

He nodded slowly. "Rachel doesn't just have an additional gene. Her entire genome was cloned."

"The only clone Ohnenrai Genetics created that survived to adulthood."

"This is the sample sent back from the harvester?"

"Zant. Based on the amount of Azatem bacteria in homo sapiens' DNA, we determined the Azatem were on Terra before we were. We still don't know why."

"You have a theory?"

"Look at the name the woman gave."

"Yazadami." He considered that. "Why would she have the name of an Ohnenrai god?"

Ahremena folded her arms. "I think the Azatem named her. They were trying to create a god. It makes sense if you think about it. They're the Azatem, the Unborn. They are, from a certain point of view, immortal."

He shook his head. "You're saying these bacteria are not only organized, but they have a culture? A religion?"

She shrugged. "More like a goal."

He scratched his jaw. "Did they get the idea from studying our culture?"

"Maybe. Or by combining it with Terran religions? It's immaterial." She closed the file. "The choice to share this or not with Rachel I leave to you."

They were silent for a moment until she leaned forward. "What do they say to her?"

Instead of answering he said, "I'll keep this to myself for now. But I hope we're making the right decision. I don't want to lose a family that I've just discovered."

Ahremena dissected him with her scalpel gaze. "You returned from Terra a very different man."

"A better man."

She went to the door. "That remains to be seen."

Ehtishem watched the door close behind her. He picked up the puzzle piece and turned it this way and that, considering. "We are one," he murmured, running his finger over the curves and bumps of the wood. Care was necessary to fit all the pieces into place.

PART TWO
IRON

ELEVEN

HUOREM SHOVED up his sleeves like he was getting ready to arm wrestle and asked, "Should we hold hands, Barethri?" He winked at me.

Ahremena dismissed his suggestion with a wave of her hand. "The Azatem appear not to need a physical connection. Intensity of emotion, however, may be a factor."

We were in her lab, testing non-verbal communication.

"Why are we doing this, Sarem?" Gohra asked. I would know her anywhere by the white Draxtu-Mainyu symbol branded into her dark, shaved scalp. She was playing daspa with Mahzel, the tiles clacking on the low table between them.

"I want to determine the extent, if any exists, of Barethri Rachel's connection to those soldiers with Azatem DNA from the zosh's genome. I also hope to understand how the Azatem are communicating with her and if it's an attempt to control her." She turned back to Hu and me. "Begin with a strong desire, Barethri."

"Ooh, think of something embarrassing." Huorem waggled

his brows at me from where he lounged in his chair like a rag doll.

I gave him the finger. "Very funny, cannon fodder."

"Focus." Ahremena adjusted a monitor sitting on the table beside us. It read our vitals from the implanted trackers in our brains.

I shot her a dirty look; she'd earned a permanent home on my shit list. But Ehtishem thought her experiments had merit, so here I was. "Okay," I muttered and stared at the aluminum tabletop between Hu and me. "A strong emotion." I glanced up. He was staring at the same general place. *Happiness. What makes me happy?* Pearl came to mind. *Pearl, Pearl, Pearly Girly.* I visualized my daughter herding chickens with Audie and Jack, heard her laughter and Goat-Goat's protests, the dogs barking, the flutter of feathers and squawking complaints.

"Do you feel any connection with your soldier?" Ahremena asked. "Aevadasa, do you sense any change?"

"Nava," we replied simultaneously.

I concentrated on my emotions, but nothing indicated I'd connected with Hu. I sighed. Frustration was an emotion but not a productive one. *Happiness. Pearl.* I closed my eyes and, unbidden, the memory of holding my infant daughter for the first time flooded me. The relief when I'd pushed her out, the greater relief when she'd cried. Putting her to my breast and the euphoria when she'd nursed. The exhaustion and the unadulterated love I'd felt gazing down on her.

"Aiya."

I opened my eyes at Huorem's exhaled word. He wore a wide-eyed, dreamy expression.

"I think that worked," I said. My spine tingled and the hair on my arms stood on end. *Weird.*

"Quite well, I believe," Ahremena said as she took notes.

Hu shook his head and cleared his throat. "What were you thinking about?"

I matched his grin. "Pearl's birth." The monitor beeped and registered our vitals.

Ahremena studied the information. "Surprisingly effective. You're both significantly relaxed." She nodded. "Try someone you're less familiar with. A negative emotion this time."

I straightened in my seat. This was dangerous territory. If I strayed too deeply into my worst memories, I could experience a flashback.

"Gohra." Ahremena beckoned the lanky munitions tech forward. She settled in the chair that Huorem abandoned. Ahremena input her tracker code and recorded a new set of baseline readings. "When you're ready."

"Gimme a minute." I'd never be ready.

Gohra folded her hands upon the table and, like Huorem, stared at a spot somewhere between us.

Okay, Rachel, you can do this. Anger, go for anger. If I avoided fearful experiences, I'd be all right. It couldn't be a mild memory, that much was clear. When had I last been furious?

This time the memory was swift and brutal. It was Cyrus's death, and it hit me with the same amount of force I'd used to crack open his skull. I hadn't looked away from Gohra, so when I flinched she did too. With her wide-eyed gaze fixed upon me, I pushed back from the table, my chair screeching on the metal floor. "I'm done." This time, instead of tingling, my spine burned.

"Barethri." Gohra's hand on my wrist stopped me. "Whatever that was, and you don't have to tell me, the guilt you feel is unwarranted. That was revenge fairly and swiftly administered."

I stared at her. "How do you know?"

"Because I recognized that emotion." She gestured toward the other soldiers. "That's a kind of hate we've felt our entire lives."

"You picked that up?" Gohra and Huorem nodded, their expressions grave and hard. They'd been feeling the same raw fury, yet not one of them had shown it. I covered Gohra's hand with my other one. "Is this difficult for you?"

Her brow furrowed. "Difficult? You mean experiencing your emotions?"

"You're all so controlled." I looked down. "Before I met the zosh, I didn't think any of you were capable of feeling emotions."

She squeezed my hand then sat back. "We had you fooled."

Mahzel said, "We're just better at masking our feelings, controlling them, and venting them completely when it's time."

"And when is that?"

"In battle," Huorem replied with his usual irreverence.

Mahzel added, "Focus is what we learn, Barethri. We focus our rage and use it as a weapon."

Ahremena was looking from the soldiers to me to her compad. She nodded. "That's what you need to do, Rachel. Focus your emotions *and* theirs. If the zosh hopes to retrieve you from *Maso*, our forces must fight past a lot of enemy bio-weaponry to succeed."

"I'm supposed to convert everyone's emotions into a weapon?"

She cocked her head, considering me. "We know you can broadcast your emotions, but can you collect them from others?"

Stig stood. "My turn." She was tall and beautiful, with enormous brown eyes, ebony skin, and a surprisingly quick smile. She'd have been a fashion model, if she'd been born on Terra. But I'd sparred often enough with her over the last six months to know she was much more than a pretty face. Stig was a beauty and a beast, a fast and deadly combatant.

Gohra gave up her seat. I exhaled and scooted my chair into place. After the monitor registered our baselines, Stig nodded and said, "Let's stick with pleasant emotions, Barethri."

"Zant." I glanced at Ahremena. "Any idea how I'm supposed to do this?"

"Try," she ordered without looking up.

Stig nodded and closed her eyes. I did too and cleared my mind.

At first there was nothing then warmth started at my scalp and spread down my spine. The tingling sensation began, like ants on my skin. I perceived happiness, but instead of feeling it, I observed it as a ribbon of yellow sunshine. Something in my brain seized the ribbon and pulled it, followed it, and I had the strangest sense that I could absorb it, make it mine. A part of me wanted to. It wanted to gorge on those emotions, swell with them, and rob Stig of all her feelings.

Another part of me knew that was wrong. Very wrong. I opened my eyes and slammed the door down on our connection.

Stig's eyes opened wide. "Aiya."

Ahremena looked at us and back to her readings. "What just occurred?"

I shook my head, unsure how to answer. Stig replied for me. "Barethri Rachel had control of me. She could have stolen my — joy — if she'd wanted to."

Gohra and Huorem shifted in their seats. "Both of you felt that power too?" the geneticist asked. They nodded. Ahremena turned back to me. "Was that your perception, Barethri?"

I nodded and swallowed. My mouth felt cottony.

"Very interesting." Ahremena turned her compad to face us. "When Huorem and Gohra first engaged with Barethri

Rachel their brain waves synchronized with hers. However, when she engaged with Stig, their brains reacted in distinctly different ways. The barethri's brain waves slowed and lengthened and she entered a meditative state. Stig's impulses began steadily, came into synchronicity with hers, but devolved as their connection persisted." She lowered the compad and turned to me. "Does that match your experiences?"

"Zant," I said. "But I don't like what I did to her. It felt like I was stealing her emotions."

Stig said, "I think you were."

Ahremena sat back. She looked like a cat that had captured a bird. "Now that we have a better understanding of your current abilities, we'll focus on boosting your control." She surveyed the soldiers. "Mahzel, you're next. Let's help the barethri learn vairim."

Huorem found me in the supply depot, his whistling announcing him before he came through the doorway. "Coming to the hamistayeca, Barethri?" He took the full bag I was dragging and hefted it onto the rack with an easy swing. "The zosh promises a good match."

"Show-off." I rubbed my sore palms on my pants. "Zant, but part of me thinks it's a bad idea."

"It's not," he said, grinning. "What's a 'show-off'?"

"A person who likes to be noticed."

"Ah. An apt description then." He flexed his substantial muscles and preened.

I laughed. "It's not considered a good thing."

"I don't see why not."

"Of course you don't."

Gohra and Stig were my assigned guards for the day, so his

arrival surprised me. "Why're you here?" I asked as the two female soldiers, Huorem, and I reached the lift lobby. It was unusually crowded, but I received preferential treatment, something I'd never get used to.

He grinned then asked Gohra, "You're playing, right?" as the lift doors closed and Stig directed its computer to take us to one of the ship's transportation hubs.

She nodded. "Zant. Got marked this morning. No way I'm gonna miss this chance to break skulls." She slammed her fist into her open palm. The white Draxtu-Mainyu symbol glowered down at me from her dark-brown scalp. She looked more intimidating than ever and I was glad she was my ally. I'd hate to have her as an enemy.

The lift stopped and we exited into bustle and noise. "Marked?" I asked as we weaved through the crowd.

Gohra replied, "The hamistayeca team leaders mark four players, then the remaining fifteen on each team are picked by random draw." She bounced on her toes and stared eagerly down the long line toward the tracks. "Hu, I'm gonna run to the Forward Launch Bay. Gotta limber up and I can't stand in this line."

Huorem and Stig laughed and sent her off.

"How far is the run?" I asked as our line crept closer to the tracks. Her kinetic energy had me jittery, or maybe it was the collective excitement humming through the ship.

Hu squinted then shrugged. "It'll take her about thirty minutes."

"Decent warmup."

For once, the crowd ignored me, more fixated on the hamistayeca than on the alien in their midst. Truthfully, I'd found that *Pohru-Mahrko*'s soldiers were far less curious about me than *Dathusha*'s citizens were. Noise and excitement washed over the platform, a seething basin of anticipation and agitation in need of release.

"Is the entire crew going to this thing?" I was grateful for the two large guards keeping open space around me. Being in a crowd of Ohnenrai was a claustrophobic experience. I couldn't see past all the tall, broad bodies and the air grew stale if no one moved for long. It was too easy to imagine being crushed.

"All non-essential personnel," Stig replied. "The FLB will be packed tight."

"Engineering redirected air circulation to keep the crowd cool and breathing," Huorem added, laughing at the look on my face.

"This must be some game," I said.

"Oh, it is," Hu replied as we moved a few feet closer to catching a ride.

After we finally reached the Forward Launch Bay, we stood in another long line and slowly snaked into the cavernous area. Huorem explained that transports and equipment had been moved into storage or hoisted overhead. I resisted the urge to run when I craned my head up to see a phalanx of massive troop ships suspended over us.

Heavy, green barrier walls formed a square arena in the middle of the bay and tiny, black rubber beads the size of BBs covered the floor. Terraced platforms surrounded that on all sides. The first level of platforms had bench seating, but all the others were standing room only. Judging by the smiles and laughter, the grunts didn't mind.

I tugged Huorem's sleeve and he and Stig leaned closer to hear me. "How will a ballgame help our situation? I mean, why would anyone want to play games right now?"

Stig squinted at me, as she often did, as if I were an enigma to be puzzled over and figured out. "Everyone aboard this ship is a soldier, Barethri. And when you hit an Ohnenrai soldier, that soldier hits you back. Harder. And keeps hitting until you can't get up. But *Pohru-Mahrko* is wounded, so instead of hitting back, we're running away. No Ohnenran likes running from a fight. It's not in our nature or our training. So every soldier you see is looking for a chance to hit someone or something. That's where hamistayeca comes in."

Huorem nodded. "It's all about hitting. Hard. So your opponent can't get up."

I looked from one to the other. "All of you have anger management issues."

Huorem shook his head. "Nava. We're just crazy."

Stig suddenly pumped her fist in the air and shouted, "Drax-*tu!*"

Instantly, the whole bay reverberated with the word as thousands of soldiers bellowed, "Drax-*tu!*" over and over, and pounded their fists against their chests and each other.

When it finally stopped, my ears kept ringing. The crowd's excitement was infectious. It wrapped around my brain and rushed down my spine, warm and tingling like when I sensed Stig's joy during Ahremena's experiment. But instead of yellow, this thread of emotion was red with excitement, orange with anticipation. I pushed against its allure, afraid I'd plunge into that well of feelings and happily drown.

Along with what seemed to be an endless parade of personnel, we made our way to the platforms. The rumble of the crowd vibrated the floor even more than *Pohru-Mahrko's* engines did. I craned my head to take in the scene. It was the first time I'd seen the majority of the ship's soldiers gathered together. It was a terrifying sight.

I tugged Hu's sleeve. "How many people can fit in here?"

"Three hundred thousand," he called over the rumbling crowd. "I'd guess we're looking at two hundred ten thousand right now."

"Wow." It looked like a full house was turning out for this game.

Stig scanned the crowd, her gaze pausing on a raised row of seats at the edge of the arena. "It's been too long since the zosh played. We want to see our leader in action."

Huorem led me to that raised platform and along the first row of benches. I spied Mahzel standing beside a cluster of empty spaces, his weapon in hand.

"Ehtishem's playing?" I smiled at Mahzel as we reached him and sat.

Huorem nodded and saluted as several division leaders and Ahremena sat behind us. "The troops need to see that their zosh is fighting fit. They need to know that being on Terra," he glanced at me, "and with a Terran, hasn't softened him."

"I see."

Mahzel said, "This will be a rough match."

"Zant." Huorem flashed a toothy grin at his comrade. They reached across me and thumped each other with heavy fists, blows that would've broken my ribs and collapsed my lungs.

I shook my head. "Has everyone forgotten he almost died?"

"That was six months ago, Barethri," Stig replied with a dismissive wave of her hand, "And this is the zosh we're talking about."

I frowned. "That's supposed to explain his idiocy?"

The three of them nodded.

A roar rattled the stands and echoed back from the FLB's overhead as the players emerged through the crowd at opposite ends of the arena. They wore close-fitting trousers and shirts, one team clad in dark green, the other in burgundy. They all had wrapped knuckles and wrists but no other protective gear.

Huorem scanned the field then pointed. "There's the zosh, Barethri."

Like so many of the other players, Ehtishem stooped, gathered a handful of beads from the floor, and rubbed them between his palms. He wasn't the largest among the players, but he was definitely up there. Broad shoulders and cut muscles, Ehtishem had put on bulk since he'd returned to duty from his protracted stint on Earth. When we'd met he was impressive compared to the Terran men I knew, but now he had the chiseled physique of a superhero, and I definitely wasn't complaining about the view.

"Isn't the other team worried about playing against their leader?"

Huorem shook his head. "Everyone's equal on the hamis-tayeca grounds. If you aren't willing and able to give and get a beating, you have no business being out there."

Ehtishem and his teammates — all clad in dark red — spread out across the north end of the arena. He paced before his team, taunting the opposing force and whipping up his teammates. The green team's captain came forward to match the taunts with his own.

Stig howled like a wolf and a hundred thousand other voices joined in.

Huorem laughed and shouted, "The show I promised is beginning, Barethri."

When the arena quieted I asked, "What language are Ehtishem and the other captain speaking? It's familiar, but not Ohnenrai, right?"

Stig said, "It's Ohnaia."

Mahzel added, "The root language of Ohnenrai, the warrior's tongue."

The chaotic taunting turned into a back-and-forth chant with stomping, chest thumping, and war faces. The two teams grimaced and snarled, stuck out their tongues, stared wide-eyed, and bared their teeth. They slapped their hands against their thighs and chests, clapped and gestured, creating a rhythmic display of strength and unity meant to intimidate their opponents.

"That's pretty terrifying," I said.

"Exactly," Mahzel replied. Beside him, Huorem stamped his boots and roared along with Ehtishem's team. He stuck his fingers in his mouth and whistled so sharp and loud I had to cover my ears. All around us, groups of soldiers joined the war chants and thumping displays going on in the arena and the entire FLB vibrated with the sound and fury of it.

With the teams and spectators whipped into a frenzy I felt in my bones, a referee — dressed in yellow — marched to center-field, a yellow ball about the size of a soccer ball tucked beneath his arm. He saluted both sides and was saluted in return by the players and the crowd. He placed the ball upon a white marker, turned, and strode to the field's edge. He raised his arms and the crowd began to count down from twenty-five by fives — following the segments of the Ohnenrai twenty-five-hour day:

"Ushin!"

"Frashin!"

With each count the referee lowered and raised his arms, urging them to bellow louder and louder.

"Tishrin!"

"Dvarin!"

The players took ready stances, flexing their fingers and staring their opponents down.

"Aevin!"

The crowd roared, "Adhem!" The referee spun to face the field and the melee began.

Soldiers kicked and punched, elbowed and kneed each other. They shouted obscenities, wrestled, and threw each other down. No one went out. No one backed off. There were no time-outs and, apparently, no fouls.

"Is there a point to all this bloodshed and madness?" I shouted to Stig over the roaring crowd.

"Get the ball into the opposing goal. There are two rules: If a carrier throws for the goal and misses, a point is awarded to the opposing team. And no eye gouging."

I laughed. "Seriously? No eye gouging? That's it?"

"Zant."

The crowd, the violence, the frenzy had me buzzing. A heady mix of emotions swirled around the arena, an epidemic of bloodlust fueled by frustration. I should've been afraid, but the mix lacked hatred. The soldiers around me and on the field were having *fun*.

And so was I.

"Is there a strategy? All I see is forty soldiers brawling."

Huorem flashed me a grin. "Get the ball into the goal."

Mahzel added, "What other strategy do you need?"

"It's a war zone."

"Nava." Hu waved my concern away. "No one's ever died playing hamistayeca. I don't think."

In possession of the ball, Ehtishem, Gahlen, Tinish, and Gohra roamed behind their team at one end of the field like a pack of hungry hounds. They shouted, passed the ball back and forth. They shoved away encroaching opponents and looked for an opening to run down the field.

"Look! He's running it!" I leaned forward and pointed as Ehtishem charged through the melee.

With Gahlen and Tinish barreling ahead and Gohra on his heels, the zosh punched and shoved opposing soldiers, elbowed through a defensive line, and reached halfway into the green team's territory before four players dragged him down. As he hit the ground, he tossed the ball to Gohra. She leaped over the pile of bodies, twisted away from two more soldiers and, with her compatriots knocking aside foes, reached the goal and slammed the ball into the net.

"Nice!" I shouted and clapped. "Yeah! Wooooo!" I turned to Mahzel and raised my palm. "High five!"

He looked puzzled, so I showed him how to do it.

"Why do you slap palms?" he asked.

"I dunno. We just do." I laughed at his confusion and thrilled at Gohra's joy, felt the triumph Ehtishem, Tinish, Gahlen, and their teammates shared.

The teams regrouped, joking and jostling as med techs tended two soldiers — one with a bloodied nose and another spitting blood and having her wrist wrapped. At least half the players had black eyes and bloody noses, several had their ribs taped, and one had been carried off the field with a broken femur.

"Zara!"

"Zenghana!"

"Zara!"

"Zenghana!"

Half of the spectators started a call-and-reply chant. Zara meant *green* and zenghana meant *watch out*.

Not to be outdone, the fans of Ehtishem's red team answered with: "Vohu Bahkem, irish-irish-irish!" which meant *Red Kings, kill-kill-kill!*

My guards joined in the chant as the green-clad soldiers took possession of the ball and wasted no time diving into the fray.

As the game progressed, the main strategy became clear — neutralize as many of the opposing players as possible by any means necessary. Soldiers tackled and pinned their opponents. One-on-one fights distracted players away from whoever was carrying the ball and cleared the way to the goals. It was bloody and brutal, and I was enjoying it way too much.

Ehtishem raced the green team's man to the wall, but the Zara player scored. Ehtishem shook his head and turned away from the goal. As he did, a green player shoved him into another Zara soldier who threw a sucker punch that caught the zosh in the jaw.

I saw red. *That bastard!* I seethed. *Kick his teeth in!*

As the crowd roared, Ehtishem turned back and caught his opponent's head and shoulder. He yanked the man downward as he drove his knee up into the soldier's face. He threw the player to the ground, landing astride him, and pummeled the man mercilessly. The crowd screamed pleasure and outrage as players from both teams waded into the fray. The game devolved into a mass of fists, elbows, blood, and curses.

Two additional yellow-clad referees joined their man on the field and forced the teams apart. But the crowd loved seeing their zosh walk away from his assailant, his face bloody from a cut above his right eye and his taped fists stained with his attacker's blue blood. The message was clear: Hit Ehtishem Mahle and he'd hit back, twice as hard. Their zosh remained a force to be feared and respected. Terra hadn't softened him and neither had I.

The players took water. Two injured men — one the man who'd sucker punched Ehtishem, the other unable to walk — were removed from the field, then the game resumed.

In the end, Vohu Bahkem triumphed over their opponents by one point. The referee's whistle cut through the roar of the crowd as Gohra made the tie-breaking goal.

"That. Was. Nuts," I said breathlessly as Stig, Mahzel, and Huorem led me from the arena. We, and the other ranking soldiers leaving the first tier of seats, received a clear path to the closest lift. I vibrated with the crowd's euphoria, felt flushed with its fever.

Hu grinned. "Told you it was a spectacle."

We stepped into the lift and Ahremena slid in beside me. "Did you enjoy the hamistayeca, Barethri?"

"I did. It was wild and a lot more violent than I'd imagined, but everyone had fun, even the players getting hurt." I shook my head at that.

"It's impossible not to feel the excitement of the crowd," she said.

"It's infectious," I enthused.

"And the power of the soldiers," Ahremena added. "They are formidable."

Everyone in the lift agreed.

"Imagine the damage even a small force could do," she mused, "if the Azatem were crippled." Her gaze slid to mine. "Avenge *Dathusha*." The lift reached its first stop. "Rescue your daughter." She exited.

I stared at the closing doors and my reflection looked troubled.

"*We are one,*" snaked into my mind, a distant murmur.

TWELVE

POHRU-MAHRKO SETTLED into orbit around Iodiq, a blue, white, and brown planet.

Time, Ehtishem thought and turned away from the external monitor. *We need more time.* Rachel was hearing the Azatem again. That meant they'd find her sooner rather than later. The ship repairs weren't complete. The attack plans and troop training weren't complete. *Not enough time.*

Timsai said, "Navigation, put us into stationary orbit above the Western Iodiq Plain."

"Zant, Thrai. Finding coordinates," the nav tech replied.

Ehtishem jogged up the steps between the raked platforms that arrayed the ship's command crew around him. Gahlen and Tinish joined him as he reached the lift. He wanted to observe and inspect the landing teams before deployment. He hadn't had that pleasure in over a decade.

As the lift descended to the launch deck, he pulled up the team assignments and noticed Pearl's name still associated with one. His jaw tightened. Standard procedure dictated that each squad consisted of nine soldiers, one commander, and a dog-and-handler team. Pearl and Audie would've benefited tremendously from the in-field experience. Now it was a moot point. He approved the assignments. Panca Seven-oh-one would go without a CN, a cathru-at-namandar.

He schooled his expression. Worrying about the girl's circumstances served no purpose. He wanted Pearl to be alive, wanted it desperately, but the chances were slim. Ehtishem couldn't decide if he should hold onto hope or face reality, so he avoided both, instead dealing with the things he could control — the water ops, comforting Rachel, *PM's* repairs.

The East Launch Bay floor vibrated. Ship engines roared, beasts awakening from hibernation. Feet thudded across the iron grating, soldiers and technicians shouted, dogs whined, equipment groaned and clanged. The bay was a microcosm of sound and movement. Swirling around all of it was the stench of sweat, ozone, and oil.

Ehtishem found Panca Seven-oh-one and leaned against the reflective surface of their troop ship, listening as Ops and Intel briefed the pilots and soldiers on the mission. He studied each member of Seven-oh-one, appreciating their focus. Throughout the launch bay squadrons received similar orders.

"Records indicate this site is one of the oldest stations established by our predecessors and it's unknown if the pump exists, let alone operates," the Ops officer said, then turned to Dvaidasa Jorinei, the unit's ground commander who moved to the front of the panca and surveyed its nine members.

"Cover each other and stay alert. We're going down without a CN, so we won't have an early warning system. Let's get in and out quick." Heads nodded and she continued, "Ehnk and Pohm, you're in first to scout and secure. No dog means no pa'yunam to set up camp, so add that to your duties once you've secured the perimeter and set the turrets. Romvi and Aihaman, you'll follow. Check the availability of water in the well and assess its quality."

"Zant."

"Leilei, Nadera, Nergis, Vehl, Fehrana. Man the pump station, assess its functionality, and complete necessary repairs."

Jorinei turned the group back to the Ops officer, nodding at Ehtishem as she did. He returned the gesture. She was good at her job, which was why Timsai had approved Pearl going out under her.

The tanker team was briefed and assigned. They'd oversee the water uptake dirtside, while crews waited aboard *Pohru-Mahrko* to empty the tanker into the warship's holding tanks. After those team members were assigned tasks, the Ops officer said, "Your transport pilots today will be Kruhz and Rivan aboard *Cathru-Ahzish*." The pilots nodded. Rivan caught Ehtishem looking at him. His attention snapped back to the officer.

Good. Stay sharp. Ehtishem slid his hand over the troop transport's hull. The surface shimmered and changed to mirror him. The multilayered armor of the Ohnenrai ships still fascinated him. Its crystalline plates played with light, like Terran fish scales did. Their mech-suits were made of similar material.

Tinish stood beside him. "How many hours do you think this'll take, fra?"

Ehtishem studied his reflection in the ship's changeable surface. "Ideally? Twenty-five. Realistically? Forty. Maybe more." He turned away from the hull. "Those facilities have been neglected for almost a century."

Gahlen was inspecting his shock rifle. "Or the locals have moved into them."

Echoing that remark, Seven-oh-one's Intel officer stepped forward. "You should've reviewed your briefs by now and know your assigned facility's specs, the surrounding topography, and the fauna most likely to eat you." The soldiers laughed, but the officer said, "That's no joke. Iodiq offers some large, nasty predators and you look like lunch. Stay alert to stay alive."

Jorinei said, "Stick close to camp. No wandering. Helmets and armor remain on and sealed at all times. We don't know if the Azatem have been here. I don't want any of you coming back as beasts."

"Some of us already are, frei," Dasa Leilei, Seven-oh-one's munitions tech, announced to jeers and laughter.

"You'll be shot on the spot, Lei," the Intel officer said then wished the unit good luck. "Ashusta, pa'nerem."

Jorinei nodded. "Remember: Va'vinas avant, va'nagava'-vant." She jerked her thumb at the waiting transport.

Ehtishem smirked. "You break it, you buy it," he muttered in English.

Every Ohnenrai soldier knew their combat mech-suit was their responsibility and their life. Designed to enhance the strength and endurance of a field soldier, the heavy-duty suits were forgiving...up to a point. Lightweight and situation reactive, the reflective armor moved like muscle but relied on nanotechnology and magstenite particles suspended in gel to prevent injury. Its closed system operated in toxic, aquatic, and null atmospheres, and it could withstand most biological, electromagnetic, and radiation strikes. The bio-suit they wore beneath regulated body temperature and interfaced with their neural trackers, their armor, and *PM's* communications system.

Each soldier also knew the Ohnenrai military "you break it you buy it" policy was a joke because anything strong enough to break their suits would break them too.

Ehtishem pushed back from the troop transport as the soldiers grabbed their gear and started checking their suits and packs. The pilots, Rivan and Kruhz, jogged away from the transport. There was no rush for Panca Seven-oh-one. They'd be one of the last squads deployed.

Already suited, Pohm donned his helmet and lowered the visor. His head nodded to some unheard beat as he instructed his suit's syscom to pull up files and run diagnostics. He elbowed the soldier beside him. "Ehnk, check out the file on the anizofstra."

Ehnk dropped his visor with a practiced nod. "Aiya, ugly bastard," he said as he saw the creature on his internal display. "Big too."

"Put that on tonight's menu," Pohm said and they laughed.

Their voices joined thousands more as troops prepped gear and boarded a hundred ships. By Ohnenrai military standards, this was a small operation. But it was critical. The soldiers were glad to be going dirtside but wouldn't mess around. Ohnenrai field soldiers were all business when their boots touched the ground.

Satisfied with the clockwork precision he saw around him, Ehtishem crossed the launch bay, nodding acceptance of the salutes he received, and took a set of stairs that spiraled ten decks up to the observation suites.

His com buzzed. Ahremena. He considered ignoring his mother but resisted the urge. There was no avoiding the woman.

"Zant?"

"Why aren't you deploying Rachel to Iodiq?"

"Why are you asking that question? Deployment isn't your realm of expertise."

"Nava, but Rachel *is*. Why not set the trap here?"

"Because *Pohru-Mahrko* is damaged and my troops aren't ready for that fight. We need more water not more blood. I'll deploy her when all systems are prepared, not a moment before. Stay out of military matters, Sarem. And stop second-guessing me or I'll charge you with insubordination." He cut the connection and shoved the com back into his pocket.

Ahremena didn't know when to quit, and she sure didn't respect rank or boundaries, especially where he and Rachel were concerned. He growled in the back of his throat. He was nobody's tool.

THIRTEEN

I WAS DRAGGING a full med pack to the day's growing pile when two soldiers strode into the depot. One of them was Rivan, the snide soldier I'd encountered on the transport from *Dathusha.*

"We're looking for Dvaidasa Dahmircan. Is he here?" he demanded.

Sweat left a dark streak on my sleeve as I wiped my brow. "In the stacks." I jerked my chin toward the door into the depot warehouse and resumed pulling the pack.

Rivan leaned on the counter and watched me. The other man disappeared through the doorway.

Sweat trickled down my back. "I could use some help with this."

He came around the counter, hefted the pack with one hand, and slung it onto one of the conveyor hooks.

"Ferahi-va." I stretched, digging my fingers into my lower back, then retrieved an empty bag and started stocking it. Antibiotic wipes. Butterfly bandages. Spray adhesive. I could pack with my eyes closed. Dahmircan and Judilei kept their depots neat and orderly. Every item had its place and nothing was ever out of place. And the two rooms, though on different ships, were identical. Always easy to find what was needed.

Rivan picked up an empty hypomatic and fiddled with it. "There's something I've been wondering about you."

I slid a suture stapler into its proper pocket. "What's that?"

He turned his back to the counter then hopped up to sit on it. "Why'd the zosh send his vira to stock med packs?"

"He didn't send me anywhere." I glanced at him as I grabbed a set of clamps. "I asked for a medical-related assignment. I hate sitting on my ass doing nothing; I'm more useful than an Elite Level house pet."

He grunted then jerked his chin toward the wall of filled med packs. "I guess so."

I opened a box of hypomatic canisters and added a dozen to the new pack.

The depot door opened and Rivan's companion glanced at me then gestured for him to follow. Rivan slipped from the counter and disappeared into the cavernous room, leaving the door ajar behind him.

"Don't call me vira," I muttered as I opened a drawer looking for a cutter. "I'm nobody's slave, asshole." I thought Dahmircan had stashed his blade there but no luck. "Like I'm some kinda pocket dog with a frou-frou haircut and a nervous condition." I shoved the drawer closed hard enough to make it bounce back open.

I scratched the back of my skull while surveying the room. "Cutter, cutter, where can I find a cutter?" I went to the open doorway to the warehouse and peered around. "Hello? Dvaidasa Dahmircan? I need a cutter." If it had only been one container that needed opening, I'd've waited, but there were four. Gauze, gloves, and suture staples were low, too.

The cavernous warehouse held rows and rows of stocked

floor-to-ceiling shelves. Boxes, containers, bags, canisters of every shape and size. I looked around and whistled low. "That's a lotta stuff." I tried not to wonder how much of it was stolen goods from Earth. Under Isphahan's command, the Ohnenrai had picked my home world clean.

"If I were a cutter where would I be?" I muttered and entered the depot. The door slid shut behind me. "Oh, great." The door panel ignored my palm and the computer requested a code, but I had nothing to enter and my compad was on the counter in the fulfillment room. "That's just won-der-ful."

Figuring someone would be along to let me out, I began poking into drawers and bins. Nothing. Nothing. Nothing. "Ah-hah!" The sixth drawer yielded a cutter. I shoved it into my back pocket and wandered the aisles until I spotted another door at the far end of the warehouse. Its access panel glowed green, so I trotted that way, maneuvering around a phalanx of empty stock carts.

"Dvaidasa?" Hopefully, he wouldn't be pissed that I was in the stacks. I'd once thought Ehtishem was the biggest Ohnen-ran, but Dahmircan topped even him. Still, I was just doing my job and he wasn't so intimidating after his kindness during the attack.

As I reached the door something heavy struck the other side and I jumped. "Je-sus!" Whatever it was, it slid down and hit the floor. The door retracted. Dahmircan fell backward, his head striking the metal floor. His blood and spittle flecked my boots.

The two soldiers stood over him. Rivan held a sparking baton — some kind of energy weapon. Our eyes met.

"Shit!" I turned and bolted.

Feet thudded behind me, long strides.

I yanked the carts away from the wall as I dashed up the

aisle. A crash and a curse followed. I whipped around a corner and ran flat-out.

Where was the hell was an exit? All the damned aisles looked alike.

Light ahead. A distant open doorway between two rows. I stopped fast, slipped, hit the floor. Scrambling to my feet, I changed directions and raced toward the escape route.

The second soldier appeared between freedom and me. I slammed on the brakes and turned around. Rivan skidded to a stop behind me.

Midway to freedom I was hemmed in.

Nowhere to go but up. I leapt, caught a ledge, and hauled my carcass upward. "Hu! Mahzel! Help!"

Rivan grabbed my foot. I yanked boxes and containers from the shelves. He batted them away and lost his grip. I went higher. Metal clattered. Plastic cracked and crunched. I rained down supplies and climbed. Boxes thudded. Glass shattered. A bottle of something spilled. I reached the top and scrambled along the shelf, pushing boxes and plastic containers off each side and crawling on my hands and knees toward that open door.

"Help me!"

Rivan's face appeared near my right hip.

I grabbed the cutter from my pocket and flicked the blade open. "Don't you fucking touch me!" I slashed back toward his face.

He ducked almost fast enough. The blade left a thin line of blue blood across his cheek. He didn't even flinch. Instead, he pinned my arm against the shelf. His hand twisted. Pain shot from my wrist to my shoulder.

"No! Let go!"

"Kruhz, va dar hei." He ordered his companion to catch me,

then he shoved me sideways off the shelf, yanking the cutter from my hand as I tumbled over the side.

I screamed. The other soldier caught me, but the bastard immediately let go. I hit the metal floor face-first and tasted blood. I tried to get up. He flattened me with a knee against my back and a hand at the nape of my neck.

"Get off me! Mahzel! Hu!"

Kruhz stood and pulled me up.

Rivan swung over the top shelf and dropped to the floor. He reached for my arm.

"Don't touch me!" I knocked his hand away.

Quicker than I could react, Kruhz seized the front of my coveralls and shoved me against the shelf. I saw stars as my head smacked metal.

Rivan removed a tube from a pouch on his belt and nodded toward me. "Hold her still."

"Shit!" I struggled harder as I recognized the syringe he slid from the metal tube. "No! No-no-no!" The frenzied dance of the microscopic alien bacteria within it was unmistakable. I slammed my head forward and caught Kruhz's chin. He cursed, but his grip only tightened and he pinned me with his body. "Not yet! Don't do—" The soldier's hand over my mouth cut me off.

Rivan yanked up my sleeve and pinned my arm against the shelf. He jabbed the needle into the crook of my elbow and pushed the plunger. The Azatem streamed into me.

The three of us didn't move.

I held my breath. My heart pounded in my ears.

The ship's engines thrummed.

Nothing happened. What were we expecting?

Kruhz's grip on my mouth eased.

I snarled, "You stupid motherfuckers."

"We are one."

My brain overloaded and my body went haywire. "Oh shit."

I started shaking. Memories careened through my head. A fever came on like a blast furnace. A migraine made my teeth feel like they were retreating into my skull. Pain tore through me like my nerves and muscles were being put through a paper shredder.

I reached out, blinded by the agony and the memories playing out in my mind's eye — my parents' deaths, Cyrus attacking me, Pearl's birth, Jack dead. One of the soldiers said something I couldn't make out over the ringing in my ears. Then there was nothing but the replay of every moment of my life and the emotions that accompanied them.

"Momma!"

I grabbed the hot barrel and swung the gun back. Two dogs hit the car's hood, stopped. They crouched and whined, their ears back and tails tucked. I froze. What the hell? All the dogs cowered. They retreated up the road.

I slid to the ground, slapped the shotgun barrel, but the pump remained immobile. "Fucking c'mon." I jiggled the pump without luck. "Shit, shit, shit." Giving up, I pulled open the car door as I looked left, right, into the trees, up the cliff. A low vibration traveled through the ground, up my legs, all the way to my teeth.

"We are one."

"What is that?" Pearl clung to Audie and stared out the windows.

Now the low, rhythmic thum-thum-thum of massive, otherworldly engines joined the vibration.

"Get out!"

Audie barked. He ran.

"Audie!" Pearl scrambled after him.

I raced after her. "No, baby! Let him go!"

"Frayan! Frayan!" Somewhere a man was shouting for people to move.

"Get out!"

"Get off me! Mahzel! Hu!"

Kruhz pulled me up. Rivan reached for my arm.

"Don't touch me!"

Kruhz shoved me against the shelf. My head smacked metal. Rivan held the syringe. "Hold her still."

"Frayan! Frayan!"

Boots thudded, metal jangled, leather creaked.

"Hold her still."

"We are one."

"Momma!"

"Mem kam-va, Rahzhel, upairi anghu."

My past and my present separated into their proper order as I regained my senses. But my head took up the rhythm of an Ohnenrai gunship's engines, adding pressure and pain to confusion. My spine and muscles joined the chorus. Everything ached and memory turned to reality as I became lucid.

I bit my tongue hard against pain and nausea, and listened. Engines thrummed and my aching body trembled along with them. Above me, men and women called orders in Ohnenrai. I risked a look at my surroundings as the voices became muffled. I was lying in the dark forward hold of an Ohnenrai transport, directly below the cockpit.

"PM Command, Panca Seven-oh-one is on the ground."

"Surun-ta, Cathru-Ahzish. Pull back to cover tanker at 48.79018056 north by 122.43575278 west."

"Surun-ta, Control, pulling back to cover tanker. *Cathru-Ahzish* out."

Holy shit.

"We'll circle out, drop our cargo, then return to cover the tanker's landing."

A man asked, "How are we gonna explain the deviation?"

"Easy. *PM* Command, this is *Cathru-Ahzish*. We have movement warnings. Be advised we're circling out to investigate."

"Surun-ta, *Cathru-Ahzish*. Remain in radio contact and report your findings."

"Surun-ta, Control. *Cathru-Ahzish* out."

My hands were manacled in front of me, and my mouth was taped. The tape, in particular, was a pisser and hurt like hell as I pulled it off.

"Doesn't this endanger the ground forces?"

The engines roared and the ship accelerated and banked hard.

"Zant. Which is why we're making it fast."

Beeping filled the small area. One of the soldiers said, "Get as low as you can." His voice grew louder as he opened the hatch above me. It was that prick Rivan.

I closed my eyes as the ship's engines slowed and deepened.

"You want me to set down?" the pilot called. It must've been Kruhz.

"Nava," Rivan replied. "Just get low. I'll open the door and push her out." He'd entered the small forward hold. "A few feet won't cause much damage."

I rocked as the ship shuddered and banked.

"*Utha*," he cursed. "Kruhz, don't you know how to fly?"

The pilot laughed. "Better than you can walk."

"Gawmezh." That meant bull piss. The soldier laughed and unfastened the straps holding me. The ship steadied, something rumbled and scraped — metal on metal. Frigid air blasted into the hold. I sucked in a deep breath and opened my eyes, grateful to have the nausea ease.

Rivan's back was to me as he leaned out the ship's open cargo door. I flexed my hands and feet then sat upright. My vision tunneled. Pain pressed against my skull from the inside out. I blinked through it and watched his back.

"This is as close as I'm going to those cliffs," Kruhz called.

Rivan turned toward me.

"You're coming with me, asshole." I launched at him.

But my trajectory changed abruptly as the pilot shouted and the ship bucked and spun. There was an explosion and a blast of heat. I hit metal, then the floor knocked the wind out of me.

"What was that?" Rivan shouted as he regained his feet, his face and hands bloody. He swung back to face me.

Kruhz's voice was calm as he sent a distress call. "Command, this is *Cathru-Ahzish*. We're under attack in the third quadrant, unidentified enemy. I repeat unknown enemy weaponry in the third quadrant. Command, *Cathru-Ahzish* has sustained heavy damage. We are going down. I repeat, *Cathru-Ahzish* is going down."

I crouched against the wall opposite the open cargo door and looked for a weapon. Black, oily smoke filled the ship as it shuddered and whined like a terrified dog.

"Brace!" Kruhz shouted.

Rivan lunged toward me. I dodged. A second explosion pitched the ship on its side and into a spin.

I screamed and grabbed at nothing as I plummeted through the open cargo door, tumbled through the air, and slammed into water. Struggling to the surface, I fought to keep my head above the waves as the current pulled me away from the crippled transport. It was so low I saw Rivan's wide eyes as he dangled from the open cargo door.

An armored dragonfly the size of a bus hovered around the ship and stabbed its scorpion tail into the transport's open gut. Throwing off flaming debris, the ship came around and slammed into a rocky cliff. Grinding metal shrieked and moaned. The Ohnenrai ship, like some dying, drunken beast, performed a wobbly pirouette.

I gagged, kicked, fought for breath and battled the insistent current. But my bound hands, heavy boots, and the frigid water worked against me. The waves grew rougher, the current faster.

"Shit!"

I struggled toward a rocky overhang and grabbed for it. The current pulled me past. I searched for another handhold but was pushed under the water. I popped back up, twisted around. Something snagged my manacled wrists. I jerked to a stop. The water kept coming and I struggled to stay above its flow. Caught on a jagged outcropping, the manacles were friend and foe as wave after wave crashed over me. I couldn't free my wrists, couldn't escape the current.

Worse yet, flaming fuel and debris were heading my way, setting the sparse vegetation along the river's edge ablaze.

"Fuck-fuck-fuck!" I kicked and struggled, was pulled under then, somehow, found purchase on a rock beneath the outcropping. The water grew warmer. Oil gave it a rainbow hue. Its chemical stench stung my nose and eyes. Shredding my fingers and nails, I grabbed the stony ledge, pushed and pulled, and hauled my waterlogged carcass onto the outcrop just as flaming debris reached me.

Only my sopping wet clothes kept me from catching fire. But I wasn't safe. The water's edge was aflame. I twisted my bleeding wrists free, straddled the outcrop, and shimmied back to the shore. Then I ran.

I crashed through flaming brush, drenched sleeve over my face, moving upward along a worn path I hoped was created by gentle, plant-eating animals instead of transport-killing hell-beasts.

To one side of the trail, water tumbled over and around boulders. To the other side black-and-gray rocky cliffs rose. The air was frigid and I shook from adrenalin and the cold as the path turned steep and winding. Acrid smoke billowed from the crash site. I gagged at the stench of burning oil. I swallowed my gorge, took a breath, then lost it and puked river water and my lunch in the weeds. "Christ Almighty." I spat, wiped my mouth, and kept going.

As I rounded a switchback, the hum and snap of Ohnenrai weapons, shouts, and an unearthly screeching rose over the river's tumult. On the next ridge, the transport's massive attacker squared off with the squad Rivan and Kruhz must have dropped. If a dragonfly and a scorpion had a giant, armored, hell baby, that would be it. The soldiers had the thing down, but it had taken out two of their unit before they'd fried its wings and half its legs.

At a sharp whistle, the soldiers fell back into the dark entrance of a cave. Its rusty doors had been ripped from their hinges. Huge furrows were gouged into the ground in front of the entrance. Blood and flesh littered the area. The monstrosity had torn apart those soldiers who'd gotten in the path of its mandibles, undeterred by their heavy mech-suits.

"*We are one.*" The voices — the Azatem — were back.

I kept climbing, hoping to another entrance to that cave. I had to get the manacles off, which meant I needed those soldiers. And I had to get word back to Ehtishem. The latency period was over. The Azatem Code had been triggered and the beacon was transmitting. *Pohru-Mahrko* had to get the hell outta Dodge. I swallowed a lump. All his careful planning was screwed. He couldn't save me from the Azatem now.

"I'm sorry," I whispered. "I hope you know how much I

love you." Cold, wet sleeves weren't worth shit when it came to wiping away tears.

The path grew steep. Snow clumped beneath brown scrub. My fingers cramped, my teeth chattered, my body shook. I was getting hypothermic. *Gotta get warm.* I focused on the path and picked up my pace. Hopefully movement would keep me alive long enough to reach those troops.

The pebbles beneath my feet became rocks and the rocks all around turned to boulders. And rising above, the boulders became mountains — stony spires knifing the sky, their wind-hammered flanks so sharp not even snow clung to them.

I finally stumbled over a small ridge and found a wide-mouthed cave, shelter against night's growing darkness.

Light and raised voices came from the opening. I stopped in the shadows just at the edge of the light. At the entrance, a female soldier I didn't know stood with a whining shock gun pressed to Rivan's head. Blue blood covered the right side of her helmet and mech-suit. "—compromised the entire mission and all our lives," she was saying.

Rivan, hands up, spat blood and replied, "I don't know what you're talking about, Leilei."

A dvaidasa stepped between them, grabbed the front of Rivan's flight suit, and slammed him against the cave's rocky wall. "You left the squadron unprotected. Ehnk and Pohm are dead because we didn't have air support."

Rivan remained maddeningly calm. "Kruhz picked up movement on his sensors. He circled out to investigate. Another anizofstra brought down *Cathru-Ahzish.* Probably the mate of that dead one."

A command came from behind me. "Get your hands up."

I slowly, painfully raised my manacled hands as the soldier came around to identify me. I mumbled, "Surprise."

Her stunned silence and hesitation lasted long enough to

tell me I wasn't part of the squad's orders. "Zhek," she said and re-sighted her rifle.

I lowered my hands and stumbled into the pool of light. Everyone, but Rivan, was fully-suited. They turned and stared at me. His eyes looked like they'd pop from his skull.

"Somebody shoot that lying prick," I slurred. The soldier put her arm around my waist as I slumped against her.

"Secure Rivan," the commander ordered. "Fehrana, remove those manacles from the barethri. Vehl, get heating blankets around her and someone find her dry clothes, water, and food."

I nodded to Fehrana, the soldier supporting me. She helped me sit. I held up my shaking, cuffed hands as she pulled a lock reader from one of her mech-suit's compartments.

Someone shoved heating packs under my armpits and placed them in my lap. A thermal blanket was wrapped around me. I recognized Dasa Aihaman from the medical bay after the Azatem attack as the med tech pressed a thermos with some sort of warm, sweet liquid to my lips. "Drink," he said. I took a gulp. The cold and chaos had befuddled me, but the warmth and sugar were thawing my mind, muscles, and tongue quickly.

"We are one."

The squad's leader crouched before me. "I'm Dvaidasa Jorinei. How did you got here, Barethri?"

I jerked my chin toward Rivan. "That asshole and some dick named Kruhz abducted me from the MSD."

Jorinei faced Rivan. "Explain."

"I had orders," he said.

"From?"

"That's classified."

The dvaidasa's eyes widened and the surviving members of Panca Seven-oh-one muttered. Their voices echoed in the cave, like the murmur of waves in a seashell. She asked, "Does the zosh know about this?"

"Of course not. He'd never approve it."

Jorinei pulled her MaP and stuck it under Rivan's chin. "Who recruited you?"

The man remained silent.

Shit, I thought. *It doesn't matter who's behind all this.* Only warning *Pohru-Mahrko* about the Azatem was important. "Dvaidasa?"

Jorinei started to turn but three sharp whistles from one of the scouts by the cave mouth grabbed her attention. "Report," she said.

"Nadera's picked up two more pa'nizofstra heading our way, frei."

"How far out?"

Nadera appeared at the cave mouth. "Five miles and closing fast."

With a nod, the commanding officer shoved Rivan toward two of her men. "Collar him." She gave a series of short whistles and the soldiers started packing and moving, silent and efficient. She strode to a soldier who was hunched over a piece of damaged equipment. "Get that com relay up, Romvi. We need to contact *PM*."

"Working on it."

"How long?"

"With a company move? Probably another thirty minutes after we reach the next stop."

"Zhek," Jorinei cursed beneath her breath. "Okay, deal with it later. Right now find us another route out of these caves."

His visor turned opaque as Romvi muttered commands to his suit's internal syscom. He shook his head a few times then nodded. "There's a secondary cave mouth five-point-eight kilometers southwest of us. I'll mark the route and share it with the squad."

The commander called, "Leilei, set motion charges on the entrance. We'll cut off their access and their heads."

"Zant, frei."

"We're going deep, pa'nerem. I want all of you kicking up dust in five minutes."

The whole company was hustling.

"We are one." Damn, they were getting louder and that meant closer.

"Dvaidasa?" I tried to get her attention again.

Vehl dropped a bio-suit and socks beside me as Aihaman pulled a bag of cleansing cloths from his med pack and removed one. "You've got a cut beneath your right eye, Barethri," the med tech said and reached toward me.

I grabbed his wrist. "Rivan shot me full of Azatem bacteria before we left *Pohru-Mahrko*."

Aihaman sat back on his heels. "You don't seem infected."

"My immune system is weird. But that doesn't matter. You all have to return to *Pohru-Mahrko* and leave Iodiq."

"I'll let you close that wound yourself." He opened his pack and pulled out the stapler then said, "Dvaidasa, can we speak?"

Jorinei strode over. "Make it quick."

"Tell her," Aihaman said to me and I explained the situation, adding, "Leave me and get back to *Pohru-Mahrko* immediately."

The dvaidasa studied me. "Why did Rivan infect you? And why should we leave?"

"Because the Azatem Code's been latent in my system. That injection made me a beacon for the Azatem. They're coming here. Fast."

Rivan stared at me, apparently unable to summon the vairim to control his shock. "Zhek." He looked at his comrades. "I didn't know that's what was in the syringe. I thought it was a sedative. Jori, you have to believe me. I didn't know."

Jorinei slowly stood. "How long before they reach the planet?" I shook my head. "Utha," she muttered. She folded her arms and lowered her chin, considering her options. She glanced at me again. "What was the zosh's plan?"

"To repair *Pohru-Mahrko* and ambush the Azatem. I wasn't supposed to be activated until the ship and troops were ready."

"But now he's lost any chance of controlling the engagement and *Pohru-Mahrko* is unprepared." Jorinei looked long and hard at Rivan. "Alright. Every Ohnenrai soldier has clear orders to keep you safe, Barethri. Now we know why. You're a biological weapon. Until we can contact *Pohru-Mahrko* and receive new orders, we'll remain your protectors." I started to protest but she cut me off. "If we die following the zosh's commands, then we'll die defending our people. We're soldiers, Barethri, death is what we do best." She turned and called, "Right, maibyo pa'haxan?"

"Drax-*tu!*" The cave echoed with the panca's shout. She'd called them more than her squad. She'd called them her friends.

FOURTEEN

POHRU-MAHRKO HAD LOST contact with Panca Seven-oh-one. They'd landed and entered the pumping station, but there'd been nothing for over two hours. That violated standard protocol of hourly check-ins. Worse, they'd lost the squadron' ship. *Cathru-Ahzish* had gone down. The ship came under attack, from what was unclear. One pilot and two dasas were confirmed dead, their trackers had off-lined and their vitals had flat-lined.

Fuck. It was such a perfect Terran word. Ehtishem understood why Rachel favored it. And it was ideal for this situation. He'd set things in motion just by touching her. He had to keep from doing it again. A daunting proposition considering his vairim weakened daily where she was concerned.

He refocused on Iodiq. "Timsai, who's closest to Station Seven?"

"Already ahead of you, fra." The thrai pointed at one of many lit displays. "Panca Five-oh-one aboard *Merekha* just arrived on scene."

This was the thrai's operation. Ehtishem was there for the

troops. He wanted them to know they had his attention. "Ash-ush," he murmured.

Timsai clasped his hands behind his back. "Trackers show the remaining soldiers are alive. Vitals are elevated but stable."

Ehtishem nodded. What had happened at Station Seven? This should've been a routine operation. That they were maintaining com silence suggested their attackers were still in the vicinity or their relay went down when Dasa Ehnk was killed.

He glanced at the heads-up display, taking in the ground-level view of the other units going about their tasks, nothing extraordinary happening as most worked on testing, activating, and pumping, while others found and assessed food supplies. Panca One-oh-one's first water tanker was already aboard *Pohru-Mahrko*. Panca Five-oh-one had reported low water tables and toxic levels of beryllium and arsenic contamination in their aquifer. They were dismantling the pump when Timsai rerouted them to Station Seven.

"Suxra, Zosh?" a young trainee offered Ehtishem a cup.

He nodded and took it, sipped the red tea, then frowned. He needed something with a kick, not a whimper. Suxra usually did the trick, but this was weaker than piss in a rainstorm.

His mood darkened a little more.

He took in the shadowy command deck. Troop handlers relayed orders between the dasas and their dvaidasas, mech techs monitored vitals and diagnostics, and the engineers kept up a steady murmur as they directed the pumping ops.

Timsai nodded to Ehtishem. "Zosh, we have *Merekha's* feed. Screen Fourteen."

The display showed a bird's-eye view of *Cathru-Ahzish's* wreckage, lit up by *Merekha's* searchlights. It lay at the base of a rocky cliff and was partially submerged in a river that skirted the mountain before turning sharply downward in a headlong crash toward the Western Iodiq Sea.

One of *Merekha's* pilots said, "*Pohru-Mahrko*, you need to see this." The view skewed as the ship's officer refocused his feed on a cave mouth. "This is the entrance to Station Seven, fra." Huge metal doors were twisted and torn outward from their frame. Metal and debris blocked the entrance, along with the massive, mutilated carcass of one of Iodiq's nastier predators.

"Anizofstra." Timsai crossed his arms and met his leader's gaze. "Now we know what downed *Cathru-Ahzish*."

Ehtishem squinted at the screen. "I didn't know they grew that big."

"They don't according to our data." The thrai tapped his com officer. "Tell *Merekha* to gather tissue samples. Carefully. There may be Azatem bacterial contamination." The man nodded and relayed the order.

Ehtishem murmured, "Genetic manipulation?"

Timsai nodded. "That's why I wanted the troops fully suited at all times."

"Zosh."

Ehtishem turned from the screen. Gahlen had spoken as he and Tinish strode across the command deck. They stopped when they stood toe-to-toe with him.

"Va'gaosha aeva," Tinish said, his voice pitched low. The message they brought was highly confidential.

Ehtishem met Timsai's gaze. "May I use your consult room, Thrai?"

"Of course."

Ehtishem and his guards exited the warship's bridge into the small, adjoining room. When the door whispered shut behind them, Gahlen proffered his compad. The heavily

encoded message had originated from Mahzel. It turned
Ehtishem's blood cold:

Dvaidasa Dahmircan is dead. Barethri Rachel was
abducted from Pohru-Mahrko, *possibly by Pa'dasa*
Rivan and Kruhz. Tracker trace indicates she is on
Iodiq. Please advise.

He slammed the compad against the table's edge. The
screen shattered. Parts careened around the room. The paper-
thin device bent over his fist and he threw it hard enough to
lodge in the padding of Timsai's chair. He stood, head down,
hands fisted, fighting the urge to tear the table from its bolted
pedestal and kick chairs through the floor-to-ceiling portal.
Finally, he turned to Gahlen. "Ask the thrai to join us."

While he waited, Ehtishem stared at Iodiq. Rachel was
down there. Unarmed. Unprepared to survive that planet's
environment.

Pairika, I'll find you. And I'll kill whoever's responsible for
this. They can't hide from me.

Timsai entered. He glanced at the pieces of broken compad
and his damaged chair.

Ehtishem relayed the news.

"Rivan and Kruhz. Could Panca Seven-oh-one be a part of
this?" the thrai asked. "It would explain their com silence."

"Unknown," Tinish replied. "The visual record from the
MSD was disrupted. We only have a record of Kruhz and
Rivan entering the room. There's a gap of twenty-two
minutes."

Timsai said, "Now Kruhz is dead. What are Barethri
Rachel's coordinates on Iodiq?" Tinish pulled up her tracker
location. The thrai took the aevadasa's compad, glanced at the
readout, and showed it to Ehtishem. "She's with Seven-oh-one."

"Utha." *If Rachel dies...* Ehtishem straightened and buried that thought with a great many others. Tension shimmered and distorted his vision for a moment, but his self-control held. Zosh Ehtishem Mahle was a master of vairim. He had to be. He turned to his most trusted advisors. "Gahlen, tell Huorem and Mahzel to report here. Now."

"They've departed for the planet's surface, fra."

Ehtishem grunted, unsure if he wanted to kiss or kill Rachel's bodyguards. He appreciated their commitment to recovering her, even if it was their lapse that had permitted her abduction. "I want regular updates from them."

"Zant, fra," Gahlen replied.

"Do we know *Merekha*'s pilots?"

Tinish tapped his compad then shook his head. "Not well enough for this." He paused and ran through a list, tapping on names and entering orders. "I've activated Berk, Deniz, Stig, Anchal, and Gohra."

"Ash-ush. Send them to my quarters for further instructions. And bring in Sarem Mahlei too. I have questions."

Accompanied by his team, the zosh left the room, crossed the command deck, and boarded the lift. Timsai remained behind to oversee ops.

Gahlen swiped his compad. "Stig and Gohra have a mid-level worker in custody for questioning."

"Who?" Ehtishem asked.

"Dvaidasa Judilei."

"Rachel's supervisor in the CMSD? She has no business being aboard *Pohru-Mahrko*."

Gahlen met his gaze. "Exactly."

Stig and Gohra were waiting when Ehtishem reached his quarters. Judilei was with them, shackled and hang-dog, and no one said anything about her swelling eye and bloodied nose as they dropped her at his feet.

He crouched. "Every detail. If I think you're lying or hiding something, I will beat it out of you."

She swallowed and nodded. "My job was to get Barethri Rachel aboard *Pohru-Mahrko*. Rivan and Kruhz would wait for Huorem and Mahzel to leave her in the MMSD. Then Dvaidasa Dahmircan would be incapacitated. The barethri would be caught, drugged, and delivered to *Cathru-Ahzish*."

"You know Dahmircan is dead?"

Her expression turned stony. "That wasn't part of the plan."

"Was leaving you behind to take the blame part of it?"

She failed to hide the bitterness that tainted her reply. "Nava."

Only the knowledge that Judilei's testimony would be needed later kept Ehtishem from detaching the woman's head from her body. But that self-control was hard won. He'd garnered a great deal of satisfaction from sending her teeth skittering across the floor.

That struggle got harder when Tinish proffered a syringe and a protective metal tube stamped with an Ohnenrai Genetics code. "This was found in the depot. It must be the sedative they used."

Ehtishem took the empty syringe and held it up. Light winked off the dregs of bright yellow fluid inside. He clutched the glass. "Gahlen, get someone to Rachel's quarters immediately. I need to know if there's a protective case and a syringe like this on the galley counter."

Gahlen stepped back, got a soldier on his com, and explained his need. "Double-time," he said, "this is your only concern, Dasa."

Ehtishem glared at Judilei. "Who orchestrated this?"

"I told you all I know, fr—" The Ohnenrai word for *sir* turned into a gasp as Ehtishem's fist snapped Judilei's right clavicle. "My only job was to get her onto *PM* in time for the next dirtside mission," she said through clenched teeth.

Gahlen swiped off his com and said, "There's no syringe in the barethri's quarters."

Ehtishem's fist met the woman's other clavicle with the same disastrous result. "I personally approved you to interact with Rachel in the CMSD. You betrayed the Ohnenrai, Judilei." He held up the syringe. "This isn't a sedative. It's Azatem bacteria. You and your co-conspirators just told our enemy exactly where to find us." The vial creaked within his grip. "Who's responsible?"

Judilei stared at her leader, all vairim broken as horror and pain contorted her face. "Sarem Mahlei," she rasped.

Ehtishem's blood turned cold. "Ahremena. Why did you conspire with her?"

She sagged. "I've waited a decade for a live birth. Paid money I couldn't afford on my measly salary, but I won the last lottery for your DNA. I finally had a live fetus with the ultimate genome and a quality surrogate. I finally had something only the Elites possess — immortality for my genome." She looked up. "The sarem threatened to take it away."

"Rivan and Kruhz won the lottery and faced the same threat?" He couldn't believe what he was hearing. His DNA had been commoditized, fetishized, and weaponized.

She nodded. "Zant, fra. She held that over all our heads."

"You should've come to me. I would've helped you. All of you. Now?" He shook his head. "There's nothing I can do for you."

"With *Dathusha* gone," Tinish said, "you've just wasted your life, Judilei."

"And lost that Elite DNA you covet so much." Ehtishem didn't bother controlling his anger as he snarled, "You betrayed your people for immortality and destroyed everything for everyone."

"But there's still a chance we can recover the ship," she said, a plea in her eyes, blue blood crusting her nostrils. "Isn't there?"

"Not without our weapon," Ehtishem replied. "Not without Rachel. Not without *Pohru-Mahrko* repaired and her troops healed." He turned his back on Judilei. "Cage her before I kill her." Two detention soldiers were summoned to lock up the woman Ehtishem had trusted to obey his orders and keep Rachel safe. His sense of security slipped as Judilei was taken away. "Locate my mother. *Now.*"

Tinish answered, "Already on it, fra. Security is bringing her up from the Nerem Deck lab."

Gahlen muttered, "This is madness."

Ehtishem said, "She weaponized my DNA in more ways than one."

"She used it to make military decisions."

"Zant." Ehtishem straightened his shoulders. "She committed high treason in doing so." He looked down. Judilei's blue blood stained his floor. "Someone clean that up."

Two security soldiers arrived with Ahremena. They hadn't shackled her, much to Ehtishem's regret.

She looked icier than usual. "What's this all about? I was running a time-sensitive test when these two barged in. That data will be ruined. I'll have to start all over. This summons is very inconvenient, Ehtishem."

He planted his feet and crossed his arms over his chest. "Sarem Ahremena Uahdimei Mahlei, you're accused of committing high treason against the Ohnenrai people."

Her carefully controlled mask didn't break. "Really? Based on what evidence?"

"The testimony of Dvaidasa Judilei."

Ahremena met his anger still with an unflinching regard. "I don't know who she is."

Rachel had told Ehtishem that his rage was like the split-second of utter silence and abject terror that preceded an Ohnenrai orbital bomb strike. He certainly felt that way hearing his mother lie without hesitation. Her voice and expression held no hint of regret or shame. Clearly she believed she was beyond reproach or punishment, that she knew the best path for the Ohnenrai, military leadership and experience be damned.

"What exactly am I accused of doing?" she asked.

"Coercion."

"That's not treasonous," she said.

"It is if it results in the loss of our only weapon against the Azatem."

She considered him through slitted eyes. Dropping all pretense of innocence, she replied, "Rachel's not lost. She's serving her purpose."

Ehtishem's tone was even colder than hers. "What made you think you had the authority to deploy her?"

"Because you didn't have the strength to do it."

"You damned fool."

"She's the only weapon we need. The Azatem will take her and stop dead, instinctively driven to ignore all other DNA. You've seen it in the lab, Ehtishem. Her only purpose is to lure them into mutational meltdown. Your only purpose was to deposit her in their path. But you failed. I told you to drop her. I told you not to become attached. You did anyway, and I won't watch our people suffer and die because you're flawed. The attraction you have toward her is my fault, so I found a work-around. Now, recall your troops and let's leave Iodiq before the Azatem arrive to claim their prize."

Ehtishem considered the high shine of his black boots. He straightened. He met her cold gaze. "Sarem Mahlei, I find you guilty of treason against the Ohnenrai people, the Office of the Ohnenrai Command General, and Ohnenrai Military Command." He drew the MaP from his hip holster and shot Ahremena in the chest. She stumbled back against the wall and slid to the floor, leaving a bloody blue streak on the way down.

"Why?" She stared at the spreading stain above her heart.

He holstered the gun and squatted before her. "Because I never loved you."

Ahremena had designed him to love but gave him no reason to love her. He was her creation, her tool, her weapon, her prize. But he'd never been her son. Love and family he'd gotten from Rachel and Pearl. He wasn't about to give them up. Ehtishem watched his mother gasp, writhe, die, and he felt nothing.

He looked at his officers. "Does anyone have a complaint about the sarem's execution?"

Gahlen asked, "What about her genetics work, fra?"

"We have other geneticists. But Rachel's our only functioning weapon against the Azatem." Even if he didn't love her with every fiber of his being, he'd be a fool to abandon their best chance of defeating their enemy.

Tinish nodded. "And we don't know if *Maso*'s populace is the only colony. There may be more Azatem spreading across the galaxy."

"Exactly."

Berk, Deniz, Stig, Gohra, and Anchal arrived. They said nothing about Ahremena's body. Gahlen programmed Rachel's tracker code into their coms while Tinish briefed them and issued orders to the armory to outfit them.

"You know what to do, pa'nerem." Ehtishem sank to the couch and rubbed the back of his neck as a sickening wave of helplessness swamped him. He wouldn't give in to it. He couldn't. "Leave me. I need to think." Without a word, his most loyal soldiers filed from the small quarters, taking Ahremena's body with them.

Retrieving Rachel was a suicide mission. Ehtishem scrubbed his palms over his face and groaned. Had she been in the very ship he'd stood beside while he listened to the ops officer brief Panca Seven-oh-one?

"I won't leave you to die alone." He didn't know if he and Rachel could stop the Azatem, but they sure as hell could slow them down. They could buy *Pohru-Mahrko* time to escape. They could do enough damage inside *Maso* to give the Ohnenrai a fighting chance. Maybe they could even free *Dathusha*.

He stretched out on the couch and contemplated the empty metal tube. So many lives were counting on Rachel. He opened a channel on his com and reached Timsai.

"Zant, Zosh?"

"Evacuate all our troops from Iodiq immediately. I want *Pohru-Mahrko* to break orbit and find another place to hide as soon as all personnel have returned."

Timsai nodded. "And Rachel?"

More than ever, he needed to know she was safe. He needed to find her and protect her. "I'm going dirtside to get her." He didn't say that he wouldn't return. He cut their connection.

Understanding the nature of the Azatem Code and the biological need driving the Azatem to be together forced Ehtishem to analyze how much of what he felt for Rachel was love and how much was alien DNA influencing his behavior. He cursed mentally, wishing Ahremena had kept that knowledge to herself. Instead, she'd planted doubt in his mind. He knew why. His mother hadn't wanted him to experience love's power because it threatened her influence over him. And when she'd realized she'd lost that battle, she'd sought other ways to control the outcome of the war.

Ehtishem closed his eyes and willed his brain to shut up. The time for worrying was behind him. Now was the time to rest, eat, prepare. The time for action was coming.

FIFTEEN

WHEN OHNENRAI SOLDIERS looked at each other via their helmets, they saw rank markings superimposed on the insides of their visors — yellow, green, red, and blue bands indicating commanders, techs, etc. Their bio-suits were color-coordinated and their mech-suits were marked to indicate rank and identity, too. It was how I knew at a glance that Jorinei was the panca's commander, a dvaidasa, and a tactical officer.

Around me soldiers shouldered packs and equipment. Vehl was their engineering tech, and Fehrana and Nergis were weapons specialists. Romvi handled communications and navigation. Aihaman, who I knew from the trauma bay after *Maso's* attack, was a munitions specialist like Leilei, in addition to being the panca's med tech. Nadera was the recon scout. I watched them and fingered the dry clothes. They'd be way too big and the last time I'd been naked in a crowded room I'd been too doped up to care. But I was painfully lucid now.

"Bio-suit first, Barethri," Fehrana said. "You haven't got anything we don't, except paler skin. No one's gonna notice or care if you're undressed."

She was right and I was freezing my ass off. I shucked my boots and socks, stood, peeled off the wet jumpsuit and struggled into the bio-suit. Everything sagged, but I was warm and dry. My boots still squished, but the socks repelled the water and kept my feet dry. I rolled the ankles and sleeves on the new jumpsuit and joined Fehrana. "I can carry something."

"You know how to handle a MaP?" Jorinei asked as she straightened from closing her pack.

I nodded. "I've trained with Huorem and Mahzel."

The Ohnenrai mass ammunition pistol was a high-speed, high-impact weapon. It simultaneously fired three small projectiles it sheared from its metal ammo block and it could remove a man's head and both arms with one shot. A little more impressive than the crusty old shotgun I'd used on Earth.

She unhooked the pistol and holster from her suit and handed them to me, then dug an ammo belt from her pack and said, "Spare ammo blocks. Don't shoot anyone on our side."

"I only kill bastards and bad guys."

Fehrana arched an eyebrow. "You've killed?"

"Five times." I cinched the belt, but it still hung low on my hips. I looked like a spaghetti western gunslinger. "It's not something I'm proud of."

The soldiers around me nodded, which surprised me, though it shouldn't have. I'd lived with the Ohnenrai long enough to know their military women and men weren't the B-movie bad guys I'd believed them to be when I was young and they were occupying Earth. But old prejudices die hard.

Jorinei shrugged on her pack. "Sometimes it's kill or be killed. We all know that." Her mass ammo repeater rifle went onto her shoulder. "Charges set?" she asked Leilei. With that soldier's affirmative, she called for her squad to move out. "Arfera, pa'nerem." She put me in line between Fehrana and Vehl. Rivan was at the back of the group, weaponless and with his hands still manacled and an electronic collar around his neck.

I glanced at him. Regret and doubt sloughed off him like dander. Weird that I sensed it. Was my connection with the soldiers strengthening because of the Azatem? "What's with the collar?" I asked Vehl.

"Security. If he leaves his warden's side without permission, forty milliamps will make sure he doesn't go far."

"Oh." I looked at all the soldiers. I couldn't get much read on Nadera or Romvi, but the others radiated confidence and focus. They didn't show the weakness coming from Rivan. The two I couldn't read, I guessed didn't have any of Ehtishem's DNA.

The soldiers released a small saucer-shaped drone. It lit the way, tested the air for toxic gases, and monitored for movement on our route, sending its readings to the soldiers' helmets. We traversed twisting tunnels that sloped downward, sometimes gradually, sometimes with jagged drops. We scrambled over boulders as big as compact cars, squeezed through damp crevasses, and saw the most astonishing rock formations.

Curtains of pearly-white minerals hung from some cave ceilings. Others grew bluish crystals, each larger than Ehtishem. Yellow crystalline petals draped over rocks, curling and twisting into fragile flower-like shapes amid strands of glassy shards. Water made the gray walls black and shimmery and the path dangerously slick. Soft green pinpoints of light speckled the ceiling — bioluminescent fungi and the worms that fed on it — an underground constellation on an alien planet. The air was cool and damp but not stale, and the deeper we went, the colder it became until our breath plumed around our faces.

"It's beautiful down here." My voice echoed through the passage and the soldiers around me murmured agreement. We moved carefully, as if we were in an underground cathedral surrounded by the works of great artists — nature's sculptures and stained glass.

After we'd walked for what felt like miles, Jorinei led us into a relatively wide and flat cavern. She raised her hand. "This is the Western Wail. We'll rest and eat here."

The walls were smooth and striated — gray stone with narrow white crystalline veins that shot through it in jagged patterns, like lightning through storm clouds.

"Why's it called the Western Wail?" I asked Fehrana as we set up sleeping pads and blankets.

"When the winds up top blow from the west, they seep through cracks in the mountain, hit this room, and make the creepiest wailing sound I've ever heard," she replied, the timbre of her voice high and surprisingly girlish.

"Do all of you know Iodiq well?"

"Only from training holos. This continent is thoroughly mapped. The Ohnenrai military built the pump stations and dry storage facilities, and they trained here whenever they stopped to take on water. There used to be a shipyard, too."

A distant rumble and a sprinkle of dust from the cave ceiling stopped me. "What was that?"

"The explosives I set at the cave mouth just blew. Looks like our anizofstra decided to take a closer peek than was healthy," Leilei replied, her husky voice completely unlike Fehrana's.

"Check for movement," Jorinei ordered.

Nadera pulled out her tracker. "I'm seeing some motion in the cave mouth, but it's erratic. Probably falling rocks, possibly the anizofstra struggling."

"Probably and possibly aren't acceptable. Check for heat signatures."

"Too much stone between us and the entrance, frei," Nadera replied. "I'm surprised I can get any read at all."

A scowl flitted across Jorinei's face before her expression settled into field soldier neutrality. "You and Leilei return to that last choke and see if you can get a heat signature from there. Stay in com range."

With a salute, both women shouldered their MaRRs and jogged back the way our group had come, their helmet lights bouncing irregularly until they disappeared around a bend.

Aihaman crouched before me. I knew him by the thin, red stripes on his helmet and armored biceps. "How are you feeling?" he asked, his voice slightly amplified and buzzy through his helmcom.

"Good," I said. "Strong and lucid."

He leaned a little closer. "I heard something interesting about you from one of the med techs working with Sarem Mahlei."

"Oh?"

He studied me long enough to make me feel like squirming, especially since I couldn't see his face. Finally, he asked, "Can you manipulate emotions?"

Crap.

This was dangerous territory. "I — um — maybe?" Honesty was the best policy, I decided. "Look. I can sense the emotions of people, some more distinctly than others. Anyone who has the zosh's DNA comes through clearer. I'm not sure if what I do can be called manipulation, though. I've only tried it once. I think it's less control and more amplification. I guess." His faceplate turned transparent and he scrutinized me. He was older than his companions, his hair silver around the temple. "Does it matter?" I asked.

"Matter?" He sounded puzzled. "What do you mean?"

"Does that knowledge change your opinion of me, our relationship to one another and to your squad?"

He mulled that, watching Romvi as the soldier extracted the parts of the broken com relay from his pack. "Nava." Aihaman turned back to me. "It could be useful if things go badly down here."

"You're expecting trouble?"

He flashed a quick grin that reminded me of Ehtishem. "I'm an Ohnenrai field soldier, Barethri. I always expect trouble." His smile turned to a brief scowl as his gaze caught Rivan. "Except from within our own ranks." His visor darkened again.

A strange chittering sound echoed into the chamber and made the hair on my arms stand on end. "Jeez, that *is* creepy," I muttered, assuming it was the wind Fehrana had mentioned.

A thunderous explosion followed, the floor shuddered, and Jorinei's com came to life with Fehrana's voice. "Leilei's dead, frei. She blew the cave to stop them from entering, but I don't think it's going to keep them out for long." Her breath came fast; she was running.

"Anizofstra?" Jorinei asked as the soldiers stood and checked their weapons.

"Nava. Something much smaller but in massive numbers. I've never seen them before."

"Get back here, dasa. We'll seal this cave as soon as you're here." She signaled for Aihaman. He began setting explosive charges on the cave ceiling around the entrance as the other soldiers broke camp again.

Fehrana appeared, her reflective armor coated in blue blood and mud.

I stood. "Are you injured?"

"Nava. This is Leilei's blood."

"Utha," Nadera cursed.

"Let's move out so Aihaman can blow that entrance,"

Jorinei said. We formed up and began climbing over the jumble of boulders leading from the opposite end of the cavern into another, pitch-black, narrow chamber. As I reached flat ground, a *whoop-whoop* and chittering echoed through the cave. The wild cacophony sounded like the call of baboons. I hated that sound.

A shout followed then Jorinei began firing her MaRR, its red-hot tracers lighting up the dark cavern. Romvi climbed the boulders to join her. I covered my ears as Fehrana led me toward a cliff and a dark maw beyond it.

The soldiers had lowered their combat visors and they'd gone to tactical communications mode. Which meant I had no warning before Fehrana threw me on the ground, covered my ears with her hands, and crouched protectively over me. A flash, rumble, and dust cloud meant the entrance to the cave had become rubble. As the dust swirled around us, she stood and began firing.

Jorinei and Romvi leaped over the boulders, vaulting them like they were the size of park benches instead of the size of cars. Aihaman wasn't with them. Nadera, Vehl, Romvi, and Fehrana fired at the creatures that had passed the entrance before the explosion.

More tracers lit the cavern. My ears reverberated with the thud of the MaRRs. I clapped my hands over them when Fehrana stood and opened fire. But what had my attention were the monkey-lizard things scuttling across the walls and ceiling. They had huge, yellow eyes and curling prehensile tails, mouths filled with jagged teeth set in almost-human faces. And they were heading straight for me. Were they Azatem? Or more of Iodiq's creatures? I didn't want an introduction, yet a strange pull bloomed in my brain and a shiver ran down my spine. They were repulsive and terrifying, but part of me wanted to go to them.

"Azatem," I said though not even I could hear me over the weapons fire and screeching. Hundreds came on in waves, undeterred by the deaths of their companions. With them came an overwhelming sense of yearning. They were one. And I was one of them. I couldn't fire on them, couldn't harm them.

But I was equally compelled to stay with the Ohnenrai soldiers around me. They were my guards, my companions. I couldn't let them die. I should protect them like they were protecting me.

"Get it off!" Rivan shouted. A critter clung to his leg, its teeth and claws sinking into his calf and shin. The man was weaponless and unarmored.

Jorinei calmly blasted the thing away, but the damage was done. Blue blood seeped from the punctures in his flight suit. She released his manacles and deactivated the collar, then yanked him behind her.

More and more critters came through the dust and debris. The soldiers reloaded their weapons and jettisoned red-hot heat sinks. The bodies were piling up. The cave stank of ozone and hot metal, body odor, and the musk of the critters. Still the monsters poured in and met their deaths. But they were gaining ground and a cliff dropped off behind our group.

Someone crouched beside me. Rivan. His eyes were bloodshot, his hands shaking. He held up a harness and gestured toward the cliff. "Can you rappel?"

I shook my head. He turned his back to me. "Climb aboard. I'll wrap an anchor line around you, but you need to hold on." When I hesitated, he looked at me. "I made a mistake, Barethri. Let me try to fix it."

His regret and sincerity washed over me. He was infected and he knew it. The Azatem bacteria assaulting his immune system spread pain throughout his body.

Cripes, it's aggressive.

I climbed onto his back. He stood and wrapped a strap around my hips and his waist. "Hold tight," he said. "We're going down fast." He threaded a line through anchors attached directly to his flight suit, swung over the cliff, and plunged us into darkness.

There was nothing to see. I held tight as my stomach flip-flopped. The saucer probe shot past and lit up the side of the cliff. Above us, the other soldiers were following down the line as two more explosions ripped through the cavern.

More of the critters came. They died and were replaced by others. I pulled the MaP Jorinei had given me, ignored the protest in the back of my brain, and started picking off the creatures. Yet, they moved unerringly toward me and were almost on top of Fehrana as she paused to reload above us.

Three jumped on her and I shouted, "Leave her alone!" The monsters stopped and stared at me. They were confused. They only wanted to reach me, to protect me. "Holy shit," I muttered as a light went off in my brain. They thought they were saving me. I could use this. "Go back!" I ordered and pictured them climbing up the cliff. "Leave me!"

Seconds ticked by, then a few well-placed shots from Nergis made up their minds. Still other critters clung to the walls and cliff edge, watching and chittering, rocking to and fro.

"Go back!" I repeated.

They complained.

We reached the bottom of the cliff and squeezed through another crevasse barely wide enough to accommodate the soldiers' armor. That entrance was blown, too, as we descended another cliff. When we finally stopped, Rivan collapsed. Bloody blue tears traced his cheeks. Blood ran from his nose. He groaned and shook, his agony unmistakable even if I hadn't been able to feel it. "Jori," he rasped, "kill me."

The dvaidasa crouched beside him and shook her head.

"You brought this on yourself, Rivan, and possibly the rest of us." She stood and stepped back. "This is the voice and visual record of Dvaidasa Bindi Jorinei." She reported her location, the date, and the circumstances of Rivan's impending death.

He looked silently at his compatriots. His pilot's suit hadn't protected him from the Azatem bacteria driving those critters to a frenzy. He'd screwed all of us with his stupidity and gotten his fellow soldiers killed. He'd earned and received just punishment. But, maybe, he also deserved a little compassion. "Dvaidasa?" I stepped close to Jorinei. "Can't you end this before it gets horrible?"

"Why should any of us pity him?" Her visor turned transparent. She looked perplexed. "Why do you?"

"Because someone convinced him and Kruhz that my death was the only way to save the Ohnenrai. It doesn't excuse him, but does he have to suffer? I mean, he thought he was saving his people. I'd probably do the same thing in his place."

"I wouldn't." Her visor became opaque again. "Ohnenrai soldiers don't second-guess orders. Rivan's were to protect you. He and Kruhz should have asked their commander or spoken with the thrai, if they had doubts." She turned away. Distant echoes of the infected critters filtered down from above. "Let's move, Seven-oh-one."

As the other soldiers turned away, I pulled my MaP and placed it at Rivan's feet. He met my gaze, his pupils so dilated his eyes were all black. It made him more unreadable than ever. "Don't make me regret this," I whispered in Ohnenrai then joined the departing group.

SIXTEEN

THE VIBRATION of his compad awakened Ehtishem from a dream filled with fire and blood. "Talk to me."

"Huorem, here." He and Mahzel had reconned Pump Station Seven.

"Go ahead, Aevadasa."

"We have the results of a prelim analysis on one of the anizofstra that attacked Panca Seven-oh-one. It's positive for Azatem bacterial DNA."

Ehtishem scanned the data Huorem transmitted. "The thrai was right. That explains their size. Okay. Proceed with caution. Assume anything you encounter wants to eat you. I'm suiting up and coming dirtside."

Mahzel appeared on the screen. "We're sending in a probe to see what other horrors the Azatem have created. As long as Barethri's and the soldiers' vitals hold steady, we'll move forward with a careful survey and hold our ground on the surface until you arrive."

"Ushta. Keep me informed. Call for evac if things get

messy." Ehtishem closed the link then called *Pohru-Mahrko's* command deck.

"Zant, fra?" Timsai appeared on screen.

"Status on the water ops?"

"We've cleared sixty-three wells. Pumping is finished and half our teams are already home. Dry stores yielded five hundred forty-one tons of grain and seeds and two hundred thirty-eight tons of protein discs."

"That's good news."

"Any update on Rachel?"

"We've located Panca Seven-oh-one but are unable to establish direct communications. They've gone deep. Inform the remaining dirtside troops to evac double time. I want them off the planet now, Timsai. The Azatem are down there."

"That's unfortunate."

"You're a master of understatement, Thrai."

"We'll pick up our pace."

Ehtishem went to his small galley. He wasn't hungry, but he knew to eat while food was available. He gave himself ten minutes, then it was time to suit up, pack up, and load up on weapons and ammunition. A plan was forming in his mind, but to make it work he needed enough munitions and supplies to last for months. If there was one thing he and Rachel were good at, it was surviving in the wild with nothing but wits and grit.

After cleaning his dishes, he donned his bio-suit and his uniform and pulled a travel backpack from his locker. He also retrieved the parcel he'd brought with him from *Dathusha*. He opened it, removed a fold of blue silk, and secreted that in his bio-suit's only breast pocket, then he packed clothing, dental tabs and personal care kits, and an extra pair of boots. He slung the pack over his shoulder and went to Rachel's quarters where he gathered the same items for her. On the galley counter, he found the pieces of the puzzle box he'd given her. Ehtishem added them to his pack. He'd assemble the box on the flight down to Iodiq.

His next stop was the armory.

The dasa behind the security barrier snapped to attention. "Fra," the young woman said. "How can I help you?"

Ehtishem dropped his bag at her feet, leaned on the counter, and surveyed the available weaponry. He needed something powerful but light with ammunition that would last over a long period of time and not be compromised by the extremes of Iodiq's environment. "I need two repeating MaRs, three MaPs, and enough ammunition to last for one duty rotation. Four hunting and survival knives, a garrote, and twenty-five pounds of malleable explosives with timers and detonators."

The dasa stared at him then blinked and said, "Zant, fra." She started gathering the weaponry, inputting each item into her database as she brought it out from the secure room and laid it on the counter. "That's a lot of weight from the ammunition, fra."

He nodded. "That's why you're going to bring my mech-suit out, too." He jerked his chin toward the ammunition vests and belts on the wall and added, "Give me two vests and two belts; one my size and one sized for an adolescent. Put the remaining ammo in a heavy bag."

The mech-suit would allow him to carry up to a thousand additional pounds and that meant the ammunition, survival gear, and weaponry, though formidable, would not be problematic as he and Rachel outran their pursuers. "I also want trip-wires and sensors."

The dasa hustled to fulfill her leader's orders. To her credit, she never questioned what Ehtishem was checking out or why. She simply recorded each item as she loaded it into a heavy duffel bag, the vests, and the ammunition belts.

"Do you want assistance with your suit, fra?" she asked as she wheeled Ehtishem's suit storage case around to the front of the counter.

"Nava. I've got this."

Pulling the case behind him, he stopped at the MMSD for a med pack and survival kit, then moved on to the mess supply for rations. Lastly, he went to the Forward Launch Bay and left all the gear and supplies with Gohra and Stig before returning to the command deck.

"Thrai, a word in private?" he asked and led Timsai into the consult room. As the door closed he said, "*Maso* will be here soon."

"How can you be certain?"

"Because Ahremena activated Rachel."

Timsai's eyes widened, an unusual display of shock for him. "Aiya."

"Indeed. She's a beacon calling them. They will pursue her above all other objectives. Which I'm counting on," he added as Timsai sucked a long, slow breath. "They'll give up the hunt for *Pohru-Mahrko* for the sake of obtaining Rachel. I'm going dirtside and ordering all remaining soldiers to return to *PM*. Upon their docking, you'll immediately break orbit and head for the Fisk Juncture at maximum speed. Once there, complete *Pohru-Mahrko*'s repairs. Rachel and I will remain on Iodiq and do our best to keep the Azatem occupied. Come back when the ship is battle-ready. We'll give you the element of surprise that was lost when Rachel was injected and dumped."

Timsai shook his head. "How long will it take to retrieve her? I'm sure we can spare a day or two."

"This ship cannot be orbiting Iodiq when the Azatem arrive, unless you want to end the Ohnenrai here and now, maibyo haxan. *Pohru-Mahrko* is leaving. That's an order,

Timsai." He held his oldest friend's gaze. "You command the Ohnenrai now."

His expression graver than ever, Timsai nodded. "I won't fail you, fra."

"I know."

"What about Pearl?"

"We have to assume all aboard *Dathusha* are lost." Saying it aloud knifed him, but he didn't let it show on his face. He had to leave with steadfastness.

Timsai grasped his shoulder. "It doesn't end like this, Ehtishem."

Ehtishem nodded, but he was certain it did. Eventually, the Azatem would catch him and Rachel on Iodiq, well before *Pohru-Mahrko*'s repairs were completed. Timsai slowly saluted, the fingers of his right hand touching the outside corner of his right eye, his left palm slapping his thigh.

Ehtishem returned the salute, held his oldest friend's gaze for a long moment, then left *PM*'s command deck with Tinish and Gahlen. They joined Berk and Deniz in the Forward Launch Bay. Stig and Gohra were prepping *Eshmahe*, a small, heavily-armed transport, when he arrived with his entourage.

"Listen up," he said. They stopped loading gear and gathered around him. "Consider this a suicide mission, pa'nerem. If you leave *Pohru-Mahrko* now, she may not be here when you return. If you set foot dirtside, there will be Azatem-infected creatures waiting to kill you or worse. You don't have to sacrifice your lives today. Rachel Pryne has always been my mission, not yours. You won't lose my respect or my friendship if you choose to remain aboard *PM*. I don't require aid from any of you. I can retrieve her and Panca Seven-oh-one without your help. But the Ohnenrai need good soldiers."

Gahlen nodded. "They also need a good leader."

Ehtishem said, "You have the thrai now."

"And we're grateful to know that *Pohru-Mahrko* will be under his capable guidance, fra," Anchal said. "But we're staying with you."

Stig murmured her agreement and added, "We're family."

"And *you've* always been *our* mission, fra," Tinish added.

SEVENTEEN

WE ENTERED A LONG, low tunnel. The unit jogged bent over. Vehl brought up the rear, his lanky body folded in half. He had a way of moving that reminded me of a wind sock, all loosey-goosey and relaxed, limbs made of rubber and moving to their own music.

Fehrana was behind me. "I saw what you did for Rivan," she said.

"I'm not a soldier. I don't have to obey anyone's commands," I replied over my shoulder.

"I hope it doesn't come back on us."

"Me, too."

For a while only the sound of boots on stone and the jingle and creak of gear filled the void.

The tunnel ended in a larger cavern and Nadera turned to block the exit as she emerged. "You should've kept your weapon, Barethri," she said.

"Do you disagree with my decision?"

"Nava. Only that you should've shot him so you wouldn't

be unarmed now." She stepped back and started placing explosives around the narrow opening.

"Wait, Nadera," Jorinei said. "We're running low on munitions and can easily hold this position." She gestured toward the opening. "That'll fill up with bodies if they come this way." She turned to Romvi. "Status on the relay?"

"I still need at least thirty minutes to get it functioning, and we're so deep it's unlikely to connect with *PM* or even the surface."

Jorinei nodded. "Get to it. Fehrana, Nadera, Vehl, and I will take shifts covering the entrance."

Nadera frowned. "Frei, the path forks twenty-five meters from here. We could be ambushed if we remain in one place for too long."

"Understood, dasa, but we need to give our civilian a rest. She doesn't have a mech-suit lifting most of her weight."

I'd copped a squat and hadn't even realized it. I nodded my thanks to her.

Jorinei crouched before me and her visor cleared. "How did you halt that attack? The Azatem are relentless. Once they latch onto something they kill it, consume it, or possess it and drive it until it drops dead or encounters another creature and mutates again. But you confused their hosts and made them turn back. How?"

"I don't know exactly. Sarem Mahlei said I was designed to be recognized as one of their own."

"And they'll keep coming for you?"

I nodded. "'Fraid so."

She drummed her fingers on her armored thigh. "Good to know." She turned and went to Romvi's side. "Get this relay up. We're running out of time to contact *Pohru-Mahrko*."

He didn't look up as he replied, "Working on it."

Nadera joined them, glanced at me, then said, "Are we sure about keeping her with us?"

"We have our orders, dasa," Jorinei said, an edge to her voice that I wasn't sure was only for her subordinate.

"But if she was designed to destroy the Azatem, shouldn't we leave her in their path?"

"Nava. We proceed with our standing orders until we receive new ones."

I studied the five remaining members of Panca Seven-oh-one. A dark-yellow ribbon of fear connected them. Overtaking their confidence, it shimmered around them like heat rising from a desert road. Even Jorinei, who held to their orders, followed them out of a need for certainty. I brushed grit from my hands. "Nadera is the only one of you who doesn't have the zosh's DNA in her genome, right?"

The soldiers stared at me and Nadera slowly nodded.

"How do you know that?" Fehrana asked.

"Aihaman knew this but didn't have a chance to tell any of you. I share your emotions. Those of you who have the zosh's DNA give me a stronger read. I know you're all worried, wondering if you should've abandoned me, orders be damned. Even Jorinei isn't so sure." I sat back against a boulder and shrugged. "Maybe you should. Maybe not. It's the Azatem DNA you carry that's amplifying your emotions to me. And that's what allowed me to confuse those creatures. I'm drawn to them almost as much as I am to you. But I'd rather do what I can to keep you alive and give you confidence than hang out with a bunch of mini Sleestaks."

"A bunch of whats?" Vehl asked, his face as slack as his body.

"Sleestaks. They were creepy creatures on a 70s TV show. My dad showed me an episode. Gave me nightmares for months." He still looked puzzled and I said, "Never mind."

"How can you make us confident?" Nadera asked.

I patted the ground before me. "Sit down."

"Why?" She considered me, her eyes narrow with suspicion.

"Because I can ease your anxiety."

Her chin jerked up. "I'm not anxious."

"Yes, you are. All of you are." I tilted my head toward the floor in front of me. "Just sit. Give me a chance to help."

She crossed her arms. "How do I know you're not going to infect me?"

I sighed. "You saw how fast the Azatem overtook Rivan. You'd all be sick by now if I had a transmittable infection. I don't. My genome was engineered by your own geneticists to neutralize the bacteria. I won't give you Azatem cooties."

"That's why the zosh went to Terra for you," Jorinei said.

"Zant. I'm a biological weapon designed and built by Ohnenrai Genetics."

The dvaidasa stepped around Nadera and sat opposite me, her mech-suit humming with the movement. "Work your magic, Barethri."

I locked onto her emotions with startling ease. Her anxiety was as stifling as Midwest humidity in August, but I pulled it from her anyway. It took only a few heartbeats and left my spine tingling.

When I released her mind, she stared at me, wonder and relief emanating from her. "Aiya." She exhaled the word and tilted her head to indicate the rest of Panca Seven-oh-one. "Do that for them."

One-by-one I helped the other dasas. Nadera was hesitant, so I left her for last. Taking her anxiety was harder and I sat heavily after I was done. But looking up at the soldiers, blue confidence shimmering around them and their shoulders no longer bowed by the weight of worry and fear, I knew I'd done the right thing. My hands shook, my ears rang, my spine was on fire. I needed to get rid of their anxiety before it triggered another flashback...

"That's weird," I muttered.

"What?" Fehrana asked.

"I haven't had a flashback. I didn't even think about it."

"What's a flashback?"

I cocked my head. "You're so lucky not to know from personal experience." I swallowed and fisted my trembling hands. "It's a memory so traumatic and vivid it feels like I'm reliving the moment when I'm remembering it. I'm trapped between then and now and I don't quite know what's real. It's... awful." I looked down. "Sickening. Crippling."

She stared at me. "Barethri, I—" She shook her head. "How do you have those memories yet still go on? Aren't you afraid?"

"That's what's weird. I couldn't escape those memories for the longest time. Until I met your zosh. He made me feel safe for the first time since I was a child." I glanced around the cavern. "I should be scared shitless right now. I'm a gazillion light years away from Terra, separated from Ehtishem, and terrified for my daughter's safety." I lowered my hands and straightened. They'd stopped shaking as the anxiety dissipated. "But, I'm *not* scared. I'm pissed off." I met her gaze and added, "Forget scared. I'm way beyond that." Boots scraped grit as Fehrana shifted. "Here's the thing, dasa. Being mad or scared keeps me alert." I leaned forward. "I don't want to get comfortable. That'll get me killed. I've never been comfortable in my life."

"What about *Dathusha*?"

"Nothing I can do about it. And worrying just makes me crazy." I laughed and the hollow sound echoed around the chamber. "I guess that's how all of you've been able to deal with your situation."

"Zant." Her boots scraped closer as she slid down the wall to a prone position. "No point worrying or getting angry about what's already happened. We're all going to die someday."

"True, but I'd rather not die by being eaten alive."

"Or worse, turned into a mindless tool for a bunch of bacteria," Vehl added from across the narrow cavern.

Fehrana said, "Good point."

"What's that?" Jorinei asked Nadera as they studied a map of the cave system. Her voice filled the silence. "It's not on my charts."

"Unsure. It's not labeled."

Jorinei grunted then addressed the squad. "Listen up. The probe came back with bad news. The route we planned to take shows movement sixty meters ahead. There's a divergent path a few meters from here, but it runs into a choke eleven meters in."

"Want me to check it out?" Fehrana stood, brushing grit from her hands.

Jorinei nodded. "Stay in com contact. You shouldn't have to go far before you reach the choke. See if it's passable."

"Zant." Fehrana jogged into the upward sloping tunnel, the saucer-shaped probe leading the way and her helmlight throwing off strange, jolting shadows.

After a few quiet moments, her call came through the soldiers' coms. "The path is easy, frei, and there's an opening at the top of the choke. It's wide enough to squeeze through and opens onto a massive cavern."

"Any movement in there?" Jorinei asked.

"Nava, but I see daylight through an opening in the ceiling. I think we can climb up and out."

"Stay put," Jorinei told her. "We're coming to you."

The colors inside the cavern were incredible — red, blue, gold, green, orange, purple, and massive swaths of black, its edges tinged with rust. Every surface was a different hue. It was like standing inside a rainbow that had shattered as it hit the walls.

But the cavern's beauty wasn't what stopped us in our tracks. That honor went to the incomplete Ohnenrai warship sitting before us, awaiting the return of its builders.

Huge metal supports were in place to ensure the cavern's structural integrity and the floor of the seemingly endless space had been flattened. The ship was in pieces, but its name was evident on its hull.

I couldn't read Ohnenrai and was about to ask which ship I was looking at when Vehl said, "That's *Ayan-Kanya*." Awe filled his voice and he didn't bother with vairim. None of them did as they scrambled over the boulder-strewn entrance to reach the ship, leaving me in the dark.

I sat down, bemused by their excitement as they thumped each other and shouted, "Drax-*tu!*" Apparently, Christmas had come to Panca Seven-oh-one and the Ohnenrai, hopefully not too late. They circled the cruiser-carrier, their lights reflecting, bobbing, and arcing over its metal structure, growing fainter and brighter as they ran the length of the completed sections.

Finally, Fehrana, Vehl, and Nadera climbed up to me. "Apologies, Barethri. We didn't mean to leave you in the dark," Fehrana said as she helped me navigate the boulders while her companions started blocking the choke.

"What's this place called? I've never seen anything like it."

"It's the Havafna Caldera," she replied and shook her head. "It's not supposed to exist."

"What do you mean?"

"All our records say it collapsed."

I looked around at the magnificent, jagged beauty of the dormant volcano. "Looks like someone screwed up the reports."

She shot me a sidelong look and said, "Or falsified them."

Secrets and lies. It seemed the Ohnenrai had a lot more of them than I'd ever expected. "Why would they do that?"

She shook her head. "To protect this ship? To have some kind of advantage in knowing where it was? Who knows. Whoever did it may be long dead."

Another shout went up. This time it was Romvi. He'd found a working relay among the tools and components left by the engineers and techs. He paired it with his com and sent a coded status report to *Pohru-Mahrko*.

He immediately received a coded reply and read it aloud, "Location acknowledged, Panca Seven-oh-one. Evac not possible. Shelter in place."

"Utha," Fehrana cursed.

"There's a scrambled repeating message too," Romvi said. "All personnel return to base ship. Alert Level One. Report to action stations. This is not a drill." Closing the link, he turned to Jorinei but was interrupted by the distant report of a MaP.

A faint but familiar *whoop-whoop* drifted down from behind the choke.

"Well, shit," I said.

"Vehl, Nadera, Romvi, see if there's a way up to that vent," Jorinei ordered as she pointed at the distant beam of sunlight shining through an opening far above us. "Fehrana, you and the barethri are with me to scout another escape route closer to the ground."

EIGHTEEN

MAHZEL AND HUOREM were picked up from the primary base Timsai had established on Iodiq's Judit Plateau, northwest of Station Seven. Once en route to the pump station, Rachel's guards updated Ehtishem and the squadron.

"*PM* just transmitted a status report from Panca Seven-oh-one, fra," Mahzel shouted over the carrier's engines as he transmitted the information to the squad's helmet systems. "Barethri Rachel remains with them and is uninjured."

Ehtishem nodded and scanned the data. "They've lost half the squad — Ehnk, Nergis, Pohm, Leilei, and Aihaman." The soldiers seated around him shook their heads. Those were heavy losses.

Mahzel continued, "They also reported Azatem exposure killed Rivan. The remaining soldiers and the barethri went deep for safety and are in the vicinity of the Havafna Caldera."

Ehtishem grunted. "That exists?"

"According to Panca Seven-oh-one it does."

"How long to reach them?"

Huorem replied, "Hard to say. I ordered them to shelter in

place. But we're reading a massive amount of movement in their vicinity. Seven-oh-one reported the natives are Azatem infected and highly aggressive." He whistled low and nodded toward the transport's exterior monitor feed.

The ship circled the cliff where the anizofstra had crippled *Cathru-Ahzish*.

"Aiya, that's big," Deniz muttered as they got a good view of the beast's carcass.

Huorem nodded and pointed to a mound of rubble sheared from the mountain's face. "Seven-oh-one blew the entrance to slow the attackers."

Berk called from the co-pilot's seat. "No chance of getting through that way unless we blast our way in."

Tinish shook his head. "And further destabilize the cave system? Bad idea."

"I'm searching for alternative entrances closer to the Havafna Caldera," Stig said as she studied her maps and the data returning from the ship's ground-penetrating radar.

"Watch for more predators," Ehtishem said as the ship skimmed the planet's surface, following the terrain's peaks and valleys. They were vulnerable so low and without backup.

"Nidah." Stig told Berk and Deniz to slow down. "There we go," she murmured as she adjusted the external sensors. "Fra?" She gestured toward an overhead screen. "This is the western end of the Havafna volcanic chain."

"That volcano looks intact," Mahzel muttered. "All our reports say the caldera collapsed."

Ehtishem met the aevadasa's gaze. "It seems we were misinformed."

"Wish I could say I'm surprised," Huorem added.

"Me too," Ehtishem replied. How much of his knowledge was based on half-truths and misinformation? The same craving for influence that had made Ahremena betray his orders had been in play for generations among the Ohnenrai elite. It did nothing to aid their cause, from his point of view.

The ship slowed to hover over a rock-strewn tunnel at the base of the dormant volcano. There were narrow vents on this side of the caldera where gases had escaped, all now clogged with rocks and debris. Long ago, a fissure had formed at the lower end of the magma chamber and the lava had drained, leaving the caldera intact and baking the inside to form a massive hollow.

Ehtishem studied it, slowly nodding. "That's a promising opening."

"Zant at nava," Stig countered. "See the piled gravel and soil to each side of the opening? There's a good chance we're looking at a masanopla tunnel."

Gahlen shook his head. "That opening's too big. They don't grow to that size."

Ehtishem crossed his arms. "That's what we said about the pa'nizofstra."

The pa'masanopla were armored, slug-like creatures that hunted by stunning their prey with a barbed, venomous, multi-branched tongue. They engulfed and digested their meals much like the Azatem pa'vikeret did.

Tinish magnified the view and said, "No slime trail."

"That doesn't mean it isn't occupied," Stig replied.

"But it's more likely to be empty."

Ehtishem considered the opening. "How close does this put us to Panca Seven-oh-one?"

Stig called up an overlay to show the mountain's mapped tunnel system. "One hundred seventy-one meters below the summit and approximately three hours behind Seven-oh-one, fra."

Six identification codes appeared at the bottom of Ehtishem's visor, Rachel's among them. He considered the map. The signals indicated Seven-oh-one was moving away from the caldera.

"Why are they heading deeper?" Gahlen muttered. "They were ordered to shelter in place."

Stig reconfigured their readout. "Motivation." The ID codes had been replaced by moving colored dots. Each dot signified organic matter, and a very large group of something was pursuing Panca Seven-oh-one. She shifted the view on all their visors. "This tunnel system meets Seven-oh-one's route in multiple locations. If we move fast, we can intercept them here, putting ourselves between them and those critters, and exit the tunnel system down here or up here for evac." Flashing green and red X's indicated the various locations she'd addressed.

Ehtishem pushed away from the console. "Gear up. We'll take this opening and defend Seven-oh-one from whatever that is," he touched the mass on the screen. He turned to Anchal, Berk, and Deniz. "Keep this location clear. If an Azatem harvester shows up don't engage. I want you to evac the area. Rendezvous only if it's safe. We'll signal you when we know which exit is clear."

He gripped each soldier's hand in turn. "Don't waste your lives, pa'nerem."

"Zant, fra," the gunner and pilots replied.

Ehtishem and Stig left the pilots' cabin, passed through the narrow passenger compartment, and dropped into the transport's belly where Mahzel was already stowing weaponry, his mech-suit humming. They stripped to their bio-suits and donned their responsive-armor mech-suits.

All three loaded ammo and clipped weapons into magnetic holsters on their hips, thighs, chests, and waists. They shouldered their packs and put on their helmets.

The green lights of his face shield readouts glowed as Ehtishem activated his mech-suit's diagnostics and bio-electrical system. His own body's energy powered it and a few laps around the deck charged the suit's kinetic power supply.

Gohra absently scratched the dog head branded on her scalp as she checked each of them, scanning their suits' diagnostics against her medcom and making sure their neural links had synced with the transport's and *Pohru-Mahrko's* computers. Behind her, Stig, the nav and recon officer, confirmed she had correct readings on their trackers.

Berk's voice came over Ehtishem's com. *"Eshmahe's* holding steady at twelve meters, fra. All scopes are clear. We await your signal."

"Alright, let's hit the ground, pa'nerem. Eyes on the sky until we clear that cave entrance, then watch the ceiling. I don't want anyone getting a shoulder ride from an uninvited guest."

He gestured to his soldiers, directing them into formation. "Huorem and Mahzel, you're on point. Stig and Gohra cover our rear. Tinish and Gahlen with me. Stay close. Stay loose. Let's get in, find our people, and get out fast."

To a chorus of "Zant, fra," Ehtishem said, "Pop and drop, Anchal."

The ship's gunner wished them good luck as he released the cargo door. "Surun-ta, pa'nerem."

A siren sounded, a red light strobed, and the transport's belly doors parted. Ehtishem and his team dropped twelve meters to the ancient lava flow, their mech-suits taking and distributing the impact with the ground as each soldier tucked, rolled, and came up armed. The transport circled, her anti-grav washing over them without effect.

Stig and Gohra leading the way, the team of Ohnenrai soldiers followed the black, ropey stone into the dark cave, their face shields automatically adjusting to the changing light and their helmlights engaging to illuminate the surroundings.

"There's your masanopla," Stig muttered as they skidded

down a steep slope and encountered a massive, armored carcass in the wide rear of the cavern. Once larger than their transport, the creature had been reduced to a hollow exoskeleton and scattered cartilage.

Ehtishem considered the remains and the cavern. Water oozed from the rocks, ran down the walls in dark streaks, and dripped from the jagged, rust-colored ceiling.

"Lunch for those pa'nizofstra?" Huorem asked, his gun and gaze sweeping the cavern.

"Nava. Something else did this," Stig replied as she toed a pile of bones, then stooped and held up a skull, its spinal column dangling from strands of desiccated fur and sinew. The skull was small and flat-faced with enormous, protruding canines. "Something almost humanoid with a nasty bite," she gestured at the bony spine. "And a long tail."

"Native to Iodiq?" Ehtishem asked.

"Not on any list I've ever seen, fra."

He frowned and immediately schooled his expression. "Let's go. Keep your motion sensors on. I don't want any of those critters sneaking up on us."

"Or dropping down on us," Mahzel added.

The clack and whine of priming shock rifles joined the thunk of loading mass ammo and all of it echoed around the cavern.

The bones clattered as Stig dropped them. She consulted her com and jerked her head toward a dark slit at the rear of the cave. "That'll take us to the magma chamber where Seven-oh-one last reported in."

"Can we bypass it for a more direct route to intercept whatever's following them?" Ehtishem asked as the team followed the nav officer.

She studied her readout then nodded. "There's a branch

just ahead. It'll be a sharp drop but will put us on the same path they took."

"If those nasty critters are following Seven-oh-one, we're looking at an ugly fight," Gohra said.

Huorem hugged the heavy-load MaRR slung across his chest. "That's why I brought Baby."

"Drax-*tu!*" The company shouted and slapped their palms against their armored thighs.

Ehtishem nodded and said, "Iristahe, va tarshta maibyo zaste."

"Frena mem nava tarshta-va," they replied. Death should fear them because none of them feared death's touch.

As they slipped through the dark opening and descended a sharp, twisting path, Ehtishem patted his MaRR. An aggressive unknown species and unusually large native creatures — they didn't bode well for what moved ahead of his small team in the dark.

Mahzel launched a fist-sized saucer drone to lead the way. It slowly rose and fell as they descended into the mountain's dark depths.

Huorem started whistling, the sound echoing in the small space.

"Hu," Ehtishem said.

"Zant, fra?"

"Stop whistling or I'll cut off your lips."

Gohra snickered.

"Zant, fra."

"If those critters aren't native, how'd they get here?" Stig's voice was loud in the ensuing silence.

"Azatem," Ehtishem said. "I'd guess they're a new form of ground troops."

Stig wasn't the only member of their team whose reply was a curse.

They found and used the rappelling lines Panca Seven-oh-one had left behind. At the bottom, they discovered piles of dead critters, an Ohnenrai com, and a MaP's jettisoned heat sink.

Huorem ran a registry check on the sink. "Checked out with a pistol registered to Dvaidasa Bindi Jorinei."

A glint of metal flashed near the wall. Gahlen stooped and retrieved a mangled shock collar. "Utha. It takes a lot of strength to tear off one of these."

Ehtishem nodded as he ran a check on the unit. "This was registered to Dasa Rivan, who was reported killed by Azatem exposure." He scanned the cramped area. "So where's his body?"

"Torn apart?" Gohra asked.

Mahzel shook his head. "No blood or body parts."

"Dragged off," Stig said.

Huorem sneered. "Who cares?"

"I do," Ehtishem replied. "Tinish, is his tracker still online?"

Tinish entered Rivan's ID into his com then shook his head. "Vital signs have flat-lined, fra."

"I didn't ask about his vitals. I asked if his tracker is active."

Tinish changed to another screen then cursed under his breath. "Zant. Active and located between Panca Seven-oh-one and that larger group."

NINETEEN

THE HAVAFNA CALDERA'S vent had proved too high to reach. Pressed for time, our group had squeezed through a crevasse, hoping it led to an exterior vent. We made steady but hasty progress upward, searching for another way out of the caverns. The critters' whoops and chittering followed us at every turn, sometimes terrifyingly close. We reached a small hall where the exit tunnel had collapsed, restructuring the charted route. Jorinei sent Romvi to check the path and its structural integrity while we waited and listened to the sound of death approaching.

"Another choke," he said via com as he jogged back toward us, his helmlight casting dancing shadows on the hall's distant ceiling and close walls.

Jorinei huffed. "Nadera, what's our other option?"

The recon officer stood beside a two-meter fissure in the floor. "There's another exit south of here and about half a day on foot."

"Wide open or well hidden?"

"Both. A sinkhole, but not easily spotted based on the available intel. They'd have to be looking for it."

Jorinei frowned. "They will be."

"Eresh," Nadera agreed and stared at the schematics on her visor for a moment, then indicated the fissure at her feet. "This chimney leads to another exit. Almost undetectable until you fall into it. It's a shorter distance, but the way's difficult."

"Worse than being eaten or turned into a Sleestak?" I asked and the soldiers muttered agreement as we gathered around the dark maw.

Fehrana jerked her chin at me. "Too difficult for the barethri?"

"That little Terran's tougher than all you ahzish put together," Nergis said, surprising me.

I shot him a grateful smile. "I'm not sure about that, but I'm motivated to keep my hide away from those critters and their pointy teeth."

Jorinei gestured toward the hall's entrance behind us. "Is there enough ordnance to blow that opening?"

Vehl studied the cave, all his slack gone. "Not the main entrance, but the chimney can be blocked easily."

Fehrana must've transmitted the schematics to the team via helmcom, but I was grateful for her description; I knew it was for my benefit. "It's a short drop into a low-ceilinged horizontal passage. We'll be crawling for a long way, then another long vertical drop. The route steps down like that, in total darkness, until we reach a steep chimney. Ascend that and we'll be out."

"It sounds horrible," I muttered.

Fehrana's faceplate turned transparent and she grinned at me. "Worse than being dinner?"

"Well, no. But that doesn't mean it'll be a party."

Vehl smirked. "You're not giving up, are you, little Terran?"

"Not a chance, cannon fodder."

Romvi said, "Critters are on the move. Time to go."

"Let's get to it, pa'nerem." Jorinei pulled a rope from her pack. "Vehl, get ready to blow this once we've cleared the bottom."

The engineer scrutinized the shaft. "Surun-ta, frei," he said and started prepping explosives.

Even as he spoke, Panca Seven-oh-one's remaining soldiers settled into the vertical opening. Their backs wedged against one wall, their feet against the other, they shimmied downward into darkness.

Fehrana gave me thick gloves and wrapped something like duct tape around my knees. When my turn came, she and Nergis fashioned a harness with Jorinei's rope and secured me. But the descent was surprisingly easy once I got over being scared shitless. At the bottom of the shaft, we started a hands-and-knees crawl in pitch black held at bay by the glow of shock rifles and helmet lights.

Someone began singing an Ohnenrai song I'd never heard about the moons of Ohnenrah. The song pushed the darkness back and all the group sang, not missing a word even when the vertical shaft behind us was blown. Someone passed me a cloth to wrap around my face against the dust.

Time became irrelevant and, soon enough, I joined in the chorus. More descending chimneys and more horizontal shafts awaited. The pattern went on for hours, but every time my chest tightened and the tunnel felt too close, one of them called encouragement and reassurances.

Finally, the interminable song was replaced by calls: "Yahz!" and "Aiya!" as Jorinei and Vehl squeezed through a narrow fissure. They'd reached the final ascent. The shaft was clear and lit by a ray of sunshine, blinding after the long darkness. Then came a long wait while each soldier ascended.

As I got closer to the opening, it became clear how deep we

were. In the same shimmying manner we'd descended, the fighters ascended a shaft that stretched the length of several football fields. Light shone down from far, far above, and I squinted to see a small face in the opening when it was my turn to climb. Once again, I was given a harness, but this time the burden was on me to walk up that wall.

"Well, shit." There was a long way ahead.

"You can do this, Barethri," Fehrana said.

"I know, I just don't want to." I looked down at my legs and said, "Okay, getaway sticks, let's escape this hell hole." The opening of the shaft was just above my head, so one of the fighters boosted me up until I caught a metal handhold someone had hammered into the stone. The rope was pulled tight from above. I exhaled and began the longest climb of my life.

By the three-quarter point my whole body was shaking. I stopped, leaned my head back against the stone shaft and breathed through my mouth to control wave after wave of nausea. I clung to one of the metal inserts and squeezed my eyes shut, as much from the sweat stinging them as from exhaustion.

A rope brushed my shoulder as it sailed past and Jorinei's voice carried up the chimney. "I'm coming up to help you, Barethri."

I opened my eyes. *No. She shouldn't be worrying about me.* "C'mon, woman, get this done," I muttered and pushed off, ignoring the nausea, ignoring the shaking, ignoring the pain in my legs and arms, the numbness in my fingers. Daylight was above and I had to escape to see the sun and Ehtishem, and Pearl, again.

"Swing low, sweet chariot, coming for to carry me home." I started singing, the rhythm moving my legs and arms, one over the other, inch by painful inch.

"Swing low, sweet chariot, coming for to carry me home. I'm sometimes up, I'm sometimes down. Coming for to carry me home?" I spat dirt. It was up my nose and in my ears, I was sure.

"But still my soul feels heavenly bound. Coming for to carry me home." My palms burned. My shoulders, back, and legs burned. Even my fingernails ached, but I kept climbing and singing.

"Swing low, sweet chariot, coming for to carry me home. Swing low, sweet chariot, coming for to carry me home." My pant leg caught on one of the metal inserts. "Shit," I muttered, tugging hard. It wouldn't let go. I leaned over, stretched, reached, cursed. Somehow I managed to make my arm and fingers long enough to get to it. I freed myself, blinked more sweat from my eyes, and resumed the hymn and the climb.

"I looked over Jordan and what did I see? Coming for to carry me home." I focused on the song, on the sunlight, on escaping that damned mountain and breathing fresh air again.

"A band of angels coming after me, coming for to carry me home."

Hands caught me beneath my arms, lifted me up, and set me on a log beside a scraggly tree. Someone pressed a canteen to my lips and I drank and drank even though the icy water made my teeth hurt. Even the bug paste Romvi offered tasted good.

Fehrana sat beside me and scanned my vitals. "I once heard the zosh say you're the toughest Terran he ever met."

"I believe it," Jorinei said.

I just nodded, too tired to smile but damned grateful to be free of the darkness.

Nadera stood on a small rise, scanning the terrain. She cursed and headed back toward us. "We've got movement, Jori."

Jorinei turned to the recon officer. "Where? Show me the scan."

"All around us," Nadera replied and the dvaidasa cursed too.

Romvi stood and shouted, "Hold your fire!" just as an Ohnenrai troop ship rose from behind the mountain's summit.

Fehrana blocked me from the worst of the ship's anti-grav wash as it circled the squad, but my guts still felt jellied.

Nadera sighted her MaRR down the hillside. "Movement at thirty-five degrees!" Jorinei and Fehrana brought their weapons up to point at a narrow vent hidden among boulders and brush.

"Hold your fire! Friendlies in the arena!" crackled over their helmcoms. "Repeat, friendlies in the arena!"

An Ohnenrai helmet appeared at the vent's opening. A soldier climbed free of the rift, followed by more.

"Utha," Fehrana murmured. "If I'd had any doubts before, now I *know* you're important."

She and the rest of Panca Seven-oh-one snapped crisp salutes as a fourth figure emerged from the rift, the dog symbol and seven stars on his mech-suit's biceps unmistakable.

"*We are one.*" The Azatem voices were back and they were loud. What fucking timing.

I stood on wobbly legs. "Ehtishem, you stubborn jerk," I said in English. "You shouldn't be here."

"I'm relieved to see you're alive, too, Pairika," he replied also in English as he reached my side and returned the soldiers' salutes. He caught my arm gently, despite his mech-suit's powerful grip, and drew me away from the soldiers and the landing transport. "Nava, nava, *Eshmahe*," he said in Ohnenrai, communicating with someone aboard the ship.

Jorinei approached and asked for orders. "Ka'ngho va'sanghem, fra?"

"Ar hamem antara *Eshmahe*, dvaidasa." Ehtishem told her to load everyone aboard the small ship as it landed nearby. She obeyed immediately, urging Panca Seven-oh-one toward the transport. Ehtishem spoke again to whoever was communicating with him via helmcom. "Mem visdi." He paused, then gave orders. "Sadayeiti adha, *Pohru-Mahrko*. Hayem angho maibyo asanghem."

I grabbed his arm. "Why are you ordering *PM* to leave?"

"Wormhole formation," he replied in English.

"Could it be *Dathusha*?" I knew it was the Azatem even as I asked that.

He shook his head. "If Ahnoru got free, he'd go to the Fisk Juncture, not Iodiq."

"We are one."

He took his helmet off and turned to his soldiers, addressing them in Ohnenrai. "I've ordered *Pohru-Mahrko* to break orbit. This is where we go separate ways, pa'nerem. The Azatem want Rachel, but our people need you. This is a direct order," his voice softened, "and a personal request." I swallowed a lump as Huorem and Mahzel reached us. "Leave Iodiq now. I've ordered Thrai Timsai to the Fisk Juncture for repairs. When *PM's* ready, you'll return here." He looked down at me. "We'll be waiting."

Huorem looked like he'd defy the order, but our gazes met and he lowered his head. Ehtishem returned their salutes as each soldier boarded *Eshmahe*. Anchal tossed several large duffels and a backpack to Ehtishem. The ship lifted off and he shouldered the bags.

I felt like I couldn't breathe as the transport receded from view. Would I die never hugging Pearl again? Nor seeing my Ohnenrai friends? Would Iodiq's Azatem-infected creatures tear Ehtishem apart the way they had Pohm and Ehnk? Would they possess him the way they had Rivan?

He pulled off his gauntlets and caught my hands. "We'll be fine, Rachel."

"You don't know that."

"I believe it."

"Is belief enough?"

He placed two fingers beneath my chin and tilted my head back. Our gazes met. "Do you trust me?"

"Unquestionably."

"Do you love me?"

"God, Ehtishem, you know I do."

"Then we have trust, love, some big guns, and a lot of explosives." He kissed me. "Let's go deep before Iodiq's creatures track you here."

We slipped into the corkscrew tunnel that had led him back to me and I saw just how heavily armed he was as he set explosives to blow the entrance then lowered his packs into the darkness. The *whoop-whoop* of Iodiq's critters inspired me not to bother with questions or doubts. We were stuck on Iodiq. As much as I thought he was an idiot for staying behind with me, I was damn glad not to be facing those nasty little shits alone.

"We're doubling back?" I asked.

"Zant. If we get above those things, we can reach the Havafna Caldera first and hole up inside *Ayan-Kanya*."

"You saw the ship."

"I did, and it was a welcome sight." He caught my gaze. "Almost as welcome as seeing you."

I swallowed. "They'll tear it apart to get to me."

"Not if I can activate her field generator." We slid down and emerged into a narrow, twisting tunnel with a high ceiling and smooth walls. "Can you jog?"

"If it's run or be caught by Sleestaks, I'm running my ass off, Stranger."

"Good. Later you can tell me what Sleestaks are."

Ehtishem picked up the pace. His jog meant I *was* running. But that was just fine because a familiar and sickening whine had followed us into the tunnel — Azatem reapers.

He triggered the explosives to seal the entrance and the whine disappeared. "*Pohru-Mahrko* will handle the pa'vikeret from orbit before she leaves for Fisk," Ehtishem said over his shoulder.

"Then why are we running?" I panted. Damn him for being so fit.

The path split and he stopped. "Because we don't want to be close to the surface when the orbital bombardment begins." He faced one direction and inhaled, then the other and did the same thing. "Stay here. I'll be back." He took the left-hand path and disappeared around a sharp bend, leaving me in total darkness.

"Oh, seriously? This sucks." There wasn't even any bioluminescence. I willed my heart to stop trying to pound its way out of my chest as I leaned against cold stone. I prayed *Eshmahe* had escaped the Azatem and Iodiq, hoped *Pohru-Mahrko* wasn't engaged in a battle she was too crippled to win. "Please keep them safe," I said to the darkness. My words echoed back, as if someone, somewhere was thinking the same for Ehtishem and me.

The Azatem decided to chime in. "*We are one.*"

"Shut up," I muttered and stared into the dark.

Finally, a faint glow lit the distant path and boots scraped dirt. He turned the corner. I exhaled a breath I didn't know I'd been holding. But he shook his head as he passed me. "Rock fall has it completely blocked." He headed down the other path, once again plunging me into darkness.

This time my thoughts strayed to Pearl. I'd worked so hard to keep worry, fear, and grief at bay. Ahnoru and Sree were with her. Audie was protecting her. I had to have faith that she was alright.

"Momma?"

I covered my mouth to stifle a sob. I swore I could hear her in my mind, just like I heard the Azatem.

"Momma, I'm scared."

"Oh, god." I slid down the wall to crouch, leaned my head back, and smacked it hard on the wall. "Ouch. Shit!" I swallowed a sob.

"Are you alright?" Ehtishem emerged with the light.

"Nava," I whispered.

"You will be." He pulled me up. "You're still the strongest woman I know."

I shook my head. "I don't feel strong. I feel tired and scared and worried."

"Strong doesn't mean unfeeling. You're still merely Terran."

I would've laughed if I'd had any humor left in me. "But Pearl. Ehtishem, she needs me, I know it. I should go to her."

"You will, Pairika, when we're ready to deploy. *Pohru-Mahrko* will return. Then we'll find *Maso*. We'll free *Dathusha*. We'll rescue Pearl."

"But—"

"Trust me." He held my gaze. "Please."

All I could do was nod. He wiped the tears from my cheeks, his hands still so gentle, despite his mech-suit's heavy gauntlets. "Ready?"

"Zant."

"Ash-ush. The path slopes steeply downward and turns back on itself, but the air remains fresh. We'll have to cross water further down."

I blew a stray strand of hair out of my face. "Lead the way."

"Steep was an understatement," I muttered as I clung to his back.

"At least it's vertical."

"Not all of it was and you damn-well know it. Those horizontal faces were terrifying." We reached the bottom and I unbuckled the straps holding me against him as the saucer probe he'd deployed hovered above our heads.

"Rachel." He turned and caught my waist. "I won't leave you to face the Azatem alone. I promise you that." He lifted me off the ground and crushed me to him. "I promise."

I wrapped my arms around his broad, armored shoulders and we held onto each other. Our lives were so intertwined that it no longer mattered where one of us ended and the other began. "Mem kam-va, Ehtishem."

His grip tightened. "I love you, too," he replied in English.

But as I relaxed against him, let serenity fill me for a brief moment, the distant excited calls of the critters pulled me back and made us look upward as one. They'd found our trail and wouldn't be slowed by the descent into darkness.

He let me go and considered the cave diagram on his helmet's visor then triggered his helmlight and shined it into a narrow tunnel. "If we follow that passage, we'll come to water. Maybe crossing it will slow them."

We took the route to a stream, fording the middle of it until we reached a low opening. The echoing rush of water drowned out the critters' calls.

"The stream's flowing freely, so I doubt this narrows, but I'm going to check." Ehtishem handed his MaP to me and disappeared under the water. That part of the cave was rich with glowing blue larvae and I stared at the walls and ceiling, more of that amazing underground starscape. The glow of his helmlight shimmered and distorted as he returned. "The ceiling is low and you'll be underwater for a few feet. It opens to a low cave, but that leads to a wide cavern. It's tight, but should be comfortable for you."

"Okay." I handed him the pistol and stepped toward the stream, but a familiar *whoop-whoop* and chittering filled the cave. "Dammit all to hell."

Ehtishem pushed me at the cave mouth. "Go."

I didn't need more encouragement. I sucked a deep breath and sank into the frigid water. With his hand against my back, I pulled forward hand-over-hand through the opening. Pain cramped my fingers from the icy water. *Cold is nothing. I've had plenty of ice baths.* We emerged from the duck-under and I could almost stand.

"Keep going."

I didn't argue with the command in his voice and the muted chatter and calls coming from the adjoining cave. I came into the wide cavern he'd promised, but Ehtishem had stopped at the mouth.

"Keep moving back." He tore open a package and quickly kneaded it — the same explosives Panca Seven-oh-one had used. I climbed out of the water and moved away from the opening, hoping he'd given himself enough time to join me.

Ehtishem charged out of the dark, a flash and rumble behind him. The heat and shockwave hit me, but there wasn't time to react as he turned and fired his MaP at two moving points of light — glowing eyes. There was a shriek, echoed by others. Something scuttled across the ceiling. Ehtishem fired. Another shriek followed. Something caught my arm, something dry but sticky. Above me loomed huge yellow eyes and an almost-human face. I screamed. It echoed me, its mouth wide, eyes emotionless. It lifted me off the floor.

"Ehtishem!"

"I can't get a shot," he replied, his voice maddeningly calm. "Use your knife."

I was way ahead of him and buried a blade in the thing's skull. The sticky bastard howled and dropped me. Ehtishem's MaP flashed. The creature flew backward into oblivion as I hit the cave floor. It knocked the wind out of me. Sharp pain stabbed through my ribs. I'd landed on jagged rocks. I curled into a ball, unable to breathe or talk, trying not to puke. He stood over me, sweeping the cave with his helmlight and tracers as he obliterated any critters that had survived the explosion.

"Are you conscious?"

"Fuck," I gasped.

"Can you stand?"

"Fuck you."

"Later." Ehtishem inspected one of the twitching attackers then picked me up and moved into the cavern.

I didn't protest being toted around. Everything hurt too much and the monkey-lizard-man-whatever-the-hell-that-was had freaked me out. "Are they Azatem ground forces?" I wheezed out when Ehtishem stopped hiking and set me down.

"Must be. There's no record of anything like them on Iodiq. Any new injuries?"

"Bruised ribs. Maybe cracked. Damned rocks."

He caught my shaking hands between his. "You did well. Kept calm."

"Bullshit. I screamed my damn head off."

"I'd scream too if some big-eyed critter yanked me off the ground."

I snorted and winced. "Oh, shit. Don't make me laugh. It hurts."

"Sorry." He kissed my forehead. "But laughing's good."

After we sat in silence for a few minutes, he said, "We need to keep moving. Can you walk or should I carry you?"

The shortness of breath had eased. "I think I can make it on my own two feet. My ribs still hurt like hell, but I'm pretty sure nothing's broken."

"Ash-ush."

I stood with a groan, hating every little movement. "Get us out of here, Zosh."

He consulted his map, scanned the cavern, and grabbed my hand. "This way, Barethri."

TWENTY

EHTISHEM FOUND a cave overlooking a long valley. The drop from its opening was sheer and at least a hundred meters to the ground.

Rachel gazed out from its mouth. The valley floor stretched below fading into the hazy distance, its brown, wind-scoured desolation broken by murky, rust-rimmed pools. Vapors rose and gray-green sludge bubbled. "Jesus. This side of Iodiq looks like the kind of place where life crawled out of the muck, stood, and roared, 'Where's my breakfast?'"

He grunted. "An adequate description. Iodiq's natives aren't soft and cuddly, even less so with Azatem modifications." He unrolled a thin, thermal blanket and draped it around her shoulders. "Sit."

She did, slowly and with a groan. She wrinkled her nose. "Stinks too, like overcooked eggs."

He dropped explosives into the chimney they'd ascended to reach their haven. A distant explosion, the floor shifting, and a cloud of dust meant the pursuing horde wouldn't gain access that way. "Time to eat and rest," he said.

Rachel stretched her calves. "I'm not sure how much more of this Bucky McGillicuddy and Kicks McGee can take."

"Who?"

"My legs."

"You named your legs?"

Rachel snorted, winced, and rubbed her ribcage. "Yeah. It's a Terran thing."

"Huh." He handed her a canteen and unpacked another thermal blanket, some tablets, and a round canister. "Drink." He still didn't quite understand Terran humor.

"Way ahead of you." She tipped the canteen and drank deeply, lowered it, and watched as he replenished ammo on his belt and kit.

With his weapons reset, he unscrewed the lid from a canister, upended it, and removed two brownish, dry disks, then resealed the container. He passed her one and swigged water from the canteen.

"Mmm, bug pucks. My *favorite*." Ehtishem's lack of expression must've conveyed his lack of amusement because she laughed, despite her sore ribs.

"Why am I always pushing you to eat?" he asked as her humor died.

She considered the hard brown cake. "Two reasons." She sniffed it and frowned. "Number One: This is far less appealing than gnawing off my own flesh. Number Two: More than half the times that we've sat down to a meal, either you've been a dick or offered me something that smelled like dirt."

"Ah. So I'm responsible?"

"Of course. I'm too perfect to be the root of all this trouble." She gnawed at the cake.

"Well, you have to admit they taste slightly better than they smell." He tore his cake in half and popped a piece into his mouth. He chewed and watched her struggle to tear off a chunk with her teeth. "Here." He pulled a small tin cup from his pack and poured water into it. "Let it soften."

She dipped the cake in the water. "You must have mastodon jaws."

He gave her a broad, toothy grin.

She matched it. "How can you be so relaxed? You're not like this shipboard."

He offered her the canteen. "I only have two people to worry about right now. There's no more I can do to help *Pohru-Mahrko* or *Dathusha*, so they're not my focus. I have a different type of concern up there," he pointed heavenward. "There's you and Pearl and eight million other lives counting on my decisions. Here my mission is simple: Keep you alive and the Azatem away."

She stared at him and the hunger in her eyes had nothing to do with food. "What is it about you that makes me want to screw you every time we're stuck on the side of a mountain?"

Ehtishem paused in eating, the rest of his protein disk halfway to his mouth. He flashed her another grin then said, "Eat. Drink. Rest. As tempting as *screwing* sounds, you're exhausted and there's not much time for you to recover before the critters figure out how to reach us. We need to stay several steps ahead of them if we're going to get back to *Ayan-Kanya*."

Rachel tore off some of the softened cake with her teeth. Water made it gummy. "Mmm, tastes like starvation."

He sat beside her and wrapped his arm around her shoulders. "We could try roasting one of those critters."

"Oh, barf." She shivered. "And give up these delicious insect steaks? Don't be ridiculous." She saluted him with her dinner and added, "This is some real gourmet shit."

He uncapped another canteen and dropped a purification tablet into it. "I'm glad you approve. We're having the same thing tomorrow. For every meal."

She rested her cheek against his armored biceps. "How long do you think we'll be stranded?"

"Months."

She jerked straight, winced, and hissed at the pain of it. "*Months?*"

Ehtishem capped the canteen, gave it a good shake, then tossed it back into his duffel and turned his head to kiss her temple. "Timsai needs time to reach a safe port, gather materials for repairs, and fix the ship. She can't withstand another battle like that last one. *Maso*'s weapons outclass *Pohru-Mahrko*'s significantly."

She eyed the cave entrance. "How will we stay safe? The Azatem know where I am. How the hell are we gonna keep ahead of all those critters and reapers and harvesters?"

"I told you. We'll gain access to *Ayan-Kanya*. I have her activation codes. She'll have enough power to keep us warm during the winter and hold the critters at bay until we're rescued."

Darkness slowly consumed the world beyond the cave's mouth.

"Why would your people return for us?" Her voice sounded small.

"Because Timsai is my very stubborn friend. He'll send in a small rescue squad and cover them with an excessively-large protective force."

"It's good that he'll return for you, but this is why I exist."

"He'll return for us." The words came from him with iron-clad conviction.

"That goes against the plan and the survival of your people." She tore another chunk from the disk.

"You're vital to the survival of my people. We'd be fools to assume the Azatem aboard *Maso* are the last of their kind. You're the only weapon we have against them. Leaving you behind risks everything. The Ohnenrai still need you. Timsai knows that."

"I wouldn't come back, if I were him."

"You're not and he will. I know my oldest friend. He'll return." He scooped her onto his lap. "You can always trust Timsai to do what's best and right for the Ohnenrai, and your continued survival among us is just that, best and right."

"How long have you known him?"

"We trained together from boyhood."

"One of the survivors of schooling with you?"

Ehtishem nodded. "He's more than capable of doling out bruises."

"I'm sure. Otherwise you wouldn't have made him the thrai." His hand rested atop her stomach and she fingered his scarred knuckles. He laced his fingers with hers, marveling at the white crescents of her nails, each like a sliver of moon. "I can't figure him out," she murmured.

"Is there something to figure out?"

"Well, yeah. I see him watching me. I'm not sure he approves of me being with you."

"Why do you think that?"

"He's so damned cordial. I can't relax around him. I feel like he's scrutinizing me, but not the way your mother does. It's different with Timsai." She shrugged. "I dunno. Hard to explain."

He leaned back to get a good look at her. She blushed under the directness of his gaze. He loved the way her cheeks turned rosy. "Timsai's jealous," he said.

Her green eyes widened. "Jealous? Of what?"

"You."

She squinted at him, confused. "Me. What the hell does Timsai have to be jealous about? I don't get it."

He smirked. "Frena dam asmanaca."

"I am not stupid as stone, you big jerk." She slapped his arm, but he only laughed.

It felt good to laugh. "So you *were* listening to my conversation with Sree."

She gawked. "You knew?"

"Of course. And you were supposed to be in your quarters when we were talking." His arms tightened around her. "Clearly, you weren't."

"Nope. I was eavesdropping." After a moment, she continued, "Timsai's jealous. Of *me*?" She shook her head. "The only things I have that he doesn't are a child, a vagina, and you."

"He's never expressed much interest in having a child or a vagina."

Rachel straightened, evidently surprised, and Ehtishem began to laugh again as she stared. "Wait, wait," she said. "I didn't know he's gay."

He sobered. "There's no 'gay' or 'straight' among the Ohnenrai. We want whomever we want. Timsai prefers male companionship and is attracted to me." Ehtishem rested his chin on her shoulder and murmured, "I prefer females. Those are the facts."

They were quiet for a moment. "It's really that simple?" she asked.

"Zant. Why wouldn't it be?"

"Poor Timsai."

"Why?"

"To be so close to the person he desires and know he'll never have you. That must be painful."

Ehtishem shrugged. "He has my friendship, my respect, and my loyalty. That's more than most Ohnenrai get from me. Timsai has many close companions. He isn't lonely."

She relaxed into his armored embrace. "How did a people

who can be so accepting spawn the Purist movement and kill so many of my people?"

He wished he could feel her warmth through his armor. "Remember that Ohnenrai creation legend I told you, the one that says we're gods of war?"

"Yeah?"

"It also says all other beings exist only to enable our evolution into Yazadami."

"What's that?"

"The supreme being responsible for the universe's creation, transformation, and destruction."

She turned her head to peer at him. "A cyclical god? I didn't know the Ohnenrai had one of those."

"Don't all cultures?"

"Seems like it." She turned back and stared out the cave mouth. He followed her gaze. The sky was full of unfamiliar stars. "And they make it an excuse to do horrible things to other people."

"Timsai respects you. He says you're good for me." Ehtishem slid his fingers through her short hair, pleased when she shivered under his gentle touch.

"That's what Pearl always said about you." She looked down and swallowed, stiffening at the emotions that came with thoughts of her missing daughter.

He rested his chin atop her head and tightened his grip, hoping to calm her turmoil. "I am happy when I'm with you, Rachel. Happy and myself. I've never had that with anyone else." She gentled him in a way no other person did.

But the pain of not knowing what was happening to her little girl wouldn't be quelled. She started to tremble. "You have to let me go," she whispered.

"Nava." His arms tightened around her as if to hold her back from what she was about to say.

"She's not here." Rachel gestured around the cave, her voice rough and tight. "But she's never *not* here." She touched her chest. Her sadness and desperation tore into him. There was no vairim where she was concerned anymore. He felt everything she did. Her pain, her grief, her fear, her guilt. Her anger.

She pulled against his grip. "Is Pearl alive or dead? Is she afraid? Is she suffering? Not knowing what's happened to her has trapped me in a psychological prison. I can't move forward until I do everything possible to put this horrible not-knowing behind me. And if she's gone, I have to avenge her, Ehtishem. I need revenge, like I need to breathe."

He didn't loosen his hold. "I feel your suffering. I can't block your emotions, Pairika. You've torn down those walls. And I share that torture of not knowing about Pearl and everyone else aboard *Dathusha*. But I'm asking you to endure that pain with me a little longer. We're so close to being ready." He closed his eyes, pressed his lips to her hair. "I can't lose you to the Azatem, too."

"I know. But how can I wait? When I think about sitting here on my ass doing nothing to save Pearl, to protect her and destroy them, it makes me so angry." She broke away from him and stood. "I'm pissed off, Ehtishem. At the Azatem. At having to wait." Silent tears streaked her face. Her voice broke when she added, "I'm pissed off at you." She twisted her fingers together. "And I feel guilty about being angry with you because I know you're in an impossible position. I know you're suffering, too. But I-I can't help it."

He held her gaze, didn't flinch away from that anger. "I understand. You have many reasons to rage at me and your situation. I'd rather you rage than give up and collapse under despair." He'd seen that on Terra. Logan's stepmother had been so broken by hopelessness that she couldn't react, and it had killed her. She'd died a horrible, fiery death. He couldn't stomach the idea of Rachel being that helpless, that catatonic.

But she did collapse, slumping down against him again, a flower wilting in winter's cold darkness. "The only hope I cling to is the hope of getting aboard *Maso*, finding Pearl alive, and destroying them. Every goddamn one of them. It's hope from vengeance, and that's a mean thing, Ehtishem. It's a kind of hope that rots you from the inside out."

He pulled her close, wanting to comfort her, ease her suffering, lessen her pain and anger.

"I was just beginning to feel like my world had become a stable place. This yanked the foundation out from under me. I feel like I'm falling and there's no bottom. I feel like I'll be falling forever unless I do this." She gripped his hands, unexpectedly tight. "Please." She searched his face. "Let me go."

"What you're asking, Rachel." He shook his head. "I don't know if I can do it. The thought of leaving you behind twists me up inside."

"If you love me, you'll do this for me."

He looked away. "Don't."

Her nails dug into his flesh, but he didn't mind the pain. "I need to know one of us lives."

A distant screech and a series of chittering barks carried into the cave — the sounds of something dying and something dining. She shivered.

Once again she ran her fingers over his knuckles, crisscrossing the fine lines and fat scars that marred his brown skin. Ehtishem was a warrior, born and bred to be a conqueror. And he'd never felt so helpless. He swallowed.

"After Ahremena told us about the genetic drive compelling me to protect you, I thought about my feelings for you." He turned his hand over and she traced the lines on his broad palm. "Were they only hormones and chemical markers?" He closed his hand to encase hers. "Nava, Rahzhel. Nava. I love you. I loved you the moment I first saw you, the day you were born and your mother placed you in my arms. You were tiny and fierce and I loved you more than I thought I could ever love anything or anyone. That's a kind of love I've never felt for anyone else. And you don't know how long and hard I searched for you after Isphahan destroyed everything. How much it kills me to know you've suffered and still suffer." He lowered his head until it rested against hers. "You gave everyone hope. The only healthy infant after decades of trying to develop an Azatem Code carrier. You don't know what a miracle you are."

"And you were created to protect me."

"Zant. But I've always loved you."

"Why? I'm the queen of messed up emotions. I hear aliens talking in my head. I'm a weapon, Ehtishem. A set-it-and-forget-it."

"Not to me."

"But—"

"*Nava.*" He held her against him. "I would destroy the universe to keep you safe." He pressed his lips to her hair. "My feelings for you aren't a genetic flaw. They aren't weaknesses, no matter what Ahremena said. You're my strength, Rachel. You're my purpose."

TWENTY-ONE

I LAY atop Ehtishem's chest, listening to the screeches and whistles of Iodiq's natives as they greeted the dawn. He was studying the cave's ceiling. The rising sun's orange glow flared like fire in his dark eyes. It lit the strong lines of his cheekbones and jaw, the soft curves of his full lips and broad nose.

His gaze drifted to my face. He trailed his finger from my temple to my jaw tracing the mahle vine that twined and twisted across my skin and marked me as his to protect. The tattoo had kept me safe when he'd needed every safety measure he legally could get, but he'd never treated me as anything less than his equal. Ehtishem cradled my head with his hands and kissed me. He didn't care that I heard our enemy in my mind. He didn't care that I got emotional and flew off the handle, that I was more than a little weird, even for a Terran.

"I have something for you." He reached for one of his bags, searched a pocket, and pulled out the wooden rose puzzle box.

"Oh!" I sat up. "You finished carving it."

His lips twitched into a smile. He captured my hand and placed the box on my palm. He'd completed it with the central bud. I fingered the smooth, polished petals. Every cut was precise, every curve was perfect. "It's beautiful and amazing and...and the nicest gift I've ever received." I swallowed a lump. He was so damn good to me.

He studied my face. "When did you last receive a gift from a man?"

"Never." I looked away from the intensity of his gaze and mumbled, "Except presents from my dad when I was a kid."

"You're supposed to open it." Keeping me on his lap, he sat up and took the box. "Slide this petal to unlock the puzzle." He moved the last piece — a curling petal — until the central bud popped up with a little click. Ehtishem then twisted the entire flower until the central bud dropped back into place. Then he slid the first petal home, lifted the rose up and off the box, and presented the inner portion to me.

Pale-blue silk lined the inside and nestled within was a band of stardust — a ring seemingly carved from the heart of the Milky Way. There was no other way to describe it. A perfectly round ring of sparkling microscopic stones reflecting color and light from every angle. No metal encased them. Rather the precision of every cut and the tension of each placement held them together, like gravity locks the moon, the Earth, and the sun.

My breath caught. It was the most beautiful thing I'd ever seen.

He made a little noise in the back of his throat and put the lid aside. He lifted the ring from its bed, captured my left hand, and slid the band onto my ring finger.

I stared, hypnotized by the ring's fire. Never in my wildest dreams had I imagined ever receiving such a gift.

He gave my hand a little shake and I looked back at him. There was a mischievous glint in his eye, a little smirk curving his lips. "You said you wanted one in case I got my big carcass killed in some stupid battle."

I swallowed, too stunned to think. "Ehtishem, I-I-I don't know what to say."

"I don't want you to be my property, Pairika. I want you to be my partner, my equal."

I looked at the sparkling ring and murmured, "How can I accept this?" I met his gaze, "Look at where we are."

I started to take the ring off, but his hand on mine stopped me. "Our circumstances don't matter. I'm thinking about our future. I love you and I want you to be my wife."

"I know, but—" I sighed.

"What?"

"You love me so much that you won't give me up, no matter how much that hurts both of us."

He ran his fingers through my hair. "Giving you up goes against logic, but even worse, it tears against every fiber of my being. I can't imagine my life without you."

The struggle, guilt, regret showed in his eyes and through his touch. He said there was no vairim where I was concerned; that went both ways now. I felt his anguish, like a knife in the ribs, and it only sharpened my own pain.

Ehtishem would not abandon me to the Azatem. He truly believed we'd destroy those monsters together or not at all. But what if he was wrong and we all died? As much as he couldn't stand to lose me, I couldn't stomach the thought of a universe in which he no longer existed.

"That ring is my promise to you, Rachel. I won't stop until the Azatem are gone and you're safe."

He brought his lips to mine, a slow, deep kiss. I pressed against him, and longing sparked, spread, heated me. "Get that mech-suit off before those critters find us," I said against his mouth.

"Zant, frei." He was all too willing to oblige. Ehtishem's hands were on my breasts, his tongue was in my mouth. I fumbled with the catches on his armor and cursed beneath my breath. I needed him inside me now and the damned suit was in the way.

He stopped my fingers, placed them against a hinge, murmured, "Press here." I did and the joints separated, a smart, simple design.

"Easy access," I said against his mouth.

He smiled. "You like that?"

"Mm-hmm. I'm developing a new appreciation for Ohnenrai design and engineering."

"Me too."

This time I took control of our lovemaking, sped and slowed him, demanded his fingers, his tongue, his mouth. He drove me beyond sensibility until there was only the feel of his body beneath me. And for a little while I didn't care if the whole world burned as long as he could remain inside me until the end.

After we made love, we lay between the thermal blankets, me atop him because Ehtishem wouldn't let me sleep on stone; he wouldn't let me be cold or lonely. He idly twisted one of my short curls around his finger and studied my face. His finger stopped. He held my gaze, unblinking, deciding, weighing his words.

"I know that look," I said. "It means there's something on your mind."

He slowly nodded. "Information I've kept from you because Ahremena kept it from me."

Shit. "Nothing good ever comes after a sentence like that." I swallowed. "O-kaaay. What is it?"

"You're a clone, Rachel. The original Terran you're created from was aboard the Azatem harvester my father's great-grandfather destroyed in Ohnenrai orbit. She was captured and brought aboard *Pohru-Mahrko*, but she died soon afterward. The woman had a high level of Azatem bacterial DNA in her genome. That's what Ohnenrai Genetics isolated and manipulated to create your functional Azatem Code. It's the thing that differentiates you."

"I'm...not human?"

"You are one hundred percent human."

"We are one."

I ignored them. "Human but a clone," I said and pushed upright. "But I look like my mother. I have her wavy brunette hair and her pale skin. And I'm tall like my father and have his Dutch nose."

"Your parents looked like you, Pairika, not the other way around." He touched my nose and murmured, "I always wondered why Ahremena chose men and women who looked similar." He booped my nose. "I assumed it had to do with a specific set of genetics. And I was right but for the wrong reasons."

"But you said my parents' DNA was used to create me. You said my mother lost seven fetuses before me."

"She did. Of that I'm certain. Your parents and I were told their DNA was the basis for each fetus. Apparently, Ahremena and Ohnenrai Genetics lied."

"Why?" I pulled my knees up and hugged them. "Why hide that from everyone?"

"To protect their research, she claimed. Maybe that's true. Maybe not. She's dead, so we'll never know." He folded his hands behind his head. "Does it matter?"

"That she hid it? I don't know." I picked a scab bridging the back of my left knuckles. "It matters that I'm not who I always thought I was." I looked up. "If I'm not my parents' daughter, who am I?"

He considered the question, then asked one of his own. "Why does DNA make a difference? Why *aren't* you their child?"

I rested my chin on my knees and contemplated that. "My mother never took me to see a pediatrician. She was a doctor and didn't need to consult anyone else about my health. That's what she told me anyway. Now I wonder if she was hiding this." Blood welled along the line of the scab. I frowned; I knew better than to open a wound. "Did she know I was cloned? Did my dad?"

"I don't know."

"A clone. I remember when rich people were cloning their favorite pets," I muttered. "That was right before you guys showed up on Terra."

"We've been visiting Terra for centuries."

"You know what I mean." I stretched out at his side, but Ehtishem lifted me to lay atop him again.

"What is family? I thought I knew." I drew circles on his muscular shoulder. Sunlight sparkled off the ring. "Were my parents even my parents? Can I call them that?"

He caught my hand. "Zant. You know exactly what makes up a family and you taught me. It's why I executed Ahremena."

"Wait. What?" I pushed up. "You killed your mother? Why?"

"She wasn't my mother, she only claimed the title. You showed me what a mother is to a child. You're firm but supportive, encouraging Pearl to challenge herself and be independent. You trust her enough to let her make mistakes. You hold her to a high standard and yourself to a higher one. You care enough to discipline her but with moderation. You show her that it's acceptable to apologize when you make mistakes, that making mistakes is a normal part of life and learning. And you comfort her. You sacrificed whatever was necessary to guarantee her health and security."

"But those are just what parents do, Ehtishem. None of that's unusual."

"It is for an Ohnenran — aside from discipline — and it's inconceivable for Ahremena. I didn't learn she and Zainabahn had contributed the majority of my DNA until I was seven years old." He shook his head. "I was in the training center with Timsai and three other trainees when she strode in, sat, and observed. The tahkaesha asked if she required assistance. I'll never forget her reply: 'Nava. I've come to assess what's mine.' Then she summoned me forward and directed me to 'prove' I was worth the trouble I'd caused."

"What did you do?"

"Threatened her life."

"Oh." I pressed my cheek to his chest. "She should've left you alone."

His short laugh rumbled through my ear. "Eresh. Maybe she'd still be alive."

I peered at him. "But her bitchiness isn't a reason to kill her."

"Of course not." He squinted in the sunlight. "I executed her because she disobeyed clear and direct orders to protect you. Sarem Mahlei decided she knew military strategy better than I did and that I was her greatest mistake, a disappointment after all. She used threats to bend Judilei, Rivan, and Kruhz to her will. My mother is the reason you're on Iodiq. And her actions got our soldiers killed and our civilians captured. She endangered the survival of all the Ohnenrai."

"Oh," I repeated. I should've been shocked, but I couldn't muster any emotions over her treason or her death.

He studied me. "Does her execution upset you?"

I sucked the blood off my torn knuckles. "Apparently not. Maybe I'm too numb to be surprised or upset by anything you throw at me. Is that weird?"

"I don't know. And, if it is, I don't mind." Ehtishem hugged me. "I love you no matter how weird you are."

I laughed. "Now, you sound like a Terran."

He smiled. "That's not such a bad thing. Some of my favorite people are Terran."

"And some of mine are Ohnenrai."

We fell silent again for a while. Squawks, squeals, and wild calls drifted up from the valley floor. Iodiq was awake and her natives wanted breakfast. My aching body wanted more sleep, but my scrambled brain refused to rest. Way too many questions caromed around inside it.

"You saw my birth?"

He shook his head. "I wasn't in the room."

"But you held me?" It seemed so weird. He wasn't that much older than me. Or was he? Wormhole travel had distorted the Ohnenrai timeline. Ehtishem was twelve years older than his peers because he'd been left behind on Earth. But his people had witnessed historical events on my world that I'd only read about in books. It was too much for me to grasp and put into perspective. Too many wormhole jumps. Too much time distortion.

"We came and went from Terran orbit. Decades aboard *Dathusha* were centuries for Terrans."

"And during one of your stops, my mother came aboard and birthed me."

"Zant. And she placed you in my arms." He brushed my

hair off my forehead. "A tiny creature with the potential to save both our worlds."

"'And though she be but little, she is fierce.'"

"*A Midsummer Night's Dream* by William Shakespeare. Your parents introduced me to the Bard." He twisted my hair around his finger again. "I like that play. It's absurd, but I enjoy it."

"*We are one.*"

I sighed. "Absurd like my life."

"I'd assess it as unpredictable more than absurd."

"Ironic without being amusing." He said nothing and I added, "Bittersweet, too." To that, Ehtishem just nodded and tightened his arms around me.

TWENTY-TWO

EHTISHEM LAY with Rachel stretched out atop him. Arms around her, he reveled in the weight of her body on his, the sweet smell of her skin, the soft tickle of her short brunette curls against his neck. He didn't sleep in the field. Long before his dozen years on Terra, he'd learned to doze in combat and awaken instantly, alert and battle-ready. But she slept deeply, her breathing slow, her muscles lax. Though the sun was high, he was loath to wake her. She'd pushed herself hard to keep up with Panca Seven-oh-one.

He pressed his lips to the top of her head and closed his eyes. He couldn't lose her. He *wouldn't*. There'd been a time when the survival of the Ohnenrai had been the impetus driving his life. That had ceased to matter the day he'd stood in the woods on Terra, watching as she'd scrubbed violence and violation from her skin.

He wanted only to protect her. Nothing else mattered. "Utha." His grip tightened.

She murmured, turned her head, and blinked bleary green

eyes at him. "What's wrong?" she asked, her voice thick with sleep.

"Nothing. Go back to sleep."

She closed her eyes. "You're a terrible liar."

He grunted.

She raised her head and studied him. "Worrying about things won't fix them. And we haven't lost all hope. There's still a weapon."

"I can't let the Azatem have you, Pairika. There must be a way to wield that weapon without destroying you." He pressed his palms against his eyelids and muttered, "I just need to think of it."

"I'm not really into the whole idea either, but I'd rather try and fail than *not* try and fail anyway."

He lowered his hands to rest them on her hips. "I've been trying and failing all my life."

"Oh." Rachel chewed the inside of her cheek then gave him a fake smile. "Well, you do it so well, why stop now?"

He blew out a breath, then laughed. "You have a tip," he said in English.

"A tip?" She looked puzzled. "Oh, no, a *point*, Ehtishem. I have a *point*."

He returned to speaking Ohnenrai. "Zant, that's what I meant. American slang still confounds me."

Rachel's humor disappeared. "If Pearl's alive, promise you'll take her back to *Pohru-Mahrko* and raise her. She may never forgive me."

"Especially if this doesn't work," he said. They laughed, but the sound was humorless. "I promise." He sat up, lifted her off him, and stood. "But there must be another way," he repeated.

"It's why I was created. A weapon that's been generations in the making. But, damn, it'll suck if it fails and I croak for nothing."

"Generations in the making?" He cocked his head, thinking. "That could work."

Her eyes narrowed. "What could?"

He talked as he donned his bio-suit and armor. "The Azatem won't recognize you as a threat. Which means you can board their ship without being stopped."

"Yeah. And?" She shrugged into her bio-suit, too.

"Generations," he repeated. "My father's great-grandfather succeeded in blowing up a harvester, but he failed to stop *Maso-Vohu*. Not because he couldn't, but because he didn't know to wait and target that ship. We do and we can." The parts of his mech-suit snapped together and whined as they connected to his bio-suit and routed power through all their systems.

Rachel paused in lacing her boots. She looked up, realization in her eyes. "You want me to plant a bomb aboard *Maso*?"

"Zant." When she didn't jump up and down and clap her hands, he added, "And escape before it explodes."

"Ohhh. I like that idea better."

"I hope."

"Annnd you ruined it." She swallowed and started chewing the inside of her cheek again.

He hated seeing the return of that self-destructive habit. "Stop that."

"Stop what?"

"Hurting yourself." He crouched and took her hands. "I can't guarantee you'll survive, Pairika. I can't guarantee any of this will work. But better to try and fail—"

"Than not try at all and fail anyway. Yeah, I hate it when my words come back to haunt me. And so damn quickly this time."

Ehtishem began to say something, but an unnatural silence had replaced Iodiq's cacophony and his instinct for danger shut him up. He pressed a finger to his own lips. She nodded and remained silent and still as he crept toward the mouth of the cave. A quick glance told him the story and it didn't have a happy ending. Critters climbed up and skittered down the sheer cliff toward their location.

"Utha." He jerked back as a shadow winked between him and the sun and a blast of air kicked up enough dust to obscure the dim cave.

"Shit!" Rachel grabbed the back of his mech-suit and yanked him sideways as the massive iridescent claw of an anizofstra scraped the cave floor at Ehtishem's feet.

"Go-go-go," he whispered, grabbing his packs and guns. He herded her toward the back of the cave.

Zhek. Why hadn't he checked their one vulnerable point sooner? *Stupid and sloppy.* He needed to be better than this if he was going to keep them both alive.

The silence of the creeping Azatem critters ended. They chittered and screeched as Iodiq's enormous predator attacked them.

"That anizofstra's looking for breakfast. It'll keep the critters distracted for a little while," he said.

"We're trapped?"

"Nava." He pointed toward a hole in the cave ceiling. "We go up."

"How the hell are we gonna do that?"

"I'll boost you up. Then I'll follow."

She stared at the dark narrow opening. "You're shitting me, right?"

"That's disgusting and impossible. And one of the worst Terran sayings. Also, nava, I'm not. There are handholds. Once you get your body into the chimney, you can shimmy up using your legs and your back. I'll stay behind and enjoy the view."

"Fuckity-fuck-fuck-fuck," Rachel muttered as he boosted her into the darkness.

"Climb."

"I am, trust me. I can climb and cuss at the same time, you know." Whooping and chittering echoed into the cave. The critters had provided the anizofstra with an ample breakfast, but still more of them had survived the attack. "Jeez Louise. Did those little bastards multiply overnight?"

"Apparently. Or more were dropped by pa'vikeret." He pulled a MaP from the holster on his left thigh and passed it up to her. "Use this to clear the way ahead of you. Please don't shoot downward. I'll cover our rear."

"Gotcha." She holstered it. "So far I don't hear anything above."

Ehtishem couldn't say the same for what was happening below. He wedged his feet against the rocks on opposite sides of the chute, pulled his other MaP, and flicked off the safety. "Keep going." There was barely enough room for him to fit in the hole, and he'd had to leave his bags behind. Two MaRRs were slung across his chest, but there was no room to aim and maneuver the large rifles, so the pistol was his weapon of choice in the narrow space. No matter, the targets were numerous and un-missable.

"You'd better be behind me," she said.

The chittering and howling overcame his answer. And if she'd repeated herself, he couldn't hear her over the thunder of the super-heated chunks of metal his pistol was hurling at the critters as they attempted to scale the chute.

She kept climbing. He shimmied upward slowly, firing all the time. The pistol was overheating. He needed to jettison the sink and reload, but the critters just kept coming. Their sheer numbers and blind devotion to their cause were astonishing. His MaP's sudden shutdown as it jettisoned the heat sink before going critical was unfortunate. Before Ehtishem could pop the secondary heat sink into place, something caught his left foot. His mech-suit registered an error on his visor, then metal groaned, popped, and something sharp sank into his left calf.

"*Utha.*"

"What?"

The chittering rose to a frenzied pitch. Clawed fingers grasped his legs and feet and yanked him down with surprising strength.

Rachel screamed.

He hit the ground, slammed the new heat sink home, and fired in every direction but up. She was shouting, but her words were indistinct. He couldn't even look up to see if she'd cleared the chute. He just fired and fought. Aiming was unnecessary, there were so many beasts coming at him.

Four mech-suited soldiers dropped feet-first into the frenzy, their MaRRs blazing as they waded toward him through living, dead, and dying critters. Relief surged through him at the sight of Huorem, Tinish, Stig, and Gahlen. It was followed by annoyance that they'd disobeyed his direct order.

Shrieks and smoke filled the cave. There was a pause in the barrage of gunfire.

"Dammit! Don't kill them!" Rachel's command was distant and staccato as the gunfire and screeching started, stopped, and restarted. Ehtishem was confused. Did she mean he shouldn't kill the creatures? The soldiers had blazed a perimeter around him. The critters had backed off. The cave walls bled. Gore dripped from the ceiling.

She kept shouting commands down the chute as a rope dropped from above. "Protect me from the anizofstra! The soldiers aren't a danger!"

Ehtishem realized she was controlling the critters. Between

the decimating gunfire and her commands, they ranged back and forth, chittering and howling, apparently confused by her orders. Some retreated toward the cave mouth, obeying her directive to attack the monster from Iodiq. But a sizable group remained around the soldiers.

Ehtishem assessed his guards. All were unscathed except Huorem. "Zhek." The aevadasa was bleeding from a horrific neck wound where the creatures had torn open his suit at the shoulder gap and bitten him. Only his suit's auto-balance and his own sheer determination were keeping him upright.

Ehtishem grabbed his swaying friend. "Hu—"

Huorem met his gaze and yanked two grenades from his suit's stores. "Up and outta here, fra." He glanced upward and whispered, "You've gotta take care of her."

Ehtishem closed his eyes. Hu, who'd made Rachel laugh, who'd saved his ass on the battlefield and always had his back. Not Hu. He sucked a breath and nodded, then pressed his forehead to his wounded friend's. "Ferahi-va, maibyo arshno, maibyo haxan." He thanked Huorem as his brother, his friend. He, Gahlen, Tinish, and Stig pressed their fists against Huorem's chest and said, "Drax-tu." They ascended the rocky chute again as Hu began whistling weakly and firing into the critter crowd in controlled bursts. Smoke and dust streamed past Ehtishem and, for once, he was thankful for Huorem's whistling even after he could no longer hear it.

"Wait, Barethri." Mahzel's voice came from above. "They're coming."

Ehtishem emerged through smoke and dust. Jorinei helped him then knelt to pull Gahlen up, too. Stig and Tinish followed.

Gohra emerged from a bend in the passage ahead of their gathering.

"Where's Hu?" Rachel asked.

"Dead on his feet," Ehtishem replied as he met Mahzel's gaze. Grief flickered in the aevadasa's eyes, then it was packed and stored with so many other horrors and losses.

"We can't leave him," Rachel said, her voice wavering.

"Rachel." Ehtishem grabbed her elbow. "We have to go."

"Nava." She pulled back, but he didn't lessen his grip. "Nava! We can't leave him to die here!"

Ehtishem jerked her around and loomed over her, his voice low and angry as he said in English: "He's infected. They'll change him. They'll make him their puppet. It's a fate worse than death. Huorem's going to blow the cave and all the critters within range. We need to move. Now."

"But—"

Mahzel touched her arm. "Hu made his choice. Honor it by surviving."

Stig, Tinish, and Gohra pushed a massive stone over the hole to the cave as Mahzel threw Rachel over his shoulder. Jorinei supported Ehtishem. Their group ran full tilt through twisting tunnels, away from Huorem's tomb. Rachel's sobs accompanied the hum of the mech-suits and the crunch of grit beneath their boots.

Hu's grenades detonated. The floor heaved. Another, larger explosion followed immediately. The rocks all around them squealed and groaned. More explosions continued as Ehtishem's abandoned munitions went off. Dust and rumbling filled the air, grew to a roar. The dust became rocks.

"The cave's collapsing," Stig warned.

"Move!" Ehtishem shouted.

Rocks thudded around their feet, bounced off their armor. Mahzel shifted Rachel into his arms and hunched over her. Dust obscured everything, but the noise eased, the rockfall lessened.

They kept running until the passage opened to another

cave, this one full of milky blue cave pearls. Dust followed them, but the cave-in didn't.

Mahzel put Rachel down. She wiped her sleeve across her face, leaving dirt streaks behind.

Gohra dropped a med pack at her feet. "The zosh's wounds need to be tended. You're the most qualified med tech in our group now."

She stared at it, nodded, then turned to assess Ehtishem's bites and scratches as he removed his damaged boot. "Jesus. You're bleeding like a stuck pig." She fished a tourniquet from the medical pack and worked it just below his knee.

"I'm not going to die from this wound," he said absently as he studied a map Stig had shared to his visor.

"If it needs a tourniquet, it needs immediate tending. If I had a tranquilizer I'd shoot you in the ass right now, you stubborn bastard."

Gohra snorted and Ehtishem gave her a look that threatened to melt her face.

"How the hell can they tear through our armor?" Vehl muttered as he considered Ehtishem's wound.

"Pretty impressive jaws and claws on such little buggers," Stig added.

Rachel said, "This wound's down to black bone." The critter's teeth had torn apart his muscle where it narrowed into his ankle and nearly severed the tendon that went up the back of his calf. "I can't do an adequate job. This needs microsurgery. I can stabilize the tendon, but it's a patch job at best."

"If I can limp, it'll do." He pushed away from the stone, put his weight on the leg, and grimaced. Tinish ducked under his arm. Gahlen caught his other side.

The group climbed, following a gradually ascending path that led to a volcanic vent on the west side of the mountain chain.

They emerged into daylight among blackened boulders and petrified tree trunks and the soldiers spread out. Their perch overlooked a wide valley bisected by the river *Cathru-Ahzish* had crashed in. Volcanic rocks and broken forest gave way to scrubby grass and wetlands along the river's edge where the terrain flattened.

"Scout a landing site for *Eshmahe*," Jorinei ordered, sending Romvi and Nadera downslope, while Stig and Gohra headed up toward a plateau.

Mahzel said, "Gahlen, get your relay up and contact Berk and Deniz. We need immediate evac."

"Zant, fra." The aevadasa had already opened his pack.

Ehtishem said, "Jorinei, Mahzel, explain why you disobeyed orders."

Mahzel answered, "We voted to be insubordinate, fra."

"This isn't a democracy, it's a military operation," Ehtishem countered. Tinish and Gahlen settled him on a fallen tree.

"Well, *I'm* glad you're here," Rachel said. "Take him back to the ship." Ehtishem opened his mouth to object, but she met his gaze and said, "With that wound, you'll only slow us both down and get yourself killed. Go back to *Pohru-Mahrko*, get your leg and that ship fixed, then get your ass back here and save me." She swiped sweat, dust, and tears from her face. "And try not to make it another twelve-year wait."

The soldiers fell silent. Watching their zosh, awaiting his reaction.

Ehtishem growled. "I'm not giving up that easily." He stared at his bandaged leg, blue blood slowly seeping through the white pressure wrap. "I would appreciate a nerve block when that transport arrives."

TWENTY-THREE

EHTISHEM SAT on a fallen tree while I doctored his leg. A shout broke the peace. Nadera and Romvi were running up the slope toward us. Howling suddenly filled the air and the clearing erupted with the whine and thump of Ohnenrai weapons as a wall of critters appeared over a rocky rise behind the two soldiers.

Ehtishem twisted and yanked me backwards. We landed behind the log. The cries of a wounded soldier joined the howling as Nadera was overrun. Her MaRR fired wildly, spraying the area with molten projectiles and Romvi went down under the barrage. There was a thump and wood splinters stung my left cheek. Ehtishem rolled, taking me with him until we were behind another tree. He covered me with his body and said, "Head down. Don't move."

How the hell could he sound so calm?

The bone-rattling buzz of pa'vikeret joined the firing and howling.

"*We are one.*" The Azatem in my head were as loud as the weapons and the critters.

I snarled, "Goddamn it!"

"Are you injured?"

"Nava! I want a weapon."

"Here." He pressed his MaP into my palm then belly-crawled to Jorinei. She lay facedown in the grass, a hole blown clear through her from chest to back. I hadn't even seen her get hit by the stray fire. He checked her pulse then took her MaRR. The weapon's vents hissed as he popped them open. He rose to a crouch then froze as a figure came up out of the tall grass before him.

Rivan.

I stood and aimed at his chest. "No closer."

He raised his hands and stared at me, a strange, longing expression on his ruined face. He was gaunt and bloodied, his flight suit tattered, his skin peeling away from his scalp and face. Worst of all was his black gaze. The whites of his eyes and his brown irises were gone, replaced with watery blackness.

Ehtishem kept his weapon trained on his former soldier. "What do you want, dasa?"

Rivan's speech was garbled. His teeth were missing or broken and he drooled as he spoke. "Give me the repeaters, fra. I'll hold 'em back as long as I can." Though I couldn't tell where he was looking, I had the distinct feeling that his gaze remained on me when he added, "I need to fix my mistake."

Ehtishem watched him, unmoving, ready to kill.

"You'll protect me from the Azatem?" I called.

"Zant." Rivan shifted toward me but was stopped by the muzzle of Ehtishem's rifle in his face. "We are one and you need to be protected."

"From the Azatem or the Ohnenrai?" Ehtishem asked. Rivan licked his lips. Blood and spittle ran down his chin. He lunged toward me. Ehtishem blew his head off.

"Oh, god." I swallowed bile.

Ehtishem grabbed my elbow and pulled me up the hillside, away from the thing that had been Rivan.

Huorem. Now I understood.

"Everyone else all right?" Ehtishem called.

Tinish, Gahlen, Mahzel, and Vehl offered a grim chorus. "Zant, fra."

Gohra and Stig joined us as we ran away from the valley floor and the approaching horde. The soldiers reloaded their weapons and replaced spent heat sinks as they retreated.

"Back into the dark?" I asked and looked at Stig as we reached the opening into the mountain we'd only just escaped.

She shook her head. "Nava. Movement down there." She stepped forward and pulled a grenade from her pack. "Fire in the hole!" Our group picked up the pace as she dropped it into the vent.

The explosion sent a dust plume skyward. The ground shuddered. The opening slowly collapsed as we continued toward the upper plateau.

The howling, screeching, and humming grew louder.

"We are one." The voices in my head were loudest of all.

I tried to stop. "Ehtishem, leave me." He said nothing, but his grip tightened on my hand. "They don't want to hurt me." He pulled me onward.

"I'm aware of that." He glanced down at me then over his shoulder. "And I don't care," he replied in English.

"You're being an ass."

Gahlen had the com relay deployed. A faint sound came from it as we put a group of large boulders between us and the critters. He said, "Go ahead, *Eshmahe*," and listened. "We're trapped. Azatem ground forces are closing. We're two meters from the landing zone. Do you read our marker?"

Bringing up the rear of our group, Tinish, Vehl, and Mahzel began firing. Ehtishem and the other soldiers joined them. I pulled my gun and added to the madness. For every critter we obliterated, a dozen more appeared.

"Where the hell are all these bastards coming from?" I shouted. No one answered. They couldn't hear me above the guns, the creatures, and the goddamn buzzing pa'vikeret. That humming was in my head, vibrating my skull and rattling my teeth.

The steeper terrain slowed the reapers, but the critters kept coming, bounding over rocks, skittering across the jagged terrain, not even pausing as their compatriots were blown apart by Ohnenrai projectiles.

Gahlen shouted into his helmet's pickup. "Zant! Immediate action is required!"

No sooner had he said that than the ground started shaking and the rocks reverberating with the hum of Ohnenrai engines. Small stones hopped around our feet and skittered down the hillside. *Eshmahe* appeared over the cliff face, her anti-grav washing over us. The critters slowed, stopped, retreated toward the oncoming pa'vikeret.

"Be advised, the zosh is wounded," Gahlen shouted into his helmcom.

The ship dropped low, her doors opened, and two mech-suited soldiers — Anchal and Fehrana — dove out. Ehtishem signaled for the transport to clear a perimeter. *Eshmahe* rose and opened fire on the approaching reapers and critters.

Fehrana added molten slag to the projectiles obliterating the Azatem-controlled creatures surrounding us.

Anchal approached, his suit compensating for a limp that was evidence of an old wound. "Let's get everyone to that plateau for retrieval, fra." He eased the zosh's arm over his shoulder to take some weight off his injured leg.

Ehtishem didn't loosen his grip on me. "What's the situation?" he asked.

"Seventeen pa'vikeret dropping critters and on a trajectory to intercept us. *Pohru-Mahrko* deployed *Amava* and *Zavareca*, and all three ships have engaged an Azatem harvester in orbit. It's giving the thrai some trouble."

"So Timsai disobeyed my last command and dropped our destroyers to take it down?"

"Zant, fra."

Our whole group moved to the far edge of the plateau as *Eshmahe* forced the pa'vikeret back and obliterated the critters. I tried to hang back, tried to find a chance to lead the enemy away from the man I loved and the people I respected. But Ehtishem's grip didn't lessen.

The Azatem raced up the valley, some disgorging critters, others absorbing their fallen bodies. The transport hovered a meter above the ground, her jump doors open. Mahzel, Anchal, Vehl, and Fehrana hopped aboard.

Ehtishem grabbed my waist. "In, Rachel."

"You, too."

"I'm last."

"Don't be an asshole. You're wounded."

He lifted me up to Mahzel, who transferred me to a seat.

"Goddamn it." I raised my hands. "Why is he like that?"

Mahzel replied, "He's always had an inflated sense of responsibility for everyone on his team. Easier to get aboard and not fight him, Barethri. It will make things go faster."

The last dasa climbed aboard as the transport rose. Ehtishem grabbed an anchor strap and made to swing up to the doorway. But as his fingers caught hold, critters emerged from beneath the ship and swarmed him.

"No!" I shouted. "Let him go!"

He plunged to the ground, landing on his back and crushing some of the little beasts beneath him. He shook two more off and came up, gun in hand, but more surged toward him.

"Circle, circle. Zosh Mahle is down," Mahzel ordered. "Zosh Mahle is down."

"Surun-ta. I have visual. Coming around," Berk replied.

Deniz said, "Watch our grav-wash."

Mahzel anchored me against the seat with his arm as Tinish and Gahlen went out the door. Mech-suits protecting them, they tucked and rolled with the impact of the ground, unfurling like steel insects, their MaRRs aimed and ready to deliver molten-slag death. But they couldn't get a clear shot.

Ehtishem fired again and again. The critters kept coming.

Eshmahe opened up on the critters surging toward my lover and his protectors. Blood and screeches filled the air, a vaporous, dark-red cloud. Still the critters came on and now the gut-twisting hum of more pa'vikeret joined the hellish cacophony. Tinish and Gahlen directed their fire at the closest reapers, but they couldn't stop the damned things.

A traitorous part of me didn't want them to. Like in the cave with Seven-oh-one, I was torn between alliances, terrified for Ehtishem and enraged that he stood between the critters and me. "Jesus Fucking Christ," I muttered, shaking. Hands over my ears, I rocked back in my seat, fighting the fear, rage, and suffering coming at me from every angle.

Suddenly, the dark metal barrel of a plasma cannon filled my vision as Vehl leaned out the door at a terrifying angle. Gohra held his belt and braced back on her heels, and Stig, in turn, grasped her belt and a metal strut. With the weapon held as steady as the stone cliffs around us, Vehl aimed.

The world slowed to a crawl.

Vehl shouted, "Drop!"

Ehtishem, Tinish, and Gahlen hit the ground.

Three hollow thumps sounded. My ears popped. Three

reapers exploded in balls of blue fire that engulfed the closest critters, too.

"Yahz!" the soldiers cheered.

I slumped in my seat, equally relieved and horrified.

Gahlen pulled Ehtishem up, lifted the zosh's arm over his shoulder, and they moved toward *Eshmahe* as Tinish followed.

The transport's com crackled. "*Eshmahe*, be advised. *Zavareca* is prepping orbital plasma bombs. I repeat, OPBs coming in."

Deniz replied, "Nava, *PM*. The zosh is on the ground. Do not deploy OPBs. Repeat, do not deploy OPBs."

"Understood, *Eshmahe*. *Zavareca* is standing by."

Two more pa'vikeret erupted in fire and slurry, and the transport was rocked by the blowback of the explosion even as a third reaper disintegrated. But still more came.

Ehtishem, Tinish, and Gahlen were pulled aboard, and the ship was airborne again.

The zosh braced against the overhead struts. He shouted over the ship's thrumming engines and the screech of the critters. "Deniz, get *Pohru-Mahrko* on the com." Dark-red mist coated his mech-suit. Anchal proffered a rag. Ehtishem wiped critter blood from his face and hands, tossed the rag out the open jump door, then pulled the door closed.

"*PM* is in the arena and fully engaged," the pilot answered. "Her crew says you owe them leave, Zosh."

"Gawmezh, I do. They disobeyed orders." Ehtishem lurched forward to the flight cabin, leaving a trail of critter blood in his wake. "Brief me." Only the Ohnenrai mech-suits kept all aboard from becoming infected.

"I've got *Pohru-Mahrko* on the com, fra. Patching you in." Deniz passed an earpiece to Ehtishem.

He'd lost his helmet in the fray and was damn lucky to have

Azatem immunity. The thought of him becoming something like Rivan made my breath catch.

Clutching the cabin doorway as the ship swung around, he said, "Zosh Mahle here, go ahead *Pohru-Mahrko*." He listened for a minute, his expression unreadable. "Ushta. Damage?" Silence, then, "Zant. We're coming in with Azatem exposure. We require full decontamination and quarantine for the transport and all personnel." Silence, again. "Zant, zant, Timsai. Aevadasa Gohra can describe the injuries." He nodded to Deniz who relayed the com to the med tech's helmet.

Eshmahe lurched sideways. The pilots cursed. The transport's engines whined and my head smacked the crash cage as the ship spun on her axis.

"We are one."

"No," I whispered. "I'm not like you. Go away. Leave us alone."

No one heard me and the Azatem didn't care.

"We've got ballast," Berk called. "Losing altitude."

"What did we snag?" Ehtishem asked.

"Nothing, fra. Critters snagged us. I'm trying to shake them."

"Utha."

The ship rocked from side-to-side and spun. "We've lost communications," Deniz announced.

"Level out," Ehtishem ordered. He turned to his ground troops. "Get us free."

Berk said, "There goes Stabilizer Three."

Stig, Vehl, Fehrana, and Tinish grabbed MaRRs. Anchal anchored the four snipers to the ship's struts then pulled open the jump doors. He and Gohra manned the transport's mounted Mass-affect Repeater Cannons. Mahzel unholstered his MaP and braced between me and the open door. The transport tilted wildly.

Like a living tower, critters clambered over each other to reach the sides of the ship. They clung to its armaments, pulled off equipment, and clawed at the hull.

"We are one."

I covered my ears as four rifles and two cannons started blasting away the creatures.

More blood. More tissue. More screeches and howling.

A flash of light and the ship shuddered and whipped sideways. Vehl crashed against Fehrana whose next volley went wild and blew holes in the floor and walls of the cabin. Stig flew out the door only to be whipped back inside by her safety strap. She hit the overhead, the floor, and was slow to get up, even with her mech-suit's assistance.

"We've lost pressure in Engine One," Berk announced.

"Those larger pa'vikeret are firing on us," Ehtishem said and pointed at something. "Anchal, Gohra, concentrate cannon fire on them."

"Aiya," Vehl cursed as he helped Stig to stand. "Since when are reapers armed?"

"Since now," Mahzel replied.

Gohra and Anchal opened fire on the Azatem monstrosities with *Eshmahe's* cannons.

"You okay, Barethri?" Fehrana asked as she regained her position, jettisoned her MaRR's heat sink, and reloaded an ammo cartridge.

I nodded, surprised by my own self-control. The blood and violence, the voices in my head and conflicting loyalties, all of that should've had me fetal in a corner, flashing back over my entire adolescence. "Are you?" I asked.

Blue blood splattered the inside of her visor and was smeared from her nose down to her chin. She flashed a bloody grin. "Just another day in the Ohnenrai military."

"We are one."

Dark-red blood drew my attention to Ehtishem. Fluid and tissue dripped from his mech-suit. Only it wasn't dripping but creeping, clumping, striving to rejoin the colony.

"Christ Almighty," I muttered.

"We are one."

That explained how their attacks seemed endless. I met Ehtishem's gaze and saw my own realization reflected in his grim expression. This wasn't going to end for the Ohnenrai until I took the fight from their hands and set them free. This was what Ahremena had shown us. This was their reality, *my* reality. We hadn't finished the job. The critters had scented me like hounds on a fox and nothing would stop them from returning me to their colony. They thought I was part of them, that I was Azatem family.

That knowledge centered me. I knew what I had to do. And I wasn't afraid to do it. It meant Ehtishem would be safe. My Ohnenrai friends would be safe. Hu, Jorinei, Aihaman, Leilei, and all the other tens of thousands — *millions* — of deaths wouldn't be in vain.

It meant I might be able to rescue Pearl. And it meant her death would be avenged, if I couldn't.

"We focus our rage and use it as a weapon." Those were Mahzel's words. They told me I was right. I grabbed my bodyguard's arm. "Don't let the zosh follow me."

He looked from me to Ehtishem. He nodded, his expression grim.

"Barethri?" Fehrana asked as I released my harness and lifted the crash cage. The open door was on my right. I stood. "It's okay." I found Ehtishem's gaze again and said in English: "There's no other way."

His eyes widened. The ship lurched again. He shoved Mahzel aside and grabbed me. "You don't have to do this," he shouted over the screaming engines and pounding guns.

"You know I do."

He kissed me hard, deep, and I almost didn't let go. I almost let resolve crumble and slip through my fingers.

Pearl.

The thought of her solidified my determination. "I love you," I said in English.

He released me. It was killing him, I saw it in the hard set of his jaw, felt it in the desperation of his kiss. Letting me go was the hardest thing he'd ever had to do. Failure warred with determination and a heartbreaking sadness in his eyes. But we both knew I had to go. I couldn't dishonor the sacrifices he and his soldiers had made to get me to this point. Aihaman, Jorinei, Huorem. Especially Huorem, my friend, my protector. I couldn't let his death be meaningless.

"I love you," I repeated against his lips as I kissed him one last time. Then I shoved him away and stepped back, through the open doorway, into midair.

I tumbled, saw ship, sky, ground, critters, ship, sky, ground.

I was snagged by the open arms of a thousand Azatem-infected critters, fell again.

My body whipped around, my head snapped back, my stomach lurched.

Ship.

Sky.

Ground.

Critters.

Snagged. Held.

The world slowed as strangely sticky fingers cradled me. We fell.

Critters released the ship and dove after me.

The pa'vikeret stopped firing.

I looked up.

"Rachel!" Ehtishem knelt in the doorway. Hands held him

back. Our gazes met for a second before my vision was blocked by a cloud of critters wrapping me, hugging me, protecting me. They'd break my fall with their own small bodies, sacrifice themselves to keep me alive.

Ahremena was right. The Azatem wanted me, not the Ohnenrai. Not Ehtishem.

"Strike when you need to," my father had said.

Double-edged sword.

"We are one."

Howling. Screeching. Chittering excitement.

No fear.

Nothing.

TWENTY-FOUR

"HOLD YOUR FIRE! HOLD YOUR FIRE!" Mahzel shouted. "Barethri is on the ground!"

Released by the wave of critters, *Eshmahe* lurched sideways and whipped around. Shrill alarms sounded. The pilots called instructions to each other and their passengers. Ehtishem stared at the jump door as Stig closed it. Soldiers and equipment were scattered around the transport's belly. Critter blood slicked the floor and walls. Smoke hung in the cabin and the stench of hot metal, melted flooring, and ozone stung his nose.

He patted his pockets, but what he suddenly wanted was missing, lost to Iodiq. He grabbed Gohra's arm. "Get me a com."

She yanked one of the thin devices from its holder on the side of Deniz's seat and passed it over.

The ship leveled out. Tinish said, "Ten more pa'vikeret have joined the ground forces, fra, with another ten inbound." As if to emphasize his warning, *Eshmahe* veered to avoid enemy fire, and Tinish added, "The armed ones."

Berk said, "Orders, Zosh?"

"Don't get shot down." Ehtishem activated the com's tracker mode then stared at its flashing yellow lights as he racked his brain for Rachel's tracking code. "Aiya." What was it? "Zhek!"

"PNA625969," Mahzel said. He knew Ehtishem's mind, always had.

Ehtishem entered the code. The device immediately registered Rachel's tracker. "We're still above her." He gestured at the closed jump door. "Fehrana, Mahzel, Gahlen, Tinish, recover Barethri Rachel."

The soldiers stood and exchanged their weapons' spent heat sinks for fresh ones. But before they could activate the door, Berk shouted, "Incoming! Taking evasives!"

A flash lit up the world outside the transport. Heat and sound filled the cabin. The ship juddered, surged upward, and banked hard, throwing Ehtishem and his soldiers across the cargo hold. He hit the metal wall and two mech-suited soldiers landed atop him. Ehtishem's skull cracked on a strut. One of them crushed his chest and the other pinned his wounded leg. Ehtishem gasped and fought blackness as pain tunneled his vision. The soldiers scrambled to get off their zosh. Their heavy suits were as much weapon as protection by sheer weight alone. Every Ohnenrai field soldier had used the armor to crush enemies in just the way Fehrana and Mahzel had flattened him.

Another explosion rocked *Eshmahe* and the pilots cursed as they corrected the path of the ailing transport to escape the barrage of Azatem fire.

Deniz called, "*Pohru-Mahrko*'s hailing us."

"Go ahead, *Pohru-Mahrko*," Berk responded. He listened for a moment then replied, "Nava, hold those bombs. Barethri Rachel is on the ground."

Ehtishem shook his head to clear tunneling darkness. He

sucked a breath, cursing against pain — his ribs were broken. Again. He pushed away from the transport's wall. "Does anyone have a visual on Rachel?" he rasped.

"Nava, fra. The area's swarming with critters and pa'vikeret."

"Fra, we can't stay here. *Eshmahe's* guns have overheated. The ship's an easy target."

"What about Rachel's tracker?" He'd lost the com. "Someone find her signal."

Mahzel grabbed Ehtishem's shoulder and got in his face. "Fra, *Pohru-Mahrko* needs you."

He bared his teeth at his aevadasa, grabbed his throat. Rachel's bodyguard. The failure. He should crush the man. Mahzel had let her be abducted, had gotten his own partner killed. Ehtishem pulled his MaP from its holster. He pressed it against Mahzel's bloody faceplate.

His aevadasa didn't flinch. His gaze didn't waver. But his voice softened. "We have to leave Iodiq, Ehtishem," he said. "We can't recover Rachel today. But we can save *Pohru-Mahrko*. We can come back stronger and finish the war, but only if we survive this battle."

Ehtishem snarled, an animal sound, a killer's sound. Just a twitch of his finger. Vengeance was so close.

But...

Rachel hadn't blamed Mahzel. She wouldn't want him killed. And the loyal bastard was right. She wanted Ehtishem to leave her, to return stronger, recover her after she'd crippled the Azatem and avenged Pearl.

Fuck.

Ehtishem swallowed. He lowered the pistol. "Take us to *Pohru-Mahrko*, Berk."

"Zant, fra."

The ship banked and rose, shaking violently as she escaped the planet's atmosphere.

But Ehtishem's heart stayed behind, too heavy to leave Iodiq.

Still gagging on the fat, bitter pill of failure, Ehtishem hobbled into the lift that would take him and his team up to *Pohru-Mahrko's* command deck. He'd been through the decon showers and had threatened to kill med techs determined to confine him to a med bay while he relayed orders to his embattled thrai. He'd watched helplessly from quarantine as the only operational Ohnenrai Tarad-class super-heavy cruiser-carrier and her deployed destroyers fought to stop the Azatem harvester from retrieving pa'vikeret from the surface of Iodiq. *Pohru-Mahrko* had a strong signal from Rachel's tracker. She was still alive and dirtside.

On the command deck, Ehtishem gripped his chair arms until they creaked while two med techs repaired his leg and he focused on his ships and crew.

The senior med tech loomed over him, arms folded and expression uncharacteristically disapproving. "Fra, I insist you receive a nerve blocker."

Ehtishem met the man's stern gaze. "Administer it and I'll snap your spine." The nauseating pain from his leg was keeping him sharp and angry. There was no room for worry about his injury. If he could stop the harvester from retrieving the pa'vikeret, then Rachel would remain on Iodiq and rescuing her would be a simple matter of following her tracker.

"But, fra—" The tech's words ended with a strangled squawk. Ehtishem had his collar. He yanked him close.

"Shut your mouth. Fix my leg."

He released the tech with a shove.

Timsai's steady hand prevented the man from tumbling down the command deck's tiered levels. "The pain keeps our zosh focused," he murmured to the tech. To Ehtishem, he said, "The harvester is on a trajectory to ram us head-on. I defer to your expertise in evasive maneuvers, fra. You have *Pohru-Mahrko*'s con."

"I have *Pohru-Mahrko*'s con," Ehtishem confirmed. "Projections, Helm," he called to the ship's pilot.

"On screen, fra."

Lists of calculations and a plotted trajectory appeared on the deck's curving central screen. Ehtishem studied the numbers and figures, nodded, and called out a series of orders to the battle ops crew. "We'll turn *Pohru-Mahrko* ass over elbows. Helm, nose down ninety degrees. On my mark, fire sustained thrusters to hold our position and compensate for torpedo fire. Weapons, on the Thrai's mark, fire heavy torpedoes from all rear batteries targeting the harvester's belly. We'll gut her as she passes overhead."

The crew affirmed their orders.

Except one aevadasa who asked, "Ass over elbows, Zosh?"

"Nose down, tail up," he replied.

"Ah. Zant, fra."

Ehtishem sat back and glanced at a side monitor displaying Iodiq's blue, white, and brown surface.

Rachel, distract them, even if it's only for a minute. Buy me time to attack.

Her tracker continued to function. Her vital signs were strong. They hadn't killed her. They wouldn't. They thought they were protecting her. They thought she was one of their own.

They were dead wrong.

Rachel was *his* lover, *his* family, not theirs.

As if reading Ehtishem's mind, Timsai addressed the crew. "Barethri Rachel remains alive and her presence is dividing their attention. She's buying us time to stop that harvester. Let's make her efforts worthwhile, pa'nerem."

"Twenty-six kilometers until impact."

"Torpedoes loaded. All rear batteries standing by."

The Azatem harvester came at them, looming larger on their screens.

"Fire North thrusters," Ehtishem ordered. "Weapons, are we still out of range of her guns?"

"Firing thrusters."

"Out of range for fifteen, fourteen, thirteen..."

"Hold the yaw and roll steady, Helm."

"Zant, fra," *PM*'s pilot replied.

"Torpedo thrust compensation calculated, Zosh."

"Twelve, eleven..."

Ehtishem said, "Call out the pitch."

"Sixty degrees, fra."

"Ten, nine, eight..."

Pohru-Mahrko dove as the Azatem ship neared, the maneuver's forces countered by *PM's* gravitational compensators.

"Seven, six, five seconds until we enter their range."

"Approaching eighty degrees, Zosh."

Tension and focus showed on the faces surrounding Ehtishem. "Do we have a visual?" he asked.

"Three, two, one..."

"Eighty-five degrees."

"Nava, fra," an officer replied. "We can't get a visual with these rapid pitch changes. Syscom won't bring it up."

Timsai asked, "Is her belly in range?"

"Ninety degrees."

"Helm, fire thrusters to hold our position," Ehtishem said.

"Range confirmed, Thrai."

"Fire aft torpedoes," Timsai ordered. "Full salvos. Auto-targeting."

The med techs hit a nerve and Ehtishem's chair arm cracked beneath his grip. "Are you almost finished?" he said through gritted teeth.

"Salvos away."

"Zant, fra, but it's only triaged," one of the med techs replied. "This wound requires surgery."

"Thrusters compensating for torpedoes."

"They're not releasing countermeasures, Zosh."

"No return fire, fra."

Ehtishem murmured in English: "Whatever you're doing, Rachel, it's working."

The med tech asked, "Fra?"

Ehtishem stabbed a finger at him. "You. Leg. Finish."

He swallowed audibly. "Zant, fra."

"Second salvo ready."

"Fire torpedoes," Timsai ordered.

"Steady at ninety degrees."

"Torpedoes away."

"One hundred percent strike rate."

"Still no return fire, fra."

"Torpedoes ready."

"Fire torpedoes," Timsai repeated.

An alarm sounded, shrill and insistent. A proximity warning.

"Wormhole formation. We're in the emergence field."

"*Pohru-Mahrko*'s taking auto-evasives, fra," the pilot said, her voice admirably calm. "She's locked out manual controls."

"Dammit!" Ehtishem cursed in English as *Pohru-Mahrko*'s computer seized control of navigation, thrusters, and the engines and accelerated away from the wormhole's estimated coordinates.

"Override," Timsai commanded, but everyone on deck knew it was too late. The proximity override was only disengaged when the ship was hooked into a wormhole convoy. In combat, *PM* was programmed to save herself and her crew.

The pilot shook her head. "The system's locked for another forty-three seconds, fra."

Ehtishem slammed his fists against the chair arms and ground his teeth as the wormhole gave birth to *Maso-Vohu*. The planet, Azatem battlecruiser, and the harvester receded as *Pohru-Mahrko*'s computer carried them farther away from danger. The harvester swallowed a squadron of pa'vikeret as the transports broke from Iodiq's atmosphere.

"Override available in twenty seconds. What are your orders, fra?"

As *Maso-Vohu* emerged from the wormhole, the massive ship opened her enormous front docking bay and took in the harvester.

"Second wormhole forming."

"Aiya," a jump tech muttered. "How can they open one while still emerging from another?"

There wasn't enough time. Even if *Pohru-Mahrko* had been undamaged from their battles with the Azatem ships, even if she'd had wormhole capabilities ready to deploy, they couldn't align a lock and power up the jump ships in time to intercept the escape wormhole.

"Awaiting orders, fra."

Ehtishem fished a wooden worry disk from a compartment on the side of the command chair. He rubbed it between his thumb and fingers.

Timsai watched him, hands clasped behind his back, expression passive but eyes compassionate. He knew. They all did.

"*Maso* is entering the second wormhole, fra."

"They win this battle," Timsai said to Ehtishem.

He nodded. "But not the war."

To the crew, Timsai said, "We cannot intercept now. Ferahi-va, pa'nerem."

Ehtishem pocketed the worry disk. "Thrai, I'd like to see a damage report and repair status when I come out of surgery. We need teams to sweep Iodiq's western quadrant for Azatem biologicals. Once the field is clear, send technical teams to the Havafna Caldera. We did find one pleasant surprise during all this mess. Panca Seven-oh-one's surviving dasas can fill in the details. And I want them to receive commendations and advancement."

"Understood." Timsai nodded to his assistant to see that the zosh's orders were carried out.

"And, Thrai?"

"Zant, Zosh?"

The command deck crew continued to call out status reports.

"*Maso-Vohu* has cleared the event horizon."

"I've lost Barethri Rachel's tracking signal, fra."

Ehtishem finished, "Ferahi-va, haxan."

"Va'kanikar, maibyo haxan," Timsai said.

"The event horizon is collapsing. Wormhole has closed."

Ehtishem permitted the med techs and his guards to help him into the lift. A last glance at the screen showed only Iodiq floating in a field of stars.

Maso-Vohu was gone.

Rachel was beyond his grasp.

Ohnenrai Genetics' weapon was working. He had to believe it. He couldn't exist in a world where Rachel's sacrifice was in vain. He didn't know how he'd find her, but he would. He *would*. It was a promise he made to her and himself. He'd find her and together they'd obliterate the Azatem.

PART THREE
STEEL

TWENTY-FIVE

"MOMMA?"

It was library quiet except for my daughter's voice in my mind.

Pearl?

I gasped and opened my eyes. Creatures loomed over me. I shrieked, lurched away, and tumbled off a low platform. Entangled in a white sheet, I landed hard on my naked ass and a cold floor.

Three humanoids watched my retreat. They were tall, long-limbed, and broad-shouldered with skin the gray-brown hue of wet sand. The creatures had large black eyes set in flat faces and looked kinda Ohnenrai, kinda not. They were identical and female and weirdly expressionless.

Pearl wasn't with them. I surveyed the room, but she wasn't there. I swallowed. She existed only in my mind and memories. "Azatem?" The quavering word rasped from my sandpaper throat.

"Azatem." The middle alien's sweeping gesture encompassed herself, her companions, our surroundings.

All three creatures bowed their heads and held out their slim, spidery hands toward me as they murmured, "Yazadami." Their voices were surprisingly rich and melodic. I hadn't expected monsters to sound like that, like Etta James.

Yazadami. The Ohnenrai god? *Me?* I touched my chest with a trembling finger. "Yazadami?"

They met my gaze with those blank eyes and bland expressions and confirmed my guess with reverence. "Yazadami." All three stepped back, gestured toward a low table, and left the room.

I sat on the floor clutching the sheet to my chest and staring at the portal they'd gone through. I desperately wanted Ehtishem, desperately remembered I couldn't have him, and desperately regretted my own stupid sacrifice.

I twisted the sparkling ring on my finger, relieved to still have it. "You are, without a doubt, the biggest dumb-ass, Rachel Elizabeth Pryne," I said. It wasn't true, of course. What choice had I had? None. Ever. I'd bought him time to escape and myself the only possible chance to find out if Pearl was alive. That's all that mattered, the people I loved.

I pulled the sheet around me, tucking and tying it to keep it tight, and explored the chamber, my bare feet slapping the pale floor.

Flesh-colored walls surrounded me. I'd fallen off an expanse of padded platform, a bed I guessed. Beside that and the table, the room contained a cushioned seat, a curtained area hiding a shallow bath and, of all things, a lidded chamber pot. I also found two boxes — one empty and one filled with the same kind of loose gowns the Azatem wore. I put one on. It was white, sleeveless, and had a plunging back. My captors had worn theirs over a fitted bodysuit, but they hadn't given me anything more modest than the gowns.

"Jerks," I muttered, weak bravado but the only defense I had.

The portal — the one way in or out of the room — wouldn't yield to me and had no apparent handle, access panel, or sensor. It felt warm and rubbery and had operated more like a membranous valve than a door when it had opened for the Azatem.

The room was oval, its ceiling vaulted and the walls strangely ribbed and irregular. It seemed organic, grown rather than built. It was like being inside the ribcage of a living thing. A single viewport stretched its entire length and beyond that were stars and an unfamiliar blue planet with no obvious land-masses. I saw no sign of *Pohru-Mahrko* or debris to indicate the ship had been destroyed.

Thank god for that small miracle, I thought. Maybe I was wrong and all the people I loved were dead, but I'd cling to illusion just as desperately as I was clinging to sanity.

The low table and padded chair sat before the window. On the table were a jug of water, a filled glass, a lump of spongy, pale-green bread, and what looked like turkey jerky.

"Yazadami." I mulled and ate, figuring they weren't going to poison me. The bread tasted like wheat grass and the jerky was gamy, salty, but edible. The water was cool and clean, filtered, and I drank all of it.

I considered the food, clothing, room. It seemed my captors had provided everything they thought I needed to survive.

"Not everything, assholes," I murmured. "This isn't home. You're not family. And I am *not* one of you."

I sat on the bed and stared at the strange planet. Three moons orbited it. Did they have names? Everything was surreal. My universe was not only spinning, it was threatening to throw me off into the weeds. But I still wasn't scared. Angry, yes.

Freaked out? Definitely. Resigned? Eventually. I blew out a long sigh.

Double-edged sword. Strike when you need to.

"I am," I said to my father's memory. "But this feels like death by a thousand cuts."

I stared out that window for I don't know how long, listening to the subtle sounds of the ship. It whooshed and thumped, hummed, purred and seemed more and more like a living thing.

"I'm Jonah," I announced to no one, "and I'm the Jonah of this ship." I laughed at the irony. "And I'd better find a way to keep my sanity."

The portal opened, interrupting my weird musings. Two Azatem women stepped into the room and took up positions on either side of the entrance. I waited, but they remained silent and no one else followed them.

"I guess this means I'm supposed to go?"

No answer.

Warily, I approached the portal. The women stood, impassive guards. Two more Azatem occupied guard positions outside the room and one waited between them. As I stepped through the opening, she turned and strode along an arched hallway. I followed and the four guards accompanied us.

Either I was going to my doom or I was gonna get some answers. "Where are we going?"

No response. Not even a glance. *Maybe they don't understand English.*

The way spiraled gently downward and grew increasingly populated with identical Azatem women. It didn't escape my attention that they were moving in the same direction as my little escort. Their footsteps combined with the brush of their clothing, the ship's thrumming and whooshing to create an undulating sound wave.

I studied my surroundings as we descended. Wide, bony bridges connected external chambers to the central spine like spokes on a wheel. The spine rose at least a hundred levels above and another hundred below us. Thousands of Azatem streamed across the bridges, ascended and descended the central path, all heading for the same bright opening in the spine dozens of levels below us.

Maso was all curves, hollows, and ribs. The winter when I was nine, my father had found an enormous empty wasp nest in our storage shed and had cut it open to show me its structure. It had a central column with chambered disks stacked like pancakes around it. That was how the Azatem ship was structured — a spine with stacked floors of chambers rising around it, bony bridges connecting them.

While the Ohnenrai were aliens to me, their ships had offered much that was familiar, in no small part because they'd stolen many things from my home world. The Azatem, though humanoid, were thoroughly, unnervingly alien.

Being surrounded by them made me edgy. "It's a surprise party, right?" I said just to hear my own voice break the unbearable silence.

Still no reaction. These bitches had invincible poker faces, but beneath their masks, all the Azatem were excited. That's what was making me jumpy. I felt it like I'd felt the emotions of my Ohnenrai companions aboard *Pohru-Mahrko* and again in Iodiq's caves. Their excitement and — triumph? — buzzed through my brain, sucked me in, an almost feverish seduction.

"Ugh." I rejected that addiction, drew on Ehtishem's example of vairim to find self-control and to push their elation away as we cleared the threshold of the opening in the spine.

A sea of gray-brown expressionless faces turned toward me. I balked like a donkey facing a pack of rabid dogs. My escorts stopped and waited.

Inside the chamber, the walls curved and twisted overhead to rejoin the central spine. Perforated like honeycomb, the architecture offered a view all the way to the distant overhead where a transparent membrane gave a glimpse of the stars outside *Maso-Vohu*'s armored red hull.

A low oval dais occupied the middle of the chamber, surrounded by the standing Azatem. Like the orderly curving pattern of a sunflower's seed head, all the rows of the chamber whorled inward toward the dais. The Azatem woman who'd led me from my chamber proceeded to the platform, stepped up to it, and faced me. She said nothing, didn't beckon, but I sensed her desire. She wanted me to follow her. She wanted me to sit on the lone padded seat there.

I scanned the room. While the Azatem remained a silent sea, their emotions raged like a storm-tossed ocean. Excitement, success, fulfillment. A sense of destiny being achieved. What I didn't find was anger, hatred, or violence.

I had no idea what would happen if I sat down, but I wasn't getting any answers standing in the doorway.

"Going to hell in a hand-basket," I muttered and followed the only path to the room's center. I stepped onto the dais, sat on the stool, and tried not to flinch as the woman arranged the folds of my gown to fall gracefully around the stool and expose my feet. She stepped back and demonstrated how I should let my arms hang loose at my sides.

Once she was satisfied, she stepped down and faced her sisters, and made a pronouncement in what sounded like the Ohnaia Ehtishem and the other players had chanted during the hamistayeca.

I understood only a handful of words: Azatem, Yazadami, sevishta — which meant very strong — and bahkem — which meant gods or rulers.

The room was filled with an eerie muted clicking as the

Azatem tapped their fingers together, apparently their sign of approval.

Then, one-by-one, the crowd shuffled forward. They merged into two pathways that curved around the dais and permitted each of them to touch my feet, my arms, and my back. After running their bony fingers over my skin the Azatem put their hands into their mouths.

After flinching away from the first few touches, I closed my eyes, swallowed hard, and fought a growing urge to capture their emotions. The temptation was great; they operated as a single entity with a singular focus, and a single orange ribbon of self-satisfaction connected all of their minds. I concentrated on Pearl's smiling face, remembered the hum of the bugbots pollinating the flowers in *Dathusha*'s gardens and the flicker of sunlight through the trees surrounding Suffer. I recalled the strength and gentleness of Ehtishem's hands.

After what felt like hours, I resorted to counting each touch and schooled my body and brain not to react. I blocked the Azatem's satisfaction and exuberance, struggled not to feel the same tingling sensation, the same emotional bond as I'd experienced with the Ohnenrai during Ahremena's experiments and the hamistayeca, and on Iodiq with Seven-oh-one.

I turned a clinical eye to their actions. They were using touch transference to integrate my DNA into themselves. That also explained the chamber pot. My DNA came off my skin. It was in my saliva, my urine, even in the air I breathed.

Gross.

The leader of my escort was the last to touch me. She ran her fingers over my skin, stared at them for a long moment, then raised them to her lips and met my gaze.

This is my body. This is my blood. This is your death, I thought.

On stiff legs I followed the guards back to my room. More

food had been set out for me while I was gone. The bed was made and clean towels waited in the bathing area. My escort left without a word and the portal still refused to obey me.

I pulled the white dress over my head and left it on the floor then poured bucket after bucket of cold water over my body trying to wash away the feel of bony alien fingers sliding over my skin.

When my teeth ached from clenching and my skin burned from the cold, I dried off, dressed, and sat on the floor before the window.

The planet my bio-mechanical prison orbited presented a bright edge, the light of some distant star setting its curve aglow. The wall-length window separated me from the black emptiness of space, a darkness emphasized by the strange planet's vibrant blue hue, a color so like Earth's twilight sky.

Out there, somewhere, Ehtishem waited and wondered. If he was still alive.

I bit the inside of my cheek until it stung and I tasted blood.

As I'd sat in that chamber, each Azatem woman running her fingers over my skin, I'd explored their presence in my mind. The difference between the Azatem and the Ohnenrai was individuality.

"Gohra's mind is hers alone. Stig's is hers, Mahzel's his. No one shares their thoughts," I murmured. The Azatem were different. They were like the critters from Iodiq. When I felt their excitement, it was the emotion of one entity. Ahremena said the Azatem were colonial, and that seemed to mean their minds were too. They were individual creatures making up a single organism, a super-organism. A family? Maybe.

"What makes one strong makes all of them strong. Same for what makes them weak," I told my reflection.

I was vulnerable, too, though. Their pull on my mind and emotions proved that. I'd need to take precautions to remain separate from them and not fall under the influence of my own genetic design. I was Rachel, but I was also a clone of someone else; someone they'd influenced and maybe even created.

"Yazadami," I murmured. That's what the Azatem had called my predecessor. "Do they think I'm the woman the Ohnenrai took from the harvester? Or do they think I'm a god?" I shook my head at that. "I'm no god. And I'm definitely not a savior. I'm just a woman, a mother."

A weapon.

I sighed.

Ehtishem said Yazadami was an old Ohnenrai god. The supreme being responsible for creation, change, and death. Or something like that. How did the Azatem and the Ohnenrai end up with a common god? How did the Azatem make the jump from worship to resurrection? And why was I stuck in the middle of the mess?

I straightened. "So the Azatem want me to create, transform, and destroy? Fine. I'll be their Yazadami, their false god." I smoothed the folds of my dress. "And I'll give them exactly what they deserve."

The locked portal said I was a prisoner, not a guest. These were near-solitary confinement conditions and I had to assume they'd last a long time. This was a game of attrition I planned to win and that meant surviving with my mind intact.

Routine, mental and physical exercise, and a way to track the passage of time. Those things I could control. They'd keep me sane, stop me from falling into the trap my DNA had set.

"My life prepared me for this," I said to the empty room. "Isolate me? I did that for eight years in Suffer. Touch me against my will? That was every day with Cyrus. Make me a murderer? Been there. Done that."

Those were small ordeals. But this? This was the real trial.

This was a test of my mother-fucking soul and I *would* endure until the deed was done.

I looked past the portal to the bright blue planet. "Cyrus couldn't break me. Neither could Isphahan or Ahremena. The Azatem won't either. I am steel forged in a crucible of cruelty."

I met my reflection's gaze.

"I'm Rachel Elizabeth Pryne. My daughter is Pearl Ellenore Pryne. My partner is Zosh Ehtishem Zain Mahle. I was born in San Diego, California, in the United States of America on the planet Earth, in the Milky Way Galaxy. My mother was Ellenore. My father was Joseph. And I will survive."

TWENTY-SIX

EHTISHEM NEVER THOUGHT he'd regret the limited broadcast range on the personnel trackers implanted in all Ohnenrai brains. But he did now because many nights, like this one, he lay in bed staring at his blinking com as it tried, and failed, to pinpoint Rachel's location.

That glowing yellow code blink-blink-blinked, mocking in its interminable indifference.

One hundred twenty-four days had passed since she'd been taken from him.

"I will find you, Pairika," he murmured, thumbing off the com and sticking it to the magnetic wall holder beside his bunk. That was a promise he would keep.

But how? He'd spent four-plus months trying to figure that out.

He rolled onto his back, clasped his hands behind his head, and stared into the dim room. *Pohru-Mahrko*'s engines thrummed through him, a rhythm as familiar as his own heartbeats. Pale blue light from the wall chron reflected off the galley's metal counter, interrupted by the blocky shape of *The Collected Works of William Shakespeare.*

The metal tube holding Azatem cells had rested on the galley counter in Rachel's quarters until Rivan and Kruhz had removed it, used it, and turned her into a beacon calling the Azatem. Those bacteria had followed the Azatem Code, unerring in their hunt, unwavering from their path, undaunted by anything he'd thrown at them. They'd known exactly where to find her because they'd had a long-range tracker of their own inside every one of her cells.

But Ehtishem didn't have anything like that.

Or did he?

His eyes widened and he grunted as if smacked by Sree, as if his old trainer had slapped the back of his skull and snapped, "Don't be dense, Ratheshtolo. Ahremena gave you a good brain. Why don't you use it better?"

"Why indeed." He rolled off his bunk. "Syscom, lights twenty-five percent." The lights came on as he snatched up his compad, accessed Ahremena's data, and started pacing while he searched.

It didn't take long to find what he wanted. *Azatem Code and Emotional Manipulation.* He retrieved the information and began reading.

By the time the first duty rotation came up, Ehtishem had a plan based on a hunch, which wasn't much to go on and certainly he'd never walk into battle on such skimpy ground-work, but his resources were scarce. "Beggars can't be choosers." He recalled that Terran saying and another one about wishes being horses. He shook his head. What he needed now wasn't sayings but soldiers. He sent a message to Mahzel: *I want to see you, Stig, Gohra, Vehl, and Fehrana at oh-nine-hundred in Cen EXO.*

Mahzel acknowledged the request and Ehtishem pulled a clean uniform from his locker.

They were going to find Rachel. And they were going to use the Azatem Code to do it.

Ehtishem leaned against the edge of a table in the briefing room. He considered his black boots as the gathered soldiers settled around him. The toes were scuffed; he hadn't noticed before. He should've. A scowl flitted across his face, automatically schooled to oblivion. He looked up, looked from face to face, folded his arms. "Theoretically, all of you have an established non-physical bond with Rachel Pryne. Mahz, Stig, and Gohra, I've read Sarem Mahlei's notes from the emotions experiments you participated in. I want to know if you truly believe Rachel linked with you." He turned to Vehl and Fehrana. "I've read the debriefing notes on Panca Seven-oh-one's time on Iodiq. I want to know what you experienced and how you connected with her."

The one soldier missing from the experiments was Huorem. Ehtishem didn't dwell on his friend's death or on the memory of Rachel's palpable grief. Hu's absence was a painful maw no one could ever fill. Ehtishem missed the smug bastard and his annoying whistling every day.

Stig cleared her throat. "It was one of the strangest experiences I've ever had, fra." The other soldiers nodded.

"How so?"

"The barethri pulled emotions out of me and," she paused, scratched the back of her short-shorn skull while she considered her words, then continued, "and she could've kept taking them, I think. If she'd wanted me to be miserable, she could've stolen all the happiness right out of my brain."

Fehrana said, "That's exactly what she did for us on Iodiq. We were panicking, to be honest, fra. Those critters were on our asses and we were getting slaughtered. I really thought we were lunch. I've never been that scared in battle. Somehow Barethri Rachel knew we were losing our vairim. She called us out, one by one, and she just took that fear and replaced it with confidence. It was just—" She shook her head.

"Unreal," Vehl finished. "If I hadn't experienced it, there's no way I'd believe someone could do that. No way."

Ehtishem nodded. He believed it. "I understand, pa'nerem. I've experienced the power of her influence first-hand. She's had a profound effect on my behavior." He gripped the edge of the table. "It's how she was designed. Sarem Mahlei made many mistakes. She was unconscionably arrogant and danger-ously subversive, but she was an outstanding geneticist. She created a deadly weapon. Hopefully, she also gave us a method of locating that weapon for recovery."

Mahzel said, "You think we can track Barethri Rachel because we've connected with her?"

"That's my hope."

Fehrana clapped her hands against her thighs. "When do we start?"

"And how?" Stig added.

"Now, but I'm as much in the dark on this as you are." Ehtishem folded his arms. "I'm open to suggestions."

Vehl flopped back in his chair. "Syscom, lights ten percent. Project *Pohru-Mahrko*'s current location."

Ehtishem straightened as a holographic depiction of the Milky Way Galaxy filled the briefing room. Yellow stars; blue, brown, and orange planets; grey moons; and white nebulae appeared all around them. Two red points located *Pohru-Mahrko* and *Ayan-Kanya* at the edge of one of the galaxy's spiraling arms.

Mahzel peered into the starscape while Stig and Gohra slowly moved around the room. Vehl remained seated and Ehtishem's gaze drifted from point to point. This felt like the right approach, but no matter where he looked, none of the locations called to him.

"That little Terran has a lot of power in her," Gohra muttered. "A lot of power and a lot of rage."

"You felt that too?" Vehl asked.

Mahzel replied, "Zant. You should've seen her vent her anger on the zosh." He arched a brow at Ehtishem. "I recall food being thrown at you, fra."

"And a threat of castration," Ehtishem added.

Vehl and Stig laughed. Gohra murmured, "Ferocious woman."

Ehtishem nodded. Ferocious, and iron-willed, and everything he'd ever wanted in a lover. His gaze traveled the Milky Way. His soldiers wandered and perused. *Pohru-Mahrko's* engines thrummed.

Vehl stretched, stood, and ambled through the stars. Stig sat on the floor, then laid flat. Gohra straddled a chair. Mahzel simply stood, hands clasped behind his back, his gaze moving methodically from point to point.

Time passed. The universe expanded, carrying Rachel farther away.

"She's not in this galaxy." Ehtishem suddenly knew beyond question.

His companions murmured agreement. They stretched, yawned, rubbed their eyes, rotated stiff shoulders and massaged sore necks. The wall chron showed they'd been there for almost three hours. He frowned. He had a ship inspection in thirty-five minutes.

Mahzel said, "Syscom, expand star map to include the known universe."

The density of stars brightened the room until the individual points couldn't be discerned. Vehl cursed beneath his breath. Squinting he said, "We need to be more systematic in our search."

"Agreed," Ehtishem replied. "Syscom, show all galaxies ten billion light years in all directions from *Pohru-Mahrko*'s current position."

"That's more manageable," Mahzel said as the room darkened again.

"This search could take a long time," Stig said.

"It'll take as long as it takes," Gohra replied.

Ehtishem nodded. "Consider this your new duty station, pa'nerem." He pushed away from the table. "I'll inform the thrai of your reassignment and I'll spend as much time beside you as I can manage. Work together to narrow the field. Let's find that weapon and put an end to the Azatem threat."

"Drax-*tu*," they replied in chorus.

Mahzel took charge. "Move these tables and chairs to the perimeter." The group started rearranging the furniture as Ehtishem exited the room.

Now they were getting somewhere.

Within his military, the hunger to find and ambush the Azatem had Ehtishem's soldiers working double shifts to complete *Pohru-Mahrko*'s repairs and get *Ayan-Kanya*'s systems one hundred percent functional. He wasn't the only Ohnenran who wanted to finish what Rachel had started.

Like *PM*, *Ayan-Kanya* was a Tarad-class super-heavy cruiser-carrier, but she was a third-generation ship, which made her an altogether different, larger, and deadlier beast. Using the corvettes as haulers, Timsai's engineers had gotten her parts into Iodiq orbit then assembled her enough to be space-worthy in thirty-three days. Her systems remained minimally functional and all able-bodied crew were scrambling to ready her for warfare. But once Ehtishem had seen her impressive main guns and advanced wormhole array, he wouldn't let her rot another day in the Havafna Caldera.

"She's barely habitable, but she'll make wormhole travel more efficient and she'll have some serious thunder in her belly," Timsai remarked before they'd left Iodiq.

Now aboard his personal transport, Ehtishem flew around her hull, inspecting her fully-assembled external systems. Her reflective surface hid her well, made all the more effective by her sleek organic curves.

But *Ayan-Kanya*'s wicked weapons arrays were what drew his critical eye. The technicians said her hyper-velocity weapons were intact. It was a technology both awesome and terrifying, and they were incredibly fortunate to have found her.

Aevadasa Sezenei co-piloted. "Wish we had her schematics." *Pohru-Mahrko*'s Chief Structural Engineer had taken on the job of completing *Ayan-Kanya*'s build while her lieutenant oversaw *PM*'s final repairs.

"What's the word on those arrays?" Ehtishem asked.

"They're close to being fully functional, but stabilizing the reactor was the first priority and proved to be trickier than expected. The entire housing had to be rebuilt. Really, we're fortunate she didn't fail during the first test jump, fra."

"Hmph. Have you maxed the engines?"

"Not yet. But the reactor's solid and stable now."

"Ash-ush."

Tinish eyed the ship. "Looking forward to taking command of her, fra?"

"Thrai Timsai will have that privilege. *Pohru-Mahrko* will remain our capital ship."

Sezenei nodded. "She may be smaller and war-weary, but she's a tough, reliable lady."

Gahlen murmured, "That she is."

Their transport came around the aft of the modern cruiser-carrier and Ehtishem guided the small ship into *AK*'s open forward belly bay.

"Interior work's ahead of schedule," Sezenei remarked. "We were able to salvage all the communications systems, and retrofitting her water purification went faster than expected."

"Good."

She was a massive predator whose innards remained exposed. Skeleton and nerves laid bare, a body open for maggots to crawl through, picking out the dead pieces and leaving behind what worked. But these maggots were bringing life to the beast. Bugbots crawled through her computer boards and bio-systems like Terran ants. Technicians crawled through her structure wielding plasma arc welders like surgeons.

They made him think of Rachel, bent over his bleeding and broken leg, exacting and relentless in her dedication to removing all traces of infection from a wound that should have killed him. He'd never told her just how much agony he'd been in. He never would. She probably knew he'd been wearing a brave face for her benefit.

The Terran foreman, Lot Jones, was Rachel's friend. He'd been in the Pacific Northwest Sector compound where Ehtishem found her. Ehtishem didn't like the man, but he respected him. They'd worked together to get most of the imprisoned Terrans off *Dathusha* and back to their home world before Isphahan had gotten wind of the scheme and shut down the operation. He appreciated Lot's loyalty, determination, and skills, rewarding him and a handful of other Terrans with work alongside Sezenei and the Ohnenrai crews assembling *Ayan-Kanya*. Lot proved capable of wrangling his own people and standing up to the Ohnenrai without making enemies of either.

As Ehtishem dropped from the transport to the bubble deck, Lot put his fingers in his mouth and gave an ear-piercing whistle. Within seconds he had the entire crew's attention.

"Zosh on deck. Watch where you spit!" He waved them back to work as his Ohnenrai assistant interpreted.

Ehtishem nodded and said in English, "Thank you for that courtesy." Despite fans and the ventilation system on high, residual ozone from the welding irritated the workers' sinuses. They were supposed to wear masks, but the Terrans complained that the Ohnenrai-sized apparatuses were ineffective and uncomfortable. Some of them wrapped bandanas around their faces, but most just snorted saline. The ship was an echo chamber of hissing welders, clanking and groaning metal, and guttural snorting as the techs cleared their sinuses and spat.

"No one wants spit in the eye." Lot adjusted his cap and nodded at Sezenei. "Where's that water you promised me, frei? We got the paradox coupler back in place yesterday, finished reinforcing the inner-hull and have the atmosphere functioning ship-wide. I'm told the command deck's now fully functional and your HV arrays are ready for testing."

"Working on the water," she replied. "I know the ship's dead without it."

"Good to hear." The Terran man nodded. "I'll give you a tour since this lady will be out of my hands soon."

The engineering chief begged off the tour as Ehtishem glanced at his chron. Two hours until supper. He wanted to spend more time with the star map before hitting the gym and his bunk. "You've got thirty minutes, Lot." Tinish and Gahlen followed as they climbed aboard a waiting skiff.

Ehtishem studied the arching overhead. "Did the bots double-check the main beams?

"Zant, fra, and confirmed the joints are solid all the way to her nano-welds. Nothing short of a supernova will rattle her."

Ehtishem listened and questioned and, most importantly, looked. The construction crew had dismantled the hull scaffold, reusing it in other parts of the ship as the framework for interior walls. They'd saved the finish work until after they departed Iodiq. As the skiff entered the ship's primary personnel accommodations deck, he tapped Lot's shoulder. "Stop here."

The skiff landed in what would soon be one of four mess halls.

Ehtishem inhaled, sucking the air over his tongue. He turned to his guards. "Do you smell that?"

Gahlen nodded and Tinish replied, "Taste it too, fra."

The Terran sniffed the air, his head high like a dog trying to scent the way home. "What should I be smelling?"

The zosh answered, "Traces of sulphur. Your sinuses are too dry to pick it up. The scrubbers are malfunctioning."

Pulling an atmospheric reader from his pocket, Lot took a quick reading. "That's not good." He contacted the senior atmo engineer. "There's a problem in North Mess."

"Doubtful," the man replied.

"Definitely." Lot sent his readings to the engineer. "Get your team down here and fix this. I want a status update on the hour."

"My team doesn't take orders from a Terran. *I'll* redirect them once they've completed the dry storage hookups."

"You'll redirect them here now. I won't have anyone breathing blood on my watch, especially not Zosh Mahle."

"The zosh?" the engineer said.

Lot turned his com so the Ohnenran could see Ehtishem, who ignored the man's hasty salute.

The senior engineer said, "We'll get right on it."

"I thought so." Lot cut the communication.

Ehtishem turned to Gahlen. "Make a note that I'm removing him from his position. I don't trust a man who places the well-being of soldiers second to dry goods."

Lot nodded. "We're in agreement on that, fra."

Once the atmo engineering crew had normalized the readings, Lot took Ehtishem to the command deck.

"I want to know if you're getting pushback from the crews," Ehtishem said as he returned the salutes of his soldiers on deck.

Lot nodded. "So far it's been subtle, but not a problem I can't tackle. But, honestly, your people are hard to read. That makes it tricky for me to see the push coming before I've been shoved."

"I've heard that before."

"No doubt from Rachel." Lot chuckled, then stiffened when he realized the zosh wasn't sharing his amusement. "I apologize, fra."

Ehtishem didn't look at him, didn't give the slightest tell to reveal his reaction. "Apology accepted. And you're not incorrect." He clasped his hands behind his back and pinned the Terran with a steady stare. "I find it strange that anyone concerns themselves with my private affairs."

"Conjecture, poker, and daspa are the only entertainment most of these people have." Lot indicated the crew crawling in, out, and around the command deck. "Terrans are notoriously nosy about their neighbors." He risked a glance at Ehtishem and added, "I imagine you're hemmed in by curiosity, fra."

Ehtishem studied the Terran foreman for a long moment before replying. "I'm accustomed to tight spaces." He surveyed the area, suppressing a smile as he watched two Terran boys and their mother crawling into the small service space that ran beneath the deck. Usually Ohnenrai technicians relied on bots to run those cables and wires, but having few of those at his disposal, Lot had authorized his crews to utilize the smallest Terrans capable of performing the job. Ehtishem had seen women and children crawling around the ventilation system, too.

Ayan-Kanya was coming together quicker than he'd anticipated. He didn't regret his decision to put Terrans to work side-by-side with his crew. It would take the Ohnenrai far in overcoming xenophobia. There'd been incidents, but fewer than he'd expected. Lot's suggestion of distributing decks of cards and sets of daspa tiles had been genius. Both the Terrans and the Ohnenrai enjoyed games. There was even talk of a tournament.

He nodded, satisfied with the ship's progress. Soon she'd be battle-ready. Soon his small group would pick up Rachel's trail. Soon they'd have a rescue and their revenge. "Show me Weapons Control," he said.

"With pleasure." Lot gestured for Ehtishem to precede him.

TWENTY-SEVEN

"EIGHT HUNDRED SIXTY-EIGHT." I carved another hash mark into the wall, an ongoing count of days that spanned the room. "I'm Rachel Elizabeth Pryne. My daughter is Pearl Ellenore Pryne. My partner is Zosh Ehtishem Zain Mahle. I was born in San Diego, California, in the United States of America on the planet Earth, in the Milky Way Galaxy. My mother was Ellenore. My father was Joseph."

I'd spent two years and three months with the Azatem, being the poison in their system, an addiction without a cure. All the while, I was dutiful. I let them collect their precious DNA. I attended their creepy grope fest every day. I wore the clothes they provided, ate the food they brought, and clung to my sanity while waiting for Ehtishem to find me or the Azatem to die.

Every day I awoke expecting them to realize I was a monster in their midst. Every day I saw fewer of their kind roaming the bridges and paths, felt fewer of their bony fingers on my skin, sensed fewer of them in my mind.

Every day I expected them to read my thoughts, figure out the bomb the Ohnenrai had planted in their midst, and turn on me, the clone created to kill them.

"Not today, I guess," I muttered and plaited my hair. It reached the middle of my back.

Next step in my daily routine was exercise. I pulled the back of my dress hem forward between my legs, brought it up, and tied the ends at my waist to make a jumper of sorts, then I planked on the floor, hands shoulder-width apart, legs straight. One hundred pushups. "One, two, three..."

Followed by one hundred sit-ups, one hundred squats, one hundred jumping jacks. And, if I wasn't interrupted, I'd repeat the cycle until I was bored or too sore to continue. Ehtishem would be proud. But, really, what else was there to do? I couldn't leave my room. I had no companions, no purpose.

Except death.

"Eight, nine, ten, eleven..."

Repetition. Routine. Mental and physical exercises kept me sane. Mostly. They kept me from wondering how much time had passed for Ehtishem and how much longer I'd have to wait. And they distracted me from the ever-widening wound Pearl's loss had opened in my mind.

"Fifteen, sixteen, seventeen—" I paused mid-pushup and stood, brushing my palms on my dress as the chamber portal opened. My primary Azatem caretaker entered, the one I'd named Sandy.

"You're early," I said. She gave me the usual bland look, bowed, and ignored me.

I'd found tiny differences among my half-dozen regular caretakers and used those traits to name them. Sandy and I were equal in height and build, and after years of continually integrating my DNA into her genome, like all the surviving humanoid Azatem, she had green eyes and a heart-shaped face.

But her skin remained the gray-brown hue of wet sand, hence her name. Of course she, like the rest of the Azatem, would never have a white mahle mark on their faces.

I thought of Pearl's bright smile, her infectious laugh. They'd never have a beautiful daughter.

I touched the ring Ehtishem had given me. They'd never have a powerful lover.

I crossed my arms. They'd never be me.

Sandy replaced my dirty clothes with clean ones, exchanged my chamber pot for an empty one, and cleared my morning dishes. After the introductions on the day I'd arrived, none of the Azatem had said anything to me. Not. A. Word. Their silence was deafening, maddening, louder than any sound I'd ever heard.

I spoke English and Ohnenrai fluently, other languages, too, though they were slipping away with disuse. But the Azatem language escaped me, not because it was particularly alien, but because they refused to converse with me or even in my presence. How do you learn a language if you never hear it?

Unlike me, Sandy and company could come and go as they pleased. Though I was their savior, I was also their prisoner and most of my days were spent staring at the same walls, ceiling, floor, the same blue planet outside my window. My caretakers, however, did what they wanted, even though I told them to piss off on a regular basis.

The one named Honey entered and offered me a new gown. She'd earned that name because she seemed a bit sweeter than her sisters, occasionally making eye-contact and, rarely, smiling.

"It's green," I said. It was a sickly shade of cabbage, to be precise. "Why is it green?"

Honey met my gaze. Honey smiled. I was pretty sure

Honey only pretended to be dumber than a box of rocks. But was she trying to fool me or everyone else?

"Fine, whatever." I took the dress and stripped. I'd lost all modesty amid the Azatem. They didn't care if I was naked, so why should I? The green might mean they planned to make me lunch today. Or maybe it meant they'd reached some mutational milestone. Or maybe someone had the brilliant idea of dyeing some fabric. The change should've excited or worried me but I couldn't summon the will to give a whooptie-fucking-doo.

Two more caretakers arrived, Lucy and Ethel. Lucy's name was suggested by the reddish hue of her hair. And Ethel was so named because she followed Lucy everywhere.

They were here to put up my hair and like a good little prisoner, I sat at the table and closed my eyes while the dynamic duo brushed it, carefully preserving every loose strand. The hair would be added to the ship's water supply. The same fate awaited my nail clippings and my wastewater, something I tried not to think about whenever I was drinking.

The daily routine never changed. Six Azatem body servants entered uninvited, provided food and clothing, and prepared me for the daily pawing. They accompanied me to the grope fest and marched me back to my chamber afterward.

Mind-numbing days passed, each marked by a number carved into the wall. My room remained lit for twelve hours then plunged into darkness for another twelve.

I amused myself by imagining I heard Pearl talking about her day. How she'd trained Audie to be extra quiet. How Ahnoru was growing hybrid fruit in Ehtishem's garden so everyone had something other than bugs to eat. How she'd found a place where she could see the stars. Sometimes I cried for hours, convinced I'd lost the war against madness just as surely as I'd lost my daughter and my lover.

Beside the green gown, something else was different. Honey had taken up a guard position usually occupied by Peaches.

"Ah," I said in Ohnenrai. "I see natural selection spoiled Peaches. That's good. The strong grow stronger; the weak die."

"Yazadami," Honey murmured reverentially then looked down at the floor under Sandy's sudden scrutiny.

I'd also noticed not all was equal inside the hive mind these days. The sisterhood had developed a hierarchy. The undertakers and janitorial staff dealt with waste, refuse, the bodies of the dead. The nurses cared for the Azatem when they were encapsulated for mutation. The caretakers saw to the feeding, clothing, and defense of all their sisters. And my caretakers — the priestesses — had seized a position above all others. They controlled access to me, guarding it like misers. Everyone got an equal share of my DNA. Except my caretakers, of course. They got extra helpings and protected the privilege with their fists.

As the passing days had turned to weeks then months, I'd discovered I could explore my captors' emotions, as long as I did it when I wasn't being groped. During those hours, their frenzy was too alluring and I had to shut out everything or fall into that deep, addictive pool. But times like this, when it was just Yazadami's priestesses, I eased back on the vairim and tested their emotional state.

Honey was agitated by Peaches' failure. So were Lucy and Ethel. But Olive and Sandy were gratified. Her death proved their superiority. They'd begun to see their sisters as competition. A sense of individuality was a recent development among the Azatem, and it was an unexpected weakness I was all too happy to exploit.

Strike when you need to.

"Too bad. I liked Peaches. Still, survival hinges on more than just powerful genes," I mused. "Sometimes the strongest are those who fight hardest to live. You gotta do whatever it takes to outlast your enemies. That'll decide who ultimately rules."

Sandy and Olive watched me, their gazes keen. Those bitches caught my drift, even if they didn't understand Ohnenrai.

That meant it was time to start playing favorites.

Ethel was fussing with my hair. "Too bad it wasn't you." I slapped her hands away and stood. "Let's get this shit over with," I announced in English and headed for the door.

As our group moved along the wide spiraling path toward the gathering hall, an Azatem sister I didn't know kept pace with me. She side-eyed me, glanced at the priestesses, then darted close and touched my arm.

Sandy pivoted and slammed a weapon into the woman's face. It was a short, electrified baton and the blue spark it emitted made her screech and jerk like a broken marionette. Olive barged her away from me. Clawing at her burned face, she stumbled across the walkway and collapsed against the inner wall, sobbing and twitching.

I held my breath and looked straight ahead. I was a god. I was above caring about suffering and need. I didn't smell the stench of burned flesh and hair. I didn't see my own vengeance at work. I hadn't just vomited a little in my mouth, hadn't swallowed acid bile. My stomach wasn't a fist and my skin wasn't cold and clammy.

No. None of that.

I was a god.

After the groping, I returned to my chamber and scrubbed the intrusion from my skin. Too bad I couldn't scrub my brain and my eyeballs. I wanted to forget the violence enacted by Sandy and Olive. Would that woman survive her wounds? I'd never seen scars or wounds on any of the Azatem. Did they destroy the wounded, the sick, the infirm?

"Probably." That was an ugly truth.

Toweling my hair dry, I emerged from the bathing area, my bare feet slapping the cold floor. I stopped, stared, slowly lowered the towel.

The room's portal was open.

No caretakers were present and no one stood guard. Someone had replaced all my white dresses with green ones. They'd left food and water on the table, they'd changed my bed linens. And they'd left the portal open.

"Ooh," I whispered, "someone's gonna get busted."

I stood at the opening, watching the Azatem go about their day and debating the wisdom of making a run for it. Not that I really had anyplace to run to but freedom was mighty tempting, even if it was an illusion.

Someone would catch unholy hell for this mistake. That should've bothered me, but the lure of new horizons was too tantalizing not to take that first unaccompanied step.

I cleared the threshold. The portal closed behind me. I froze.

In the years I'd been aboard *Maso*, I'd never been outside my chamber without Olive, Sandy, and Honey.

I took a deep breath, pushed down panic, and struck out, determined to take advantage of this momentary release.

No one came near me, spoke to me, touched me. They looked away quickly when I caught their eyes and they gave me a wide berth, kept at bay by fear of my caretakers' vengeance.

Maso was bigger than any city I'd ever visited, much bigger than *Dathusha*. I stuck to the path that spiraled around the spine and descended as far as the gathering chamber. Once there, I stood at the turn beyond that massive hall and considered my options. Continue downward or cross one of the bridges and explore some of the antechambers that I'd glimpsed in passing? Foot traffic lessened in the lower levels from what I could see, and I didn't want to get lost in the ship's endless maze.

"Antechambers, it is," I muttered and crossed the next bridge to a dimly lit passage. It dead-ended in a rotunda with portals all around. I winced as I bit into my cheek, perpetually raw from a habit Ehtishem hated but I couldn't break. I considered the doorways then moved to each one, trying to trigger them to open. The fourth portal yielded and dim light spilled out.

Nothing in my lifetime of messed-up experiences had prepared me for what I saw.

I'd blundered into a metamorphosis chamber. Neat rows of chrysalides lined both sides of a walkway. Human-sized, pearlescent, and shaped like fleshy sarcophagi, most of the chrysalides were translucent and light-colored, ranging from cream to golden in hue, and subtly throbbing with life. But several sat like black, gangrenous wounds, emitting the putrid stench of rot. One was open and two Azatem nurses stood beside it, staring at me. I'd caught them in the midst of removing one of their dead sisters.

"Oh, shit." I backed out fast, turned, and ran. I'd just seen the result of my DNA's disruption of Azatem hybridization: Non-viable nightmares with my half-formed face, decomposing organs, and buckled bones.

That was what Peaches had become.

Terror constricted my chest. I wiped my sleeve across my eyes and swallowed a sob.

The bridge curved and sloped downward. Light dimmed

until the hall I was following was nearly dark. Azatem foot traffic had thinned to none. I slowed, stopped, looked around.

"Hell-and-a-half." I'd taken many wrong turns. I leaned against the wall to catch my breath and calm my nerves. "Where the hell am I?" My voice echoed back, shaky, muted, and unhelpful.

Maso-Vohu was a weapon, a house, a laboratory, a cradle and, I now had to accept, more and more a tomb. Like Iodiq's tunnels and caves, the red monolith had a naturally-formed structure; the body of some beast the Azatem had enslaved, mutated, and made their home, symbiosis at its worst. They added more and more machine to what had once been a free being. What remained was a bio-mechanical monstrosity.

A small portal filtered dim light into the hall. I peered through it and saw the blue planet from a new angle. I'd gone much farther into the ship's guts than I'd realized. I stared at it. When they'd brought me aboard, the Azatem had stopped all exploration. They'd ceased all acquisition of new DNA. *Maso* ceaselessly orbited the planet because only my genes mattered to the Azatem now. The race for hybrid vigor compelled the rapid mutations and deaths taking place in chrysalides all over the ship. Instead of demonstrating superior qualities with the introduction of my supposedly top-tier genome, the Azatem were drinking the Kool-Aid, committing mutational meltdown, and spiraling toward annihilation.

I was committing slow genocide, a fact I hadn't wanted to face.

"No regrets," I whispered into the void. "No. Regrets." Regret was for the weak and I had no use for weakness.

Yet regret sank its teeth into my conscience. "No, they started this." I recalled *Pohru-Mahrko* under attack. Blood and gore flowing down the drains in the ship's trauma bay, the nasty mutated Azatem critters scuttling through Iodiq's dark caves with their enormous staring eyes, sharp claws, and sharper teeth. Huorem blowing himself up and Rivan's rotting face and staring eyes. Ehtishem being jerked down into the hole, their howls and screams like coyotes catching their prey as they sank their teeth into his calf and tore it open.

"Stubborn bastard." I missed the man so much, I ached thinking of him, doubled over with need to hear his voice, feel his strong arms around me.

I looked at the ring of stardust encircling my finger and packed away those memories then turned instead to Pearl. She must've been terrified when *Dathusha* was captured. Her absence burned a hole where my heart had been. Dwelling on my daughter becoming a meal for the Azatem had left me huddled in a corner for hours many times. "No. No." I shook my head, clenched my fists. "Don't go there, Rachel." I shoved thoughts of her away too, which was a solution almost as painful as the problem.

So I stumbled onward, my footfalls echoing as I rounded a curve and reached another portal. It opened at my approach. The pungent scent of death was subtle but unmistakable. Covering my mouth and nose with my gown's neckline, I stared into a massive launch bay. Its overhead arched to triple the height of the other levels and rounded into the walls. Much larger chrysalis-like structures, dark and dead, occupied half the storage space. Some had been emptied, their occupants left to rot on the floor. Dead reapers. In the distance I saw an enormous harvester, also black, unmoving, lifeless. Were they dying because of exposure to my DNA, too? Or was it a lack of care by the dwindling Azatem humanoid populace?

I turned away from the leather-skinned, metal-boned monstrosities. I'd been carried to *Maso-Vohu* in a reaper's slimy guts and that memory threatened to shake loose my tenuous vairim.

Stepping back, I found a ladder. "Okay. Up." At the top, I opened a hatch and emerged onto a long catwalk. My feet thudded a hollow rhythm and I looked down, realizing I was above that huge launch bay and could see into it through the grating. At the other end of the catwalk, I found another portal. It opened at my approach and I staggered through, too shocked by what I saw to think of anything but moving forward.

Dathusha.

Like a massive beached whale, she lay on her side, torn open from stem to stern, the victim of a vicious attack. Tran-screte, wiring and conduit, huge magstenite support struts, furniture, pieces of transport rails and smashed bullet cars spilled from her belly. Broken bits of what had once been a home to millions lay in heaps. Fire had blackened gaping wounds up and down her sides. What I didn't see were skeletons, and I didn't know if that was something to feel hopeful or hopeless about.

"Pearl," I whispered.

"Momma?"

I swore I heard her in my mind and called louder, "Pearl?" A mixture of hope and panic tightened my chest.

"Yazadami."

I squeaked and whirled around, my heart hammering.

Sandy stood just inside the portal, a baton in her hand. Jeez, she was stealthy.

Like a child caught snooping for Christmas gifts I blurted out in Ohnenrai, "Someone left my room portal open."

She looked past me to the ship, her gaze drifting up and over the hulking metal carcass of what had once been my home. Her attention returned to me and her disapproval came across, a blue-black ribbon of oppression wrapping around me and squeezing. She gestured for me to follow her and started back through the opening. No explanation, no accusation, no room for discussion.

I hesitated, considered defying her, but I wasn't sure she wouldn't use that weapon to stop me. I sighed and trailed her, but not without looking back and wondering.

Pearly Girly, are you really here?

TWENTY-EIGHT

"COORDINATES ARE ACCEPTED AND LOCKED. The tethers are strong. Formation is stable. We're entering the wormhole now, Zosh."

"All systems report normal."

"FTL readings are holding steady. *Pohru-Mahrko* and *Ayan-Kanya* report hull stresses and engine readings in the normal ranges."

The strange warping of Ehtishem's insides meant *Pohru-Mahrko* was passing through folded space six months after Rachel's disappearance. *PM* was second to enter the wormhole, tethered behind *Ayan-Kanya*. While *Pohru-Mahrko* remained the flagship, *Ayan-Kanya* had the most advanced internal faster-than-light drives of any ship that had ever existed in the Ohnenrai fleet. Timsai had her command and was shepherding her sister ship through the wormhole.

A shrill klaxon sounded and the deck lights turned amber.

"Event horizon forming. Exit in twenty seconds."

Ehtishem nodded. "Keep all hands at their action stations.

Ayan-Kanya will drop the tethers and we'll begin weapons tests upon event collapse."

A chorus of "Zant, fra," filled the command deck.

This was more than just a test of *AK's* FTL drives. Ehtishem and Timsai were determined to be battle-ready before the next confrontation with *Maso-Vohu*. They'd scheduled ongoing systems tests and crew drills for both ships. They would not be caught with their pants around their ankles again.

"Exiting in five, four, three, two, one."

Ehtishem scanned his crew. All were focused. *Ushta.*

"We've cleared the event horizon. Wormhole collapsing."

The Fisk Juncture offered a spectacular view of a binary star system enclosed by a massive ring of glowing orange gas and dust. It also offered asteroids aplenty for target practice and Timsai already had *Ayan-Kanya's* HV cannons blasting away. Cousin to *Pohru-Mahrko's* weapons, *AK's* hyper-velocity arrays used smaller ammo launched at rates ten thousand times greater than *PM's* cannons could manage. She produced destruction well beyond any other Ohnenrai ship's capabilities. Like *PM*, she was significantly smaller than *Maso*, but *Ayan-Kanya* had enough muscle to tear the Azatem battleship in half.

"Com, hail *Ayan-Kanya*," Ehtishem said. "Helm, watch her debris field. Do we have shields at maximum power? Someone show me exteriors."

"Hailing *Ayan-Kanya*, fra."

"Forward shields at full power."

"Exteriors on screen."

Ehtishem considered the view that appeared on one of the larger overhead screens. *Ayan-Kanya's* HVCs were obliterating asteroids the size of troop transports, turning them into dust.

"*Ayan-Kanya's* responding to our hail, fra. On screen now."

Timsai appeared, an uncharacteristic glee in his eyes. "Enjoying the show, Zosh?"

"It's impressive, Thrai. Getting any instability from those cannons?"

"Nava. Wish I could meet whoever designed her dampers. We're running smooth and quiet over here."

"Ash-ush," Ehtishem replied. "Leave a few rocks for us, nerem."

"Will do." Timsai saluted and ended the conversation.

Ehtishem settled back in his command chair and said, "Let's go to tactical and find some targets of our own, pa'nerem. We can't let the thrai have all the fun."

"Going to tactical."

"Targeting acquired."

Ehtishem said, "Fire at will."

―――――

Five even tones sounded throughout the ship, signaling the end of Gray Watch and the beginning of Black Watch. Ehtishem reached forward, stretching the stiffness out of his back and shoulders. He should've been asleep. He'd returned to his quarters just as Gray had gone on duty, but his churning mind kept him awake and on the sofa, carving an ushika from a piece of basswood. Now it was passing the middle of the night and he still wasn't tired.

His neck crackled as he rotated his head. The fifth tone faded.

He stood, shrugged into his coat, and left his quarters with the rough sculpture and his woodcarving kit in hand. He nodded to the soldiers who'd drawn guard duty outside his door. They followed him, silent, respectful, as he wended his way through *Pohru-Mahrko*'s guts to reach one of her mess halls.

Some of Gray Watch were filling their bellies, and he returned their salutes as he perused the available meal options at a long counter occupying one end of the open room. Bugs and suxra, the usual, although someone had sliced the pucks into wafers and baked them until they were crisp.

Gohra stood behind the counter. "They taste the same, but the texture's different."

"Change is good." He accepted a small bowl of them from her. "I thought I reassigned you."

"You did, fra, but I can only stare at a million points of light for so long."

He grunted. "Change is good?"

She replied, "Zant," and added a mug of suxra to his tray. "Can't sleep?"

"The body is willing, but the mind is occupied."

She jerked her chin toward the soldiers seated around the hall. "There's a lot of that these days."

"Nerves will do that to you. Might be time for another hamistayeca." He considered the rise and fall of murmured conversation, ignored the gazes that landed on him then slipped away. The crew's edginess hadn't escaped him, though he'd hoped the past week's wormhole jumps and military exercises with *Ayan-Kanya*'s crew would help.

"Wouldn't hurt, but what everyone really wants is to bust some Azatem heads."

"Me too. We owe those bastards." He handed the mug back to her. "Dump that into a thermos. I'm heading for Cen EXO."

She obliged and bagged the chips for him, too.

The halls were empty as Ehtishem made his way to the briefing room. When he entered, he found Mahzel leaning against the table, arms folded, brow furrowed.

"Can't sleep?" The star map filled the space, the only illumination in the dim room.

The aevadasa pushed away from the table. "Nava. You?"

Ehtishem shook his head. He extended the bag and gave it a little shake. "Bug chip?"

"Do they taste any better this way?" Mahzel asked and fished one from the bag.

"Nava."

Mahzel ate it, considered, shrugged. "The texture's different. That's a change I'll embrace. I'm tired of disks and gruel."

"Hockey pucks and bug paste." Ehtishem crunched on a chip. "That's what Rachel calls them. She's not a fan."

"I remember. She said they taste like starvation."

Ehtishem laughed. "She has a way with words."

"I miss that." Mahzel took another chip. "Her bluntness."

Ehtishem saluted him with a chip of his own. "So do I, nerem."

"I'm sorry I failed, fra." Mahzel stared into the room, his expression dispassionate but his voice low and surprisingly mournful. "I don't deserve to be called your friend."

Ehtishem put the chips aside. Their novelty had worn off. "You earned my friendship long ago, Mahz. A mistake can't undo years of dedication."

"That mistake cost Huorem's life. It resulted in the barethri's abduction."

"We're all guilty of failing." Ehtishem gripped Mahzel's shoulder. "I'm an expert at it. But we can't let failure stop us. We can't let guilt paralyze us."

"Nava," Mahzel said. "May as well curl up in a corner and die, if we're going to give in to self-pity."

Ehtishem clasped his hands behind his back. "Rachel would kill me if I did that."

Mahzel nodded. "No doubt about that." He moved to the

center of the room, sat on the floor, and laid back. "Syscom, push out ten billion light years from the last ending position." He folded his hands behind his head as the star map adjusted and another mass of unfamiliar systems replaced a roomful of planets and stars that had been considered and discarded by Ehtishem's team.

"Still no Rachel," Ehtishem murmured and rubbed his fingers over his right temple. He had not exactly a headache, more like pressure, a sudden nagging discomfort. He stared into the field of stars, not really seeing them or anything else.

"You alright, fra?"

The question brought his gaze to Mahzel. Was it best to answer that with the truth? Or did his aevadasa need a lie to comfort him? "A bit tired," Ehtishem replied, deciding Mahzel deserved the truth. He could handle it. He'd seen his zosh in some pretty bad spots and stuck by his side. This wasn't different. He massaged his temple again, stared into the starscape again.

Where are you, Pairika?

Mahzel sat up, draped his arms over his knees and stared in the same direction. He cleared his throat.

"Zant?"

"I—" Mahzel hesitated, squinted, continued in a bit of a rush, as if he wasn't sure how Ehtishem would react. "I keep wanting to look in that direction, fra." He jerked his chin in the same direction Ehtishem was facing.

Ehtishem looked from his aevadasa to the stars and planets Mahzel had indicated. "So do I." As if that realization was behind the pressure in his head, Ehtishem's discomfort eased.

Mahzel stood and came to his side. They considered the tantalizing possibility that they'd discovered the first hints of Rachel's location and simultaneously nodded.

"Ash-ush," Ehtishem murmured.

"Let's not say anything to the rest of the team."

"Wait to see if they corroborate our hunch independently?" Ehtishem fished another chip from the bag. "A good idea."

Stig and Vehl joined them an hour into the morning's Yellow Watch. During the first week of their group's activities, they'd agreed that a quorum was adequate to declare a sector clear and move the starscape forward, so Vehl's first comment upon entering Cen EXO was, "Quorum reached last night, eh?"

Ehtishem and Mahzel had spent the remainder of Black Watch narrowing the scope of their search. They'd concluded that Rachel's location wasn't among the stars and planets represented, but they had a clear sense of direction to pursue. They'd found her trail.

Stig had a bowl of gruel and stood shoveling it into her mouth as she slowly surveyed the map. She chewed, swallowed, shoveled in another bite, her gaze roaming systematically around the room until her focus reached the same direction that had pulled Ehtishem and Mahzel so clearly only hours earlier. She started to look past it but tilted her head and returned to that quadrant, frowning. Spoon midway to her mouth, she stared then moved unerringly along the path of stars and planets toward the edge of the map, stopping when she reached the wall.

Meanwhile, as had become his habit, Vehl ambled up and down the length and breadth of the room. Instead of looking at the lights, he looked at the floor. He said it helped him *feel* the right direction. Or, at least, he'd hoped it would. So far nothing had come to him, but he was unwavering in his certainty that it would.

Stig turned to Ehtishem and opened her mouth to speak,

but he silenced her with a gesture and a nod toward Vehl. She nodded and waited, her meal forgotten as she alternated between watching her peer and studying the path that was so clearly calling her.

As Vehl approached the quadrant, Fehrana and Gohra arrived. Gohra had brought suxra and mugs for all of them and another bag of bug chips. Vehl crossed the path and continued to drift along, no hesitation or sign of any change.

Ehtishem schooled his expression and fought disappointment. He was so certain, but he wanted validation from the rest of the group. He didn't want to send *Pohru-Mahrko* and *Ayan-Kanya* on a search for a needle in a haystack without a firm consensus that they were at least searching the right farm, even if there were a billion haystacks and a billion trillion pieces of hay.

Instead, he pulled the ushika carving from his pocket and focused on that. He was shaping its delicate, rounded ears, carefully notching the wood and removing tiny chunks to get the right depth.

Fehrana walked directly into Rachel's Quadrant and stopped, her eyes wide and expression twisted up with puzzlement. Gohra watched her, equally puzzled.

Vehl suddenly stopped, looked up, and pointed at Stig. "We need to go that direction."

"Zant!" Stig said, nodding like one of those weird bobble-headed figurines some Terrans kept on their desks.

Ehtishem suppressed a smirk. He hadn't thought of those strange little toys in years.

"Oh, good," Fehrana said. "I'm glad I'm not the only one."

"You're not," Mahzel replied. "The zosh and I noticed it when we changed the map last night. "The pull is unmistakable."

Ehtishem watched Gohra. She was the only one who hadn't confirmed their hunch. "Gohra?"

She met his gaze. "I'm not sure, fra. There's...something. But I'm not sure about the location or what it is exactly."

"What does it feel like?" he asked, fingering the wood, feeling for rough spots.

She frowned, schooled her expression back to neutral, then pressed her fingers agains her temple, just like he had early that morning. "Pressure here," she said.

"That's what you described," Mahzel said to Ehtishem.

He nodded. "It feels like your brain is trying to pull you."

Gohra nodded. "Zant." She massaged her temple. "It's not painful, just strange. Like my brain wants to escape my skull."

"*Sounds* painful," Vehl remarked and Gohra laughed.

She shook her head. "Hard to explain."

Ehtishem nodded. "Eresh, but I understand." He surveyed his team. "I think we have our first solid clue." He pulled his com from his coat pocket and contacted Timsai.

His friend's face appeared against a darkened room. Sleep thickened his voice. "Problem, Ehtishem?"

"Nava. Sorry to wake you, but there's something we need to discuss. Can you come to *PM*?"

All the sleep had fled Timsai's face. "Zant. Give me," he peered at his chron, "fifty minutes."

"Ash-ush. Meet me in Cen EXO."

Ehtishem closed the connection. A smile slowly curved his lips and he let it. Rachel was out there. He felt it. His team felt it too. They wouldn't stop until they brought her home and turned those Azatem bastards into ash.

TWENTY-NINE

I'D HEARD NO MORE from Pearl since discovering *Dathusha*. I didn't know why she'd fallen silent. Maybe she'd never actually spoken. Maybe she was a figment of my splintering mind. The only way I'd find out if my daughter was alive or if I was completely nuts was to get aboard that ship.

I gotta get past Sandy and the Sister Squad.

They'd kept me under even closer supervision since my escape, one or two of them standing guard at my door at all times. I tore another chunk of bread from my morning roll and shoved it in my mouth, thinking about Pearl and *Dathusha*. I had to escape my prison.

I started to chew, but something tugged at the corner of my lip. "For Christ's sake," I muttered and fished a strand of wavy hair out of my mouth. It had grown long enough to snag my fingers, was always in my face, and knotted like a rat's nest at night. My hair had become one more shackle, and I was sick of the attendants messing with it.

I pushed the plate away, propped my elbows on the table, my chin upon my hands. "Stupid, hair. I'm tired of eating you,"

I muttered as it fell like a curtain around my face. I blew it away. It drifted back. Story of my life.

I ate almost as much of my hair as the bland Azatem food. I curled my lip and considered the bread, then the jerky, the bread again, and my gut lurched. "Shit." I sat upright because eating my hair had sent my brain off on a weird tangent and a truly horrific thought had crossed my mind and gotten stuck.

There'd been almost eight million Ohnenrai citizens aboard the mother ship when she was captured. The ship had been largely intact when I found it. Those people went *somewhere*. And now I was swallowing my gorge because I'd also wondered where the Azatem were getting their food now that they were in perpetual orbit and my brain had come to a nightmare conclusion.

The bread? That was probably safe, probably made from vegetable matter. But the jerky? That was *meat*. "Oh, Jesus, oh, shit." I knocked the plate from the table. Its clatter echoed through the room. The bread rolled under my chair. "Shit-shit-shit!"

I lurched away from the table and made it to my chamberpot in time to spew the few bites I'd swallowed. After the food was gone, my guts kept trying to expel every meal I'd ever eaten aboard *Maso*, until there was nothing but a thin string of yellow spittle hanging off my lower lip.

I didn't even have enough energy left to cry, so I curled up in the corner where the wall met the viewport and hugged my knees.

"Maybe I'm wrong," I rasped, shoving my hands into my hair and pulling until it hurt. "God, let me be wrong."

But *Maso* was huge and its inhabitants weren't starving. My meals were always the same, which meant they were manufacturing nutrients on board the way the Ohnenrai had churned out their bug paste and pucks.

A little groan escaped me accompanied by more cramps. I swallowed a sob down a throat fried by stomach acid.

I had to think of something else. This was a horror I couldn't keep contemplating, so I shoved it down a deep, dark hole. It would fester there, but I couldn't unpack it anymore or I'd unpack my sanity with it and there'd be no getting that sorted and stored once I tumbled off that cliff.

I sat up, my back against the cold viewport.

The ship's ribbed ceiling curved overhead and down to meet the edges of the entrance portal. I was the heart that beat against its prison inside a behemoth's ribcage, had been for one thousand two hundred forty-six days. I did the math, a welcome distraction. Almost three-and-a-half years with the Azatem.

I hugged my knees and sighed. I'd awakened feeling morose that morning and my mood didn't look like it would ever improve. Each day it got harder to stay positive. All the death was getting to me. The death and the silence and the god-awful touching. The knowledge that *Dathusha* was near yet unattainable and feeling certain that Pearl was still inside that ship, fighting to survive, terrified of being discovered. And, maybe worst of all, the terrible possibility that I was wrong and she was dead and I was fucking crazy.

And now the damned food. That was the last straw.

I stood, hunched over with another wave of cramps, then forced myself upright and staggered to the portal.

The opening had two halves, almost seamless when closed, warm and vinyl-like. I pushed my fingers between them and pulled, hard, harder, hard enough to snap my fingernails and tear my skin. They didn't move. There was some give in their fabric but zero sign that I'd separated them even a hair's breadth.

"Open, damn it!" I kicked them and succeeded only in

bruising my toes, then jarring my knee as I kicked again and again until my hips and back ached, then I turned away, shoved my hands in my hair again and screamed. I went to my knees, pressed my forehead to the floor, screamed and screamed until I was hoarse.

Nobody came. Nobody cared. Maybe they enjoyed watching Yazadami go nuts. Maybe it made Sandy and Olive feel godlike.

That thought brought me upright and I laughed, an unmistakable edge of madness to my humor. "You think you're better than me? Stronger than your chosen god?" The chamberpot filled with sick sat in the corner and I grinned at it. I must've looked completely off my rocker. But, oh, the irony; that was delicious. The Azatem were in for a rude surprise. And it looked like I'd be around to watch their disaster unfold, to shove it in their faces, to gloat and laugh.

My mood took another sudden downturn. "Ehtishem?" I said to no one. "Where are you?" I turned to the viewport. "I thought you'd be here by now." A swirling cyan storm crept across the face of the massive blue planet, my unchanging view. "You'd better find me before I lose my mind," I whispered.

I twisted the ring around and around on my finger. It was looser than it had been when I'd come aboard *Maso*. "Maybe my sanity is gone already. Maybe he never really planned to return." I pulled the ring off, held it up, the blue planet's storm centered within it. "No," I snarled. "No. No. No!" That wasn't true. It couldn't be.

"Maybe you're watching from afar. Waiting for a sign of weakness." I laid on my back and studied the room. Brown striations streaked the walls. They weren't there when I arrived. The ship was deteriorating just like the reapers and harvester, neglected by the diminishing Azatem humanoids.

"Patience, Rachel," I whispered and slipped the ring back

on my finger. Patience and persistence and faith. "He'll find you."

"I'm okay, Momma. I'm good at hiding. They've tried, but they can't find me."

I gasped and jerked upright. At that same moment the portal opened to admit Olive and Honey. They and Sandy were the only survivors of my original attendants, though Honey didn't look too good. Her serene face, so like my own but not quite right, was ashen, her eyes sunken and ringed with dark circles.

Lucy had simply disappeared after my great escape. I guessed she'd been blamed. And Ethel was the latest of my attendants to die in-chrysalis. I refused to let guilt take hold. That was two less Azatem to threaten Ehtishem and Pearl, and got me closer to reuniting with my family, closer to everyone's safety.

I scrambled to my feet and went to the table. I kicked the bread across the floor, then picked up a dull knife and faced the attendants. I held it out. "Cut my hair."

They maintained their distance and silence.

"Cut it!"

They didn't move, didn't look at the knife.

"Fine. Then you can stand there while I do it." I sat, separated a lock of brunette hair from the rest, folded it over the knife, and began to saw. The hair snapped, its ends frayed and split.

The door opened to admit Sandy. She stopped on the threshold and watched me, her expression vacillating between amused and puzzled. She had a yellow dress draped over her arm.

I kept sawing.

The three Azatem waited while I hacked off my hair. My arms and hands cramped, my index finger blistered. They and the Azatem in the gathering chamber could cool their jets. Finally, I put the knife down. My hair now fell to my shoulders and I sat amid a pile of brunette curls.

Honey and Olive began styling what was left while Sandy picked up the fallen locks.

I studied the dress she'd brought. It was a sickly shade of yellow, the color of bile, the color of my breakfast in the chamberpot.

Perfect.

When the fussing was over, we formed a small procession and headed for the gathering.

For every lit portal we passed on our downward journey, another nine remained dark. A majority of the Azatem populace had died during metamorphosis since my arrival. Yet the survivors still blissfully exposed themselves to my genes, believing they were cultivating a super species and only the strongest among them would survive.

I touched the central column as we moved downward, my fingers bumping over the rough brownish-yellow wall. When I'd arrived aboard the ship, *Maso* was pink and red, silver and white inside. But it depended upon the Azatem for food and maintenance. The Azatem depended upon *Maso-Vohu* for transportation, defense, and shelter. All were dying because of me.

I pulled my hand away from the column. I wouldn't feel guilty about the living ship's slow death. *Maso* was enslaved. Wasn't death better than slavery? Wasn't it better than being a living host for the Azatem? Wasn't death better than being infested, controlled, modified against your will?

Maybe someday I'd know the answer.

We finally reached the gathering hall and I took my place on the dais.

Where once there had been tens of thousands of Azatem

faces staring up at me, now there were maybe five thousand. Singly and in groups, they were failing to emerge from their mutational sleep. I didn't understand what triggered them to enter their chrysalides nor what it was in my DNA that interrupted some of them quickly while others, like Sandy, survived multiple metamorphoses to resemble me more and more with each rebirth.

Sandy finished arranging my dress, stepped down from the dais, and repeated the daily pronouncement. After so many repetitions and picking up a few snippets of conversations here and there during the trips to and from the gathering hall, I'd deciphered the gist of her proclamation: "Sisters rejoice. Weakness dies. Strength grows. Perfection approaches. Soon we will cast off the chrysalides and move among the stars again, the immortal, invincible ruler of the universe. We are one. We are Azatem."

They tapped their fingers together in approval, an anemic sound lost to the emptiness of the vast hall.

One by one, the crowd shuffled forward to embrace death.

Weakness dies.

I closed my eyes. I was a murderer, a monster, no better than the creatures surrounding me. Every day that I shared my DNA was a day I committed genocide. Every day a small piece of me died too and I hated my captors even more.

"I'm tired," I said as Sandy took up guard duty when we returned to my room. "I don't want company."

She didn't leave. Of course.

"Don't you listen?"

"I listen, Yazadami," I replied in a mock Azatem voice. "I just don't give two shits about what you want."

"Well, thanks a lot for that," I retorted to myself.

She ignored my insane one-sided conversation.

"What does Yazadami do each day?" I whined.

"Not a whole helluva lot," I said as I faced her. "And I do that alone. I can't think with you watching me. How many times do I have to tell you that?"

The Azatem woman's wide eyes narrowed. I imagined she was thinking I *needed* watching. There was something different in her gaze, something like...suspicion.

Damn. The paranoia's setting in.

No, that wasn't it. Sandy was creepier than usual.

"Go away." I crawled into bed and glanced at her before rolling away. She was staring at me.

Definitely creepy.

The portal opened to admit Honey. She had an armful of towels and yellow gowns. Sandy watched her replace my dirty laundry with the clean things.

I sat up and studied Sandy's expression as I said, "Ferahi-va, Honey." I'd taken to using her nickname, but not Sandy's or Olive's. I wanted them to know I preferred Honey over them. "I know I can count on you to help me. You're always kind and respectful, more godly than the rest." I looked at Sandy as I added, "There are others among your sisters who could learn from you."

Honey had reached the portal. She paused and smiled at me as it opened. Her gaze slid to Sandy and there was something unmistakably self-satisfied about the look she gave her. But as she stepped through the doorway, Sandy produced a discipline rod and slammed it into the back of her skull. Honey stumbled over the threshold into Olive, who waited on the other side. Sandy followed through, the rod raised. Olive knocked Honey to the floor.

I was too stunned to shout, too shocked to stop them. The

portal closed, but not before I heard the crunch of two more blows crushing Honey's skull. I lunged off the bed and to the opening, but it wouldn't yield to me. No one responded to my shouts, my orders and pleas. As always, my screams fell on deaf ears.

Finally, the portal opened to admit Sandy and Olive. The latter carried my evening meal on a tray. Both attendants still wore Honey's blood. Both bore serene expressions and met my gaze without concern.

Their message was clear: They were strong and ruthless. They were the ones who would become gods. They would fulfill Yazadami's expectations, and if I didn't agree with their methods, then my expectations would have to change because they were making the rules, not me.

I straightened my shoulders, raised my chin, forced myself to sneer. "Brutality isn't strength." I turned my back and went to stand before the window. Honey's murder was another death in an unending parade of them, another death I couldn't regret.

The portal whispered closed.

I was alone again.

If only I could escape my prison, reach Pearl, and find a functional transport on *Dathusha*. We could escape. We could contact *Pohru-Mahrko* and reunite with Ehtishem.

But...

Would I if I could? Would I abandon my purpose before seeing the job through to its end? Would I let the monsters live?

My face reflected in the viewport, indistinct and pallid. "Coward," I whispered. "Chickenshit." I turned away from myself and crawled into bed. "You couldn't. You know it."

I'd sacrificed too much time. I'd watched the Azatem population shrivel. My parents had lost their lives to get me aboard *Maso*. Ehtishem had sacrificed twelve years of his life to find me and get me to this moment. Millions of innocent Ohnenrai had died because of me.

Pearl. Pearl may have died because of me.

I sighed, stared at the ceiling, got out of bed, and started stretching. Staying fit was a pointless task, but I needed something to break up the monotony of my existence and distract me from the pointlessness of hope and the hopelessness of unceasing death.

Soon this nightmare would be over. Soon I'd reunite with Pearl. Soon Ehtishem would find us and take us home.

More false hopes? Maybe, but they were the only ones I had and I clung to them like I was drowning.

THIRTY

"TWO HUNDRED SIXTY DAYS, Ehtishem. How much longer can we follow hunches and experiments?" Timsai was with him in Cen EXO, surrounded by unfamiliar stars and planets, two friends leading the last of their people into unexplored space. "I'm not trying to be cruel," he added, "but how far are you willing to take the Ohnenrai on what looks more and more like a personal quest?"

He wasn't surprised or insulted to hear that sentiment, not even from Timsai. He knew the crew had growing doubts. It was only natural and the thrai was under pressure from every side. Ehtishem didn't let it trouble him. "Our directions have been consistent and focused. We have every reason to believe we're proceeding to the location of a crippled Azatem battleship." He perched on the edge of the table and folded his arms. His team stood quietly, waiting and watching the two leaders. "I know it's hard not to doubt. I do every day. But I also have a group of people who agree with each step or we don't take it." He gripped his friend's arm. "We're close, Timsai."

"But how do you know?"

Tethered together, *Pohru-Mahrko* and *Ayan-Kanya* hurtled through space, following hunches and intuition. Using a series of wormhole jumps and interstellar maneuvers, Ehtishem and his team had slowly narrowed the target of their search.

"I just do. It's how Ahremena made me, not that she knew it when she was doing it. It's the Azatem in my genome. And, maybe, more than a little faith."

"Faith?" Timsai's brows arched and he added, "How do you find faith after all we've been through?"

Ehtishem shrugged. "It's that or curl up and die." He studied the points of light filling the room. "I prefer not to give up when we've come so far and sacrificed so much, maibyo haxan." He met Timsai's gaze. "Rachel is out there, and we are very close to finding her."

Timsai considered him for a long moment. He rotated his shoulders and said, "Alright. I've never been able to argue against your conviction."

"Any time you have, it's not worked in your favor."

"Eresh," Timsai said and jerked his chin toward the holographic star map. "Show me again."

Ehtishem pushed away from the table and crossed the room. "There." At the edge of the map, he pointed at a small blue speck, a planet buried deep within a massive galaxy. The region was poorly charted. Wormhole travel would be laborious. But that was where they'd find Rachel. He was more certain of that than he'd ever been.

When he'd found the planet, he'd kept it to himself, waiting for each of the soldiers who shared a connection with her to independently confirm his belief. That had taken an agonizingly long two days.

First Vehl and Gohra had found it almost simultaneously.

"I concur," Mahzel had said, though he'd taken another day to decide it with certainty.

The last of them, Fehrana, had stared long and hard at the planet before finally turning to meet his gaze. "Zant, fra. She's there," certainty in her girlish voice.

Timsai scratched the back of his skull as he considered the distant planet. "We're talking about going deep into unexplored space, following nothing but your gut feelings and some questionable experimental data developed by a woman who undermined your authority. You're sure about this, Ehtishem?"

The entire team turned tired eyes upon the thrai. It was almost the end of Black Watch and some of the group hadn't slept for over fifty hours. They'd been pulling ten on/five off shifts in Cen EXO for weeks, driven by their growing certainty and some unexplainable need to find a Terran woman they'd all come to consider an integral part of their family.

"One hundred percent certain, Thrai," Mahzel replied.

Gohra added, "Barethri Rachel's location is in that galaxy on or near that planet," and the other searchers nodded. As the ships had gone deeper into the quadrant, they'd only grown more confident.

Timsai straightened and met Ehtishem's gaze. "Then that's where we'll go." He pulled out his com and relayed orders to *Ayan-Kanya*'s and *Pohru-Mahrko*'s crews. The wormhole coordinates needed to be calculated and recalculated.

Ehtishem clasped his hands behind his back and planted his feet. The closer they got to Rachel, the more agitated he felt. He'd carved a zoo of wooden animals to keep his fingers occupied and settle his jangling nerves.

Eight and a half months had elapsed since the Azatem took her, but the last ten weeks and two days had been a whirlwind of activity as Ehtishem's team pinpointed her location far from the Milky Way Galaxy.

It felt like forever as the ships jumped between star systems, corrected course, jumped again. Repeat, repeat, repeat. All the while he wondered how much time had passed for Rachel aboard *Maso-Vohu*. If the Azatem ship was in a stable orbit around that planet, the time dilation would've been cruel. Years could've elapsed, eating away at her faith in him.

Hold on, Pairika. I'll be there soon.

He pivoted to Mahzel and the other soldiers. "I want my assault team assembled for tactical planning at fifteen-hundred. Meanwhile, all of you get food and rest."

Timsai said, "I'll order all division leaders assembled at eighteen-hundred for an intel briefing."

The soldiers saluted and dispersed.

Ehtishem met his oldest friend's gaze. "I'll defer to your leadership on the approach and the assault."

Timsai nodded. They both knew Ehtishem's judgment was too compromised by his drive to protect Rachel. She was his priority and he needed his thrai's impassive, impeccable decision making to handle this operation. "I've already planned it. We'll approach and hold at a distance, observe the enemy, and ready our forces." He gripped Ehtishem's shoulder. "Then you'll recover Rachel."

"And you'll end the Azatem."

"Zant."

Meanwhile, aboard two command decks, nav officers, pilots, and jump techs prepared the only remaining Ohnenrai ships for their last confrontation with the Azatem. The plan was already in place, developed and overanalyzed for months.

They'd exit a wormhole as close to *Maso-Vohu* as possible but still with several planets between them to hide their emergence. From there, they'd deploy probes and utilize stealth to observe the Azatem ship and calculate another short-distance jump. Once they were satisfied with their intel and the close-jump coordinates for the wormhole exit, *Ayan-Kanya* and *Pohru-Mahrko* would jump sequentially with *AK* acting as the aggressor to draw *Maso's* focus. *PM* would exit even closer to *Maso*, drop the infiltration teams aboard *Eshmahe*, and move to aid *Ayan-Kanya* in the assault and to shelter the small transport from attack.

Eshmahe would punch a hole through *Maso-Vohu's* hull, then boarding teams would infiltrate her, extract Rachel, and blow the shit out of the monstrosity. *Pohru-Mahrko* would retrieve the transport and both cruiser-carriers would link up and escape via wormhole.

It all relied on perfect timing and an enemy crippled by Rachel. If *Maso* was fully functional, *Pohru-Mahrko* and *Ayan-Kanya* would evacuate the system immediately and never look back. Ehtishem would recover Rachel or die trying.

He considered the small blue dot at the edge of the star map and straightened his shoulders. That would not be his grave.

Four more jumps was all it took. Four and they found *Maso-Vohu* orbiting a blue gas giant. The Azatem ship gave no sign of noticing the arrival of the Ohnenrai ships.

The crews aboard *Pohru-Mahrko* and *Ayan-Kanya* were intense, quiet, hyper-focused as both ships scanned the red behemoth and confirmed life forms aboard. "A lot fewer than we've seen in the past," Timsai remarked to Ehtishem from *AK's* command deck.

Waiting aboard *Eshmahe* with his team, Ehtishem received the report from his thrai. "That's hopeful."

"Indeed," Timsai replied. He paused then said, "You're

sure you have to do this personally, Ehtishem?" He thought it was an unnecessary risk and he'd said so more than once during those four wormhole jumps.

"Certain. Rachel is my mission." He surveyed his team: Mahzel, Anchal, Fehrana, Gohra, Vehl, Tinish, and Gahlen. "I'd leave all these dogs behind, but they'd just scratch up my doors and tear apart the couch in protest."

The soldiers laughed. No one was letting him board the Azatem ship alone.

Timsai nodded on the screen. "I wish I could go with you, haxan, to watch your back like the old days."

Ehtishem cocked his head. "You are watching my back, maibyo arshno. And covering my ass."

Timsai slowly saluted. "Bring her home, Zosh."

Ehtishem retuned the gesture. "Blow them up, Thrai."

Timsai cut the connection.

"Draxtu Mainyu Family, let's end this," Ehtishem said as he turned to his team.

"Drax-tu!" they shouted as Eshmahe lifted off the flight deck.

Ayan-Kanya went in with full shields up and weapons blazing as Pohru-Mahrko covered Eshmahe's careful approach. A small explosion opened one of Maso's outer hatches just below her midline, even as large explosions lit up space and rocked the red ship.

The assault teams met no resistance as they boarded the alien vessel.

Ehtishem, Tinish, Gahlen, and Mahzel followed Rachel's tracker as they moved from the entry point into a cavernous hangar bay. Anchal, Fehrana, and Vehl peeled off from their group to follow energy readings toward the reactors and engines. They had bags full of explosives and detonators.

"You see this, fra?" Gahlen asked as their lights swept the dim interior. His helmlight rested on long lines of pa'vikeret idled on the floor. The organic parts of the reapers were in varying states of decay, some bloated, others sitting in greenish puddles of their own rotting innards.

"Looks like Barethri Rachel did her job well," Tinish remarked.

A low rumbling rose from somewhere below them. The floor vibrated.

"What was that?" Anchal asked over the com.

"Cut the chatter," Mahzel said. "Stay focused."

"Zant, fra," the soldiers replied.

Ehtishem's helmcom buzzed with an incoming message.

"Zosh, *Eshmahe* here."

"Go ahead, *Eshmahe*," he replied.

"We're tracking small transports and harvesters that were jettisoned from below the extraction point. They're drifting away from the ship and scans indicate no life forms aboard. Is that your doing, fra?"

"Nava, *Eshmahe*. Sounds like our host has noticed us. Those may be explosive decoys. Steer clear. We've encountered dead pa'vikeret but no Azatem humanoids."

"Zant, fra. Stay sharp."

"Surun-ta, *Eshmahe*. Zosh Mahle out." Ehtishem cut the connection then spoke to both teams. "We may have company soon, pa'nerem. Watch your movement trackers."

"Zant, fra."

An explosion rumbled through the ship, followed by the report of MaRRs.

"Stig here, fra. Encountering resistance in Engineering."

"Do you require assistance?"

"Nava. We've deployed the auto-turrets. But the Azatem

have blown their own cooling systems. I think they hoped to catch us in the explosion."

"Keep us apprised. Don't wait to call for backup."

"We won't," she said. "And, fra? The Azatem we've seen," she hesitated, "they look like Barethri Rachel."

"Look like her how? Explain."

"They're female, humanoid. Same dark hair and similar face, but different, wrong. And they don't speak," Stig shouted over another bout of rifle fire.

"Vis, aevadasa." Ehtishem cursed beneath is breath. "You catch that?" he asked his team. They nodded. "Be prepared for what we'll face in battle. And, remember, they're not Rachel."

They exited the hangar and followed a wide bridge across an open space to reach a spiraling path. The open area stretched into darkness with more bridges ascending far above them. The path was empty and well-worn. It wrapped around a massive central column that rose into darkness. They continued steadily, following Rachel's tracker, passing bridges that led to closed portals and encountering no enemies. Her location was on one of the outer rings of the ship. Ehtishem led his group across another bridge and through the first open chamber they'd seen since leaving the hangar.

Dim light came on as they crossed the threshold. Rifle ready to obliterate anything that moved, Ehtishem eased into the space and swept it looking for threats. Thousands of pods occupied the cavernous area, some opaque, a few clear. Racked like supplies, they stretched outward and upward as far as his eye could see.

"What is this?" Tinish murmured.

Ehtishem's gaze roamed, his attention splitting between the immediate area and the readouts projected on his visor — Rachel's ID and the movement tracker. "They look like stasis chambers. But I don't know why an FTL-capable ship would need cryo-sleep capabilities."

Gahlen peered into the closest transparent one. "There's something in this."

Ehtishem finished sweeping the area. Nothing even twitched. Turning his light onto the pod the aevadasa indicated, he stared at the thing it contained. Dark-hair, gray skin, and a face that was both Rachel's and something else. It turned his stomach.

"Utha," Mahzel cursed. "These are what Stig described."

Tinish muttered, "This place is a tomb."

Ahremena had said the Azatem would integrate Rachel's DNA into their own. Ehtishem hadn't realized that meant they'd try to become her. He moved into the echoing space, sweeping his light over the stacks and rows. Most of the chambers were opaque, but the few transparent ones offered the same disturbing view: Dead creatures resembling Rachel, deformed and rotting.

"Yazadami," he whispered.

The team passed through the area, their helmlights and weapons constantly moving, their tongues held. Their silence spoke loudly; they were spooked.

"Where's the barethri?" Gahlen asked. "In one of these?"

"On a higher level." Ehtishem pointed upward. "Let's move on."

Like air escaping a pressure seal, hissing sounded behind him. A chorus of the same sound echoed throughout the area. The hair stood on his arms.

"Utha," Mahzel repeated.

The creatures came at them from every angle. Slow and clumsy most, fast and determined some, and eerily quiet all, the Azatem women clambered from their chrysalides and assaulted

Ehtishem's team. Blind in their determination, Rachel's captors made no apparent effort to avoid death.

Mahzel deployed a turret gun and cleared a path of retreat. As they returned across the bridge, Tinish tossed grenades into the chamber and dropped two more on the bridge. The resulting explosions sent Azatem bodies flying and collapsed the span.

"Movement, SSE," Tinish called and all of them trained their guns on their south-south-east quadrant.

"We're coming up on an explosion," Anchal announced in their helms. "That your doing, Zosh?"

"Zant," Ehtishem replied as his team re-sighted their weapons. Anchal, Gohra, and Stig appeared around the path's curve. "Charges set in Engineering?"

"Ready and waiting, fra," Gohra replied. "Fehrana and Vehl found two functional harvesters in a lower launch bay and are setting charges on them. They'll meet us at the extraction point."

"Ash-ush. Let's retrieve the barethri and get out of this crypt," Ehtishem replied as they followed Rachel's signal. Eighty-seven more levels to ascend.

They crossed another bridge and entered what appeared to be a weapons depot. Skeletons littered the floor and crunched beneath their boots.

"Aiya, what a nightmare," Anchal said.

"Are those incendiaries?" Ehtishem asked, pointing to a wall of devices that looked too much like Ohnenrai incendiary bombs to be mistaken.

Stig nodded. "They learned from us."

"Not surprising, since they enslaved so many of our people," Gahlen said.

"They took Ohnenrai bodies and their minds," Tinish added, too bitter to keep it from his voice.

Lights flickered overhead, came on bright and blinding, then turned off. A portal opened behind them.

The blare of movement detectors went off in Ehtishem's ear. His team got the warning too. They started firing as Azatem humanoids erupted through the narrow portal, surging into the room like water through a cracked dam. It was Iodiq all over again. For every one they shot, ten more appeared, climbing over their fallen companions, silent madness distorting their faces.

Stig deployed her last turret gun and opened fire with her MaRR as Anchal strafed the attackers.

Ehtishem and the rest of the assault team retreated back through the outer chamber.

"Come on!" Tinish called to the two heavies.

Anchal turned to leave, but the creatures got around him. Ehtishem couldn't get a clean shot and the man went down. Stig blasted the things off him, but not before they tore off his helmet and bloodied his face. She started to pull him free. The turret ran out of ammo. The Azatem surged.

"Get out! Get out!" Stig shouted and pulled a grenade from her belt as she wrapped Anchal in a bear hug.

He grabbed her hands and the grenade. "I always hated you, woman."

"Gawmezh," she spat back at him, her arms around him in a farewell embrace. "You know everyone loves me."

Ehtishem and the remainder of his team charged down the ramp and across another bridge as the grenade detonated.

That explosion triggered the incendiaries and other munitions. The blowback knocked them off their feet. Only their mech-suits kept them alive as heat and flames engulfed the chamber and bridge. Another, deeper rumble rolled through the floor. The entire ship groaned.

Mahzel pulled Ehtishem up. Tinish, Gahlen, and Gohra

joined them and their group moved away from the conflagration. Mourn and regrets would come later.

Ehtishem's syscom beeped. His gaze went to a readout on his visor. "Rachel's moving."

"Toward us or away?" Mahzel asked.

"Toward." Ehtishem started running up the path. "Double-time, pa'nerem."

"Drax-*tu!*" Tinish called out and his fellow soldiers echoed him.

THIRTY-ONE

MASO-VOHU RUMBLED. The lights in my chamber came on, flickered, steadied. Too bright.

I crossed my arm over my eyes. "What the hell?" I muttered and rolled over in bed. It seemed like I'd just fallen asleep.

Maso rumbled, again, somewhere deep in its guts. A tremor vibrated the bed. I bolted upright and looked at the portal, expecting caretakers, but none came through it.

What was that? Were the ship's engines firing? Were we breaking orbit? Why would the Azatem do that after circling this planet for five years? Looking at the viewport answered those questions. The rumbling wasn't the massive red ship's engines. Our position above the blue planet hadn't changed.

Something else had.

"Holy shit." I tumbled off the bed, entangled in the sheet and struggling to extricate my legs so I could get to the window. My hand slapped the cool surface as I reached it. "Ho-ly *shit!*"

Sitting on the far side of the planet was a welcome sight, an Ohnenrai cruiser-carrier. It wasn't *Pohru-Mahrko*, so it had to be the other warship, the one from Iodiq.

A series of flashes emanated from her forward cannons and a volley of explosions occurred just off *Maso*'s bow.

The cavalry had finally arrived.

Uttering a whole litany of "holy shits," I lunged for the gown box and pulled on a clean dress.

Another rumble. Another shake. The lights flickered. I stopped dressing and stared at the floor. That explosion had come from inside the ship.

I jumped as the room portal opened. Olive entered. She'd lost her impassive expression and was armed with a baton. She gestured for me to join her and I didn't think she'd take "no" for an answer. Besides, I was better off being free of my prison than trapped while the battle unfolded.

Yesterday's grope fest had revealed just how depleted the Azatem populace had become. I'd counted as they touched me. One thousand seven hundred and eight humanoids.

If Ehtishem led a full assault, my captors didn't stand a chance. They only had three things on their side: the danger of Azatem exposure, the sheer size and labyrinthine structure of *Maso*, and a hostage.

Of course Ehtishem had no way of knowing how many Azatem remained alive and what kind of resistance he'd face. But he wouldn't be deterred by those factors.

There was another element working against my captors. I was healthier, stronger, and a helluva lot more pissed off than they were. And Olive was making this way too easy as she looked everywhere but at me. I yanked the stun baton from her hand. She turned, surprise on her face. I punched her in the mouth. She staggered back, surprise morphing into shock. Before she could comprehend the extent of my betrayal, I gave her a firm dose of the baton's medicine. She slumped down the wall of the spine and I took off down the spiraling path.

My bare feet slapped the bony floor and a familiar feeling

tugged at the back of my brain, urging me on. Ehtishem was here, and he wasn't screwing around. I had to find him and I had to find *Dathusha*.

Pearl! I shouted in my mind, willing her to hear me, willing her to really be alive.

Smoke stung my eyes and made me cough. I covered my mouth and nose with my sleeve and looked into the gap between the outer chambers and the spine. Fire burned below on *Maso*'s outer rim. I stuck close to the spine and continued down. Where there was fire, explosions, and destruction, I'd find Zosh Ehtishem Mahle.

Passing the gathering hall, I cut through chrysalis chambers to reach the lower launch bays faster. I tried not to look at the semi-transparent chrysalides. Someone had opened many of them, probably checking for signs of life. What they contained was mostly bilious goo, bones, and hair — the stuff of my nightmares. From what I'd observed, like caterpillars becoming butterflies, they digested their own bodies then rebuilt themselves from stem cells genetically altered by my DNA. Or tried to without success.

I entered a series of interconnected chambers and halls. Stopping, I closed my eyes and felt for Pearl. This was the way I'd gone when I'd found *Dathusha*; I was sure.

"Pearl, answer if you can hear me," I whispered into the quiet darkness.

Nothing moved. No voice spoke in my head.

The sound of another explosion rose to meet me. I didn't know if the Ohnenrai were blowing shit up or the Azatem were sabotaging *Maso*. Sweat stung my eyes, trickled down my back and between my breasts as I continued searching. It was getting hotter the lower I went.

I descended two more levels, then heard the buzz of

Ohnenrai orders coming across helmcoms and the distinctive hum of shock pistols, the thud of MaRRs. Ehtishem's voice rose above it all.

"Fehrana, Vehl, what's your status?" he asked.

Light and sound filtered through the grated catwalk beneath my feet.

Fehrana answered. "Just finished planting charges on the harvester, fra. Heading for the extraction point."

"Ash-ush. *Eshmahe*, any sign of enemy ships?"

"Nava. They're still not engaging with *Ayan-Kanya*, fra," Berk replied.

"Fra?"

"Go ahead, Gohra." Ehtishem turned his attention to his explosives tech.

"The heat down here will destabilize the charges if it continues to rise. I recommend evac as soon as possible."

"Understood."

I spied a hatch near the end of the hall. I came through one to a catwalk on the journey to discovering *Dathusha*. If Pearl was alive, she was close. So was Ehtishem. My heart threatened to thud right out of my ribcage.

I glanced down and spotted him through the grates. Kneeling, I put down the shock baton and thrust my arm down to get his attention. "You took your time getting here," I called in English. My voice echoed in the eerie silence of the massive launch bay below.

Ehtishem looked up. His visor turned transparent and he gave me the biggest, most beautiful smile I'd ever seen. "Hello, Pairika."

"Hello, Stranger." My voice caught. "You're late."

He pressed his hand to his chest. "My apologies. We were delayed."

I swallowed a lump. "*Dathusha's* on board, Ehtishem. Pearl's hiding inside her."

His expression changed from relieved to surprised to something else before he asserted vairim and it turned neutral. "Are you sure?"

I hesitated. Was I? "I saw the ship. It's largely intact. We're close to where they're storing it."

He reached toward me. "Come. It's better if we get caught up away from the explosives."

"I'll be right down."

"Draxtu team, Barethri Rachel has been located. Time to go home," Ehtishem said into his helmcom.

Home. I clenched the grating. "But we need to find Pearl."

"Zant, fra," soldiers answered.

"Momma? What's happening?"

I jerked upright and turned, certain I'd heard Pearl that time, certain of her location.

Sandy loomed over me, the shock baton in her hand. "We are one, Yazadami."

A flash of blue electricity. A yelp of pain. A thud. That's what Ehtishem saw and heard.

"Rachel." He choked on the word. But calm immediately flooded him, the calm of a seasoned Ohnenrai field soldier, the calm of a lifetime of vairim. He started firing off orders. "Mahzel, evacuate all personnel immediately."

The aevadasa saluted and relayed the order.

Tinish asked, "What about the barethri?"

"I'm getting her," Ehtishem replied, his voice calm but firm. "I'll move faster alone." He located four possible exits from the bay, looked up, and calculated a three-story distance to reach the overhead catwalk. Pipes and protrusions ran parallel to it. A rotting harvester sat nearby. "Tinish, Gahlen, launch me up there." He pointed at the Azatem ship.

The pa'aevadasa had done this maneuver many times. They squatted before him, their hands laced together to create a platform. He backed up, took a running start, planted his boot in their hands, and was launched upward, boosted by their mech-suits' power. Ehtishem hit the harvester's roof ledge and hauled himself up. Another three strides and he jumped, caught the pipes overhead and, hand-over-hand, reached the catwalk.

His soldiers headed for the launch bay's closest entrance and the hole their transport had punched through *Maso*'s hull. Ehtishem knew none of them wanted to leave him and Rachel behind, but they also wouldn't risk disobeying their zosh's orders again. Besides, he was right; he could move much faster alone. Whoever had incapacitated Rachel wouldn't escape him. They were burdened with her unconscious body, would be even more burdened with her rage when she came to, and destroyed by his when he caught up with them.

The pipes groaned beneath his weight but held long enough for him to tear the floor grating free. It clattered to the flight deck far below and he hoisted himself through the opening and onto the empty catwalk.

He surveyed the area, spied a ladder hatch and a closed portal at the far end. The tracker told him Rachel was that way, so he reached it, unholstered his MaP, and started blasting molten metal at its locking mechanism.

I groaned. Every inch of me hurt. Something smelled burned and I was pretty sure it was me. Sandy. That bitch had cooked me. I pushed up to my knees, stood, and looked around. *Dathusha's* broken hull stretched into the darkness before me, and the portal behind me was closed. The thudding coming from the other side of it and the growing striations in its surface told me Ehtishem was out there and determined to blast the mechanism clear off its frame.

A flicker of blue light was my only warning as Sandy lunged at me from the darkness. I dodged the humming shock stick, but she pivoted and came at me again. I ducked. She slammed the baton into the wall with a resounding thud. Electricity arced off a strut and I yanked my hand away.

She should've been tired and weak, but she wasn't. Nor was she the badass she used to be; she was much worse. She came at me a third time, the stick whining, deadly.

But I was more pissed off and determined than ever.

I blocked the blow with my left hand and punched her in the kidney with my right, shoving away from her and keeping a close eye on her weapon. She said something, a curse maybe, and faced me, wariness in her eyes.

"That's right, bitch," I snarled. "Yazadami was created to fight dirty."

Mahzel's words resurfaced from so long ago: "*We focus our rage and use it as a weapon.*"

Sandy had my face, my figure. She was a perfect clone and as mortal as the rest of her doomed species, even if she wasn't showing weakness yet.

The only way to survive was to disarm her. "I destroyed the Azatem," I said in Ohnenrai, a sneer plastered on my face.

She hissed and tensed, watching, waiting for me to make the next move.

"I'm a biological weapon, designed by the Ohnenrai and sent here to kill. You All." Her eyes widened. "And I've relished watching every single one of you *die*."

Sandy lunged, but I moved in and intercepted her arm. The weapon shocked my hand. My fingers weakened. She brought it back toward my head. I ducked. The shock stick singed my hair as it whistled past. Sandy lunged forward, the baton raised for a killing blow.

I straightened and stepped into the attack again. I stopped her blow with my left arm, struck her face with the side of my palm, twisted my fingers into her hair. My other hand grabbed her wrist. I yanked her down and sideways. Her head slammed into a metal hydrant jutting from the wall. Bones cracked. She gasped and dropped the weapon. I hauled her back, slammed her into the hydrant again, and threw her to the floor. She looked up. Blood coated her face. I kicked her in the mouth. Blood splattered my bare feet. I broke two toes, but I barely noticed.

"It's Doomsday, bitch!" I grabbed the baton and slammed it into her skull.

"I want my life back!" Bones crunched.

"I want my freedom back!" Gore flecked my gown.

"And I want my face back!" A tooth skittered across the deck.

Ehtishem's gloved hand stopped my next swing. "She's dead, Rachel."

Blood dripped from the baton. It stained my feet, was splattered across the floor and smeared all over my hands and dress.

Sandy no longer had my face. There was only blood, flesh, and white bone.

"Jesus." I dropped the weapon. It clattered to the floor. The sound echoed through the dead space.

"Zosh, we are leaving," Mahzel called over the helmcom.

"We're on our way," Ehtishem replied. "Hold the door."

"Jesus-Jesus-*Jee*-sus." I wiped my hands on my gown. In the bay's dim light, the blood made them look gangrenous.

"Pairika." Ehtishem gripped my arms and gave me a little shake. "We have to leave. *Now*."

I blinked at him. "Leave?"

"We're blowing *Maso* apart. *Pohru-Mahrko* and *Ayan-Kanya* are waiting to obliterate it. There's only minutes to reach our transport before this thing's vaporized."

"But Pearl." I waved toward *Dathusha*'s carcass. "We can't leave her."

Confusion crossed his face. "She's dead, Rachel." He turned me to face the mother ship, and his voice was gentle as he added, "They're all dead. You have to accept that."

I jerked out of his grasp. "No, they're not. Pearl's alive. I've heard her in my mind, just like I heard the Azatem. Ehtishem, she's alive. Audie's alive, and Sree and Ahnoru and others. They're hiding in there!" I jabbed my finger at the broken ship. "We can't leave them!"

Mahzel announced, "Five hundred fifty-eight seconds, fra."

Wordlessly, he scooped me up and over his shoulder. "We'll be there in five hundred forty-eight," he said.

"No!" It took a Herculean effort to get free of his grip, but I did and landed on my ass. As he pivoted, a flicker of motion in the darkness caught my eye.

"Momma, wait!"

Pearl leaned from one of *Dathusha*'s broken viewports. Barking echoed from somewhere behind her.

A sound came out of me, a strangled cry.

Ehtishem exhaled a stunned word: "Utha."

I was up and running, even as another portal opened into the bay and a crowd of Azatem females charged toward me.

He shouted, "Rachel, wait!"

I reached an open gash in *Dathusha*'s belly.

A figure lurched at me from the darkness. Olive? A baton sparked. Pain arced through me. I hit the deck, stunned.

Pearl screamed.

Ehtishem shouted, "Run!"

THIRTY-TWO

RACHEL ROLLED AWAY as the Azatem woman brought the baton down again. Sparks arced off the floor. More Azatem raced toward her, cutting Ehtishem off. Pearl stared at the chaos, confusion and terror twisting her face. "Get out of here!" he shouted at the girl. She looked at him then dropped through the window opening, disappearing back into the ship.

Rachel dodged another blow and kicked the woman's feet out from under her. "Stop her!" she shouted, pointing the other Azatem toward her attacker. "Protect me!"

The crowd slowed, stopped, a nervous mass. They looked from Rachel to the woman with the baton to Ehtishem.

Rachel said, "Payback's a bitch, Olive."

The female alien's eyes widened.

Rachel pointed at the woman and even Ehtishem felt the command in her words as she said, "Kill her. Protect me. He's no threat, but she's trying to hurt me."

The other Azatem seemed to swell with the power of her attention. They charged in mass toward the woman with the baton.

Olive scrambled up and ran into *Dathusha's* open wound, apparently realizing Rachel had more sway than she did over her enraged sisters.

Mahzel's voice came over Ehtishem's helm. "Zosh, we have got to leave. Where are you?"

"Pearl's alive," he shouted as he pushed through the mass of Azatem. "There may be other survivors aboard *Dathusha.*"

Rachel ordered, "Don't harm him! He's one of us."

"*Dathusha?*" Mahzel replied, surprise clear in his voice. "She's intact?"

The Azatem milled about, touching Rachel's arms and back, fawning like dogs. They didn't stop Ehtishem as he crashed through their ranks. "Zant," he ordered. "Delay the charges."

"Get Pearl," Rachel commanded him.

He nodded and moved past. Her words created a compunction to obey unlike anything he'd ever felt. It was a disconcerting experience, but he wouldn't fight it. The Azatem watched him warily. They weren't a threat to her, of that he was suddenly certain.

Servos whining and boots thudding, he thundered past her and into the ship. When Pearl had been brought aboard *Dathusha,* Isphahan had put a tracker in her brain. Ehtishem hadn't approved, but now he was grateful for his uncle's greed and cruelty as he switched his suit's system to tracking the girl. He'd be damned if he was going to let that Azatem monstrosity harm his daughter.

His helmlight came on in the dim conditions and he triggered the movement tracker. Immediately, targeting superimposed three green dots upon his face-shield. They were moving away from him — Pearl and the Azatem female. Barking echoed through the hull. The third dot had to be Audie.

He was in the Ar-Pan, the military service corridor that ran between the exterior hull and the ship's interior rooms. "Syscom, overlay *Dathusha*'s schematics." The computer in his suit obeyed and he immediately recognized his location. He was close to his own civilian quarters.

Now oriented, Ehtishem's footfalls echoed as he pushed his suit to maximum speed. Fire doors had been triggered throughout the Ar-Pan, but some had been forced open. He followed Pearl, Audie, and the Azatem woman, gaining on them with each long stride.

Suddenly the signals veered away from the corridor and toward the top of the ship. Ehtishem slowed. An explosion had mangled a large section of the Ar-Pan and the surrounding area. He scanned the passageway and spied a service panel in what should've been the ceiling. With the ship on her side, it had become a crawlspace. Pearl and Audie had gone that way. The alien woman followed.

He was only moments behind them, but the space was empty when he entered it. He checked the trackers and saw why. Pearl was putting distance between herself and her hunter. Reaching the Nest, she snaked through its maze of corridors and smaller quarters, once again heading toward the top of the ship. Her knowledge of *Dathusha*'s altered terrain was her advantage.

"Fra, we can't deactivate all the charges," Mahzel said in his ear. "Three hundred seventy-four seconds remain. I suggest you hurry."

"Can you get to Rachel?" he asked.

"Already did, but she's refusing to leave."

"Of course she is." Two more movement signatures appeared on his tracking screen. Ehtishem cursed mentally. Friends or foes? His com crackled and he heard a voice he'd thought was gone forever.

"It's about time you lazy p'ahzish showed up."

"Ahnoru?"

"Still alive and kicking, fra."

"Can you keep this broken bucket of bolts in one piece when we launch?"

Somewhere ahead a door screeched on heat-warped tracks. Ehtishem charged toward the sound, a door at the end of a hallway. It was locked when he reached it, but the mechanism failed with the application of mass-impact molten slag. Aided by servomotors that amplified his own brute strength, Ehtishem pulled the door off its track and revealed a room strewn with broken furnishings and an upturned existence. Anything not bolted down when the Azatem attacked had become a projectile or trash. A closet door hung open.

"You want me to pilot *Dathusha*?" Ahnoru sounded shocked. "We have no engines, fra. Only twelve percent of her interior is pressurized."

"I didn't ask if you could fly her, only if she'll hold together when Mahzel opens the launch bay beneath your ass."

Inside the closet, Ehtishem found another access hatch and a shaft leading to a small observation area atop *Dathusha*. "Top of the World," he muttered. That's where Pearl and Audie were heading.

Ahnoru said, "Aiya. You're crazy, Zosh. I don't know if she'll stay intact."

"Well, she'd better," he replied as he scrambled into the shaft. "In five minutes, *Maso*'s going to become a small sun."

"Zhek," *Dathusha*'s captain cursed again. "I'll do my best, fra."

"You always do, Fravaz." Ehtishem entered the closet and started after his daughter. "Mahzel, when I give the signal, I want *Eshmahe* to blow the doors off this bay."

"You're launching *Dathusha*? Can she fly?" The aevadasa's doubt was obvious.

"We're gonna find out. Now put me through to Rachel."

"Zant, fra. Go ahead."

"Ehtishem, did you find her?" she asked.

"I'm about to get her and Audie, and put a mass of molten slag through that Azatem thing chasing them. Get aboard *Eshmahe*, Rachel."

"Not without all of you."

"Zant, without us. *Dathusha's* taking a wild ride into deep space. I need to know you're safe aboard that transport."

"But—"

"Do you trust me?" he asked in English.

"Ehtishem!"

"Do you trust me or not, Rachel?"

"You know I do," she whispered.

"Then get off *Maso*. Please. For my sake and sanity."

"Alright," she said, her reluctance palpable. "I love you, Stranger."

"I love you too, Pairika. Pearl and I will see you soon. I promise."

Eighteen floors at full speed had him winded when he reached the access hatch to a small observation deck everyone aboard *Dathusha* called the Top of the World.

He smashed the locking mechanism until the door popped open, then he yanked it off its hinges.

He was greeted by a dog's low threatening growl and Pearl's voice.

"You're not my mother!"

She crouched in the narrow observation area. Audie stood between her and the Azatem female, his hackles up and his teeth bared. The alien raised her electrified baton and triggered it. Blue light arced through the small space. The dog snarled and slunk forward, his tongue flicking between his teeth.

Ehtishem saw red and yanked a serrated combat knife from

a holder on his hip. He commanded the dog to leave off. "Audie, apa."

The Azatem creature turned, made some guttural sound, and pivoted back. She brought her baton up to strike.

The boom of a MaP echoed in the space. The alien woman screeched as her hand exploded in a mass of blood and bone. The baton clattered to the floor, deactivated.

"Back off, asna." Sree spoke from the observation area behind Ehtishem. She'd fired the shot.

The Azatem woman turned, clutching her shattered hand. She had Rachel's face, but there was no life in her olive green eyes — a green that was the wrong shade set in a face that had all the right pieces assembled all wrong.

Ehtishem saw only a soulless monster. Three long strides closed the gap between them. He grabbed her throat and stabbed her — intestines, heart, lungs, brain. His gaze seeking Pearl, he yanked the knife out and shoved the creature to her knees. The dying thing toppled backward. Ehtishem wiped the blade and returned it to its holder as he stepped over the twitching body.

"Payu!" Pearl jumped into her father's open arms. She was clutching Molly Dolly, the rag doll Rachel had made for her eighth birthday present.

"You've grown, Ushika." She was almost as tall as Rachel.

"I'm thirteen," she replied.

He grunted at that. "Audie, va'jam." The dog came to his side, ears perked, tail wagging, eyes keen. As Ehtishem turned to leave, he pulled his MaP from its holster and fired. The Azatem creature's face vaporized. He didn't miss a stride, didn't even bother to look. He simply removed an abomination that he'd spent his entire life fighting or fleeing.

Sree holstered her weapon. A thick mass of brown burn scars covered the left side of her face. Her eye was missing. Her ear was a stump of cartilage. She limped along beside him. "It's about time you showed up, Ratheshtolo. The living conditions were beginning to get bad around here." Only the right side of her mouth moved.

"Did you complain to the captain?" he asked.

"Of course, but that bastard Ahnoru just ignored me. Right, Pearl?"

"All they do is argue." The girl rolled her eyes.

"That's the thanks I get for saving your life?" Sree muttered. "Ingrate."

"Are you injured?" Ehtishem asked Pearl.

She shook her head. "I knew you'd come back, Payu. I told Ahnoru and Sree you wouldn't abandon us." Arms around his neck, she hugged him and whispered, "I knew it."

He tightened his grip on her. "Of course I came back, Pearly Girly. You're my family, my daughter."

"Is Momma okay?"

"She's fine."

"Zosh?" Mahzel's voice came over the com, worry in clear evidence. "One hundred forty-one seconds until primary detonation. You're running out of time."

"I have Pearl, Audie, and Sree. Is Rachel safe?"

"Zant, fra. On her way to *Pohru-Mahrko*. Glad to hear Sree survived."

"Ahnoru, are you ready?" Ehtishem asked *Dathusha's* captain.

"Zant et nava," the captain replied over the com, and Ehtishem smiled when the man added, "You sure this is a good idea?"

"Blow the bay doors, Mahzel," he replied. He put Pearl down and said, "Hold onto me." He braced his feet wide and told Sree, "Grab hold of something solid, old woman." A muted rumbling sounded. Pearl closed her eyes. Sree's widened and she caught hold of his mech-suit. "*Ayan-Kanya*, this is Zosh Mahle," Ehtishem said.

"*Ayan-Kanya* here, go ahead, fra."

"Link with *Dathusha* and *Pohru-Mahrko*. We need to evac this system immediately."

"Surun-ta. Establishing link with *Pohru-Mahrko*. Readying link for *Dathusha*."

Metal groaned. The floor lurched. Pearl gasped and Audie whined. Ehtishem touched the dog's head and tightened his arms around his daughter as he looked out the viewport. *Dathusha* dropped from the massive Azatem ship's belly, pulled downward by the gravity of the blue planet. Debris floated past. Azatem women floated past, their eyes wide, fingers grasping for the ship. A golden glow enveloped *Dathusha* — the FTL link *Ayan-Kanya* extended to lock her and *Pohru-Mahrko* into a convoy.

"Wormhole opening," one of *Ayan-Kanya*'s techs announced. Timsai had kept the com open for all to hear. "Crossing the event horizon."

As the light of stars elongated around *Dathusha* and her sister ships, a bright fiery flash erupted from *Maso-Vohu's* belly, followed by more as explosions engulfed it. Ehtishem's visor darkened automatically. *Dathusha* bucked. Pearl squealed. Sree cackled gleefully. A brilliant white glow replaced the view as they escaped the Azatem ship's fiery destruction.

Dathusha vibrated and groaned. Stress fractures appeared in the viewport. They spread across its transparent expanse. Audie trembled, his tail tucked. Pearl squeezed her eyes shut and whispered prayers.

Sree exchanged looks with Ehtishem. "I'll be furious if this ride gets me killed after all I've survived!" she shouted over the sound of *Dathusha* coming apart at the seams.

Hold together, girl, Ehtishem thought. *Just a little longer*, as the vibrations grew more violent. He engaged the electromagnetic clamps in his boots to anchor his mech-suit to the floor and wrapped his fingers around Audie's harness.

"Exiting wormhole," the tech announced as space replaced swirling blue-white light. The short jump had felt like forever.

"You still with us, *Dathusha*?" Timsai asked.

"We're still here," Ahnoru replied. He sounded surprised. "Zosh?"

Ehtishem exhaled and his CO_2 monitor squealed, for once a welcome sound. "We're here." He gazed at the orange glow of the Fisk Juncture's gaseous ring. "Fisk never looked so good."

"Zant, fra," Timsai, Ahnoru, and a thousand other voices agreed over the com.

Pearl blinked at the stars, planets, swirling gases. "Can I see Momma now?"

"Can I have a hot bath?" Sree asked.

"Zant. To both," Ehtishem replied.

THIRTY-THREE

ONCE THE WORMHOLE jump was complete, Gahlen, Tinish, and Gohra ushered me off the small troop transport and into a white room aboard *Pohru-Mahrko*. Nozzles from the walls and ceilings warned me it was a decontamination shower a moment too late.

"Goddamn it!" I snarled as water and thick, yellow, stinking antiseptic soap blasted me from every angle. It went up my nose, into my mouth, burned my eyes, and that was the last damned straw.

All three soldiers were stripping to their skivvies, unconcerned about the liquid assault.

I leaned on them with my mind, using the Azatem Code the way I had with Ehtishem and the Azatem back on *Maso*. "Turn this shit off. *Right. Now.*"

They stared at me, eyes wide. Gahlen's gauntlets thudded to the floor and splashed filthy water across my bare feet.

"Turn it off!"

"We can't, Barethri," Tinish said. "It's automatic."

Gohra shook her head as if trying to toss my influence from

her brain. "We have to remove all traces of Azatem from our equipment and our bodies. We can't risk contaminating the ship, frei."

Shit. They were right. I spat and stared at the dress fabric, a sopping mess around my feet. Sandy's blood ran off the fabric and over my toes, pink rivulets mixing with the water and the antiseptic soap to create an orange pool. Soapy water ran through my hair, down my arms, off my fingers. It cleaned Ehtishem's ring and I stared at the band of stars.

"I've been through five years of hell. Five years of death," I said, releasing my command of them. "Five years of slowly slaughtering everything around me." The soap stopped. The water continued. It washed away the blood, only the blood.

After the shower, they gave me an oversized gray jumpsuit and led me through the ship. Not since the hamistayeca had I heard so much cheering and laughter, seen so many smiling Ohnenrai faces. Every soldier we encountered stopped, stared, and slowly saluted me. No matter what they were doing, they turned toward me and offered respect. Some even reached out as if to touch me.

I shied from their fingers. "Don't touch me. Please. I can't stand to be touched."

Tinish, Gahlen, and Gohra closed ranks around me. The others backed off.

They returned me to Timsai's old quarters. Gohra brewed suxra. She offered a bowl of greenish-gray chips. "Bug chips," she said.

I sniffed one. Ate it. Same bland taste.

"I'm sorry there isn't anything better." She paused at the door. "We should have a feast."

Pity. She felt pity for me. I knew it; we were still connected by the Azatem Code. Maybe she sensed the horror filling my brain, pressing against my skin and threatening to split my seams.

I plastered a fake smile on my face. "I'm sure the zosh will think of something."

She nodded and triggered the door. She started to close it, fleeing the madness oozing out of me. Too bad I couldn't escape it, too.

"Wait," I said. "Leave it open."

Gohra turned back. "Barethri?"

"They locked me in my chamber." The words tumbled out of me. "I couldn't go anywhere. And they didn't talk to me. They just...touched my skin." I shuddered.

She nodded and tapped the door controls. The access panel blinked from green to yellow. "You're not a prisoner here," she said and left.

Tinish and Gahlen stood guard outside.

I ate another chip. They were better than I'd had in a long time, not great but better. The suxra was another story. I savored that. Its warmth felt good and it tasted like *home*.

I paced from the galley to the bathing room and back, drinking suxra. Cheering and laughter rose and fell like waves. Surely Ehtishem and Pearl were aboard by now.

"Pa'nerem?" Tinish and Gahlen turned and peered into the room at my call.

"Do you need something?" Tinish asked.

Something? I needed so much I didn't even know where to begin. "Any word about the zosh and my daughter?"

"They're in Decontamination, frei," he answered. "Along with Fravaz Ahnoru, Sree, and your dog."

They're safe. I hadn't asked about the others. I felt selfish. "Do you know how many survived aboard *Dathusha?*"

"Just over six hundred thousand," he replied. "They holed up on different decks, sealed themselves into sections and set watches, scavenged in groups. I don't know if they even knew who and where others were."

"So few survivors?" It made me sick.

"Ninety percent of the populace died."

"But we beat the bastards," Gahlen added.

"*You* beat them, frei," Tinish said.

And I died doing it, I wanted to say. I killed a woman who had my face, murdered her and her sisters, her family. I did it to save the Ohnenrai, a people who'd killed my family and wiped out ninety percent of Earth's populace.

We were monsters. All of us. Killing each other to survive and failing at every turn.

I pulled a chair away from the tiny galley table and sat facing the room's small viewport, my back to the door. Orange gases overlaid the stars beyond the portal, a massive ring around binary stars. "Where are we?"

"The Fisk Juncture," Tinish replied.

"Is that far from where we were?"

"Zant. We followed your trail to the edges of known space and into a poorly charted galaxy."

"How long did it take?"

"Over eight months," Gahlen said then added, "It was five years for you?"

"Zant. Five years."

"That's a long time to hold on to hope, frei," Tinish murmured. "A long time to survive among the enemy."

I nodded. I hadn't been the only survivor. Ahnoru and Sree. "Sree's alive? I thought she was confined to the Bilge." That area had been blown apart, gutted, burned. I saw it.

Gahlen said, "I heard she escaped to protect your daughter, Barethri."

"Did she?" How could I reconcile a protective Sree with my memories of Adam's death? It seemed years ago that I'd watched her shoot the boy. I murmured, "I'm glad Ahnoru survived."

"Zant," Tinish said. "Everyone wants to hear their stories." He paused. "And yours. When you're ready to tell it."

"Maybe one day," I said.

"I understand." His boots scraped the floor. "Is there anything I can get for you, Barethri?"

The cheering and laughter started as a buzz, a mumble, a murmuring hum. Chants of "Drax-*tu*! Drax-*tu*!" joined in, clarified, swelled, waves moving through the ship toward me.

Ehtishem.

The chants grew louder, came closer. They were distracting, but they were outside my mind. My brain may have been filled with horrors, but at least there were no voices nattering anymore.

The cheers and chants became a roar.

I closed my eyes. "I want my family."

Hands touched my shoulders, broad and gentle. They pulled me up and into an embrace. "We're here, Pairika." Ehtishem slid his fingers through my hair. He tilted my head back and kissed me.

A slim body pressed against my side. "We're safe, Momma." Pearl's voice cracked. She sobbed. I pulled her close. Audie whined and licked my palm. Ehtishem held us tight.

Tears pricked my eyes and dampened my cheeks. A whimper escaped me. I thought I'd never want to be touched again.

I was wrong. I never wanted them to stop holding me. I never wanted to let them go.

Pearl took my hand. "What's this?" She'd discovered the ring.

Ehtishem looked down then met my gaze. He wiped the tears from my cheeks. "You kept it."

"Yeah," I said, the word half sob, half hiccup. "In case you got your big carcass killed in some stupid battle."

He studied my face, his eyes full of wonder and wanting and love. "Do you want to be my wife, Rachel Elizabeth Pryne?"

"Zant, Ehtishem Zain Mahle. I do."

He smiled and he kissed me. And I didn't care if the whole universe burned as long as I could hold him and Pearl and my whole Ohnenrai family until the end.

GLOSSARY

A brief guide to Ohnenrai pronunciation:

a: (ä) soft as in about, abbreviate, baklava
e: (e) soft and flat as in friend, hen, pent
i: (ē) long "e" as in magazine, figurine, chlorine
o: (ō) long "o" as in mold, open, poke
u: (oo) long "u" as in immune, use, tune
ae: (äe) soft "a" + "eh"
dh: (TH) "d" + hard "th"
sh: (SH) soft "sh" as in sheet, shine, wash
th: (TH) soft "th" as in three, with, thank
x: (aks) hard as in exit, x-ray, ax
y: (y) soft as in yam, yellow, yo-yo

Adha: now; so
Adhem: to begin; to start; to go
Afant: time
Aesh: this; that
Aeva: one

Aevim: the first fifth of the day (equivalent to hours
01:00–05:00)

Aevadasa: First Lieutenant Commander; ten thousand; a
commander of ten sets of ten thousand soldiers

Ah: to be

Ahmat: until

Ahn: the

Ahzish: snake; serpent; winged Ohnenrai serpent

Aiwiyo: water

Aiya: an exclamation of annoyance, pain, or surprise

Ajam: to come; to follow

Amat: us; we

Anagava: to get; to acquire; to buy

Anizofstra: Iodiq predatory creature

Angho: to be; is; was; am

Anghu: life

Antara: in; within; inside

Apa: off; leave off

Ar: move; go forward

Arshno: brother

Arusha: white

Aruva Pantam: Military Corridor (restricted to all but the high-
est-level personnel)

Ash-: prefix meaning 'most' or 'very'; creating the superlative
(ex. Ash-ush: very good; very well)

Ash-ush: very good

Ashusta: Good luck!

Ashaishtem: to feel grief; to be sorry; to regret; regret; grief;
sorrow

Asmanaca: stone

Asna: alien; foreigner (derogatory)

Astasca: the body

Aste: to rest; to stay; to continue; to persist

Astu: to mean; to define; definition; message

Astumana: messenger; conduit

At: and; but; then

Avabar: bringer; lure; bait

Avajan: biter; killer

Avant: it; thing

Avare: thousand

Axtica: danger

Ayan: iron

Azainti: understanding; comprehension; to understand; to know; to be aware of

Baghem: to share

Bahkem: gods; divinities; kings; rulers

Bahkshen: to forgive; to ask for forgiveness

Bamim: wishes; salutations; congratulations

Barathrishma: womb; The Womb; a park in the center of *Dathusha*

Baresh-Anghu: Top of the World

Barethri: mother; an honorific title reserved for a woman who has conceived naturally and given birth to a living child)

Bisham: to repeat

Cashmem: dog; beast; animal

Cathru-cashmem: four-eyed dog (a dog who sees in all directions)

Cithra: family; caste

Cithrai: caste

Cithrem: breeders

Da: to make; to create

Dadha: to give

Dam: wisdom; stupidity

Dar: keep/catch

Daradhem: keep going; carry on; continue

Dasa: ten; a commander of ten sets of one hundred soldiers

Daspa/Dadatspayat: "give and take" A popular game of strategy (similar to awale, but uses stacked tiles instead of seeds)

Dathusha: genesis; creation

Dosh: ten; a commander of ten sets of ten soldiers (equivalent to a battalion)

Draxtu Mainyu: The Great Hunter (spirit warrior in the form of a white dog)

Druj: lies; liar

Dva: two

Dvai: Second in Command of the Ohnenrai Combined Defensive Forces, responsible for all civilian matters, both legal and judicial

Dvarapan: Backdoor (the secondary component of the paradox lock)

Dvarin: the second fifth of the day (equivalent to hours 06:00-10:00)

Erenavi: to grant; to permit; to allow

Eresh: true; truth; honesty

Erezatem: silver

Eti: to come; to arrive

Everezika: powerless; incapable; useless; crippled

Fera: out; outward; away

Ferahi-va: thank you

Fra (Fratemo): sir

Framru: to speak; to say; to state; speech; language

Frasha: new; fresh; inexperienced

Frashin: the fourth fifth of the day (equivalent to hours 16:00-20:00)

Frayan: to move; move (a command)

Frei (Freitamo): ma'am; miss

Frena: because; as a result; to cause

Gadwha: bitch; female dog (can be used as a curse)

Gaonahe: -colored

Gatu: route; way; destination; place

Gawa: meat

Gawmezh: bull piss

Gered: to try; to attempt

Ghinvat: a game played with marked tiles

Grahm: angry

Hamem: all; everyone

Hamistayeca: confrontation; a formal challenge to settle a disagreement via unarmed hand-to-hand combat

Hamisterim: opponent; combatant

Hantaoj: receiver; person you're calling or speaking with

Hathra: unit of measure (roughly equivalent to ten inches); plural: pa'thra

Hathrem: measure of time passed (equivalent to one hour in a twenty-five hour cycle)

Hava: to have; to own

Havafna: sleeping; dormant

Havazangh: strong at birth; strong by birth

Haxan: friend

Haxsho: to lead; to train; to befriend

Hayem: them, these, those

Hei: she

Hu: a pig-like Ohnenrai animal

Idha: now

Irhish: to injure; to be injured; an injury

Iristahe: Death

Izhagatu: The Nest (the breeding center aboard *Dathusha*)

Jahika: prostitute; slut

Jaidhyantai: to need; to want; to request

Jivyam: nut milk

Ka: what

Kam: to love; to be in love with; heart; love

Kamcit: anyone; someone

Kameridha: someone who is mentally abnormal; 'brainless head'

Kanikar: to be welcome; to welcome

Kanya: maid(en); young woman

Kar: to do

Karana: to end; to stop; to cease; closure

Maibyo: my; mine

Maidhya Terasca: Central Cross

Masanopla: worm-like predator that attacks with a multi-pronged sticky tongue then engulfs and ingests its prey directly into its stomach

Maso: big; giant

Maso-Vohu: the Ohnenrai name for the red Azatem destroyer pursuing them

Meh: me

Mem: I

Menghi: to pay attention to; to think; to remember

Naema: half

Nairika: wife; woman

Nama: name

Namana: home; house

Namanyu: guardian; protector

Nava: no; not

Nerem: man

Nezish: nothing; nobody; one who is not here

Nidah: slow down

Nimru: submissive; weak

Nishidet: to sit; to relax

Nitemem: cowardly; small; low

Nyancyo: one who throws down; a destroyer; someone who is dangerously uncontrolled

Oyum: alone

Pa: creates the plural form (Ex: pa'nerem)

Pairika: shooting star; sorceress

Paiti: to move; to throw

Paiterem: husband; lord; head; leader

Pa'namandar: animal handlers (singular: namandar)

Panca: five; group of five-to-ten soldiers (equivalent to a squad)

Panca-nadasa: fifty; group of fifty soldiers (equivalent to a division)

Panca-sata: fifteen; equivalent to fifteen-to-twenty soldiers (equivalent to a platoon)

Panca set das'aeva: Squadron 701

Pa'nerem: men; gentlemen

Payu: Father

Peshana: to fight; to struggle

Pitarus: bastard

Pivatica: pollution; putrefaction; rot

Pohru-Mahrko: apocalypse

Rashnu: justice

Ratheshto: soldier; warrior (male or female)

Ratheshtolo: little warrior

Sadayeiti: to leave; to depart; to move away from; to give privacy

Samahe: black

Sarem: Councilor; authority

Sanghem: orders; instructions

Sevishta: strongest; very strong

Shathrinei: elite woman; powerful woman

Shathriyo: kingly; imperial; Elite man

Spayet: to take away; to remove

Spenta-vohyatem: compassion; empathy

Sraeshta: fairest; finest; most beautiful

Stoaca Varefshar: Butcher Bay (where slaughtered animals are offloaded, butchered, and prepared for distribution throughout *Dathusha*)

Surun: to obey (used with –ta to signal understanding of orders in combat)

Tahkaesha: trainer; teacher

Tanu: personal; sin; error; mistake

Tarad: superior; highest (Tarad-class ships are the largest destroyers in the Ohnenrai fleet)

Tarshta: to fear

Terasca: exit; cross

Thrai: Third in Command of the Ohnenrai Combined Defensive Forces, responsible for all military personnel, activities, and strategy

Thrish: three

Tishrin: the third fifth of the day (equivalent to hours 11:00-15:00)

Upairi: more than; above; over; greater

Upastan: assistant; aid; helper

Ush-bamim: Good wishes; congratulations

Ushin: the final fifth of the Ohnenrai 25-hour clock (21:00-25:00)

Ushika: a small, fierce Ohnenrai mammal (also Ehtishem's nickname for Pearl)

Ushta: good

Utha: an expletive; the effluent that leaks from a rotting corpse (Considered very offensive)

Va: you

Vairim: self-control; emotional control

Vana: please

Vangudha: discretion; care

Vanvuisha: conqueror; controller

Varet: enough; stop

Vayem: we; us

Vikeret: Reaper (an Azatem reaper ship)

Vinas: to destroy; to ruin; to break

Vira: servant; slave; property
Vis: okay; acceptable
Visdi: to see; to look
Vohu: red; blood
Yaozdhi: pollution; trash; garbage; unclean
Yahz: an exclamation of astonishment, surprise, or amazement
Yavin: concept equivalent to a Terran minute
Yunum: youngster; trainee (pl. pa'yunum)
Zant: yes
Zaste: touch
Zara: green
Zenghana: to be vigilant
Zervanin: an Ohnenrai year (382 days)
Zhek: A curse (equivalent to fuck)
Zosh: Supreme Command General of the Ohnenrai Combined Defensive Forces

OHNENRAI PHRASES

Kar-va jaidhyantai aiwiyo? *Do you need water?*
Va kanikar. *You're welcome.*
Mem anagava iristahe. *I'm getting nothing.*
Frena manaya-hei framru-hei ahn eresh. *Because she believes she speaks the truth.*
Va'gaoshrutavan. *Your compad.*
Mem jaidhyantai-va at maibyo tanu pa'nerem antara ahn Stoaca Varefshar. *I want you and my personal guard detail in the Butcher Bay.*
Vayem kanikar-va, Thrai. Vayem upaman va'sanghem. *We welcome you, Thrai. We await your order.*
Ma'shthra gatu. *The most public route.*
Ushta visdi-va. *Good to see you.*
Anghu framarez pantham, vana. *Clear a path, please.*
Marez'aste, pa'ratheshto. *Ready-rest, soldiers.*
Mem kanikar-va, fra. *Welcome back, sir.*
Ka fradat visdi-va. *What a relief to see you.*
Framru-va nama, vana. *State your name, please.*
Nama nava vaeda. *Name not recognized*

Vaxsh huxta vist. Ahngano vayaxanem vist. Zasta, vana. *Voice accepted. Face accepted. Palm, please.*

Kanikar namana. *Welcome home.*

Vangudha, vana. Va kar nav'ahn axtica. *Discretion, please. Don't forget the danger.*

Sarem Ahremena Uahdimei Mahlei hei jaidhyantai vis. *Councilor Ahremena Uahdimei Mahlei requests entry.*

Mem erenavi vis. *Entry granted.*

Ka kar 'Ratheshtolo' astu? *What does 'Ratheshtolo' mean?*

Mem ashaishtem. *I apologize.*

Gatu, vana. *Destination, please.*

Anghu framarez pantham. Idha. *Clear a path. Now.*

Ma'zaste. *Don't touch.*

Vana framru va hantaoj. *Please name your receiver.*

Mem ashaishtem, nama nava vaeda. *I apologize, name not recognized.*

Va upaman, vana. *Wait, please.*

Mem visdi-va. *Let me see.*

Va nishidet. *Sit.*

Frena va'ngho dam asmanaca. *Because you're stupid as stone.*

Va'jam. *Come.*

Aeva, aev'avare. Dva, aev'avare. Thrish, aev'avare. *One-one thousand. Two-one thousand. Three-one thousand.*

Mareza daitim vaedhem. Vayem nisirinu hayem at fratem daxshtem adha. *Prepare the property records. We'll submit them and make the mark today.*

Mem gered. *I'm trying.*

Sadayeiti amat. *Leave us.*

Bahkshen meh? *Excuse me?*

Iristahe tarshta meh. *Death fears me.*

Ar fera. *Move out.*

Surun-ta, fra. *Copy that, Sir.*

Mem kam-va. *I love you.*

Mem kam-va upairi anghu. *I love you more than life.*
Va'vinas avant, va'nagava'vant. *You break it, you buy it.*
Sadayeiti adha. *Leave now.*
Hayem angho maibyo asanghem. *Those are my orders.*
Ar hamem antara. *Get everyone aboard.*
Ka'ngho va'sanghem, fra? *What are your orders, sir?*

ALSO BY MONICA ENDERLE PIERCE

Glass and Iron Series

Girl Under Glass

The Mother Element

A Sad Jar of Atoms (short)

Rust and Ruin (short)

Militess & Mage Series

The Shadow and The Sun

A Castle to Keep

The Bones Beneath (coming in 2019)

To Give Her Heart (short)

The Apocalyptics Series

Famine

Anthologies & Collections

The Dragon Chronicles

Prep For Doom

The Doomsday Chronicles

Once Upon a Time in Gravity City

ABOUT THE AUTHOR

Monica Enderle Pierce and her characters have been kicking the crap out of evil since 2012. She writes fantasy and science fiction and her stories are filled with strong women, smart men, love, adventure, and magic. She has an English literature degree from the University of California, Los Angeles, and she lives in Seattle, Washington, with her husband, their daughter, a neurotic dog, and two crazy tomcats. When she's not sending characters into battle or off on an adventure, she's reading minds, seeing through walls, and reveling in the glorious Pacific Northwest rain.

How to reach me:
monicaenderlepierce.com
monicaenderlepierce@gmail.com